SPIRITS
OF THE
ICE FOREST

SPIRITS
OF THE
ICE FOREST

Max Davine

Tamarind Hill Press
www.tamarindhillpress.co.uk
First published in 2021

ISBN

978-1-64786-448-4

TAMARiND HiLL
.PRESS

Dedication

To the memories of Valeriya Leshcheva and Athenie
Kalos

Acknowledgements

"Spirits of the Ice Forest" is the culmination of thousands upon thousands of hours of thinking and reading. The native peoples in this story are inspired by the real Little Passage and precontact people, whom I have used as a reference for early Beothuks without expressly trying to depict them. For what I could scrape together of the Dorset-Beothuk and precontact peoples, I have to thank the tireless and extraordinary efforts of the team at heritage.nf.ca for their incredible compilation of facts about these disappeared peoples. The work of Ralph T. Pastore along with Majorie G. Forest, Donald H. Holly Jr, James P Howley, Genevieve Lehr, Ingeborg Marshall, Frederick Rowe, Frederick A. Schwartz, Peter Such, James A. Tuck, and Leslie Upton is an invaluable resource to get to know the true spirits of the ice forests, the tundras and the meadows of Newfoundland. I can't urge readers enough to go and read up on these fascinating peoples. They aren't here to tell their own stories anymore.

I also want to thank Matthew Horstead, Limuel Buidon, and George Zhong for compiling a new online resource on Beothuk peoples which was still underway at the time of writing.

The website native-languages.org was also indispensable for finding all the right letters, numbers and body parts to name my native people after. Thank you to all the many, many contributors. What an astonishing resource.

My Viking research was not as specific. Viking folklore endures today and is popular enough, while enough research out there shows how prominent a role women played in their societies, that I could indulge in ballads such as Gunnlaug the Serpent Tongue and the Saga of Eirik the Red to get a beautiful picture of their possible society from that.

On a personal note, I want to thank Peter Kalos of the Melbourne Actor's Lab for the years of training I received there; my former colleagues in the plumbing department of Holmesglen Institute of TAFE and current colleagues at Box Hill Institute, for being great enough gangs that I don't dream of escaping from my day job like most authors; and my fellow volunteer firefighters at Belgrave CFA and District 13 for keeping me alive and treating me like family while allowing me to do the same in return.

And lastly and mostly, thank you to Amanda. I love you.

Find Athenie's Angels on Facebook.

Table of Contents

Norse Terms

Althing: A Council or legislative assembly. From Iceland.

Atgier: A polearm, similar to a halberd, but with a blade in place of an axe head.

Faering: Light transport vessel.

Jarls: Aristocrats.

Karls: Peasants.

Karvi: Smaller transport vessel.

Knarr: Large, oceanic ship.

Skraelingjar: The Norse word for indigenous peoples – "savages."

Skjoldmoy: Shield Maiden, a Norse woman who takes up arms, and fights alongside the Viking men.

Thralls: Slaves.

Map of Vinland
C.E. 1000

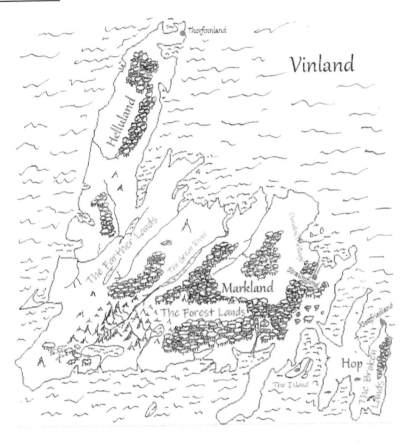

"A nation is not conquered until the hearts of its women are on the ground. Then it is finished, no matter how brave its warriors or how strong its weapons."

\- **Cheyenne proverb**

1

Straumfjord

Silence swept through the Althing like an icy breeze when the stout, muscular figure stepped through the skin curtain into the warm orange firelight. The council were struck dumb and stared at their guest. Even the thrall women stopped with their platters and ale mugs, frightened by the sudden shift from a booming symphony of disorderly chatter to intense and silent focus. Nobody had heard her horse approach. Nor had anyone heard her footsteps to the two Chieftains' lodge.

Helgi and Finnbogi sat at the head of their table. Helgi looked at Finnbogi, who did not take is eyes off Freydis. Helgi turned his eyes back to Freydis Eiriksdottir as she stood before the brothers and smiled. But no words came.

'Meat! Bread! Ale!' Helgi shouted as he clapped his hands. The women, pillaged from all over the known world and gifted to them by Thorfinn Karlsefini, nervously went back to their serving.

Helgi noticed how Freydis' eyes tracked the women whenever they passed her.

'Please,' Helgi gestured to a passing thrall and Freydis took an ale horn from her hand. A murmur had begun to pick up as service resumed but it remained in awkward, hushed tones.

'What is the meaning of this?' a councillor boomed from across the table.

'Sigurd!' Helgi snapped at him.

'We sent for the Chieftain of Straumfjord!'

'His sister will suffice...' softly came the voice of Freydis. The smile had left her but a slight smirk still remained. She turned her gaze back towards Helgi and Finnbogi and both would have sworn she looked right into them at once. '...for a clan of your standing.'

'Did you come here to insult us?' Sigurd asked.

'Is it insulting to be reminded?'

'Alright, that's enough,' Helgi said. He was careful to direct his order towards Sigurd. 'We dislike this ill-feeling that has sprung up between our clans. We wish to make an offering of peace.'

'You have built your settlement on the borders of Straumfjord,' Freydis said. 'Lief Eiriksson ordered that Markland was to be mine.'

'Thorvald's...' came the voice of Sigurd again.

'Chieftain Thorvald,' Freydis corrected, still with her smirk.

'We have yet to establish safe harbour in Helluland,' Finnbogi said. 'The skraelingjar there kill our stock and haunt us from the trees. They are hostile as the land.'

'Frightened of animals,' Freydis smiled and shook her head. 'And you expect Thorvald Eiriksson as your guest. Then go to Hop.'

'Hop is infertile,' Helgi pointed out. 'King Leif knows it.'

'Hostile and infertile,' Freydis added as she turned away from them. 'What do you think Straumfjord was when my brother the King arrived? What do you think Greenland was when my father...'

'Your half-brother,' Sigurd grumbled. 'Your supposed father.'

Freydis' eyes drew a bead on him. But again, she smiled and turned back to the two chieftains. 'Alright. Since you are afraid, you may stay in Markland. But you must move away from Straumfjord. As far away as my family's clan intends to spread our crops and our stock and our homes. We don't care where. Not near here. That is all.'

'We need to hear this from the Eiriksson Clan's Chieftain,' Finnbogi said. 'It is the law.'

'You hear it from me.'

'It is enough,' Helgi quickly said. A collective groan issued from around him but it was no stronger than the accompanying sigh of relief. 'We will find another place to establish in Markland. The bay and Straumfjord shall be Eiriksson's. Do we have peace?'

'We have peace,' Freydis said with a toothy grin. Without bowing, she turned and went back out into the night. The curtain flapped shut behind her and then her horse's hoofs faded off into the forest.

'Perhaps Thorvald Eiriksson is not as great a foe as we thought,' Sigurd half-mumbled. 'If he would agree to terms improvised by that...mistake.'

'That mistake is the half-sister of your King,' Helgi said. 'We are here because of *his* terms.'

'Come, eat,' Finnbogi ordered.

The thrall women found their enthusiasm again and the last of the stores from their voyage were served as the revelry again escalated.

* * *

The Sicilian brought the last of a succession of steaming pales of water to his tub and tipped it in. Then looked at him with those golden eyes. Dark like the amber of *Yggdrasl*. Her legs were short and full and her body stout against the cold of the night. Black hair fell like raven's wings over her shoulders. She gave him a coy smile.

'You'll stay,' he ordered.

The pale was empty and she held it close by her side and lowered her head subserviently. Thorvald emptied the scant pieces of dinner left in his bowl into the ash of his fire dish and rose from his cushions to unlace the skins that covered him.

'Help?' she said.

Thorvald looked at her. 'You know our words?'

She stared at him. There was no comprehension upon her face.

'Never speak our words to me,' Thorvald ordered. 'Never.'

The Sicilian lowered her head again.

'Help,' Thorvald said as he pinched the lace between his finger and thumb. The Sicilian's ankle cuffs rattled as she stepped closer and with her plump little hands began to untie him. He waited until she was behind him. Then slowly exhaled the hot, trembling breath. The Sicilian stayed there as she slid his clothes off. Closer to the warmth of the fire. But she came back to his front to unlace his pants. Her fingers brushed against him. Carefully. Her eyes looked up at him as she lowered his pants to his ankles. Thorvald stepped out of them. She unlaced his shoes and he lowered himself into the hot water. The Sicilian moved to his front. She started to unlace her dress...

Footsteps came hurried through the snow towards Thorvald's door.

'Back to the privy!' Thorvald bellowed as the door flew open, but it was no thrall that came blundering across the longhouse toward him.

The Sicilian kept undressing.

'Cover yourself!' Thorvald ordered while Torvard caught his breath.

'Thorvald... my Lord... your sister...'

'What has she done now?'

Torvard shook his head and pointed towards their hut. 'They...'

Thorvald had already risen from the water and the Sicilian began to dry him off. He was wet now. No time to be traipsing about outside, away from fire.

'They... beat...' Torvard was overcome with emotion and began to cry. 'My...'

'Take me to her,' Thorvald ordered while the Sicilian hastily laced his leathers back up.

* * *

Freydis' horse stood untied outside their hut. As Torvard led Thorvald to the door, it flung open and a healer woman came rushing out with a bloodied cloth in her hands. She hurried to the adjoining privy. Inside it, Thorvald could see two thralls washing more cloths in pails. He felt a tinge of brotherly fear for a moment and quickened his steps.

Inside, two more healer women quickly parted from Freydis' bedside and rose for their Chieftain. Freydis lay on the bloodied cushions. Her groggy eyes sought the ceiling in a daze while blood dried around her nose and lips. Torvard fell at her side. Thorvald kneeled beside him.

'Will she live?' Thorvald demanded.

'She is immensely strong,' one of the healers answered him, cautiously. 'But her body is bruised and bloodied. They were savage.'

'Did they...?'

'No,' Freydis wheezed with a cough. 'No, brother. I wouldn't let them.'

'It was a trap,' Thorvald said. 'Helgi and Finnbogi must be sick to their minds to set a trap for my sister!'

'They called us weak,' Freydis said. 'Said Straumfjord would be theirs for the taking.'

Thorvald rose to his feet. 'We ride tonight.'

'Brother,' Freydis croaked. 'Kill them all. Leave none alive.'

* * *

A tipsy stagger stole Helgi from his path as he ambled back towards his hut. A child chuckled. He looked up and saw his little Henrik seated on the turf bricks by his door. His hands were crossed innocently in his lap. Little feet kicked at the side of the brick. He cocked his head.

'Hello papa.'

'What is this?' Helgi asked. His son's smile became cheeky, almost sly. 'Why are you out in the cold?'

'I wanted to see you come home,' Henrik answered as Helgi stumbled up to the boy and seized him by the wrist. Henrik looked up at Helgi.

Eyes full of innocence watered in the stinging night air.

'Boy...' Helgi began. The door opened and Agnetha looked out with sleepy eyes.

'Helgi...' she noticed Henrik. 'What are you doing?'

'I wanted to see Papa!' Henrik cried.

'I told you, you could see him in the morning!' Agnetha roared as she snatched Henrik out of Helgi's grip and dragged him inside.

Helgi sighed. The boy brought it on himself. He opened the door to follow them into the ebbing warmth when a soft rumble caught his attention. He looked across his village towards the downward slope. Down beyond it was the cove and Straumfjord. All around, the men who dispersed from the Althing stopped and looked in the same direction.

The rumbling grew louder. The horse's hoofs drew near.

The bodies of every man and woman tensed at once and they scattered. They dove towards whichever hut was nearest. Helgi charged inside. He reached over Agnetha's head to fetch his spear and shield while she laid Henrik across her knee. Seeing her husband in flight, she took the boy and ran with him towards the other sleeping children.

Helgi charged back out into the moonlight as Thorvald and Gottfried rode their horses from the darkness of the forest and led a horde into the village. Gottfried wove between the huts with his battle axe; he brought it down on the heads and shoulders of fleeing men with crushing blows. Thorvald veered off in another direction. He swung his sword and took the ends off spears with a single swipe, then struck the sharp steel against the wielder's breast, neck and head. Behind them, the horde flooded the village. Thick blotches of red sprayed across the snowy ground where bodies fell.

Finnbogi ran with his family from their longhouse towards the forest. Sigurd charged in with an axe. A horse made for a hut but Sigurd swung low and cut the feet out from under it and with a blood curdling scream, it crashed into the snow. The rider was fast upon his feet. He drew an axe and swung it to divert the blow of an atgier. The Straumfjord warrior split his attacker's side with a follow up swing, who then doubled over and collapsed into the reddening snow. Sigurd saw it and cleaved the Straumfjord warrior's skull with his own axe. Helgi heard the crack over the screams and roaring of the raging raid.

The Eiriksson warriors charged toward the huts on their horses. The horses' kicking hoofs dislodged the turf bricks which collapsed the roofs and then rode inside. Screams issued from within. One burst out from Helgi's own hut, right behind him, and he turned and rammed his spear into the rider's stomach. The rider growled and curled off his horse. Helgi tugged the spear from him and pushed it into his collar. He made a gargled cry.

Sigurd swung his axe high and struck a charging rider in the chest. His body flowered open in fountains of crimson and the animal rode on.

Finnbogi picked up an atgier and swung it at the throat of a rider. But the rider deflected his blow and used an axe to cut the head off the atgier. The horse turned and the warrior dropped onto the ground then he swung his axe at Finnbogi. Helgi saw as his brother collapsed on one knee from the axe's impact and gasped as blood gurgled up from his gullet and gushed from his mangled shoulder. Helgi charged and thrust his spear into his brother's attacker. He felt the blade crack the shoulder blade. Helgi pushed harder as the warrior fell and drove the spearhead deeper.

Finnbogi laid on his back as blood bubbled up through his lips and his eyes bulged. The sight stole Helgi from the battle. He never saw Thorvald's blade swing at his side but he felt the steel hack deep into his ribs and lodge in his spine. He dropped his spear as his body crumpled. With a second blow, Thorvald severed the rival Chieftain's head and it fell into the snow.

Blood spurted from the body then it fell limp by its side.

* * *

'Miss Freydis! You need rest!' the healer woman protested as Freydis pushed the door open to let the clear sunrise into her hut. A nearby longhouse bustled with villagers. They were piling its contents in the snow outside of it.

'What are they doing?' she demanded.

'You should be resting!' Torvard cried as he came running from the privy. 'The healers said you need rest!'

'What are they doing?' Freydis asked louder as Torvard took her by the arms. As though he could physically move her anywhere, let alone back to a bed she'd spent enough time in.

'They're clearing a longhouse,' Torvard said as he tried to goad her back inside.

'The Icelanders had no horses.'

'Not for horses,' Torvard said. 'Women. Children. Thralls.'

'I told him to leave none alive!' Freydis growled as she pushed against him. Both crossed through the slushy snow.

'Freydis...' Torvard called. 'Women and children...'

'None alive!' Freydis almost shrieked.

Thorvald approached from the longhouse, still spattered with blood from the night before.

'What is the meaning of this?' Thorvald asked.

'What is the meaning of that?' Freydis pointed at the longhouse.

'We do not kill women and children, Freydis,' Thorvald said. 'We do not kill useful thralls. Go back to bed.'

'You are a coward!' Freydis spat before she turned and stormed back inside her hut.

* * *

Thorvald finally bathed but no longer lusted for the glorious body of the Sicilian. He dismissed her. The others bathed him but none of them could excite his interest either. Thorvald lusted only for sleep. His body ached. His mind roared and rattled as furious visions recounted the previous night and many nights and days before. At some point, he found himself in bed, on his back, tense and with his pulse throbbing. The thralls were gone.

Had he sent them out?

Had he been sleeping?

The sound of his teeth grinding woke him. He unclenched his fist and found that he'd made his palms bleed again. Long, steady breaths soothed the tempest. The embers in the fire dish and the silence outside told him it was deep in the night. Maybe early morning.

Screams came from beyond his door.

Thorvald grabbed his axe and charged outside.

Nothing moved beneath the moonlight but the screams continued. Was he dreaming them while awake?

No...it was the longhouse. The captives.

Thorvald hurried to the door and flung it open. Spilled candles shone dull light over the scattered corpses, some of them but babies with their heads dashed open. All of them split either in their middle, across their heads or at their shoulders and chests. Women. Children. Thorvald raised his eyes and saw the woman who ran towards him. Behind her, the dark figure swung a battle axe twice at the shoulders of a screaming girl until she'd cleaved the way down through her ribs. The woman crashed against Thorvald.

'Save me!' she cried. 'Save my baby!'

Thorvald held her in shock as she was thrust from his grip by a powerful jerk from behind. He saw Freydis force the woman down to her knees. Then with a single blow from above, she buried the axe into the woman's skull.

Thorvald watched his sister as she painfully stretched herself upright. Her face was spattered with blood and her eyes shone out from the crimson veil like green inferno.

'I told you to leave none alive,' she breathed.

2

Oonban and Family

Sunrise carried the warmer winds into the giant skins that billowed and carried the Pale Ones' big canoes back out into the endless water whence they had come. Out near the rocky shore, Madawaak could see how many people were in the canoes. They moved fast. The boatmen used every oar that could fit over the sides until the wind took up their sails.

Madawaak hurried back to the bloodied snow. Some Pale Ones still rummaged around in the houses and forced him to keep low. The beds of glowing ember still smouldered. Last night, the flames of the huge pyres had flickered above the treetops and had stank of burning fat and meat. The same Pale Ones that had slain the dead had also observed their funeral rites.

Like his people, they had laid stones. Only at the site of the burning, instead of as a marker for the burial. Unlike his people, they did not see the small things that moved or lived between the trees. They did not hear the wind or the rustle in the leaves. The way everything changed when one tiny thing did. Madawaak had spent days and nights with his courage mustered testing their perception by stalking them from just beyond the forest edge. Closer and closer each time. Each time, they had not seen him. Once, he even saw a man who dug the earth shiver as the cold spirits in the air tried to warn him that an enemy was close. But he had ignored the warning. Oh, to see how the Pale Ones hunt, with such ineptitude.

The more Madawaak watched these strange people with their hard hats and their weapons of shining stone, the more questions he had. He kept quiet and ran on the tips of his toes to the trees and then around their ruined village. Between the smashed homes, the earth was slowly swallowing the bloodstains as the snow melted beneath the radiant sun. Madawaak liked their homes. They were not of skin and tree, but earth and tree. Blocks of soil and grass dug from the ground and stacked. They were strong. Only the creatures the pale people rode upon could break their walls.

Once he got to the downward slope, Madawaak knew he could run.

* * *

The growing warmth of outside bled into Oonban's mamateek and enticed him out from under his furs. But the age of his body and the shape of his wife beside him kept him down. Chipchowinech laid on her back. Lips slightly parted as a thick lock of greying hair laid across her mouth. Carefully, conscious of his hard and calloused old hands, Oonban reached across and moved the hair out of the way. She stirred and her eyes opened slightly. The sun rose for the second time that day; now in his heart.

'Papaaaa,' came the strained voice of little Shanawdithit. He rolled back over and looked up at her. Somehow, she'd crept right up to his head without him sensing her, and she looked all too comfortable staring down at him. Even with those weepy eyes. 'Demasduit would not let me go with her.'

'Where has Demasduit gone?' Oonban asked. He didn't bother to look at his elder daughter's bed. He knew it was empty. Long empty.

'I don't know. But I want to go too.'

'How do you know you'd like it if you don't know where she is?' Oonban asked as he sat up. Shanawdithit was comfortably tiny again. He took her in his arms and sat her down on his lap.

'She likes it where she is.'

'I doubt she knows where she is,' Chipchowinech said as she rubbed her eyes and sat up behind Oonban. She kissed Shanawdithit's brow, kissed Oonban and heaved herself onto her feet. 'The God Spirits saw we had no sons, so he made one of our daughters one.'

'I want to be one too.'

'One what?' Oonban asked.

'I don't know.'

Chipchowinech ground the dried Great Auk eggs into a large bowl and drizzled the maple sap over them and mixed them into a pudding. 'Come and eat something first, little *Kobet*.'

Shanawdithit got up and Chipchowinech gave her a smaller bowl and portioned out some of the meal.

'Take it outside,' Chipchowinech ordered. Shana hurried through the curtain of their mamateek, eager to be that much nearer to Demasduit. 'Wandering is fine but with those pale devils roaming about...'

'...they've stayed in the bay thus far,' Oonban said. 'Longer than the last time, I know. But they have not spread.'

Rapid swishing in the grass outside drew near.

'Not that we know,' Chipchowinech said as she served Oonban's breakfast.

'Sir! Sir!' the cracking voice of Madawaak called.

Chipchowinech gave Oonban one of her knowing looks and portioned out another bowl.

'Come in.'

Madawaak swept under the curtain and staggered in, breathless. Chipchowinech handed him a birchbark sack of water and a bowl then he bowed to her and sat down.

'Sir...' he gasped.

'Catch your breath, boy.'

Madawaak took in a deep breath and exhaled slowly. Oonban did not miss his glances towards Demasduit's bed nor the slight change in his enthusiasm to see she wasn't there.

'The Pale Ones... massacred each other... two nights ago.'

'Massacred?'

'One village,' he swallowed a gulp of water, 'turned on the other. I saw them use their weapons of shining stone. They are clumsy. But they can sever a man in two with a single blow...'

'...ohhhh...' Chipchowinech groaned.

'I have seen it.'

'Are their numbers much less?'

'Not from the fight,' Madawaak replied. 'Their numbers were still many. But this morning I saw their great canoes sail into the big water and disappear. No more have come yet to replace them. Now they are fewer.'

'Oonban...' Chipchowinech half whispered.

'Your father will want to know how you know,' Oonban said to Madawaak.

'I will take his spear across my back if it means I have done you a service,' Madawaak said.

'Oonban...' Chipchowinech whispered again.

'Go to your family,' Oonban ordered the boy. 'Tell them we must gather a party. Men from every family we can reach.'

Madawaak left his bowl and water and leaped to his feet. The bowl still rocked back and forth and the boy was gone through the curtain and out of the village. Oonban turned to his wife. She looked at him gravely.

'The others should know. We should discuss...'

'...we should not discuss war. Not with them.'

'We must discuss something,' Oonban said.

* * *

The village of Oonban stood upon a high rocky spit. It overlooked the grassy headlands that held the bay water in which the larger Pale One village stood. Madawaak ran along the edge of the rocks and felt the salty spray of the growing swells that dashed to glittering pieces upon the dark and jagged shore. The thin wisps of smoke that rose from the smaller village that had stood at the peak of the headland were still visible. The ground sloped down as he ran inland. The trees quickly closed in around him. He wondered where Demasduit was so early in the day...

His father often suspected her of making peace with the Pale Ones. The thought stalled Madawaak's run as it struck a dark gloom into his heart. But she wouldn't. Never. She couldn't. Her father's village stood overlooking the water from which the first wave of Pale Ones had come, when they were children. Those Pale Ones hadn't ventured far. They weren't like these

[22]

ones, who moved about and were seen on the farthest coasts of the island. Those ones had been afraid of them, or so the adults often told him. They only attacked when provoked. Like when they'd been attacked by Mammasamit's village. Demasduit had been a child then, like Madawaak. Even then, she'd been a wanderer. She'd entice him from his family's mamateek and from his village to go into the depths of the forest.

He'd been afraid of bears. She'd told him a story about a boy of eight—their age at the time—who'd been so brave, he'd slapped a bear in the face and run away before it could catch him. How her eyes had sparkled as she'd spoken. Why did she stop asking him on her adventures? Had she been afraid then? Did she want someone to be there and defend her if ever she was accused of conversing with the Pale Ones? But no... she'd surely still want that. More so now since these braver Pale Ones had come. Though it hurt to consider, hurt somewhere deep in the chest than the ache of too much running in cold and wet air, Madawaak decided she must have just grown out of him.

But sometimes she'd still tell him what she'd been doing. Stalking caribou. Pretending to hunt, as though she were a man. Even following bear tracks. Madawaak thought about how her eyes sparkled when she spoke of bears... He was grateful that he got to see that...

Something snatched Madawaak's foot midstride and he hit the cold, dewy grass. The pain in his toes throbbed up and down his leg.

Oh, please don't be broken...

Madawaak rolled onto his back and looked up at the dripping canopy that flooded with golden light from the sharp eastern sunrise. The leaves above rustled. Madawaak looked down at the rock he'd tripped on and saw his toes move up and down through the skin of his moccasin. Not broken. It just throbbed with pain. He laid on his back and the wet grass soaked through to his back just like his front but Madawaak didn't care. He sighed with relief that his toes weren't broken...

'You're lucky,' the voice of Demasduit prickled Madawaak's ears and he quickly looked around for her. She ran just within the boundaries of the forest towards him. Her feet swept across the forest floor as though they didn't even touch the ground. Silent and weightless. 'You weren't running like you normally do.'

The short, lithe girl arrived at Madawaak's side and crouched at his feet where she squeezed his toes.

'Does it hurt?'

'No.'

'Good. Then you're fine.'

Demasduit stood upright and offered her hand. Madawaak took it in his and she squeezed and helped him up. Despite their near same age, Demasduit was barely as tall as Madawaak's shoulder and he was a boy of less than average size as well. Yet on her tiny frame was tightly wound muscle. He'd felt it whenever she'd attacked him... yet another thing she'd ceased to do over the past few migrations while their bodies had started to change and the demands of maturity had been thrust upon them. She smiled up at him in that excited way. Just as she had when they were children.

'You listened to me!'

Madawaak blinked. 'What?'

'I told you not to run where the forest meets the grasslands and you weren't running,' Demasduit said as she slapped him in his stomach. 'You never don't run.'

She turned and began to walk in the direction he'd been heading.

'You run everywhere,' he said.

'My feet aren't heavy as stone.'

'I'd been running,' he said as he followed. 'I was interrupted by thoughts.'

'Thoughts about what?'

You, he wanted to say. Urged to say. Oh, just say it now!

'Pale Ones.'

'You were watching them again,' she said, and stopped suddenly and turned to face him. He almost walked right into her. 'Your father...'

'Someone has to watch them,' Madawaak interrupted. He wished he could stop her thinking about his father at all. 'The bad spirits might have sent them to take our country from us.'

'It doesn't have to be you,' she told him with a glance over her shoulder. There was something wounded about the way she spoke that made Madawaak want to reach out and touch her.

'I learned from you,' he replied.

'I don't watch them.'

'No. You watch bears.'

'I watch everything else,' Demasduit said. 'Someone has to remember what it is the bad spirits want to take away from us, before we get too caught up in defending it.'

'I would die to defend our country.'

'How would that help? Nobody dead ever won a fight...'

'I would continue to defend from the side of *Kuis*.'

'*Kuis* doesn't have what we have,' Demasduit said as she brushed her hand down the front of a rich, green, dewy fern.

'Your father always asks. I make sure I know something. And this time I know something important. Your father has called a *Mokoshan* because of it.'

He grinned, boastfully. But, suddenly, Demasduit's sparkling eyes darkened.

'Well, go on! Hurry!' she roared.

Madawaak ran again.

'Don't run until you learn how!' she called after him.

Madawaak slowed his pace and waved back at her. *Concerned about me. That is something,* he thought. Some little thing. But he'd gotten distracted again... Mooaumook wouldn't have got distracted. That's what Demasduit was thinking, he figured. Mooaumook wouldn't have got so carried away trying to boast that he didn't listen to a word she'd said. Wouldn't have tripped and he'd have been running, not dawdling. Mooaumook knew how to run.

Madawaak may have been the one mustering for the *Mokoshan*, but he knew who'd wear the red ochre and bring the caribou. He knew who Demasduit's eyes would be on.

* * *

The family of Oonban would host the *Mokoshan* but it would be Makdaachk who presided over it, for it was his son who would supply the caribou. Yaseek gathered their cousins for the preparations. Chipchowinech would lead the women in grinding and mixing the ochre, witling the bone carvings and preparing the broths while the men would gather wood and stone for the fire.

'But father, see!' Demasduit objected to the order to stay with her mother and do women's work. She held up a tomahawk fashioned of purple chert. Oonban knew it was chipped from his core as soon as he saw it.

He looked at her.

'I couldn't find any of my own,' she said.

'Bring it here,' he held out his hand while Yaseek led the men off into the forest without waiting.

'Please don't break it,' Demasduit pleaded, and she held it to her chest.

'If you've done my chert justice, I won't be able to.'

'Come Demasduit,' little Shanawdithit said, tugging at the hem of her sister's tunic.

Demasduit hesitated, but pride won the day and she handed it to him. It was a sturdy tomahawk. Tied firm. The blade was razor sharp.

'You'll make more of these,' he said. 'Out of your own chert.'

'I'll go find some now,' she leaped off to follow the men. 'It'll be green and...'

'You'll help the women now,' Oonban stopped her with the force of his voice. 'You can find chert and make tomahawks when we're not busy.'

'But Papa, we're always busy!'

'I'll let you keep this,' Oonban held up the tomahawk while he glanced up at the gathering party that quickly filtered into the trees and disappeared. 'If your mama tells me you did a good job at the women's work.'

Demasduit looked at her feet.

'Dem...'

'You keep it,' she interrupted. 'I made that for you. I'll help Mama.'

She hung her head despondently and went to join the women on their benches while they worked the ochre. The sight of her so dispirited panged through Oonban's heart. But he had work to do.

'It's okay,' Shanawdithit assured her sister as she followed Demasduit over to the women. 'I'll show you how to do it.'

Demasduit will settle down, Oonban thought. *Not yet fifteen winters since she's been on this earth,* he reminded himself. *Now is the time to be firm. She'll stop behaving like a boy eventually. It will come with age.*

He used the tomahawk on the first fallen tree they found. It stripped the branches like they were wax sticks.

Velvety twilight seemed to enliven the fire once they got it going. Like a beacon, it drew the families who had heeded Oonban's call in and he saw that Madawaak had got word to six villages. Near the proud old face of Makdaachk stood a tall, muscular figure. He had an adult buck caribou dead across his immense shoulders and still stood taller than all of the others. Oonban had to look twice. He'd not seen Mooaumook since he was a boy of Madawaak's age.

He looked across at Demasduit, seated between Chipchowinech and Imamus. She had to notice him. If any man could tame such a masculine spirit and finally bring out her femininity, it would surely be Mooaumook.

'Oonban,' Makdaachk said once he'd led Mooaumook around the fire, through the gathering crowd to the patriarch. 'My son brings your family this offering, for hosting our *Mokoshan.* Do you accept?'

'I accept.'

Mooaumook carried the caribou over to the log table set out by the women and laid it on there. Then bowed to them. Oonban could not but smile when he saw the hunter's eyes linger on Demasduit as he stepped away from them to let them work.

She, however, fiddled feebly with her scraper and didn't even seem to notice him.

The women moved in to carve up the caribou and soon large chunks of its meat were roasting over the fire. The gathered families threw their wood carvings into the fire pit. The little dogwood caribous burned up and the smoke curled up with the sacrificed caribou's spirit into the night sky where it dimmed the starlight behind a hazy sheen. The men danced and prayed to the departing spirit. In song and dance, they said their thanks that it gave its life for their meal. Then they portioned out the meat.

The women ate first, for they had work to do.

The bones of the caribou laid stripped on the logs. With clubs fashioned from birch and chert they smashed at the bones and ground them down. The men took their ochre bowls. Oonban was given the largest and he approached Mooaumook who stripped to his waist and stood by the fire.

Oonban carefully spread the ochre over his cheek bones, his jaw, his shoulders and his chest. Makdaachk gestured to Madawaak, who'd spent the whole evening dawdling around the outskirts of the ground behind his family. He looked as despondent as Demasduit. Oonban had seen only glimpses of him as he passed between their shadows and the firelight up until he gingerly stepped forward.

Eenodsha gave him a little push on the shoulder. Madawaak stepped forward.

'We must honour the one who brought the *Mokoshan* together,' Makdaachk told him.

Madawaak's eyes lit up. Immediately, he looked over at Demasduit. She was busy grinding bone but Oonban saw it and knew what it meant. *The poor boy,* he thought. *Not a chance. Not a runt like him. Demasduit is small of stature but big of spirit and needs a man.*

Before Oonban, stood the pillar of muscle that was Mooaumook, stern and strong.

Madawaak awkwardly stripped down to his waist. He glanced at Mooaumook. Only a few more winter migrations, and yet easily twice the size.

Makdaachk painted one stripe on Madawaak's cheek and one on his breast. The crowd cheered. The dust and residue of the bones was gathered and put in a broth and boiled over the fire until it smelled rich with warm marrow. The broth was dished out into birchbark sacks. The congregation sat around the fire in a large circle and each took a drink in turn.

* * *

Then one man of each family followed Oonban into the communal mamateek where a smaller fire burned. The others were free to retire, but they never did. This was the younger generation's chance to mingle with each other... for daughters to meet sons... but Oonban's focus had shifted now. The men sat around the fire.

'I have seen them hunt,' Keathut said. 'My sons and nephews have watched them hunt. They are unskilled. They do not know our country. But they will learn quickly. Already they have found ways to trap great auk, penguin and the beaver. I have heard they take seals as well. It won't be long before they start to take our bears. And we will run out of food.'

'There will always be the sea,' Ninejeek stated.

'Not if they infest the entire coast,' Keathut said. 'We will be trapped inland and have to live after the caribou migrate.'

'We have a chance...' Oonban began.

'We cannot risk more of what happened to Mammasamit,' Ninejeek said. 'We migrate inland. We stay there and do not migrate with seasons anymore. These are people of the sea. They will move on like the ones that came when we were younger.'

'Not this time,' Keathut said. 'Not these ones. These ones do not have the same fear as their predecessors.'

'We will decide nothing while you two argue,' Makdaachk barked. 'Oonban has brought us here tonight. Let's hear what he has to say.'

[29]

'The Pale Ones halved their own number two moons ago,' Oonban said. 'Their dark spirits rose from their fires and trailed out over the great water even as the sun set this night. Many were killed. Another many departed on their giant wind canoes the sunrise past. They are as few now as they may ever be. If we work together... as though they are the caribou on their winter migration...'

'There is no victory against the weapons of shining stone,' Ninejeek said. 'I have seen them. I saw the blow that took our brother Mammasamit from our world.'

'Bad spirits brought them here,' Keathut said. '*Aich-mud-Yim* carried their canoes across the waves to visit destruction on our lands, on our food and on our people. The wind will blow no more for us if we ignore them. They are as the *Mi'kmaq.* Of black spirit. Only, these ones are pale like the ghosts of slain *Mi'kmaq* and they bring the weapons of other worlds to our shores. Any man who brokers peace with them should be sacrificed to the family of Mammasamit.'

'What do you say?' Ninejeek whispered.

'I say that retreat into the woods while the caribou do not roam and the bears and beavers hibernate is as good as making peace with devil-spirits,' Keathut said. 'What do we eat, when the winters come? Do we kill sleeping bear and beaver? I would die on these weapons of shining stone any death before I struck a sleeping being for my food. Not when the sea and the coast is rich.'

'We do not know they will occupy the entire coast yet,' Ninejeek said, although Oonban saw that he was humbled.

'They mean to,' Keathut replied. 'And you know it as well as I.'

'How does Oonban, brother know what happened at the Pale Ones' camp?' Eenodsha asked.

'Your son,' Oonban answered.

Eenodsha stared into the fire, pursed his lips and exhaled sharply through his nose.

'He is brave,' Makdaachk said. 'Like my son. I know Eenodsha's hurt. Brave sons make worried fathers. But without them our way of life will be lost and with it our place in this world. Mooaumook has watched them as well. He has seen them peel the very earth from its foundation to build their houses and flatten forests to make grassland for the animals they brought with them. Those they ride upon and those they keep for food.'

'What disgrace is this?' Keathut thundered with a wave of his fist. 'I have heard this as well. They do not hunt all the time. They keep beings enclosed and feed and grow them to be slaughtered. I thought it was rumour. Is it true?'

'It is true,' Oonban responded. 'Madawaak has reported this to me as well. They hunt only to know the taste of what lives here. The beings they feed upon are kept by them. They never know natural lives.'

'What do you say to this?' Keathut glared at Ninejeek.

'I am disturbed,' Ninejeek said, sombrely. 'Who could enslave a spirit and take its flesh as well?'

'Will you allow it?' Keathut asked.

'I will not,' Makdaachk declared. 'My son will not.'

Eenodsha looked at Makdaachk.

'I will not,' he said.

'I will not,' Oonban asserted. As he did, he felt his body. The age. The heaviness of the scars upon his skin and the creaking of the tissue beneath them. The pains that came and went.

Ninejeek's eyes watered. 'I fear.'

'It is alright to fear,' Keathut offered. 'If you did not fear you would be wrong of the mind and unfit to sit here with us. The Pale Ones do not fear. To fear is good.'

'They are not of one world,' Ninejeek said. 'They have conquered worlds we have never dreamed of.'

'It is true,' Eenodsha agreed. 'They have humans kept as captives and servants and their servants are different to them. Not all Pale Ones. Some are dark of skin. Some darker than night. Some look so different they could only have come from worlds more distant than we can ever measure. Fearsome peoples have fallen before them.'

[31]

'I see their canoes fill the ocean when they come for their revenge,' Ninejeek said. 'I fear that we have not yet seen the might that won them so many and so different a number of human possessions.'

'Let them come,' said Keathut.

'Let them come,' the whole council echoed.

'I will not allow it,' Ninejeek agreed, quietly.

Those who'd remained silent remained silent some more.

'It is decided,' Oonban said. 'We will gather the winter hunting party.'

'That will take far too long,' Keathut pronounced. 'Their number could recover before then!'

'We have agreed to give our lives if need be,' Makdaachk said. 'We must not strive to do so.'

'We must take them in the greatest numbers we can manage,' Eenodsha added. 'I will send my son. He will gather them as quickly as we can hope to.'

'My son will keep vigil of the Pale Ones while Madawaak is gone,' Makdaachk offered.

'We need greater numbers still,' Ninejeek pointed out. 'What of the bands beyond the Great River?'

'Bah!' Keathut waved his hand amidst a chorus of mutters. 'They are more *Mi'kmaq* than of God Spirits. They will just as soon join with the Pale Ones.'

'They will not if we offer them peace,' Ninejeek said.

'They have given us the terms of their peace,' Oonban explained. 'And I will sooner banish my Demasduit to The Island than marry her to them.'

'You limit our chances for survival, brother,' Ninejeek said.

'That is not survival,' Eenodsha objected.

Silence.

'Are you with us, Ninejeek, brother?' Oonban said.

Ninejeek nodded slowly.

3

Lief Eiriksson

The haunting bellow of the sentry horns sounded across the Greenland Fjords as the night mists settled between the jagged, rocky, half-frozen shores. Ifar the Shepherd hurried from his flock. Beyond the coast skirted by his grazing land he could see the shadowy shape of the incoming knarr as it pushed through the deepening fog. Slowly the masts emerged above it. Ifar turned towards the hilltop. There stood the magnificent earthen Mead Hall of King Lief, son of Eirik the Red. Though the karls who worked the lands already came running from the fishing houses and the farms and the lumber sites, Ifar could not pass up the opportunity. He gathered his horn from his hip and blew with all his might.

Somewhere in the hall or the adjoining longhouse, Lief Eiriksson would have heard him. The sound of their feasting, their song and the bombastic joys of the jarls' world simmered down and fell silent. Ifar could picture them in there. He'd sat on the council in his lord's stead a few times. Tasted the *kaestur hakarl* and the wine and the ale and the herbs and liquors and smelled the women brought from all around *Midgard*. They were silent now. After the sound of his horn.

Behind him, the mists parted and the dragon-head bowsprit emerged. Along its flanks, the oars rose and fell like wings and propelled the knarr that led the fleet towards the pebbled shore. The sun disappeared behind the curve of the earth. Night was deep and dark. Ifar hurried to where the small crowd had gathered as his heart pounded so fast his fingertips prickled. He'd forgotten his flock. Rain began to patter down as the faerings departed their anchored mothership and made for land. The crowd compressed around Ifar. Their torches sizzled and the light flickered beneath the stinging, icy beads of water that showered down heavier by the second.

Ifar moved in closer as the explorers climbed up the shore and made wearily for their waiting relatives. Some threw themselves bodily into their waiting arms. Others grunted and kept their heads low. They bore the weight of some terrible defeat and, for a moment, he thought he may not see her at all. The faerings went back to the knar again and again. The light rain became heavy sheets. The cold of the water was painful as it sunk through their clothing. The torches flickered and quickly faded. Then, between the crowded heads and shoulders that Ifar peered through, passed a shock of red hair that was unmistakable to him.

She was escorted by minders: her champions. Behind her followed Torvard with his eyes fixed sharply upon her heels. From another faering came their thralls. In twos they dragged their shackles out of the salty water and after their mistress. People stood in Ifar's way, but he was tall and could stretch his neck far. She passed close by. He waited and waited to see her eyes, so emerald, look towards him. But the fires flickered and died. The last dim embers faded beneath the rainfall and all Ifar could see of them was Torvard as he faded beyond their column of thralls.

Ifar kept his spirits high as he went back to regather his flock. Freydis had come home.

* * *

'It is her, my Lord,' Ulfan said as he stood dripping before the dominant seat of the Mead Hall where the Lords of Greenland held their sixth day of feasting. 'She comes in chains.'

Lief Eiriksson felt his blood turn cold.

'Bring her here,' Lief ordered. 'Immediately.'

'Not tonight, my Lord,' Bjorn Hastensson, at Lief's right hand, said softly. 'You will offend your guest.'

Lief looked across at Thorfinn Thorsson and his family and company where they spread across the tables on the left side of the Hall. They had fallen silent. Their smiles were frozen and their eyes upon their host.

'Please, my Lord,' Thorgunna, at his leftside, urged. 'Look what the Karlsefini has brought us. Do you really want more grapes?'

'She is right,' Bjorn said.

'Ulfan,' Lief called, just in time to stop him hurrying out the door. He froze there and looked back across the three fire pits that separated either side of the hall. 'Come back in.'

The faithful servant closed the door and waited.

'Go on, sit down. Enjoy yourself. All of you, enjoy yourselves.'

The women continued to serve the families that had gathered in the rich clouds of Byzantium herbs and liquors. Lief held out his horn and had it filled with Northumbrian ale. He knew what both his advisor and his wife meant. They both sat to either side of him and pushed the remains of exotic foods around on their plates and picked at bread while their horns remained full. He knew they did not care if this evening was interrupted. He knew Thorgunna didn't like grapes any less than she liked the rich assortment of herbs that had been rubbed over her meat platter. And Bjorn knew full well that, if anything, Thorfinn would jump upon the chance to speak to anyone who had set foot on Vinland.

Lief beckoned Thorfinn with his fingers.

The explorer excused himself from his sons and daughters and his band and approached the head of the Hall, where he bowed.

'I hope that my Lord is enjoying his gifts.'

'We are enjoying everything you have brought for us, Thorfinn,' Lief said. 'I ask to be forgiven for the interruption to the evening. It seems the Chieftain of Markland has chosen to exile our sister from Vinland and I am eager to know why.'

'Oh, by all means. If my Lord wishes...'

'Not tonight, Thorfinn. Tomorrow, perhaps. I will deal with her. Tonight is for the Karlsefini.'

Lief stood and held out his ale horn. Thorfinn slammed the rim of his horn into the edge of it hard enough that the wine and the ale spilled into each other.

'With permission, my Lord,' Thorfinn said as Lief sat back down. 'If you'll bring your sister...'

'...she is his half-sister,' Thorgunna corrected. 'An accident of their father's spoils of conquest.'

'Eirik the Red was a most noble man,' Thorfinn bowed.

'Tomorrow...' Lief said.

'If you'll bring Freydis before the Althing tomorrow I would like to stay,' Thorfinn said. 'They are not expecting me in Northumbria for another season, and I have supplied them for years to come. Vinland fascinates me, my Lord.'

'Grapes is all there is to find there,' Lief said.

'Grapes and skraelingjar, my Lord,' Thorfinn added. 'Rumour has spread through Iceland of the skraelingjar of Vinland. I have heard fascinating tales. Makes me think that even the Christ-heathens would part with their gold to own them. Given a hefty tax by Lord of Vinland, of course.'

Lief tapped the arm of his chair with his fingertip and Thorgunna knew he was about to make a rash decision. But she let him. Her husband's impulsiveness had often surprised her, even if it did leave them with a legacy such as Vinland.

'Of course, as my guest, you may stay,' Lief said with a soft smile. 'But please, let's enjoy some of your business before we set about making more.'

'My Lord,' Thorfinn bowed and returned to his tables.

'Thorvald is weaker towards Freydis than even you,' Bjorn said. 'I wonder if Thorfinn should be here to know what she has done to cause him to send her here in chains?'

'Thorfinn wants human trade,' Lief said. 'I can think of no person better to make thralls of free men than Freydis. We will hear what she has done together.'

* * *

'I had a lover who would grind his hips into mine,' Freydis said. She pinned Torvard's hands hard above his head and thrust

[36]

herself upon him. Still, she did not feel him swell. 'So hard I would scream uncontrollably. Won't you try?'

'It has been a long voyage,' Torvard said, shakily. He turned his head from her mouth. Freydis licked his ear.

'Come,' she said as she brought his hands down her top onto the supple flesh of her breasts. 'Feel me. Men would die to feel me.'

'I would die,' Torvard said. 'Tonight I just might.'

Freydis leaned over him and licked his neck and ground harder against his manhood.

'Slide into me. Slam against me. Feel my wetness lather you and explode into me. I want you to, Torvard. I want you to explode into my body so I can have you inside me.'

He laid there as she tried. She moaned as she thrust. But still there was no rise. The first sliver of embarrassment of yet another evening ran through her and Freydis leaped upon it as though it were a rabid boar.

'Perhaps I should fetch my brother for you,' she suggested as she climbed off him and off the bed. 'Would he excite you?'

Torvard sat bolt upright and his eyes widened with a rage Freydis knew thinly veiled terror. 'How dare you! I am tired!'

'What? Every night?'

'I work hard for you my love.'

'Your *Lord*,' Freydis said. She put on a fur and sat down to strap on her shoes.

'Where are you going?' he asked as his soft voice trembled.

'Walking,' she said.

'It's raining.'

'Walking to find a man,' she said. 'Find a boy. Anything but you.'

'You wound me.'

Freydis stood up and swept towards the door.

'What would I do with a child you'd make anyway?' she said over her shoulder. 'What child would you make? A little furry one with pink feet?'

Torvard had no response.

Freydis pulled a cloak over her flowing red hair and walked out into the rain.

* * *

Ifar woke to the sound of his privy door slamming shut. Rain continued to pitter patter down on his thatched rooftop but he could hear the intruder move about on the other side of the wall at the head of his bed. He got up and took a torch from the smouldering fire. Through the hauntingly empty longhouse, he hurried and took his axe from upon the wall.

Oh, but if it's those children again... no, he thought. They had to be taught a lesson. He'd just have to be careful.

The rain came down hard. He hunched down and ran to the door, which was slightly ajar. Inside it was dark and smelled of mould. He held the axe up into the sheet of darkness before him and took a breath.

'Who's there?'

'Can you hear me?' the female voice asked. When the snap of fright passed through him, a hot shudder followed. 'Hear me breathe?'

Ifar lowered his axe and stood before the door while the rain hammered down behind him.

'I hear you, Freydis. My Lord. What are you doing here?'

'Torvard...' she said.

Ifar held back the swell of rage.

'He makes me feel so unwanted,' she confessed. 'Do you know this feeling? Even the one who loves you cannot find it within himself to give you his body?'

'I don't know the feeling of someone loving me.'

'Oh, Ifar,' Freydis whispered. She was close now. He hadn't heard her footsteps but he sensed her near him. He held still. Longed for her to reach out and touch him. 'What a thing to say of yourself.'

'It's only true,' he said. *Say it,* he thought. *If what his heart longed for was what was meant.*

'My father didn't want me,' she said. Further away now. 'My own father. Perhaps this is why I am so repulsive to the man who married me. Even a father couldn't love her.'

'It isn't true,' Ifar said. 'You were...'

'Taken in. My father was a noble man, such was his reputation. He had to maintain it. He took me in when that poor thrall he raped died with worms in her brain. But I knew it from his eyes, not his words. His way. I knew. He never loved me. I am a creature unloved and now nobody can love me.'

'It isn't true,' Ifar dared not correct her any further. He couldn't risk it. Not without knowing it was reciprocated. 'You are loved. On your order, thirty ships went to the edge of the world.'

'And there they are without me,' she said. 'My own brother sent me home in shackles. Because I defended his honour.'

'What happened to you, Freydis?'

'The Icelanders hurt me,' she told him. 'I defended myself and my brothers, that's all.'

To see her in battle, Ifar thought, as he blinked slowly in the darkness.

'Tomorrow night the Lords will gather and I will stand on trial for defending my family's name. My family that doesn't love me. My own brother will put me on trial and decide what is to be done with me. Perhaps they will kill me.'

'Lief couldn't,' Ifar said quickly. As much to his own horrified heart as to her. 'Not his own blood. He is noble like his father.'

'That's what scares me,' Freydis said. She was close again. 'But I will defend my name. All of the people who came back here with me will bear witness against me but I will defend my name.'

'I will defend your name my Lord.'

'I ask more of you,' she said. 'I will never be safe here again, once they know what I've done. Not me, not Torvard. Nobody. Even Lief Eiriksson cannot be everywhere.'

'Where will you go?'

'Where will *we* go.'

'We?' asked Ifar, dry-mouthed and breathless.

'I will ask for ten ships,' Freydis said. Closer again. Her voice was almost in his ear. He could feel her hot breath on his neck. 'Lief will give me three. It won't be enough. But you... I don't need noble explorers or lords to come with me. I am the daughter of Eirik the Red. Whether he or his sons like it or not. I need men. Men without families. Men with courage and fearlessness who are ready to build a frontier for our people away from the claws of Christian witchcraft.'

'But my Lord will...'

'I am your Lord,' Freydis snapped. 'So you keep saying yourself.'

'Karls are not bestowed your freedoms, my Lord. We cannot just go. Lord Ketill will send ships to retrieve us...'

'Not if you all leave him,' Freydis said, close again. Softly again. 'You are respected. Amongst his karls, you are more respected than he. You can call together all of his precinct and take your own ships and come with me. He will have nothing to pursue you with. And we will not stop at Vinland. All of the New World will be ours, if you come with me. There is more world beyond the shores of Vinland than Lord Ketill could ever hope to see. And it will be ours.'

Ifar felt dizzy. The way she spoke almost made him want to say...

'If you do not,' she continued, now behind him. 'I won't last long with three ships. If I even get that.'

Ifar turned to face her but saw only her silhouette pass into the shimmering raindrops.

* * *

When Ormur of Markland told Lief Eiriksson what Freydis had done, the thought of killing her crossed his mind. Thorgunna took his wrist in her hand. He hadn't even realized he'd been tapping his finger. She didn't look at him. He looked at Freydis. She stared right at him, without ever blinking, while each of the knarr longboat's high command verified the charges Thorvald had laid out against his sister.

Silence, then, when the last witness finished her recital of the hideous crime. Lief could barely breathe. He felt Bjorn looking at the side of his face but he could not remove his eyes from Freydis. She, in turn, did not break her gaze. Those big, green eyes grew red and watery and they flickered slightly but remained fixed upon him as though she could see inside of him. See the thought of killing her that burned there.

'My Lord, you must speak,' Bjorn said softly.

Thorgunna squeezed his wrist.

'Why?' Lief whispered.

'Because while the Icelander's Althing tried to do to me what they wanted, those women and those children and those enfeebled thralls did not try to stop them,' Freydis said. 'I was not the spoils of war. They had no claim to me!'

Silence while her voice echoed through the Mead Hall. The fire pit behind her glowed red and cast her shadow across the floor, right to the edge of Lief's table. Nobody dared speak.

'Straumfjord must be protected at all costs,' she continued, in that soft, silky timbre. 'It is our first step into a true Empire. Not built on trade and negotiations but on conquest. As we speak, heathens rise against us all across Europe. Since the time of Charlemagne, we have been losing our place in this world because we have not fought for it. They send their warlocks everywhere. All across the homelands. Iceland as well. Anyone could be poisoned. Look at the lands beyond Byzantium, where they slaughtered everyone who denied their one God. What becomes of the Children of *Asgard*? They'll turn us against *Odin*. Never again will *Freyr* quench our thirsts, will *Njord* fill our sails or *Skadi* lead our hunters to anything but barren lands. The *Valkyrie* will cast us out of *Valhalla*. We will have no world!'

She finally looked away from Lief to turn her eyes all across the table. Every man and woman who sat on the council would have thought she was looking directly at them. Everyone who heard her voice would have sworn it was spoken only into their ears.

'You know it's true,' she said. 'Our ancestors saw the Roman Gods fall. Our uncles and aunts passed the nightmares of what

[41]

death Ragnar Lodbrok suffered at the hands of the heathen Aella. They do not intend peace. They burn men at stakes, they gouge out women's eyes and tear their bodies asunder and they pollute children's minds to turn in their mothers and their fathers. Time creeps on and their influence only spreads. They will turn their children against you. You know.'

Freydis was looking now at Thorfinn.

He nodded. 'It is true. I have heard many disturbing things. They especially torture women.'

'Vinland is more than grapes and wine,' Freydis pleaded. 'It is our last hope. A vestige where our way of life may be preserved far from their poison. The lands beyond it are unending. Britannia will fall. Our homelands can no longer offer us haven. We of the old world must forge our own kingdoms and assert our place on this earth. A place where they dare not venture.'

'We know the importance of Vinland,' Leif managed to croak.

'Then you know why I did what I did,' Freydis said. 'The Icelanders tried to harm me in a way only heathens would. I could not allow Straumfjord to be compromised. It is all we have.'

Thorgunna squeezed Lief's wrist even harder and did not release it.

'I will not sentence my own sister to death,' Lief said. 'Freydis, you will go back to the homelands. You will stay there in exile. You and Torvard and whatever children you make will live in disgrace for all your years and all of theirs.'

'Let me live in disgrace back in Vinland.'

'Thorvald sent you *away* from Vinland.'

'Thorvald sent me away from Markland. I will go to Hop. Or to Helluland. Somewhere else. I will expand our frontiers.'

'It is suicide,' cried Hallbera Ofeigursdottir.

'Then my sentence remains death and I will take it!' Freydis said. 'As a skjoldmoy, with a battle-axe in my hand. But I will make *Valhalla* a place on earth before it happens. I will make Vinland the gates to all of the Nordic Empire and they will be open for all eternity to those persecuted by these one-God heathens, wherever they may be.'

'We have not the recourses,' Lief said.

'Ten ships, brother.'

'Ten ships will not go with you,' Lief said. 'I gave you ten ships last time and you took thirty of the Icelanders'. Then you declare war on them and slaughter their children. What ships will go with you?'

'I will muster a fleet of fifty by the day after tomorrow,' Freydis said. 'We will go to Vinland. We will forge a frontier on Hop. Ten years, my brother. Ten years, I will send word that there is a New World for us. All of it. Then you will send a thousand knarr.'

Lief stared at her a moment. *If it would rid him of her...*

'I will,' he said.

'We will go with Freydis,' Thorfinn said. His table barked and shouted in agreeance. 'With your Lord's permission.'

Lief reached one hand across and touched his wife's knuckles. They were cold. He'd expected to let Thorfinn gather information from Freydis. Maybe take her. But for him to go under her command?

'We will bring thralls,' Thorfinn said. 'I will bring word of Chieftain Freydis' victories. You will have my word of honour that all will be true.'

'Madness,' Bjorn whispered.

'You'll be rid of her forever,' Thorgunna whispered.

'Very well,' Lief said. He felt sweat flood his tunic. Then he stood. 'Freydis, you will take ten ships, and however many others you can coerce, to Helluland or Hop. I will send word to Thorvald separately that your expedition is not to be hindered by him or by any resident of Straumfjord. You have ten years. In that time, I expect one boatload of the red skraelingjar every year from Thorfinn, or I will cut off your settlement. You will be gone by the dawn of the next night. I will never see you again.'

'Thank...'

'Don't thank me,' Lief cut in. 'Were you anyone but the blood of my father I'd have had you beheaded this very night.'

4

The Polar Bear

'Oonban calls upon us to die,' Shendeek breathed as the warm firelight beat against his stern, withered face. Sons, nephews and men married into the family flanked him to midway around the circle, where the messenger band led by Wobee of the Forest began on either side.

'The boy brings word that their number is fewer now than it has ever been,' Wobee said as he waved his hand over Madawaak.

The boy straightened up while Shendeek regarded him with eyes sunk in the depths of a long life's wisdom. His body was still frigid with cold. The warmth of the fire tingled against his flesh as though a battle raged to break the icy barrier. Outside, the wind still howled. Snow had pelted the growing hunting party as they'd come upon the first families of the Great River, as far north as Madawaak's kind ventured. They were a different people across the river, in the Farther Lands. Even this close to them, Shendeek and his people radiated an imposing aura of otherness that Madawaak had to admit frightened him. But he sat upright with his fear. Just as he was always taught. Even though the cold made him tremble.

'That boy couldn't see over the flower petals...' a son said. Shandeek silenced him with a steady wave of his hand.

'It is not by their number now that we die,' Shendeek said as he turned his gaze to the trail of smoke that crept up through the opening in the mamateek's roof. 'I have seen the great water covered in their ships. I have seen our Great River red with blood.'

Keathut groaned audibly. The sound made Madawaak blush and bow his head apologetically. The Great River people were steeped in the superstitions of the Farther Lands. But now was not the time to insult them.

'I have not been called to a hunt with Oonban or any of the Forest Fathers without caribou flocks to hunt for,' Shendeek continued, seemingly unaware of the insult. 'Not since the times of war with the Broken Lands have I sent my sons south for blood.'

'The Pale Ones are demons,' Wobee said. 'Does your fire crackle with the tears of Mammasamit's family? Does it sing to you the screams of his women as they were set upon and taken as slaves? Come more Pale Ones. Come enough that they cover the ocean. If the Great River runs red, it will be with their blood and mine.'

'The people of the Farther Lands have spoken to us,' Shendeek voiced.

'Then you have made peace with them?' Keathut spat.

'I did not say we made peace with them, I said they have spoken to us,' Shendeek asserted. 'They have told us that Pale Ones have come and gone from their shores.'

'Then they have made peace with demons,' Keathut said.

'It is often wise to do so,' Shendeek said quickly.

'What do they say?' Wobee asked.

'What have I not said? Are you not alarmed?' Shendeek asked calmly. 'Oonban calls us to die, but the God Spirits left us to die when the first Pale Ones set foot upon these lands. *Aich-mud-Yim* brings death on the winds. They carry a demon that has not yet shown its full power to us. The men of my village will join you for Oonban's hunt. But it is not because we are summoned by the Forest Fathers. It is because we know the nature of our enemy. We have no choice. If we do not die fighting, we die slaves.'

Wobee stood. The rest of the band stood with him. The men gathered at Shendeek's flanks stood as well and the two at his sides helped their old Father to his feet.

'We have seen times when men shed the blood of men,' Wobee said.

'I am too old to see any more,' Shandeek said. 'If I could trade all our memories for the battle ahead of us, I would.'

There was a respectful silence. Madawaak mourned the talking as the wind howled and the mamateek creaked and cracked.

'Take ochre for all of them,' Shandeek said to his boys. 'And for yourselves. It is the coldest winter I can remember.'

* * *

Deep in the jagged ravine the Great River carried white chunks of ice out into the ocean. They seemed luminous with the faint moonlight they caught. Wind lashed the travellers. Madawaak walked behind Wobee with his head held low in his furs and caught glances over the edge of the rocky cliffs at the water below. Around them, beyond the clearing, the dark forest brooded beneath the icy mantle that spread across its peaks. No life stirred but them. Madawaak had heard the names of their new companions but now it was too cold. Wherever their skin was exposed, it burned. The sky was streaked with black clouds that swept so swiftly across the sky it felt as though the surface of the earth might tip over. Far ahead stood the mountains. The dim lights of the village fires glowed like dim stars and guided the hunting party.

Wobee stopped and gestured towards the trees. Shelter. They had to rest for the night. There was no walking against that merciless wind.

As Madawaak and the others followed him from the towering cliffs that flanked the borderlands between their world and the world of the Farther Lands, he thought to himself, *Why this land? Of all their conquests in all the unknown worlds, why did the Pale Ones come to us?*

* * *

Morning sun calmed the winds and beams of light shattered the thick dome of cloud that settled over the woodlands. Demasduit trudged down through the snow. Below her father's village, across the grassy fields where the caribou came to graze and the

[46]

summer wolves would hunt them along with the men, the fern forest twinkled and glistened as the snow slowly melted off the fronds.

She stopped when she heard the rustling.

'How strange,' she said aloud. 'I thought I'd have to go all the way to the lake before I found game. It must be my lucky day.'

Silence met her in return.

Demasduit carefully raised her bow and picked an arrow from the quiver across her back. 'I wonder what it could be... A fox? I'll have to aim well to hit a fox...'

A little gasp. Demasduit had her pray pinned.

'Too small to be a seal,' she continued as she carefully drew back an arrow and aimed it far from the source of the sound. 'Too clumsy to be a Great Auk.'

She prowled through the waist-high ferns that gathered beneath the towering dogwood trees like water held in the palm of a hand.

'Maybe a baby seal that got lost? Maybe even a baby caribou... I've got it! I'll just take careful aim and...'

'No! Don't shoot me!' Shanawdithit's little voice cried out.

'Oh no! It's a wolf! And it's impersonating my baby sister!'

'No! It is me! It is me!'

'I don't believe you, wolf! You'd better come out and prove it!'

'Are you going to shoot me?'

'Only if you're a trickster-wolf!'

Demasduit saw little Shanawdithit emerge from the ferns beside her. The big, brown eyes were wide with fear and watery with betrayal.

'Don't shoot me, Dema...'

Demasduit slipped the arrow back into her quiver. 'Well, don't sneak up on me in the forest.'

'But I want to go catch sculpin with you,' Shanawdithit said as she stepped out of the entanglement of fronds and revealed the dark patches all over her leathers.

'Where did you get the idea I'm catching sculpin?' Demasduit couldn't help but giggle.

'You're going to the lake. That's where the sculpin are.'

Demasduit slipped her bow over Shana's shoulders. 'That's very clever of you, to know that.'

Shanawdithit slipped her hand up through the bow and Demasduit let it go. The little girl tried to spin it on her arm. 'Were you really going to shoot me?'

'Never. But I won't be happy if you make me walk all the way back to the village. Will you go?'

'I want to go with you,' Shanawdithit said casually as she spun the bow right off her arm. Demasduit snatched it up before she could.

'What do you catch sculpin with?'

'A net.'

'Is this a net?'

'It's a bow.'

'What do you catch with a bow?'

'Foxes, birds, caribou...'

'Dangerous things,' Demasduit said. 'Not things for little girls.'

'Not things for any girls.'

'Maybe some girls aren't meant to be girls.'

'But you never come back with any foxes or birds or...'

'...there's a first time for everything. Now, go home!'

'You're going to get in trouble.'

'We're both going to get in trouble if you stay here,' Demasduit reasoned. 'Even more if you follow me. Now go on! Don't make me late.'

Shanawdithit folded her arms. 'Late for hunting?'

'Yes, late for hunting,' Demasduit replied. 'Go on!'

'I won't get in trouble. You will,' Shanawdithit kicked a piece of birchbark out from under the snow and turned it over. 'I'm too little to know better.'

Her little hand reached up and touched the end of Demasduit's bow.

'I'll make you one of these if you go back to Mama and Papa right now,' Demasduit bribed.

'Really?' Shanawdithit squealed as her eyes bulged.

'Yes. Go.'

'You have to promise.'

'I promise. Go!'

Shanawdithit turned and enthusiastically ran back through the ferns towards the forest edge. Demasduit continued towards the lake.

'Dema!' Shanawdithit's voice called. Demasduit turned back. 'Are there really trickster-wolves?'

Demasduit held out the bow. 'Do you want one or not?'

'I'm going! I'm going!'

Demasduit watched until her little head was bobbing up and down across the snow-covered meadows close enough to the village that nothing would intercept her without being seen. Then, she continued towards the lakes. The crystalline mantle reduced to slush under the prickly shadows of the towering pines that filled the forest with their amber scent. Birds chirped high overhead. When Demasduit's step disturbed a bush, a rabbit leaped out and pelted off in a zigzag that kicked snow and dirt up in its wake.

It was almost as though nothing unusual had happened at all. As though on the other side of the pines she'd find the wintering grounds of Mammasamit's family. She'd break through the wall of undergrowth that skirted the shiny, still lake surface and see them up on the banks as they smoothed over the earth to build their mamateeks. For a moment, she was expecting it. The reminder that he and all of those with him were gone hit her like a punch deep inside. She walked the rest of the way sullen and unaware.

It was well into the morning before the honks and calls of cormorants and geese told Demasduit she was near the lakes. The undergrowth gave its usual wiry resistance. Demasduit grunted as the twigs and branches clutched at her skins and hair and tried to pull her feet out from under her. The banks were hard but wet. The ice sheet that would soon cover the lake was cracked and bobbled loosely about. On the far bank, Demasduit saw a thin herd of caribou gathered by the water's edge. Bound for the Broken Lands for the winter.

She took a few paces back towards the undergrowth and walked along it, rounding the lake towards them. As Demasduit drew near, the brush thinned. She ducked into the shadows of the trees and stalked the long way around. Behind where they were gathering, they'd left a trail of broken mantle and unearthed root. Along it walked the stragglers. Elderly. Sick. Inhibited by the long migration.

'I will take your pain away,' she whispered under her breath as her eyes fell upon one. It was a doe. Not old. But her gait was shaky. Wolves would pick her off as soon as they got to the vast clearings of the broken lands. If not sooner... no young followed her. She may not have bred yet.

'There will be no breeding for you,' Demasduit whispered.

A pluckier doe passed the weary one by and she stopped and looked at it. Then she stopped walking altogether and just stood there with ribs that pulsed in and out quickly. A handsome buck walked by. She took no notice. For a moment, it seemed as though her big, dark eyes had fallen upon Demasduit who slowly approached through the tree trunks.

A few of the passing caribou froze still. Their ears prickled. Air billowed thick and white from their nostrils. Demasduit crouched low and halted her advance. The weary doe was concealed behind a young pine. Demasduit slid one of her chert-tipped arrows from the quiver and primed it on the bow but did not draw back.

'Show your face to me,' she breathed. 'I will ease your...'

A spear shot out with a sudden thwack from the deeper fern forest and pierced the doe through her ribs, right behind her forelimbs. The stricken being cried out. All the others shot off towards the lakes, jumping and ducking and weaving through the tree trunks. The doe fell on its haunches. Blood burst from her mouth and haemorrhaged from her wounds. Fast upon her were three thick-bodied men. The first of them beat the doe across the head with a club and sent her body heaving to one side. While she was down, another covered her eyes. Together, the other two opened her throat and let the thick, red life pour from her onto the forest floor.

The tall, muscular man that struck with the club turned towards Demasduit. She stood upright. His strong face and sparkling brown eyes seemed to weaken before her the same way they had years ago when they'd first met only a few paces from here. Though her heart stirred, she was angry. It was hard work to stay that way. But she would; it was decided.

'You're supposed to be watching the Pale Ones in Madawaak's stead,' she said as she walked towards him.

'I can see them better from here than he could from within their camp,' Mooaumook said. Behind him, the men of Makdaachk were already stripping the meat, cutting off the insular fat and sinew and placing it in sacks fashioned from patches of birchwood bark. 'Just like the trail you leave.'

'I leave no trail,' Demasduit snapped. But she was breaking beneath her façade the longer he stared at her. The heat in her foundations was too strong. 'You knew they were coming.'

'Help us, will you!' one of the men said.

'Come on,' Mooaumook invited as he turned back to the kill. 'You think you're so adept to men's work? Let's see how you do women's work.'

The anger at the comment bubbled to the surface as dizzying lust and she followed him down to the carcass as she would follow him to the edge of the icy, rolling brine beyond the Farther Lands. They worked with red, slippery fingers to free the meat from the body. Then to strip it of anything that might retain its heat. They placed the pieces in sacks until they almost spilled over and then laboured them down to the water's edge. The fat and the skin they placed in other sacks on their own.

Demasduit followed behind the men. She turned back towards the carcass and saw the little red and black foxes had gathered. They kept a distance. Heads low. Afraid of the humans.

'Go on,' she said. 'We need no more.'

The foxes set upon the kill and crawled in and around the bones to strip what was left and eat the offcuts. *Afraid*, Demasduit thought. Even when they could see that the men had taken the meat of a caribou and would need no more. Foxes learned fast. They had learned to fear...

At the lakeside, they washed the meat quickly and laid it on dry rocks under the sun. The herd of caribou kept to themselves and drank the water and pecked at the undergrowth that Demasduit had stalked them from. But her eyes fell upon the rocky outcropping which trailed to the lakeside where they rested their meat. She felt the heat of Mooaumook's gaze. Looked at him. He'd noticed it too.

The meat was all laid out. The other two were throwing stones at the ice to break up the thin sheet even more. Mooaumook and Demasduit looked at each other. It was she who moved towards the outcropping first. Then he followed. On the other side was a soft bed of pine needles that was held there by rocks as though it were a cradle. As they had for the first time, they went there. She turned. He was already upon her. Standing over her. She felt the skin of his face brush against hers before their lips met in a deep kiss that made her issue an aching moan.

They stopped. Had the others heard?

Stones thwacked on the ice sheet.

Their mouths rammed against each other and their lips opened and their tongues rolled over each other as though their bodies could form one and melt into each other. His strong hands held her hips. Moved along her sides. She gripped his firm bicep. They kissed deeper and pressed their bodies harder together. She felt him swell against her hip. Demasduit couldn't wait. With her trembling fingertips, she unlaced his trousers and reached in to his warm, throbbing flesh. Holding him stole her breath from her. In his arms she was lowered down to the needles.

His lips explored the skin of her neck. Hot breath caressed her ear. His fingertips trailed through her hair and down her body and touched her soft flesh where she wettened for him. Demasduit's body arched in need. He cleaved between her thighs. She let out a soft moan. They pushed and fumbled the skins off each other and Demasduit's scent blended with Mooaumook's and they lay on a sheet of their clothes naked together. She took his hot flesh in her hand. She kissed him as she held it against the sensitive spots between her legs so they could feel each other's heat and he could tingle for her the way she tingled for him.

Then the exhilarating fullness and heat as he slid into her. Her fingers curled around his sides as he slowly drew out. Mooaumook held his lips near hers. He slowly slid in again and Demasduit wanted to scream.

How had they waited so long? Why had he not come for her all the times she'd played around this lake? Why not have this feeling all the time?

The need built and tensed her again and Demasduit wrapped her legs around him and drove his thrusts harder and faster. He did as she wanted. Deep and strong movements that filled her with a storm that roiled and longed to burst out of her. Then it did. She held him close and in some corner of her delirious mind remembered there were two others just in time to suppress her cries.

'Did it happen for you?' she asked. Demasduit watched him dress.

'It did,' he said. 'I better make sure they turn the meat over.'

Demasduit let him go. She wanted to lay there for a moment and just feel it all course through her body. When Demasduit knew she had to, she dressed slowly. Savoured every second of the nakedness she'd shared with Mooaumook. As she reached for her bow and quiver, she felt something cold slither quickly up her spine.

Eyes on her.

Icy fear seized her and Demasduit slowly turned towards the source of that overwhelming presence. It knew it was spotted. The great, rippling wall of white fur launched out of the pine trees and barrelled towards her. Demasduit grabbed her bow and quiver and ran for the lake. She scrambled up the rock outcropping and felt the giant paws swipe at her heels before she rolled down on the mud.

The polar bear followed her easily.

Demasduit rolled to her feet and fired an arrow. The bear was struck in the shoulder but charged down from the rocks anyway, its stride unbroken. Her ground lost. Demasduit turned and ran towards the men. The bear charged out of the forest and followed. One of the men hurled a spear. It turned aside and fell harmlessly but a few paces from his hand. Mooaumook picked up his club but his brothers held him back. Demasduit turned to fire another shot but a rock caught her heel. She crashed into the mud. The arrow launched into the sky. Demasduit scrambled to her feet to run but the massive force hit her from behind and a crushing grip closed upon her hip as she fell. The ground rocked beneath her as the monster ripping at her hip flung her from side to side.

A spear struck the bear in the shoulder. It howled and released her.

Her arrows spilled everywhere Demasduit stood and ran. The bear chased even as the spear protruded from its shoulder. The pain in her hip finally caught her and she stumbled and fell against the rocks again. She felt the hot breath of the creature close behind her. The gnashing teeth would sink through her at any moment... she crawled.

A heavy blow swiped across her shoulder and knocked her through the air. Demasduit hit the rocks and felt the warm fluid seep down her side. The bear swept over her. Another spear hit its paw. Demasduit climbed up and landed on the spear that the first man had thrown. She grabbed it in her hands and rolled onto her back and propped the end against the rocks beneath her. The bear opened its mouth to lunge on her.

The spear entered the fur beneath its jaw. Demasduit felt it run through the flesh and crash against the bone. The bear let out a blood-curdling howl of agony and retreated. It bit and snatched at the spear. The men surrounded it and rammed their spears into its body while Mooaumook rained his club down on its head until it collapsed and still he kept hitting it.

The pain in Demasduit's hip and shoulder flared and filled her with buzzing, hammering agony. She screamed out and tried to crawl away. Just as quickly, firm hands were upon her. She swiped at them. Unable to tell anymore what had attacked her. Blackness grew from the haze that consumed her mind and finally all was darkness.

5

The Winter Closes In

'The curse of *Hel* on all of this plague!' Jannik screamed as he hurled the knife into the cutting log while the maggot-infested intestines of yet another cow dangled from the slit carcass before him.

His thralls stopped their tanning of infested skins and turned to watch him.

'I told you to separate them!' Jannik screamed at his apprentice.

'None of us can tell which are infested and which aren't,' Stellan answered with a wave towards the thralls. Jannik turned towards them. They quickly busied themselves again.

'They've infested your eyes, boy,' Jannik said as he turned back to Stellan.

'They've not,' Stellan argued. Though he uncomfortably rubbed them with his finger and thumb. That was how Goran had found the ones in his eyes. 'They haven't.'

'It's in their eyes boy, all of their eyes,' Jannik pinched open the eyelids of the dead cow. The normally brown iris had become blotched with light blue and white patches. 'Check them again.'

'And what?' Stellan tested.

'Release the healthy ones...' Jannik was catching his breath. His fiery temper simmered down. He limply plucked his knife back from the stump and looked at the hideous white worms that crawled around in the dry, brown-coloured meat. The stink was nauseating. Jannik could taste it.

'Slaughter the rest,' he breathed.

'We can't...'

'Boy!' he barked. 'Release the healthy ones, I say. Or go off yourself. I'll check them with you but get them away from here. This place is cursed.'

'Why release the healthy ones?'

'Because this place is CUUUURSED!' Jannik screamed.

'What will we do for meat?'

'Hurry along, boy.'

'What about Thorvald?'

'The infestation is spreading!'

'We'll all be killed anyway, if we starve out Straumfjord.'

'I will deal with the Chieftain.'

'What will we do for meat?' Stellan said. Jannik found his sturdiness infuriating. The apprentice had not but raised his voice, while Jannik barely had a grip of himself and felt temper boiling up inside him again. 'There aren't enough healthy ones to feed Straumfjord, and you want to let them go.'

'We'll hunt for our meat,' Jannik said.

'You know they won't like that,' Stellan's voice finally changed. It became wobbly with fear. Jannik felt it too. Both he and his apprentice knew there wasn't enough fish in the cove to feed everyone, that the yeast had frozen and they were without bread, and what was salted or pickled would not last another month. Winter was only just beginning. And hunting would put them at odds with skraelingjar.

'Are we Norse people or not?' Jannik breathed. 'How long will Thorvald have us clinging to the cove out of fear of them when the rest of the world fears us?'

Jannik was already storming out.

'Come on,' Stellan called to the thralls. 'You, you and you. Help me.'

'Burn the carcasses of the infested,' Jannik warned, before he closed the door behind him.

* * *

'The seals have left,' Anders advised, while he held his leather cap in in his hands and bunched it in his white fingers. 'We are waiting for the fish to return but our spots have dried up.'

'Lief said the same thing...' Gottfried breathed from beside Thorvald.

'I know what Lief said.'

'We will keep casting our nets,' Anders said. 'Until we freeze out there. The birds no longer lay eggs on the cliff faces and the sky is silent of them. We have made stores for the winter. But we cannot promise they will be enough.'

Thorvald's head fell into his arm and he stroked his brow. To everyone in the room, the little chair was seeming bigger and bigger. Thorvald knew it. The Chieftain's lodge stirred with quiet domesticity but every glance in Thorvald's direction avoided by the working thralls was as bad to him as someone saying aloud what he knew was true. Lief had overestimated his brother.

'Go further out,' Gottfried said, suddenly. 'Why are you only fishing in the cove? The ocean belongs to us.'

'The icebergs, my Lord,' Anders answered, weakly. 'They're growing dense and more frequent. They'll smash our faerings.'

'Are you not masters of the sea?' Gottfried waved his hand in dismissal. 'Fish the oceans, man. That's what they're for.'

Anders' eyes grew wet and his bottom lip quivered. But he bowed his head. 'My Lord.'

He left and the butcher took his place. 'My apprentice is at slaughtering my stock. There are a handful that aren't infested with these worms. Our only hope is to turn them loose and hope they take to the wild.'

'Are you insane?' Thorvald slapped his hand despairingly onto his knee. 'Wolves will pick them off. Our scouts have reported polar bears moving with the snowfall.'

'Our only hope, my Lord,' Jannik repeated. 'I don't know whether we brought the worms with us or they were already here. But the worms like human flesh as much as they like cow. I have no choice. The carcasses have to be burned. There are too many pregnant women who could be exposed.'

'Then we must hunt for our meat,' Gottfried said.

'There are enough skins to last us,' Jannik. 'Enough meat too. As long as it's only to get home.'

'You are out of line...' Gottfried began.

'If you want to go home, then go to Lars and buy a boat and go,' Thorvald said. 'Explain to Lief what happened here yourself.'

Silence. Jannik licked his lips.

'I was merely stating our supplies,' he said, low and gruff. 'We hunt then.'

'We hunt,' Thorvald said, weakly.

Jannik left. When nobody came to take his place, Thorvald took a breath that felt like his first for that whole day.

'Lief emphasized the importance of not hunting the skraelingjar animals,' he said.

'Lief also emphasized the importance of harnessing the grasslands of Hop,' Gottfried said. 'The cows would have been able to graze for another month at least. On Hop the ground stays soft. Here it has got so hard that our builders cannot uproot turf to extend homes for the babies being born. Babies we can't feed.'

'We let a vital summer pass us by,' Thorvald said while his fingers interlocked and he stared at the stained tabletop in front of him. 'Those babies will not see the next one... we have found *Niflheim.*'

'We have found a rich and fertile land,' Gottfried said. 'We have to use it properly. If we take our grape seeds to Hop now, they will survive the winter.'

'How can we begin a new frontier now?' Thorvald finally raised his voice. 'Was I to predict that worms would infest our cows? What would fresh grass do about that anyway?'

'It wouldn't matter, my Lord,' Gottfried answered, calmly. 'The seals have gone to Hop. So have the reindeer and the fish and birds. We wouldn't need the cows. If there is enough game, we can subsist on the stores we have but without it...'

'Where the animals go, the skraelingjar go too.'

'If we have to slaughter skraelingjar to save the lives of our people, my Lord, then so be it. I respect your brother's wishes as I do yours. But they are not more important to me than our people.'

[59]

Thorvald closed his eyes and breathed hard through his nose.

'Tyra is with child again,' Gottfried said.

'*Odin* smiles upon you. A boy again?'

'I think a girl,' Gottfried leaned in closer. 'My son was born on Vinland. My daughter shall be too. And they shall grow up here in a strong country. They will know that no skraeling commands their people any more than a thrall would. They will know their Lords are strong. That their father serves strong leaders.'

Thorvald looked at Gottfried.

'Commission twelve karvi from Lars and take enough stores for ten families,' Thorvald said. 'Have as many atgiers, arrows and axes made as you can while Lars works. Any skraelingjar that you come across should be regarded as hostile. I want every man, woman and child that can wield a weapon to know that. You are to send one karvi a day with whatever stores you procure from the wildlife and from the seeds you grow.'

'I will send you skraelingjar thralls...'

'No,' Thorvald said. 'They will never be thralls. Kill them all.'

Gottfried stood and bowed. Then, he marched out of the lodge and left Thorvald alone with his servants.

* * *

The powerful Nubian thralls carried the karvi upon their shoulders down to the stones that rattled under each wave that crashed upon them. They set it down on the large wooden trestles. There the apprentices looked it over. Lars watched on while his crew worked on patching up the karvi that had run afoul of a reef just offshore.

One of the apprentices looked up and shook his head.

'No good for float, suh!' one of the Nubians called out.

Lars' heart sank. He looked back at the second crew.

'The hay won't form a seal,' an apprentice said. 'We can't spread the fat that far.'

'Strip them both,' Lars ordered. 'Get everything you can off the junk pile as well. Pull one of the knarr out of the water and get working on that. I will not go to Gottfried with nothing.'

'We need those to go home,' Rolf said.

'I suppose we are home...' Lars' voice trailed off as he turned his eyes out towards the cove. His body stiffened and his mouth opened as though he couldn't get enough air in for what he needed. 'Man the boats! Get out there!'

The apprentices and a few good Nubians hurried to the stocks of faerings and carried them down to the crashing brine. The waves knocked the boats out of their hands. Their bodies were thrown against the pebbles. When their bodies fell into the water, it felt like a million tiny pins plunged into their skin. But they pulled themselves up and tried again. Faering smashed in their hands. But one got through. Then two... two would have to do. The others bobbed around as splinters in the brine while the boatmen stood helpless, wet and freezing.

Out near the heads, the lone faering was quickly sinking. The one man that rowed with all his might left a slick of red behind him in the swells and raised and lowered him like a cork. Lars couldn't see whether it was his or not. He rowed hard. It was likely not.

Lars and his crew could only watch from the pebbles as the two faering that got through rowed out towards him. Others gathered on the shore and watched. The cold air was like knives in their lungs as the tension weighted on their breaths. The two rescue boats came up alongside the stricken rower and plucked him out of the ocean as the boat turned bow-up and sank. He went on one faering. The other took another ragged form from the sinking vessel right before it disappeared entirely.

'*Freyja*, not these men,' Lars whispered desperately as the two rescue faering rowed back towards the perilous breakers. Moment to moment, the shore lost sight of them. White water formed a wall that crashed down. But everyone knew who they were and what they'd been doing out there. 'Leave us these men.'

He prayed until the two faering smashed on the stones. The men were but limbs and rags amongst the thundering white foam that turned pink around one of the bodies. Onlookers rushed in to help them. Three of Lars' men, one a Nubian, were dragged to shore, as well as two fishermen.

Sudden unease roiled through the crowd as the last of the men was pulled from the waves. Both legs were gone. Ragged flesh and ripped arteries and shattered stubs of bone protruded from beneath torn clothing. The man was white and blue. Dead. But only recently. Perhaps since they pulled him from the sinking boat.

Onlookers pulled the rescuers away and dragged them towards spot fires that burned around the village, where they joined the men whose faerings had not been able to push through the breakers. The fishermen were left on the pebbles. Lars hurried to the whole man's side and saw from the trembles that were spasmodically overcoming him that he was dying. Delirium flashed in and out of his eyes. When he looked up at Lars, he seemed almost well again.

'The boatman,' he wheezed.

'What happened?'

'Sea monster,' he said. His eyes closed and the delirium stole him away. The crowd formed a circle around him and Lars. Rolf came running but stopped at the other man. He lay on his back. Mouth agape. Eyes open. Rolf looked from the corpse to Lars and back again, his young eyes haunted by violent death for the first time.

Lars kneeled by the living man.

'Tell me what you saw.'

The man just shook and stared in terror up at the overcast sky. Lars took his shoulders and shook him. He stopped trembling and slowly turned his gaze back to Lars, full of confusion.

'Tell me what you saw.'

'Fog,' he said. 'Icebergs came from the fog. We'd chased seals until something came up from the depths and poached them from us. Anders harpooned one. But they were many. They smashed our karvi against the icebergs. Sea dragons.'

The man sat up.

'The men are all sunk in the blackest waters I ever saw,' he said. Then, he crashed down onto the stones. That final look of white horror was frozen upon his dead face.

'*Ran* has taken our fishermen,' Lars said as he stood to address the crowd. He found them parted, with Thorvald and Gottfried standing before him. 'My Lord...'

'Will the knarr make Greenland?' Thorvald asked, grimly. His eyes never left the dead fishermen.

'But one,' Lars answered. 'Only under a master's hand. And she'll need work.'

'Take as many of the weak as you can,' Thorvald said. 'And all the stores you need. Take her yourself. Send word to my brother. Tell him Thorvald has failed him. Tell him Straumfjord needs immediate rescue.'

Thorvald turned and walked back towards the village. Gottfried stayed behind. He looked out to sea and whistled a single note softly through his teeth. Then he followed Thorvald.

* * *

Winds lashed and pulled at the sails unrelentingly. The sky was a thick sheet of deep grey that pelted them with icy water by morning and at night. The sun rose and set. The waves never let up. Lars kept vigil at the helm all the while, never resting, never stopping even as the bowsprit dragon's head rose and fell beneath the very waves that threatened to consume them. He was frozen to the tiller. He gripped it so tight for so long that the ice claimed his fingers and kept them clasped there while his body shivered. But the icebergs. They came from the thick wall of fog that seemed to hurl the giant, ghostly mountains at them. Lars roared as he turned them port and starboard. Not a man nor woman slept. They ran fore and aft and bow to stern repairing the damage as the sea relentlessly tore chunks from the gunwale, the hull or the deck.

Those back in Straumfjord needed him to make it. The thought kept him alive. Their eyes, their faces. The sounds of their voices. If *Ran* claimed him and this knarr, so *Hel*'s curse on Markland would be complete.

Darkness threatened him. Haunted him like his shadow. It stole his mind from his in every blink and only by effort could he seize it back.

'Not yet *Freyja*,' he kept saying, until the icy winds stole his voice. 'Not yet.'

Then, from the heaving and the crashing and the roaring, there rose the tune of a horn.

'Take up weapons!' cried Rolf. 'The *Valkyries* have come for us.'

'Turn the sails!' Lars tried to cry. Blades of agony shot up his throat and the sound failed him. He coughed and rolled his head towards Rolf.

The stupid boy finally realized he was needed. He ran to his master.

'My Lord...'

'Turn the sails,' Lars growled. 'Ships approach. No *Valkyries*.'

Lars turned his eyes to the southwest, whence he heard the dull horn issue. Just as he did, the sound carried to them again. Louder this time. Rolf's eyes widened and his face turned ashen.

'Have they followed us from Straumfjord?'

Lars shook his head. He looked again in the direction, hoping Rolf would figure it out this time. The strain of moving his neck seemed to stop his blood from flowing. He felt his veins freezing under his skin.

'From Helluland?' Rolf finally guessed it. 'There!'

He pointed. Indeed, two knarr approached. They were adorned with shields and oarsmen and untorn sails and they wove through the bobbing icebergs as though they were flying. Headed right towards them.

'Turn us about boy,' Lars said as his strength failed him and he collapsed to his knees. Rolf put his arms around the dying man. It was no good. Lars' hands finally snapped free of the tiller. But his fingers were left behind. Red icicles jutted from the stumps on his blackened palms. 'Turn us about and go with them.'

Rolf could only ease his master down to the deck. He closed his eyes and the pain was finally over.

6

On the Eve

Hollered greetings issued from outside. Another family was arriving at the village so Oonban climbed to his feet. He looked down at Madawaak, who held his vigil firm as the firelight against him and its warmth blanketed him and the still form of Demasduit, whose colour had returned but not her spirit.

'That will be nearly all of them,' Oonban said. 'You should come and accept thanks for your work.'

'When she wakes,' Madawaak said without looking at Oonban.

The old warrior spread his calloused fingers and touched young Madawaak on the shoulder before he ventured out of their mamateek into the settling stillness of mid-afternoon.

'Where is Gobidin?' cried the heavily painted Moisamadrook. His family trudged up the hill behind him while he carried a tomahawk in one hand and a dagger in the other. He looked ready for battle right away. The others looked ready to collapse.

'We have not dared to go to the broken lands,' Oonban said. 'My messengers went by the Great River and the Forest Fathers only.'

'But we hunt on the broken lands,' Moisamadrook said as he stormed around the bonfire pit to Oonban's mamateek. The rest of the swollen village tended to Moisamadrook's family. 'Gobidin must join us for the feast. They are his lands. He must be with us on the raid.'

'We are not hunting caribou this winter, Moisamadrook.'

'We shall hunt caribou,' Moisamadrook answered. He was talking to all those who had gathered around the fire pit now. The men who had migrated with Wobee to join the battle. 'I did not come all this way to slaughter a few Pale Ones and then go home unfed. We continue with the winter hunt once we are finished with these demons.'

'Do not overstate our chances, Moisamadrook,' Ninejeek warned. 'Surely you have heard of what happened to Mammasamit.'

Moisamadrook snorted and tapped the tomahawk to his chest.

'Who has held his village at the passages between the mountains where the Great River is born?' he spoke to everyone again, now with his back turned to Oonban. 'Who looks from his campfire into the Farther Lands? Who lives beneath the shadows of...'

'I have watched them as well, brother,' Ninejeek interrupted. 'Do not insult our host anymore. When we hunt in the Broken Lands, we will tell Gobidin. But, at dawn, we hunt Pale Ones, and they are not as far as the Broken Lands. They are close to us here. Close enough to see our fire tonight and know we come for them at dawn.'

'Good!' Moisamadrook cried. He hit the side of the tomahawk harder against his chest.

'And you will not go unfed,' Keathut said. 'Tonight we have polar bear.'

Moisamadrook turned, wide eyed, to Oonban.

'By your hand, polar bear?'

'My daughter's. Demasduit,' Oonban answered gravely.

'Then she must be honoured,' Moisamadrook said loudly. 'She must be made a warrior and join us against the Pale Ones.'

'She clings to life,' Oonban said. 'She has woken a few times but without memory. Without words.'

Moisamadrook placed his hand on Oonban's shoulder.

'The God Spirits will guide her back to you,' Moisamadrook said. 'Tonight we prepare for war in her honour.'

Oonban bowed his head.

Moisamadrook's family slowly mingled amongst the other tribes while the women stacked the bonfire and brought the polar bear meat down from the long sticks from which they dangled to thaw in their birchbark bags. Groups of men went off into the forest to chop the old hunting fences down for wood. The day grew darker.

Madawaak stayed by Demasduit's side. He'd only left it while Chipchowinech had to change her skins and wash her. Now he was alone with her again.

'Do not leave me, Demasduit,' he whispered. Again. 'You have given my life meaning. You have fostered my courage. You have motivated my heart and strengthened my spirit. All I have done, I have done for you. And tonight I have done great things. To fetch your eyes. If they are to stay on another then so I shall spend the rest of my life. For I do not care whether you love me. Only that you are happy and free. If it is Mooaumook who has your heart then I only hope he treats it well. Only do not leave me. Do not leave either of us. I cannot speak for him or for your family but I know that my life will be endless darkness without you.'

Demasduit's eyes snapped open. She gasped and her hands curled up in front of her chest and she screamed. Madawaak held her shoulders.

'It's okay! It's okay... you're safe!' he whispered again. Only, this time, she didn't pass out. She eased back down on the skins and breathed heavily. Her eyes searched the firelit interior of the mamateek and Madawaak could see she knew where she was. 'Demasduit. Have you come back to us?'

'There was a b...' she began, breathless. The rest did not come.

'There was. Slain by your hand.'

Footsteps thudded in behind Madawaak. He felt their presence behind him. Her family, friends, or members of the hunting party. He didn't look. She did. She looked up at all of them and tears welled in her eyes.

'Oh,' she gasped.

Madawaak knew he had to get out of her way. Oonban was first. He fell upon her in a powerful embrace. Chipchowinech followed. Weeping. Little Shanawdithit crawled up beside her. Madawaak sat behind them. He looked up at the other people

in the mamateek. Faces he'd gathered along his long journey
from which his legs still ached.

The men watched her sit upright and wince at the pain in her
hip and her shoulder. The last of the healing weed was used up.
But she rolled her arm and she moved her legs and even began
to stand.

'Not yet.' Chipchowinech caught her by the uninjured
shoulder and held her back down. 'You're not healed enough
yet.'

'She is healed enough,' Wobee objected.

Madawaak looked at the faces of the men who watched her.
Yaseek. Ninejeek. Keathut, impressed by nothing. All of them
were stunned speechless. But a graveness about them stirred
Madawaak and made him want to speak.

He could think of nothing to say.

* * *

Oonban finally left his mamateek with only Chipchowinech,
Shanawdithit and Demasduit inside. Madawaak came willingly
and quietly to join the men outside. Oonban kept a flickering
gaze upon Madawaak as he dawdled morosely around the dark
rim of the bonfire's glow. The meat of the polar bear was
distributed amongst the fighting men. They danced and enacted
the motions they would make as they slayed their enemies
tomorrow and re-enacted motions they had made as they'd slain
enemies in the past. The two dances mixed into one. Victories
come to pass and a victory of the future.

'Scouts from the Pale Ones' village will come up from the cove
to see what makes this noise,' Eenodsha said. He'd been
standing quietly next to Oonban as they waited their turn to
dance.

The loudest set of dancers yet slayed their imaginary Farther
People and retreated to their place in the circle for their share
of meat. Another group swept in and began the dance. Some of
these ones were young. Not old enough yet to have fought the
Farther People. They could only do as they would to the Pale
Ones. Oonban and Eenodsha watched the clumsy, overexcited

movements and bit their lips with nerves. Near every move might have injured one of the dancers for real.

'My son cares for Demasduit,' Eenodsha said.

'I know he does,' Oonban shuffled uncomfortably.

'He knows,' Eenodsha said. 'It's alright.'

'What do you mean, he knows?'

'He is a smart boy. He knows.'

Eenodsha broke off to dance with a group. Makdaachk appeared on Oonban's other side, while Yaseek submissively stepped aside.

'Demasduit saved my son's life, it is said,' Makdaachk said.

'No more than he saved hers,' Oonban said.

'He is a brave and strong warrior and a cunning hunter,' Makdaachk said. 'There is no better man his age or younger in all of our lands.'

'I agree.'

'Have you spoken to Moisamadrook?'

'Only briefly.'

'He and Ninejeek have similar minds,' Makdaachk said. 'They live close to the Farther People. Without a river to separate them.'

Oonban looked across the lapping tongues of flame, bright orange against the blackening night, and saw the River Fathers gathered around old Shendeek. Neither Ninejeek or Moisamadrook were amongst them. He knew they thought of themselves as different. The Mountain Fathers they called themselves. One lived in the warm seasons on the far mountain, the other on the slope that overlooked the Farther Lands. Moisamadrook often boasted that were it not for the winter migration, he would find himself amongst the camps of the Farther People.

'I remember what Ninejeek suggested to make peace with the Farther People,' Makdaachk said.

'It will never be,' Oonban said, hotly. 'Never.'

'Of course not,' Makdaachk said. 'But that is not to say that...'

Someone made a skilful move with their tomahawk. The hollers of the crowd drowned Makdaachk out for a moment. He waited.

'That is not to say that that the Farther People will not hear of the bear-slaying girl,' Makdaachk said. 'And covet her.'

'I would kill her first,' Oonban said, though tears welled in his eyes at the thought.

'You know what they believe about the two-spirited ones. That they are part gods. That they are closer to the spirit than anyone else.'

'I don't care what they believe.'

'There is a way you could deter them,' Makdaachk said. 'Two-spirits do not marry one but many. If she married a strong, brave man, and remained only with him she could slay every bear there lives and the Farther People will not want her.'

Oonban pushed the thought away but Makdaachk's eyes on him kept it there in his mind. She was young. Too young to marry. Not in body, but in mind. Still full of a need to wander and be of her own company. Oonban didn't believe she would submit to one man. He knew it was because he didn't want her to, but he didn't want her to because he believed – he knew – that she didn't want to.

'She fancies Mooaumook.'

'Does Mooaumook reciprocate?'

'He is a well-regarded man,' Makdaachk said. 'He has his pick. It will take a father's offering to still his eyes long enough to see her properly.'

The dancers had finished. The space around the bonfire was empty. The gathering watched Oonban and his company and waited.

'I will ask her,' Oonban said.

'Do not ask her, tell...'

Oonban took his group and lunged into the dance with them. Makdaachk stayed behind while the crowd roared and slapped their chests and hollered into the night.

* * *

A flattening wall of war cries blasted out towards Oonban's mamateek as Demasduit hobbled out of it. Shanawdithit followed behind her. The chord from Demasduit's tunic was gripped hard in her little hands and she stood so close as to half disappear into its folds. Chipchowinech stayed near the door and chewed her fingers. Oonban's instinct was to go to his wife, or to go help his daughter walk, but he did neither. Madawaak stood beside him, silent. The same twitches of urgency to go and help played out all over his body. But the boy held his ground. He had ground the ochre and held it in a bowl for Makdaachk.

Demasduit limped to the front of the fire and then turned. The crowd bellowed again. Shanawdithit stood even closer to her. Oonban, Makdaachk and Madawaak stepped up before her and Demasduit untied her tunic and opened it. It slipped off her shoulders and landed in a heap behind her. Madawaak handed the ochre to Makdaachk. As the elder warrior painted her body with red stripes, the onlookers hollered and cheered again.

Oonban and Madawaak stepped away and left them in the center of the circle.

Demasduit's eyes watered at the overwhelming honour bestowed upon her. What now? What would be expected of her? What would she do?

Worst of all; was this but a formality? Would everything just go back to normal for her tomorrow? The men go off and fight, hunt and explore. She'd stay at home. Grind ochre. Cut and hang meat. Make pudding.

'You will make a great Forest Mother,' Makdaachk said, as though he read her thoughts. He applied the last of the ochre to her cheeks with his thumb. 'And the finest wife my son could have.'

Demasduit froze as he whispered the last words. He stepped back and the loudest, most overwhelming thunder of cheers hit her yet. It almost lifted her into the smoke column that issued from their bonfire. Demasduit couldn't move. She felt Shanawdithit's little hands try to push her tunic back over her shoulders. But all she could think about was those words. A mother? A wife?

She loved Mooaumook. Loved his body. She grew hot even thinking about him. But marry him? Wander no more? Know no other bodies? She was short of breath. Almost dizzy.

Her eyes fell upon Madawaak, who watched her with heavy eyes. She settled. Chipchowinech took her by the hands and led her gently back into the mamateek.

* * *

But Demasduit's mind would not settle and sleep would not come. She stirred and moved about. Even though it hurt. Even though the warriors had retired with their host families to their mamateeks and gone to the sleep they needed for the coming dawn. The heavy grimness that hung in the air kept her awake. Thoughts of Mooaumook kept her awake. Mooaumook and Madawaak.

The bodies of her family laid warm and snoring around her.

Demasduit rose and wrapped herself in skins and headed out through the door. The once towering bonfire now lay in a shattered bed of embers that glowed enough to light the closest walls of mamateeks. The night's cold had settled in and sunk through Demasduit's leathers. But something drew her away from her family's mamateek. Some need sent her walking towards the cliffs that overlooked the big water.

Amidst all the revelry the weight of war hung in every heart. It was no hunt they were going on. It was battle. Slaughter. Perhaps mutual slaughter. Perhaps their own. It turned and roiled in her heart like a storm and bothered her all the more to know that she was not the only one. Perhaps if one heart was in a deluge of terror and doom, they were alone. But she doubted it. The others had simply got better at sleeping with it inside them. Such was the gift of witnessing war, she thought. They knew what to expect. Even the younger ones had heard the stories. Demasduit was woman. She would never see war unless it came to her, and then she would only be its victim.

[72]

Thick clouds had come and blocked out the moon and stars. Darkness hung like a veil before the rhythmic thunder of the big water far below the cliffs. But Demasduit knew there was someone there. He sat on the rocks and listened. Listened to the way they had come. The great, big water that reached out to distant worlds and brought strange visitors to them. Brought bloodshed to their people.

'Madawaak,' she called as she came up softly behind him.

He turned, looked at her, and then looked back out into the bleak abyss again. Demasduit's wounds hurt. But they had no bad smell about them and she was mobile enough, despite the stabbing aches. She moved closer to him.

'Thank you,' she said as she sat down beside him.

'It was Mooaumook who saved you,' he half-muttered.

'I know,' she said. 'I saved him as well.'

Madawaak said nothing. Demasduit had never found herself having to fill silence between them, but she felt an urge to now. He had never been silent before.

'I didn't save you,' she said.

'Not from a bear, no.'

'Mama told me,' she said as she pulled up the cold grass that grew in tufts along the rocky ledge. 'You never left my side. When you returned from the muster you were exhausted, but you didn't go home. You stayed with us. You watched over me and waited for me to wake up and...'

'Yes.'

'And you spoke to me.'

'Yes.'

'And I know what you said.'

'Yes.'

'And... and you know that Makdaachk has asked my father to marry me to Mooaumook.'

'I know.'

'And you know that we are the very best of friends. Are we?'

'We are,' he muttered.

'I am relieved.'

'Then you will marry Mooaumook and we will be friends.'

Demasduit sighed as the ache inside alighted again. 'I don't want to.'

'Why not? Surely you don't think you're unworthy...'

'No,' she said. 'I think I am afraid of marriage. I am afraid to be what my mother is and what all the other women are. I have heard what the Farther People would call me and I wonder if it is true sometimes.'

'A Two Spirit? It is a Mi'kmaq belief.'

'Doesn't mean that it's wrong,' Demasduit said. 'I like Mooaumook. I like to be with him...' she stopped and waited to see if he'd react. He didn't. 'I like his company. But I don't want to care for him. Or wait for him. Or grieve him when he gets himself killed.'

'Love comes in time.'

'No it doesn't. When I looked out over open country for the first time, the very first instant, I knew love.'

Madawaak didn't answer.

'You know love,' she said.

'I do.'

'I am sorry, Madawaak.'

'Don't be. If you know love, then you'll see how you saved me too.'

They listened to the waves for a while.

'Promise you'll never forget me,' she whispered.

'Will you go away?' Madawaak quickly asked. His voice cracked.

'You are so dear to me,' she said.

'And you to me.'

She held his hair and touched her face to his and then got up to walk back to her mamateek. Demasduit knew she wouldn't sleep. But what needed to be done was done.

7

The Battle of Straumfjord

Mooaumook ate the last of the sculpin strips that lay frozen on the rocks. The night clouds had parted and the world was bathed in silvery light that promised a vibrant, shimmering dawn. His hands shook. His mouth was so dry he didn't even taste the ice off the sculpin. Mooaumook dropped the last two pieces into the brine that had settled with the dawn and eased his way up towards ruined camp above.

He couldn't hear them talking anymore.

Through the tufts of grass that rustled in the breeze, he saw the broken structures. Blackened by their fire. Smashed by the beings he'd seen them ride upon. There were two such beings held by ropes around their heads tied to a portion of a fence that still stood. They sniffed at the ground. One shook its head and stomped its hoof. Those dangerous, loud, unpredictable beings. But the Pale Ones' servants, nonetheless.

How, Mooaumook thought. *How does one tame a nonhuman being?*

A faint, acidic miasma still slithered through the icy air. The liquid they used to preserve food. They'd eaten here. Recently. There was a smell of fresh ash as well. A fire recently doused. They were here. Sleeping somewhere.

On the far side of a large, broken building made of blocks of earth, there was a view of the Oonban family village. Pale Ones over there, Mooaumook figured. Sleeping there. They'd come up last night, lured by the bonfire and the noise. Mooaumook took a few deep breaths. He felt his fear and he channelled it into focus. Then, he climbed up from the ledge and crouched low and held his tomahawk in his hand. Crossed the patch of sand to the beings. Around them were tracks that hadn't been in the earth the night before. The ground was still torn up and disturbed from their battle. Mooaumook could see it was not really a battle, but an all-out slaughter such as he had heard the Pale Ones had inflicted upon the family of Mammasamit. Sickly coldness prickled through his flesh. Many died here, he could see it. But there were fresh tracks. Feet from the beings they rode upon, and others. Other feet. There were more than the two the beings had carried. Some had walked.

Mooaumook counted. Six... seven.

One of the beings snorted. Mooaumook looked at it. Upon its big, dark eyes the silver sunrise glinted. It was huge. Big even for the Pale Ones. Such a beast could surely tear them limb from lib. Break every bone in their body. Mooaumook held his hand out to its snout and touched its velvety face gently.

'There,' he whispered. 'You there. Why do you help them? Why do you let them ride on your back? You carry them. What do they give you?'

But the creature did not answer.

Clumsy footsteps staggered in the snow. Mooaumook dove down amidst the rubble of a smashed wall and clutched his tomahawk, ready to throw it. Around the row of houses, he could just see in the low light. A figure staggered out towards the incline and held his hands in front of him. A stream of piss squirted from his front. Then he crouched by the fire and made sparks with flints his hands. His breath was a stark white mist before his face. Mooaumook could see the outline of the hay he'd stuffed into his domed, shining stone hat protrude around his head like a wicked crown.

Every muscle in his body tense, Mooaumook kept low and crossed swiftly and silently towards the other side of the village. He sheltered by the large building midway and looked back. The Pale One was obstructed by the house. But Mooaumook heard him blowing on the fire and saw the flickering orange light upon the slushy snow. So he continued to where the trees curved downward. The earth formed a half-bowl against the lapping ocean. There on the innermost beach, he could see their canoes half grounded in the shallows. On the land, clustered together under the shadow of the surrounding forest and the rising hillsides, the bright glow of the fires so hot they never ceased to burn. The outlines of their buildings. The black, ghostly cloud that loomed above them all the time. As though their village itself was alive. Like thousands of red, glowing eyes the buildings looked right back at Mooaumook.

He could smell the acrid air all the way across the bay.

Back up at the village, the fire burned. But its light cast no shadow. Mooaumook walked out past the large, broken building and craned his neck to see.

A whooshing sound caused him to freeze and the arrow struck the earth between his feet with a thud. The weapons of shining stone flashed as they caught the awakening light and moved towards him. They were at the end of long poles. Held by the Pale Ones. They pointed at him from all sides and he lowered himself quickly to the ground and threw his hands up. The tomahawk lay in the dirt and slush in front of his knees. The weapons stopped short of piercing him. The huge men that wielded them held him there for a few moments and spoke in their language to each other.

Then, one of them seized him by the shoulders.

* * *

Thorvald swallowed a gulp of wine to clear the sleepiness out of his system and then turned as the sentries dragged the skraeling into his lodge and threw him before the Chieftain's table. Its feet were bound and its hands were behind its back, but still two of the strong captors had to hold it down. The little skraeling was muscular but small. Shorter than a woman. Then suddenly he looked up in defiance and snarled with aggression. The sheer fierceness of his features and the strength of his face caught Thorvald by surprise.

'It was alone,' Ingrid said. 'Otto saw it watching over Straumfjord.'

Gottfried came from behind his arras with his battle axe in his hands. Thorvald turned and reached across the table to pick up his sheathed sword from beside his chair and tied it to his hip.

[77]

Gottfried stood before the Skraeling and he too seemed surprised.

'This is what frightened Lief away?' he asked.

'What was it doing?' Thorvald asked.

'Watching over Straumfjord,' Otto echoed Ingrid's words.

'Why?'

The sentries looked at each other quizzically.

'We... don't know,' Ingrid said.

'Are you sure it was alone?' Thorvald asked.

'Bring thralls. Have them ask it what it was doing,' Gottfried said as he gestured to a sleepy looking Roman thrall and had her pour him a horn of ale. 'One of them may speak its language.'

'Lief tried it with a female,' Thorvald said. 'He had more thralls from more places than we. Nothing.'

'Are they mute? Like animals?'

'It doesn't speak?' Thorvald asked the sentries. They shook their heads. 'It didn't try to talk to any of you?'

'Not a word, my Lord. Not in any language,' Ingrid responded.

'Then it is useless,' Gottfried said. 'And too wild to keep as a thrall. Look at it.'

The little skraeling looked from Thorvald to Gottfried. Its eyes flickered between their faces and their weapons but there was no fear. Only snarling rage. All of its muscles flexed and stayed firm. Ready to fight as soon as the sentries who held it let it go.

'We can't waste having caught one,' Thorvald said. 'Lief's ships will be here soon. We can at least take him a token of our having been here.'

'If Lars even made it,' Gottfried said, softly.

'Chain it up and lock it in my privy,' Thorvald ordered the sentries. 'Make sure it cannot get out.'

The sentries bundled in and all seized the Skraeling at once to drag him outside. Thorvald massaged the ache at the bridge of his nose and leaned back against the table.

'It's a risk to keep it alive,' Gottfried said. 'It's been inside Straumfjord now. If it got out...'

'It won't get out,' Thorvald said. 'What should I do with it?'

'Kill it,' Gottfried replied. 'Hang pieces of it from the trees around Straumfjord to ward off its fellows.'

'We have a chance to know them,' Thorvald said. 'If we can take it back to Lief he can keep up his experiments with talking to it. Maybe we can return here with some understanding of their language. Or, if they don't speak, then some kind of communication.'

'I hope you're right,' Gottfried swilled his ale and then took a hefty gulp.

'Even if Lars didn't make it,' Thorvald mused as he sat uncomfortably in his chair, 'we'll soon have to hunt the forests to survive. It couldn't hurt us to have some leverage. If they attack. Some of them must know we have it.'

'Or they will try to get it back,' Gottfried said.

'They won't know where to look for it.'

'If it makes a sound...'

'Then you kill it. I'll help you dismember him myself.'

Gottfried breathed sharply through his nose but had no objection. 'It is too early in the day for this.'

He stomped back towards his arras.

* * *

As the ambrosia sunrise slowly filled the forest with early eastern light, the nimble bodies dashed through the ferns and beneath the pines and redwoods down towards the gully. They raced the light of day, moved swiftly and lightly enough that their footsteps were but a pattering on the forest floor. Barely louder than rain drops. They moved between the trees like shadows. Even the old men. Down in the gully, they moved east towards the cove. Some gentle easterly breeze must have blown in the night for many thought they could smell the harsh fumes of their fires.

Their minds were blank. The champions. The elders. The hunters from the River Families, the Mountain Families and the Forest Families. Oonban's family, Moisamadrook's family,

Wobee's family, Shendeek's family, Keathut's family, Ninejeek's family... Madawaak ran with Eenodsha. Too young and fresh to know how thin their number looked to the seasoned warrior. Absent was Mooaumook, though Makdaachk had nephews and another son Gheegnyan to run with them. But absent as well were their allies from the broken lands and the Island Fathers they'd had no time to contact. Madawaak could not look around him and see that they were a smaller force than they should be, but he could feel it of every warrior he ran with. A tension. A trembling sliver of fear in the air around them that was never there on a hunt.

Focus, he thought. *Focus as the others are focused.*

He ran.

* * *

What kind of people don't speak? Thorvald kept thinking as he waited for the council to come together and waste another day arguing. *They must speak. That skraeling in there was playing dumb.* Thorvald kept thinking about it until his teeth gritted and his fingernails scratched against the arms of his chair.

Finally, he could take no more.

He shot up from his chair and marched out to the privy, where he drew his sword Gunnlogi from its sheath and tore the door open. Thralls were startled as they prepared the council's morning refreshments. The skraeling sat chained in the corner. A few of the thralls instinctively came up flat against the wall as Thorvald stormed past them to the Skraeling and thrust the sword at his groin. The skraeling's eyes filled with terror. Thorvald stopped short, but he felt the sharp tip touch against soft flesh beneath his captive's furs.

'You know this can cleave your manhood in two,' Thorvald said. 'You know I'll do just that. And you know I want you to speak. Say words. Words! Speak! I know you can speak!'

The skraeling's lip quivered.

'Speak,' Thorvald tensed his fist around the hilt of the sword and beads of sweat broke out across the Skraeling's brow right before his eyes. 'Speak your tongue.'

The skraeling moved his lips and made an utterance under his breath. Thorvald heard something. He seized the skraeling by its long hair and held its head back.

'Again.'

'Freydis.'

For a moment, Thorvald's arm tensed to deliver the decisive blow. A trick. Trickery. It was tricking him. But he'd said what he'd said. Not a word he could have learned by any other means but...

'Impossible,' Thorvald breathed, as he weakened. The sword fell away from the skraeling's trousers. Cold shivers slowly coursed through his flesh as he stared at the frightened creature.

'Freydis,' the skraeling said again.

Thorvald backed up a few paces.

'How do you know that name?' he demanded.

'Freydis,' the skraeling said. It was clearly all he knew.

'Freydis,' Thorvald said. Breathless. He turned towards the door where the thralls still inside watched him from against the wall.

'Repeat this,' he warned, 'and I'll burn out your tongues.'

Thorvald staggered out into the snow. Around him, the trees stood still in the soft morning twilight and raised up on the hillsides like giant green ocean swells frozen before they could wash little Straumfjord back out to sea. Something sat uneasy deep in the Chieftain's gut. *Freydis,* he thought, I have to have her brought back. But the thought wouldn't stay in his mind. He kept looking at the trees. The great walls of green, speckled with snowy caps, that stood tall and all enshrouding in every direction but back out into the ocean. It was almost like they knew their age. Their power. It was almost like they were watching...

From across the village, a woman screamed.

An eruption of fluttering issued from the forest canopy in every direction. It looked like birds, at first. The long arrows as they arched through the sky and came down again. He could only stand and take a breath in. The arrow punched through his pleated leather tunic and ran through his body. The air rushed from his lungs. At first there was no pain, only the feeling of the shaft channelling through him. Then he tried to breathe in. His lungs flooded with blood. Mind-shattering agony ran hot through his body as he trembled and crashed to his knees. More arrows flew down to the earth. They hit women midstride. Men were struck by two or three at a time. Thorvald could only watch. His body failed him. The weight of the pain and the injury dragged him down to the earth. Blood gurgled up from his gullet and filled his mouth with its coppery taste.

* * *

Madawaak primed another bone-tipped arrow after his first crashed harmlessly into the roof of a structure. He found a target. He started running with an axe and a shield towards the screaming raiders who had charged down from the tree line towards them. The figure stopped and caught an arrow on the shield. Madawaak saw she was a woman. A woman in battle.

A breath in. He drew back. Ready to release... But he didn't. His fingers would not let go of the arrow. Madawaak slackened the bow. He lined up his shot. His heart trembled.

Moisamadrook's son let out a scream, raised his tomahawk high and charged in. Out of arrows. A cousin ran in after him. Madawaak still had a full quiver. He found his target again. The woman. A Pale One. The cousin charged her. She strengthened her stance and opened her posture so the raider had a clear attack on her body. Only as he leaped into the air and raised his tomahawk did she bring the shield back. He crashed against it. His weapon was embedded in the wood. In the same motion, she brought the axe, the weapon of shining stone, down onto his skull and buried it in his hair. Blood spurted out. The body fell limp. Madawaak let out a cry and drew back the arrow and fired.

The Pale One had already crouched behind her shield. A group of others joined her and formed a shell, like a sea turtle, under their shields. Long spears with blades of shining stone poked out from between the gaps.

Moisamadrook got up and charged. All around Madawaak, men were dropping their bows and running in. The shell spread and opened. From behind the shields came a volley of their arrows. The charging horde scattered. Some fell. Crashed to the ground and crumpled. Madawaak drew back the arrow and fired as the shields closed again.

All across their village, people ran from their homes down towards the shoreline. The raiders spread and encircled the defence. Madawaak cried out and forced the thoughts from his mind as he pulled arrows, picked targets and fired faster than his emotions could stop him. He fired them at the Pale Ones who ran. He then dropped his bow and charged.

The raiders attacked the shields from all sides. They leaped and twisted their bodies around the bladed spears and crashed against the shields. Their axes flashed out at them. Madawaak saw a boy cleaved in the shoulder as he charged in and he screamed out and raised his tomahawk high. The wounded boy turned as blood burst from his shattered shoulder and his head cocked to one side and he fell. Madawaak jumped past him and swung his tomahawk down behind the shield. He felt it strike flesh. Felt bone snap beneath the blow. A scream issued out and the shield dropped to one side. Raiders flung their bodies into the gap. Madawaak crashed to the ground. He saw enormous feet and chopped at them. Cut one midway through. The Pale One crashed to the ground.

The woman.

She screamed and waved her axe. Madawaak leaped on her and hacked at her chest. The stone blade hit her with a wet crack. She coughed and moaned and writhed and tried to breathe as blood gushed from her throat. Madawaak shivered with horror. Tears filled his eyes. He drew back the tomahawk and rammed it into her face again and again until the moving and the moaning and the gushing stopped. Sticky fluid covered him. He felt it run down his face. The woman's jaw was dislodged and her face caved in.

A spear came towards him.

Moving automatically, Madawaak swept it aside with his tomahawk, then leaped at the wielder and rammed his tomahawk low into the Pale One's guts. The gigantic man doubled over. More warm liquid spilled over Madawaak's hands. But he was frenzied. Bolts of lightning shot through his flesh and powered his movements. He pulled out the tomahawk and hacked into the side of the Pale One so he'd fall down. Slimy lengths of his entrails peeked through his thick skin. He roared in agony. Madawaak wanted him to shut up. He slammed the tomahawk into his neck and blood sprayed so thick across the Pale Ones' face that Madawaak could no longer distinguish his eyes from his cheeks. He hacked once into the man's face, just to be sure.

The defence had broken apart around Madawaak. His kinfolk had chased the Pale Ones off into their village. Little, red-painted bodies charged into their homes. Tore down their doors and chased those inside out. Madawaak ran into the fray. He saw little Pale One children come screaming out of their homes and tomahawks rained down on them. Men attacked. Women attacked. Madawaak saw a woman with a spear ram the blade so deeply into Wobee's nephew it sprang red from his back. Grief and rage seized him again. He ran at the woman. But she turned the spear towards him. He chopped it aside again. But she had an axe as well and brought it up towards him. Madawaak ducked and crashed against her body. The towering figure did not budge under the puny weight of him. Two Pale One men came charging in as he sprang back to avoid a swipe from her axe. Madawaak ran in terror. Two strong raiders charged to his defence. They leaped on a man and woman and left one man to shove his shield towards Madawaak.

The wood crashed against Madawaak and knocked him off his feet. The axe followed. Madawaak rolled to one side and leaped up. The shield came fast. It caught a blow of Madawaak's tomahawk and ripped the handle from his hands. He leaped in as the axe came at him. He jumped up and rammed himself into the Pale One's chest and flailed and struck him as hard as he could.

A dagger struck the Pale One in the side before he could regain himself. As he reeled to his knees and collapsed to writhe and choke on the bloodied ground, Madawaak saw his saviour.

Old Makdaachk stood with the bloodied dagger.

[84]

Madawaak picked up the Pale One's axe. It was heavier than his tomahawk. The shining stone was too much for him. He dropped it and picked up his tomahawk. They ran together into the village. Into a structure.

Inside was abandoned. They both panted heavily. Phlegm built up in their throats. The old man and the young man ran back out and charged into another structure. A little boy screamed. Makdaachk drove his dagger through the boy's throat and sawed it back and forth until the gurgling and the twitching stopped.

Madawaak was again overcome with a cold shiver. Makdaachk must have seen.

'They did no different to Mammasamit's family. They forced themselves into the women and the children alike. They hacked them to pieces. Alive and screaming. Give no mercy. That is how young warriors become old warriors. No mercy.'

The old man led Madawaak out of the house. Outside, Oonban stood near the long house with a teenage boy's hair in his fist. The boy was on his knees, facing away. Oonban plunged his tomahawk into the boy's head and cleaved the top of his skull. The body fell. Nearby, a chained woman screamed as tomahawks carved into her fleeing body from all sides. She collapsed and the raiders hacked her to pieces.

Down before them, the brine rolled and crashed on the rocky shore. The water was tinted pink. Pale Ones pushed their canoes off and climbed from the numbingly icy waters into them and paddled away. Spears and arrows shot out after them, arched in the sky and came down. They fired arrows back.

Yaseek threw a spear. He was immediately answered by an arrow through the neck. His hands gripped at it feebly as he twisted down to the ground. Salty brine swept over his body and carried him, eyes still bulging and mouth still gasping, out after the canoes. Oonban did not even look at him. He followed the others and ran down to the shoreline.

The canoes paddled further out. Out of reach of their spears and arrows.

Madawaak panted as he watched them shrink over the waves. Behind them, the village was silent. The raiders gathered at the edge of the water. Beyond the fleeing Pale Ones, a wall of fog hid the world they'd come from.

'The ocean will finish them,' Makdaachk said.

'Makdaachk,' a voice said. A young man had brought Mooaumook to his father. Makdaachk threw his arms around his son.

'You're alive!'

'I was captured,' Mooaumook told him, his voice heavy with shame.

'Say nothing of it,' Makdaachk ordered. 'Nothing.'

Madawaak turned away and watched the boats. They seemed to go no further than the breakers. The fog didn't surround them but stayed back. Behind them.

'We wait for them,' Oonban said.

'We wait for them!' Keathut cried over the other raiders.

But Madawaak saw something else in the fog. Great shapes that heaved up and down. Shadows in the gloom.

'Look!' he cried.

Then, suddenly, the enormous forms of the Pale Ones' giant canoes broke through the fog and charged towards the shore under the great sheets that carried them on the wind. The canoes the villagers had paddled out in quickly paddled again to get between the behemoths. Their commanders waved their arms in panic. They were as surprised as the raiders.

'Run,' Madawaak thundered as his flesh turned cold. 'Run!'

'Run,' Ninejeek screamed.

The raiders broke apart in terror as the giant canoes drew near and tall. One, two, three... five of them. The thwacking of bows echoed across the shortening distance and rolling waves and the dark swarm of arrows that arched through the sky blocked out the eastern sun.

Moisamadrook raised his spear high in the air and screamed. A handful of his party did the same as the arrows came down and they were covered entirely. Their bodies fell beneath the sheer weight.

The survivors ran back through the village. Droning bellows followed after them and sounded like wind come alive and roaring in aggression and Madawaak heard their war cries behind him as they passed by the largest structure again. He expected any second for the arrows to hammer down on him.

As he passed, he saw a woman dead with an infant in her hands. Some bodies, the raiders or the Pale Ones, seemed to be torn asunder or laying under reams of viscera, but this one looked merely asleep. Tears filled his eyes. His heart thudded in pain.

He knew it was his arrow.

Madawaak screamed out as he ran with the others back into the forest. He wanted to stop. He wanted to pick up that little baby and hold it and breathe warmth and life back into it. But he felt the Pale Ones' eyes as they burned the back of him. Felt their hatred. Felt them coming up from the shoreline ready to hack into his body like he had theirs. He ran.

* * *

Gottfried staggered as he dragged his exhausted body back up to the clay banks upon which Straumfjord stood. Others of Thorfinn's clan followed him from their faerings. All over the cove, unfamiliar Norsefolk dragged their karvi and faerings ashore while the great knarr that brought them listed in the receding tidewater and crews worked aboard to bring up horses, cattle and an ample amount of weapons as well as supplies up onto their decks. But the survivors of Thorvald's clan clustered around him like their saviour.

There was Jannik. There was Thorbjorn. Their wives. Children. He looked back from upon the bank and saw them climb up the pebbly beach towards him. He could not see Thorvald. But his eyes sought Tyra with an urgency that issued from his heart.

She was not there.

As the tears of knowing already gathered in his eyes, he turned and continued up to the village. The others followed him. Like lost souls that sought a beacon to haunt, they followed him.

Bodies lay scattered across the ruins. Little skraelingjar bodies and the larger bodies of their own. Gottfried led them towards the lodge as though they were a procession and men and women broke from the small crowd to rush towards familiar corpses and scream and fall upon them in insensible grief.

Gottfried kicked the body of a young Skraeling aside.

A woman staggered away and stood over the smashed bodies of a man and two children. She made no sound. Just stood there and looked at them.

Thralls lay split across their middles or bludgeoned. Thorvald's favourite Roman lay crumpled and bloody and draped in the rags that were her clothing. By the privy, Gottfried saw the body that gripped Vinland's only sword in its hand still. He moved over to it. Let what was left of the crowd to disperse on their own stunned silent time. They trembled with grief. But they wandered off to find their loved ones. Gottfried looked down at Thorvald. He looked at the blade of the sword first and saw that it was unstained.

Gottfried took a deep breath and turned him over.

The long arrow ran from his chest to his thigh where it protruded above the knee. His eyes were half open. Cold blood stained his mouth. Gottfried knelt down and pried the sword from his cold fingers and held it by the blade. He stood to find himself face to face with a tall man, dressed in fine furs and exotic leathers and with a calm twinkle in his sky-blue eyes.

'Gottfried Magnusson?' he asked with a warm smile.

'Yes.'

'Thorfinn son of Thor,' he said, and offered his glove.

'Thorfinn the Karlsefini,' Gottfried said as he shook it weakly. 'Had you come only a few moments sooner...'

'Or later?' Thorfinn said, gravely. 'It was by the intervention of *Ran* that we found you at all. One of our trade ships happened upon your messenger Lars.'

'I'm glad you came for us,' Gottfried said. 'Our Chieftain is dead. Lief should know as quickly as possible.'

Thorfinn closed his eyes and nodded the affirmative.

[88]

'I have to find my wife and son,' Gottfried said as he stepped around Thorfinn and carefully carried the sword by the blade towards the door of the Chieftain's lodge. The rest of the Karlsefini's crew wandered back from the forest's edge and they looked around in the same sullen confusion that seemed to haunt all but the Karlsefini himself. The same hatred for the twisted corpses of the skraelingjar.

Gottfried stopped when he got to the corner of the lodge. What was he going to find inside?

The skraelingjar were defeated. The axes and atgiers of the Norse fighters had smashed their bones and spilled their bodies. Some of them seemed almost hacked through by a single blow. Others spilled their brains from heads cleaved in two, or their innards from their ribcages that were opened by slashes and hacks forms words. They were not just killed; their bodies were destroyed.

Just as it was with the first tribe that crossed them.

Gottfried snorted and turned towards the door where a small crowd had gathered. One looked up and saw Gottfried. Immediately, Gottfried recognized that it was Torvard, husband of Eiriksdottir.

'Has our King lost his mind?' Gottfried asked.

'I go with my wife anywhere, my Lord.'

Before the words could sink in, the crowd parted and Freydis stepped out of the lodge. She was still adorned with her shield and battle-axe with her helmet still on her head. Her huge green eyes turned towards Gottfried. Freydis sighed.

'He sent you back?' Gottfried growled in disbelief.

'Months ago, my Lord,' Freydis said. Her eyes were now fixed upon the sword in Gottfried's hands.

'You brought her...' Gottfried turned towards Thorfinn, who'd followed him.

'Now, now Gottfried,' Thorfinn said. 'It was Freydis who led our expedition. We've been living in a settlement in Helluland, on the northernmost tip of the island. It is from there that we have brought all our supplies. They were intended to be gifts for the Chieftain Thorvald. An invitation for peace between our clans.'

'You've been living... here?'

'In Helluland,' Freydis answered. There was a hurt weakness in her voice that Gottfried hated.

'How many more are you?' Gottfried asked.

'Another thirty families remain in the north,' Thorfinn answered. 'It was Freydis who ordered weapons be brought here, otherwise we'd have none. She knew something was wrong for Thorvald to have sent Lars towards Greenland to speak with King Lief. The knarr came home and were armed and came back towards Straumfjord with all the speed they could muster.'

Gottfried looked back at Freydis. She removed her helmet and held it against her ample hip.

'I remember the last peace offering you made,' Gottfried said.

'I have another one for the skraelingjar,' Freydis answered. She turned to address the crowd that gathered around them. 'Gather up the bodies of your loved ones. We will have funerals tonight. First, gather up the bodies of the skraelingjar. Cut off their arms, legs, and heads. Mount their pieces upon stakes or hang them from trees. Create a barrier around Straumfjord their like cannot miss.'

'You do not give orders around here!' Gottfried snapped. Nobody moved. He was holding the sword.

'Come see your pregnant wife and your son, then, friend of my late brother,' Freydis stepped aside and gestured towards the door of the lodge. 'See if you feel differently.'

Gottfried stared at her for a long time. Until the cold set in and ice caressed his skin through his clothes. He felt the silence around him and forced himself past her into the lodge. He could see their bodies already. Their limbs protruded from beneath their arras and were streaked with blood. But he had to be near them. Breathless, heavy with grief, he staggered across the lodge and pushed the arras aside.

He saw enough.

Freydis and Thorfinn stood behind him.

'Do as she orders,' Gottfried whispered to Thorfinn. 'Only this once.'

The two left him in the darkness where he collapsed and let out a cry.

8

Winter

The sunset had spilled blood red light over the snowy mantle that coated all the world. Demasduit shivered. Atop the rocky ledge where she'd watched the giant canoes make towards Straumfjord, now she watched the forest and waited for survivors to appear from the shadows beneath the snow-smothered treetops. But all was still and silent. Black clouds had settled over them since noon and only parted as the sun had made towards the jagged sunset to the west.

In all that time, nobody had come back.

Destuid got up and paced up and down again. Her fingers twitched. *Pick up their trail. Follow them and intercept them on their way home...* but what if nobody came? *No one coming home. Not Papa. Not uncles. Not Madawaak. Not Mooaumook.*

The rest of the village was packing down their mamateeks. Demasduit had helped Chipchowinech and Shanawdithit with theirs and finished much sooner than the others. It was then that she'd seen the sails. Everyone else had just kept working.

Now, when Demasduit looked at the village it was all but gone. The women, children and elderly that remained of the village and their guests had already begun down across the snowy hillside towards the meadows and the forest through which they'd make their ways towards the Broken Lands. Just as they had before every winter. Except they'd always had their fathers, sons, brothers, uncles and husbands with them. Ready to follow the caribou migration.

The world felt too empty and too big without them. Demasduit had decided she'd wait for them. *Someone would come. They had to. Surely, they couldn't have got them all. Not*

Papa. Not Madawaak. They were too quick. Too clever. They'd come soon...

'We have to stay with the others,' the withered old voice of Odensook said. The mother of Chipchowinech was ancient and deeply wrinkled. Demasduit looked down at her. Those old eyes were pinched with the pains of a lifetime. A dead child. Two dead husbands. Now... the husband of her daughter as well?

No. Demasduit wasn't ready to lose him.

'They won't know we've gone,' she said. 'The snowfall could cover our trail. They may be too weak and tired to follow us.'

'Cold winds will blow this way,' Odensook said as she looked towards the north. 'Come with us. If they are alive, they will find us.'

'They are alive,' Demasduit said. 'I won't go without them.'

'Dema,' the tiny voice of Shanawdithit called from behind Odensook. The old woman looked back and saw her little granddaughter following her footsteps up towards Demasduit.

'Not any further, Shanawdithit,' snapped Odensook. 'It's dangerous up here.'

'I know it's dangerous,' Shanawdithit complained. Chipchowinech hurried up behind her and took her by the hand.

'Go on,' Demasduit said. She nodded towards the single-file migration that snaked into the forest. Already the first few families had disappeared into the darkness beneath the crimson mantle. 'Go with the others. I will catch up once I have made contact with survivors.'

'Your injuries...' Chipchowinech said.

'I'll live,' Demasduit said. 'If they can live then I can live.'

'Granddaughter,' Odensook said, softly though her voice carried over the incessant rumble of the sea below. 'None of us will leave without you.'

Odensook, Shanawdithit, and Chipchowinech were bowed and strained beneath what they had to carry, but Demasduit's mother, most of all. Her back was bowed. She gripped Shanawdithit's hand but there seemed so little strength. Hot tears stung Demasduit's eyelids as they instantly cooled against her numb face. The deep red became a magenta twilight.

'They're not dead,' she said as her voice crackled up. The ball of emotion nearly choked her. 'Not all of them.'

'They will find us,' Odensook said. 'They will need food and the comfort of knowing we looked after each other. Oonban will need the embrace of both his daughters. Mooaumook will need to know his love is safe.'

Demasduit looked down at Shanawdithit. The little one stared up at her with sad brown eyes that squinted in the stinging cold. Across the meadows, the last of the families were leaving a trail into the forest. Demasduit sobbed. She held out her arms for something to carry. But her mother, sister and grandmother dropped what they had and put their arms around her.

As they started to walk together and Demasduit was given a share of the load, she looked one more time at the big water. The great, heaving grey big water. It had carried more of them on these winds. Demasduit felt a sickliness that coursed through her veins as she remembered the boats. Like an illness. *These Pale Ones were not like the others,* she thought as she turned away and walked with her family. *These ones had come with one purpose.* Demasduit felt it as truly as were she told by them outright. No prospectors or adventurers anymore. These ones had come expressly to kill the men of the hunt. Their purpose would not end at the bay.

* * *

Night fell hard and cold and brought swift winds that cut like daggers through the blackness of the forest. The migration broke into their groups. Everyone carried fronds gathered from the sea of ferns they'd passed through in the last dying lights of day, and they hurried to make shelters from them and the snow that clumped on the ground. More piles of snow plummeted down from the canopy. The wind loosened it and the branches could no longer hold it and they crashed down with thuds onto the shelters and smashed them. Quickly, the families inside gathered the snow and rebuilt the walls. Icicles formed on the pine branches around them. But soon it all disappeared in the total blackness of night.

Demasduit only just saw the structures spread across the forest floor before the light faded completely and left them all blind. She'd thought to gather fronds. Carried them as well as half of her mother's load when it had become too much for the older woman to manage. They fumbled their way around. They dug the fronds into the snow and built the walls up between them.

Nearby, a thud. A family cried out.

'Keep building,' Demasduit instructed. She felt her way towards the struggle and helped the stricken family rebuild their shelter and they all then came back and helped complete her own. Shanawdithit cried loudly the whole time. Her little teeth chattered and her body shook beneath every reassuring touch.

Some of the children would not survive. Everyone thought it. Nobody said it aloud. Demasduit worked breathless and blind as her hands numbed to ensure that Shanawdithit would not be amongst the little bodies to bury tomorrow. The pain in her hip and shoulder were excruciating.

'Our people have enough funerals ahead of us,' she said below her breath as she felt the walls of the rudimentary structure and sensed that they were sound. 'Go. Go in.'

Odensook took Shanawdithit through the opening first. Demasduit reached out into the blackness until her throbbing fingertips found Chipchowinech's furs and they carefully crawled into their structure together. Then they built the last wall up. The helpers, Demasduit never knew how many they were, quickly hurried off to enclose themselves in their own shelter.

They would normally have been in the broken lands by now where the weather was calmer. Winds tore at their shelters. With pains like little pins in their eyes, the women rose in the night to repair the damages again and again. If sleep came at all in the intervening moments, it did nothing to rest them. Odensook curled up with Shanawdithit and wrapped them both in her furs and Demasduit could hear their short little breaths even over the wind that howled outside.

The winds stilled sometime before morning. When the sun came, the families inside kicked through their structures to feel the scant warmth that greeted them on the golden columns of light that broke through the trees.

A few guttural screams of grief arose from around the far-spread camp. Mothers cradled their still and silent infants. Families flocked around them. Without their men.

'Why are they screaming?' Shanawdithit asked as she tugged at Demasduit's tunic.

'Come on, Shana,' Demasduit took her hand. 'We have respects to pay before we go on today.'

Little Shanawdithit looked gravely on as the little ones were placed in their shallow resting places. One elderly man joined them. The families portioned out some pudding and then they gathered what they had and carried on the long walk.

* * *

Two more elders were lost in the days before they finally picked up the trail of the caribou and followed it across the narrow bridge of land that connected their country to the Broken Lands. Odensook nearly joined them, but Shanawdithit's warmth kept her alive.

Demasduit looked hazily ahead as they crossed the strip of land that the sea lashed from both sides and saw greenery in the distance ahead. Here, there were few forests. Mostly meadows and heaths. Here, she would bring down a caribou for their men. Here, they were watched over by the mightiest warrior of their people.

She almost felt safe to know Gobidin and his bands were out there somewhere. The big brothers who would protect them for the long winter as their guests. But they passed through haunted meadow now, in the vast open grassland just beyond the land bridge that connected the Broken Lands to the main island.

The long grass tilted in the ocean breeze and shone with the glossy sheen of winter. Snow capped the taller hills in the distance.

Here was where Mammasamit's family were massacred. This land had swallowed much of their own blood. None of the migration spoke as they walked through the day to cross the mournful patch where the sun shone rich and the grass grew lush. Ahead bald hilltops beckoned them to the grazing lands.

Someone far ahead cried out. The rest of their migration stopped and Demasduit held her breath as she stretched up to see past the long row of families from the mountains and the forests. The column ahead parted and a distant figure ran clumsily through the grass. It came up to his shoulders. He was just a head that bobbed up and down and moved quickly towards them.

'Madawaak,' Demasduit gasped with a shudder. Tears poured from her. She ran down through the split column of migrators to him and leaped into his arms and they embraced in the shimmering grass. The run took what little reserve of energy she had left. Demasduit's body collapsed in his grip and she felt his weakness as well and they fell together. 'You're alive.'

'Not many of us,' he said as he sat up. 'Not many.'

Demasduit looked up and saw Mooaumook standing over her. He took her hands and helped her up and their eyes met and the flood of relief and lust that poured through her weakened her all over again, but he was able to hold her up. With his other hand, he helped Madawaak stand.

'Not many,' Madawaak said again, and he turned away.

'I was so scared,' Demasduit whispered so only Mooaumook would hear. 'I thought I'd never feel this again.'

She moved her trembling hands over his body.

'I did not fight,' Mooaumook admitted as he looked away and let go of her. Demasduit saw that his fists were balled tightly. His knuckles were white. 'I was captured. Held prisoner. Madawaak and the others rescued me.'

Demasduit looked at Madawaak. He stared at Mooaumook sleepily with his mouth open. He looked as though he might say something but instead, he just closed his mouth and looked down at the grass that swept and tickled against his chest.

'There must be more,' Demasduit supposed.

'There are,' Mooaumook said. He brushed his fingers through her hair. But not gently, like he normally would. Demasduit felt his aggression in his touch. 'They are with Gobidin of the Broken Lands.'

'Your father lives,' Madawaak revealed.

The migration had closed in around them. Shanawdithit crept through the grass to Demasduit's side and put her arms around her sister's waist and Demasduit could feel Shanawdithit's tiny fingers fiddling with the strap of her belt, the way they would whenever the little one was overwhelmed or feeling shy. Demasduit put one hand on her hair. She hoped Shanawdithit would feel the great, warming relief she felt. That it would calm her. Their men were alive.

The three of them looked around at the migration and saw the hollowed faces of great fatigue, of grief, and of the empty feeling of arriving where everyone was supposed to end up but not everyone did. Mothers held bundles in their arms where once there were children. Some buried their noses in the furs as they looked at the rich landscape ahead. The grass bent in the breeze and revealed the caribou in the heaths and on the hillsides ahead.

'It isn't far,' Mooaumook called.

* * *

Gobidin of the Broken Lands sat mountainous before the glow of the fire. He inhaled through his nose and closed his eyes. Around him sat the Fathers who'd heeded Oonban's call to the raid; Wobee, Shendeek, Makdaachk, Ninejeek and Keathut and many others Madawaak could not remember the names of. The place of Yaseek was filled by his widow, Imamus. She covered her face with her hair and sat still enough to be a mound of earth. Moisamadrook's place was filled by Douajavik, a surviving nephew. All of them waited as their mighty host thought.

A few honoured raiders and hunters were scattered outside the circle. Amongst them were Demasduit, Mooaumook, and Madawaak. Demasduit curled up beside Mooaumook.

[98]

Madawaak let them have each other and stayed closer to Gobidin, whom he wanted to admire. To see the darkness of his eyes. It was long said that Gobidin had seen such horrors in his life that his eyes had darkened to the deepest of blacks and that they absorbed the light around them. But Madawaak found himself uninterested.

He'd then wanted to gaze across the circle, through the firelight, at Demasduit and Mooaumook and to fantasize about having his own arm around her. About feeling her warmth against his own side and her soft fingers splayed across his chest. But he wasn't interested in that either...

'It was a mistake,' Gobidin finally said, so softly it was barely audible above the crackle and hiss of the fire. But everyone heard him.

Oonban hung his head. Two places down from him, Keathut looked away. Makdaachk snarled.

'We did not think we had any other choice,' he said.

'Had your messengers come to me I would have persuaded them to stop,' Gobidin said. 'Did none of you consider the coming winter? Now babies are dead from the cold. Many of their fathers are down there in the Pale Ones' camp, dead so there will never be others from them. And what have you done to the Pale Ones?'

'We have sent them a message,' Makdaachk said. 'We are not afraid of them.'

'They don't care whether or not you are afraid,' Gobidin said. 'How many are they now?'

Madawaak was looking at the men of the meeting. Makdaachk. The man who'd sawed open a child's throat was now joining in grief for their own children. Pale One or not, what crime has a child committed? And Keathut who'd riled Oonban to violence. Madawaak saw the blood as he looked at their faces and heard the screams of those who'd died. The women. The women in chains, without weapons. Victims of the Pale Ones' cruelty even more so than their people. Hacked at. Torn to pieces by these men. Madawaak felt his breaths become shallow and fast. His skin heated. Visions of death and blood flashed at him from the dark corners of the mamateek and from the shadowy corners of his mind. Focus dissolved into boiling rage. Hot blood. Boiling blood. He could see it. Skin split. Organs stilled. Insides hanging out. Agony. Screams for mercy. Screams for the end. He'd seen it. Heat and pulse hotter and faster and...

'Madawaak.' Gobidin was looking at him. The question had been directed his way.

The young hunter looked around the circle again and tried to slow his breathing. Slow his heart. The rising, bubbling heat inside him seemed to simmer down and his brain cooled against his skull. It had felt like rising tide. Hot, raging fury. Like liquid flame. He could taste blood even now as it slowly faded from his tongue.

Demasduit had sat up from Mooaumook's side. She stared at him.

'Yes?' he asked.

'How many are they now?' Gobidin repeated.

'Hundreds now,' Madawaak said. 'Maybe a thousand.'

'They must have seen our firelight and...'

'Known what it was for?' Gobidin cut off Wobee. 'Let us go to our families. Rest tonight. We should all be with our families and let those who cannot grieve. Lest we be seen arguing instead of thanking the God Spirits for the remaining love we have in this world. It may not last long.'

'We will kill them all if there are millions of them,' Makdaachk said.

Madawaak found himself glaring at the old man. The boiling and the rapid thoughts started again. Hot breaths. Blood....

'This is our country! Our land! We know it...'

'This is nobody's land,' Gobidin said.

'They do not live right,' Keathut said. 'We cannot abandon all that is good and balanced to them. They will throw it off.'

'The world's revenge is slow,' Gobidin said. He was standing now and fidgeted impatiently for them to leave. 'Slower than our lives. That they do not live right is not for us to decide nor for us to avenge. We have only two choices. Survive or be

[100]

slaughtered. Consider them while you rest with your families.
Host those who have lost loved ones. They should not grieve
alone or with each other. Everyone needs to remember now
what is most important.'

The gathering stood.

'Does Gobidin mean to make peace with them?' Keathut
questioned.

'Gobidin means to survive.'

Makdaachk and Keathut looked at each other. Madawaak
caught the exchange. He got up and hurried out into the cold
darkness and let the night temper his rage as he took a few paces
away from them. The others slowly filtered out into the night
and went off to their mamateeks to stay with their host families
or to go in the mamateeks they had built to host widows and
orphans of the battle.

Keathut and Makdaachk left together as they whispered to
each other.

Madawaak turned away as the visions of sneaking into their
mamateek and splitting their own heads with his tomahawk
scampered across his mind. He stood in the dark beyond the
firelights. Nobody could see what he was thinking now...

'Are you okay?' Demasduit asked as she came up behind him.

Madawaak's heart calmed. She'd never had that effect on him
before, but he'd never known thoughts like these before either.

'You wanted to come with us,' he said. Madawaak snatched
words from wherever he could. 'But you shouldn't have. You
should never. A battle is...'

He found himself choked. Started to cry. She put her arm
around his shoulders.

'Horrors haunt all men,' she said. 'Women as well, but only
what they imagine. Women do not survive when they see battle.'

'They did terrible things.'

'They had to,' Demasduit said.

'I need to be alone now,' he said. The surprise in the way she
looked at him was felt by Madawaak as well. He was telling her
to go away. Not to stay with him, like he'd wanted all his life. But
to go away from him. Yet it was what he wanted now. Never

before. Never had he dreamed of wanting such a thing. But he knew he wanted it now. 'Please.'

'Of course,' she said.

She turned and walked back to the lights where Mooaumook was waiting.

* * *

'You cannot!' Oonban thundered as Mooaumook set off in the day's first soft light. The Forest Father marched towards him from Gobidin's village. 'You cannot go back there.'

'I have no choice,' Mooaumook said, tomahawk in hand and rucksack over his shoulder. 'There is nobody else to watch them.'

Madawaak felt one of Mooaumook's glances flicker towards him where he sat in the grass and watched the sunrise.

'Nobody needs to watch them,' Oonban said. 'There are no Pale Ones in the Broken Lands. Gobidin has assured us.'

'There aren't yet,' Mooaumook said. 'By the time there is it will be too late. There must be a sentry to warn us if any Pale Ones should come towards the land bridge or take their giant canoes in this direction.'

'It doesn't have to be you,' Oonban said. He took a gentle step closer to Mooaumook as people emerged from the village, both local and migrants, drawn by their din. 'You've been captured by them once. They will know you...'

'That is why I must go again.'

'They won't be merciful this time, my boy!' Makdaachk called as he edged up beside Oonban.

'I will die fighting,' Mooaumook assured his father. Then he turned and kept walking. A gentle southerly rustled the grass and by the time it stood upright again Mooaumook was gone from their view.

'He wants to redeem himself,' Makdaachk said to Oonban. 'He cannot marry your daughter with the shame of his capture on his mind. Not when she has almost died saving him from a bear.'

'My daughter loves Mooaumook,' Oonban said. 'I know it better than even she does.'

'But a man must have peace within himself,' the older Makdaachk said to Oonban. 'And he is right. These Pale Ones won't be as timid as the last. For all we know, they have allied with the Farther People against us. We will need to know if they move towards us... and even if they don't, we will need to know if it is safe to go home when the warmer days come again.'

Makdaachk turned and faced the small, scattered group of onlookers who kept to the confines of the village, beyond the touch of the long grass.

'I don't see any other volunteers,' he said, loudly.

The onlookers lowered their heads and dispersed back into the village and their businesses of the day.

'Even Madawaak is afraid,' Makdaachk said as he tipped his head towards the young man. Madawaak could still hear him.

'If he is caught, they will definitely come,' Oonban said. 'Maybe more of them again.'

'Then we all should die fighting,' Makdaachk said. He offered his arm to Oonban and the two walked back towards the village and left Madawaak alone out in the grasslands. The caribou were near. Leeward and slightly uphill of them, the herd grazed within range of a good arrow. The thought crossed his mind to go and see if Demasduit was okay. She might have been grieving the abandonment of Mooaumook, but Madawaak could not bring himself to care.

He did not care that Mooaumook was in danger, but he didn't want him to go either. Madawaak did not want him gone so he could have Demasduit to himself because, for the first time since he could remember, he didn't care to have Demasduit near to him. Sadness haunted him but it had no meaning or source to it. Only his aloneness, which he wanted. Like a changing tide he could paddle out of, he wanted his aloneness because of the nothingness he felt for his people and his friends and yet the more alone he was the greater the sadness grew.

He thought of asking Gobidin permission to hunt something but he didn't want to talk to Gobidin either. Words may come from him. Words he knew he shouldn't say but wanted to, badly.

He was afraid to break the silence that had hung over such aspects of the battle. Madawaak was afraid that they would turn on him and cast him out if they knew he'd broken the silence. He was afraid they'd turn on him and cast him out if they knew the part he'd played in what had happened. He was afraid they would say or do nothing at all... or that they would congratulate him.

Madawaak took a broken breath and tears warmed his eyes. If he told Demasduit... no, he couldn't. Makdaachk was Mooaumook's father. She would believe them over Madawaak, and think Madawaak was a liar. Or she wouldn't care. Either was too much to face.

'You're still alone out here,' her voice cut through the soft whisper of the breeze and startled Madawaak. She'd come over the small hill behind him, still able to sneak up on him.

'I want to be alone,' he said. But his conscience pricked him in the heart and he turned to her. Still so beautiful to him. Eyes that struck him beneath his skin. An image that melted through him, even when she looked down at him with big, sad eyes. 'You're worried about Mooaumook. I'm sorry. But you know... he feels he has to go...'

'I don't care what he feels,' she said. Demasduit moved in closer and sat down beside him. 'I care for the vigils we held last night for the men who will never come home. Nobody else seems to. They're all worried about land and hunting and Farther People and Pale Ones. Even my father only seems to care about my marriage. Not that I don't want it, but how will it happen if Mooaumook is out there spying? Mooaumook only cares about redeeming himself and spying. Or captured. Or dead. They don't grieve. They don't want to grieve for the dead.'

She looked long at the side of his face.

'And I care for the hurt I know is inside you even though I don't know why it's there.'

[104]

Madawaak opened his mouth to speak but only a surge of emotion came to his throat. He turned away from her before he could cry and watched the caribou again.

'You want to be alone, I know,' she whispered. 'So do I. Can we be alone together?'

Madawaak nodded his head. They watched the caribou together in silence.

9

Gunnlogi

Noise and rabid bodies filled the lodge on the final day of the funeral and victory celebration, and Gottfried sat sober in Thorvald's rightful seat quiet and disinterested yet again. Thorfinn sat beside him and watched as he gently turned the sword in his hands.

The tables were overcrowded. Thralls sat on their hands and knees at the corners of the tables to accommodate all those the Karlsefini had insisted were essential to the Althing. They shouted and drank themselves insensible. All around, eyes were bleary and red. Breath was foul. Men broke everything they touched and the female thralls had barely any clothes left on them. Some even bled from bites on their shoulders or scratches on their hips and rears. The shouting was unintelligible.

Light shone through the door for a moment as it opened and closed. Gottfried saw it. He waited as the entrant prowled through the rabble and dodged the flying fists or streams of noxious belches. When she finally appeared before him, Gottfried found himself again staring into the eyes of Freydis.

He stood in a fury. 'I told you to remain on the knarr!'

An eruption of cheers rattled the turf walls of the longhouse.

'You are wasting resources!' Freydis shouted.

'We are melding our clans. It does not involve you!'

'*Their* tribes are melded!' Freydis barked. All quiet, all eyes on her. The crowd focused with the intensity of the audience of a fight to the death. '*They* are not rolling around in drunken revelry. *They* are not feasting themselves into unconsciousness for their dead. *They* are out there preparing. *They* will not waste their time like you are, Gottfried.'

'The only waste of time has proven to be listening to you,' Gottfried said as he placed his fingertips on the tabletop. The sword had fallen by the side of Thorvald's seat. 'Why did we hang their dismembered corpses from the trees?'

'That will not deter them forever,' Freydis said. 'You can go on playing. I will go on preparing for the next skraelingjar attack. Perhaps I will fend them off myself.'

'Perhaps you can run along and join them,' Gottfried sat down.

'When the winter comes and you're still here with nothing to your name and still no farmland or plantations on Hop just like Thorvald was, I wonder if you will ask my advice. I'll be here.'

'Nonsense, woman!' Thorfinn said with a wave of his hand. 'I'll make another trip to the Cape of Three Forks and bring back more than Straumfjord will consume in a year.'

'It is time you returned to your settlement,' Freydis said to Thorfinn. 'Don't you think?'

'I have sent word that Baldar is to be Chieftain of Helluland,' Thorfinn said. 'You need to go and attend to your duties.'

'My duties?' Freydis turned to the Althing. 'Other than protecting my brother's lands? The people who have come to realize his vision? Thorvald could not. Not even with this man's help,' she pointed at Gottfried. 'I will lead Straumfjord to victory over the skraelingjar. I will make three countries of this land. With Gunnlogi...'

'You will never wield Gunnlogi,' Gottfried said as he lifted the sword out of the dirt.

'It was my brother's sword,' she breathed. 'It was passed to Thorvald and...'

'...And Lief Eiriksson explicitly said you were under my command,' Thorfinn cut in. 'Never to rule. Helluland is mine. Hop shall be mine as well. Whom shall lead Straumfjord? That is the will of the Althing. You have no right to take democracy from Thorvald's people and I will never allow you to take it from mine.'

Freydis tipped her head slightly back and stared at Thorfinn. But said nothing.

'The time has come to elect a new chieftain to rule Straumfjord,' Gottfried said. He held the sword in both hands and placed it on the table. 'I will not take it myself.'

'I will take it,' Freydis said.

'You were not asked!' Gottfried thundered and slammed his fist down onto the arm of his chair.

'No, let her!' Thorfinn said as he stood up and stepped around the table. 'Let them vote for Freydis Eiriksdottir. Mistake child of Eirik the Red and the offspring of his battle-spoils and who Lief Eiriksson, her own brother, exiled here as my servant.'

He walked right up to Freydis, and then began to circle her as he spoke to the Althing.

'Freydis, who would have you all warring until the end of time. Here, and then on the mainland. Again and again. Until there is nobody left. Freydis, who had Thorvald slaughter the Icelanders Helgi and Finnbogi because she was born of war and knows nothing else, and left Straumfjord at the mercy of the skraelingjar. You don't even have their women and children as thralls! She was chief advisor to Thorvald. What did she manage with him, in that time? A settlement on Hop? No. A settlement on Helluland? Not until I came along. Are there any other settlements on Markland? Why, no. Is there even one skraeling captured here? Or anywhere? No. But they're cut up and hung from trees outside! That is Freydis' vision for Vinland. A slaughterhouse.'

He turned towards Gottfried.

'Let them vote for her. Or let them vote for the man who established trade with Byzantium and Nubia, who supplies Ragnar's country, who brought civilization to Helluland. and shall do so on Hop as well before the next winter falls. I navigated waters that swallowed Lars the Boatman and his crew to come to your rescue. Let them vote for Freydis Eiriksdottir if they want destruction and war forever. Or let them vote for trade and for skraelingjar slaves that will build our bonds with Rome, Venice, Greece and Constantinople for another hundred years. For wine and ale. For spices and delicacies. Let them vote for Thorfinn Thorsson!'

There was an eruption of cheers. Gotfried stood and held out the sword Gunnlogi.

'This sword was wielded by Eirik the Red when Iceland was tamed,' he said. 'It was carried with him to Greenland and our homes were established beneath it. Upon his deathbed, it was handed to our King Lief Eiriksson. Under it, he founded Straumfjord on which we stand. It was passed to Thorvald Eiriksson, his brother, to expand upon Vinland and make three nations here. He died trying to do so. Thorfinn Thorsson, the Althing of Straumfjord has spoken. Will you accept Gunnlogi, and everything that comes with it?'

Thorfinn held out his hands again and the longhouse erupted in another thunderous cheer. Then he gently took the sword by the hilt and turned and showed it off to the longhouse and again drew their deafening roars of approval.

Freydis was already gone.

* * *

In the frosty afternoon light, she moved slowly through the ruined village left by Helgi and Finnbogi. Mooaumook kept low by the slope down into the forest of redwoods. He watched her walk as though all the world waited for her. He watched her look around with her head held regal and high, her shoulders straight and square. There was an animal strength in her body. A power and sense of security that suggested she had not come up here alone. But Mooaumook had been fooled before.

There was nobody around her. Even his hunter's ears could not detect any other feet scrunching the snow or crackling the old, charred coals where houses once stood. He plucked the string of his bow. Freydis had come alone. Mooaumook knew it. His fingertips danced across the feathers of the arrows in his quiver. Freydis stopped in the centre of the village and looked around slowly and Mooaumook knew she was looking for him.

'Young man,' she cooed softly in his language. Perfectly, as though hers was the voice that first taught him to speak. 'Have you come to me yet?'

[109]

Now he could be certain she was alone. Mooaumook pinched the end of an arrow between his thumb and forefinger. He could. Right now. Her kin would never come for her in time. There was a chance now to end this all... the sights he'd seen on the way up flashed through his mind, through his heart and through his guts. The limbs of his people. Hacked off and hung from trees. The blood frozen in crimson icicles that dangled from their glittering flesh. Their heads rammed on spikes. Faces deformed. Twisted in their final moments of agony and frost bitten with the skin flaking off. Leaving the raw tissue exposed. Torsos tied to tree trunks. Castrated. Pale Ones had done it.

The horror had been dizzying.

Mooaumook continued on but only with the thought of killing her in mind. She'd allowed it. He knew it. Amongst them, he'd seen Yaseek. His head on a pike. Eyes gouged out and bloody sockets left open and frosted over. Hatred burned in him. He could kill her now... kill her now and set their spirits to rest...

Freydis had no weapons. No shining stone on her. And he realized she'd stopped looking around. Her piercing eyes had settled on where he hid and slowly she raised her hand. Light winked at Mooaumook from her finger where she wore some ring fashioned from the same shining stone as their weapons. He slid the arrow back into its quiver. His mouth had turned dry and his hands shook too much.

'Come out, young man,' she smiled.

Mooaumook thrust his bow and quiver and his tomahawk aside and stood upright. One last darting glance for followers. But she was alone. Then, he approached her tense and ready to run. Freydis stood head and shoulders taller than Mooaumook and the closer he got, the more her size impressed him. The strange desire pulsed through his veins.

'My people,' he said, breathless. 'What have you done to their remains?'

'What I shall do to all of them,' she said. 'If they attack my village again. Your people slaughtered babies.'

'The same as Pale Ones did to Mammasamit,' Mooaumook raged. His fists clenched.

[110]

'Then we are even,' Freydis said. She smiled and showed her big, buck teeth and the green of her eyes seemed to flare with hunger. 'The villages of the Forest Fathers are quiet again.'

'They do not stay for the winter,' Mooaumook said. 'They are with the Broken Lands' Father. Gobidin. He means you no harm.'

'I wonder if your Forest Fathers can change his mind?' Freydis said as she turned away from him and walked towards the rolling ocean. 'Are they all there? In the Broken Lands?'

'I cannot account for the Farther People.'

'I can.' She turned her head and smiled at him again. 'But your Forest Fathers and the Lakes Fathers and the River Fathers, they have gone to this Gobidin?'

'Yes. They follow the caribou migration.'

'And the Farther People come down and across the Great River...'

'We never see them. Only their tracks.'

Freydis giggled.

'What is funny?'

'I know more than you do, Mooaumook,' she taunted, sweetly. 'I know that the Farther People are spending their winter in their summer homes.'

Mooaumook just stared at her.

'They're afraid of Straumfjord,' she said. 'I have given them reason to be afraid but there is something else as well. Rumour has spread amongst them. A warrior woman who slays polar bears. They call her Demasduit.'

Mooaumook tensed again. The sound of her name spoken by Freydis' silkily poisonous voice was too much. But she smiled.

'You know her,' Freydis stated. 'She's in the Broken Lands with the rest of them, isn't she?'

'What would you do?' Mooaumook asked. He wondered if he could sprint back to his weapons before she could alert the village of his presence.

'I am giving you a gift,' Freydis said. 'Fair warning. And knowledge you can take to your loved ones. They can leave the Broken Lands. Come back to their homes here for the winter.'

[111]

'Gobidin will never leave the Broken Lands,' Mooaumook warned as his stomach knotted while her plan became apparent.

'Then he may stay and defend them,' Freydis said.

'You have the forest and the lakes and the Great River,' Mooaumook said as he waved his arms over what was potentially hers. 'Can you not leave us one refuge?'

'I leave you this,' Freydis gestured to all that Mooaumook had been waving at. 'But the Broken Lands shall be mine. And I will remind you that I have given you leave to save those you care about most. Those who aren't too arrogant to listen to you.'

'What then?'

'When the Broken Lands are mine, I will send you as an emissary with the gift of iron,' she held up her ring. 'As promised. You are but two steps away, Mooaumook. Don't ruin it now.'

'It will cost the lives of more of my people,' Mooaumook said, as hot flushes erupted throughout his body. His hands began to shake.

'Not the smart ones,' Freydis said. 'They shall have iron and our allegiance forevermore. Together we shall conquer the Farther Lands. And the lands of Mi'kmaq and all the worlds beyond them. You with our iron. And with our friendship. Don't forget what this is for. Don't forget I gave this to you.'

Mooaumook wanted to vomit. He tried to swallow but his tongue was so dry it felt as though it might crack.

'Go,' Freydis said. 'Tell your families that the Farther People are staying away. Tell them it is because of Demasduit. Then come back here. Tell me when your kinfolk are migrating again. I will need you here after that for a while.'

'If my people found out...'

'They won't, Mooaumook. Not before you give them the gift of steel. Then they will make you a god. Go.'

Mooaumook didn't want to think about it. He just had to do it. So he turned and into the icy winds he ran.

* * *

'Tonight we will recruit bands to sail for Hop at daybreak,' Thorfinn said from the Chieftain's chair. The jarls of Markland were gathered and silent to him now. He held Gunnlogi by the hilt. The sharp end was stuck in the dirt. 'We will destroy all of the skraelingjar that live there.'

The Althing roared their approval.

'All except the best specimens,' he said as he raised one finger on the hand that clutched the sword. 'They are small, but they are strong. Powerful little bodies. These ones are to be taken alive. Unspoiled. They will fetch a high price in Rome. Perhaps in North Africa as well. Bring those to me and I will make you rich.'

The Althing roared again, and horns of wine and ale were raised to the Chieftain.

'Once we have Hop, it will simply be a matter of moving through the lands,' Thorfinn promised. 'Our prosperity will lure more people from Greenland and they will come to help us...'

'If you attack Hop tomorrow, you will have no bands left for the rest of Vinland,' a voice growled from the far end of the lodge.

Thorfinn's face pinched with offence. He tiled his head back. 'Who spoke?'

'I, my Lord,' a scrappy looking karl raised his hand. 'Ifar of Greenland.'

'You are not jarl...' Gottfried began.

'Am now, my Lord. Elected by my people since we left for Vinland,' he said. 'Freydis ordered me to Straumfjord.'

'Freydis doesn't give orders regarding Straumfjord,' Thorfinn said. 'Or anywhere. Vinland is my endeavour.'

'I'm simply warning you, my Lord. You'll lose it if you move on Hop tomorrow,' Ifar said. His bottom lip quivered sadly. 'As we speak, all the warriors of the Markland country are down there. They migrated with the caribou. And they're expecting Norse to appear there. They've seen what we left for them in the trees, my Lord. They aren't happy.'

'How do you know all this?' Thorfinn asked.

'I'd have to call upon an unwelcome woman, my Lord.'

'Freydis,' Gottfried choked beside Thorfinn.

'Freydis is a liar,' Thorfinn said.

'Nevertheless, my Lord,' Ifar said. His voice had lost its power, but he stepped forward, hunched and with his hat in his hands. 'Look around Markland and you'll see their fires don't burn. They're gone. All south. Maybe a thousand of them.'

'Perhaps they ran off when they saw what we did to their brothers?' Thorfinn said.

'Whose idea was that?' Ulfan probed.

Thorfinn gritted his teeth.

'When did she tell you this?'

'Minutes ago, my Lord,' Ifar said. 'I'd not been attending the celebrations. I had business building my lodging. I'm a shepherd, sir. Jannik needs my hel...'

'I don't care about your lodging!' Thorfinn said. 'I care about what Freydis thinks she knows and how she thinks she came to know it.'

'You believe her, then?' Ulfan asked.

'I don't believe her, no,' Thorfinn said. 'I am concerned about what rumours she intends to spread around Straumfjord. I am concerned about whether I should ram her brother's old sword down her throat now or if I should wait until she's back before King Lief and charged for attempting to undermine my chiefdom.'

'I wish to speak,' Ifar said.

'Well, you have been speaking,' Gottfried said.

Ifar stepped out into the centre of the Althing where all the jarls could see him.

'Freydis called upon most of us to join her with Thorfinn's expedition to Helluland, and we have lived safely there,' he said. 'It was Freydis who ordered sailors out to the knarr we saw that was besieged by the icebergs, and it was upon her order we set sail for Straumfjord. A moment later, we might have found nobody alive here. Only skraelingjar. It was Freydis' idea to cut them up and make leaves of them. A dreadful idea, yes. But one that has worked thus far. I know nothing about what happened to the Icelanders, I have only the words of Gottfried. I respect the words of Gottfried. But with my own eyes, I have seen Freydis lead us astray or into danger not once yet. And she has respected the will of the Chieftain of the Althing. She did not come here to warn us of what awaits us on Hop, she asked me to relay her message. Respect for the people who just this morning stripped her of her title. Is there anyone here who can rightly contradict my personal belief in Freydis' integrity?'

'I can,' Gottfried said. He stood. 'I saw her slaughter women and children. Take an axe in the middle of the night and massacre them against the orders of the Chieftain and her own brother.'

'I saw it too,' Astrid Ormstungu said.

'Did anyone ask her motivation?' Ifar asked.

'I ask the Althing,' Thorfinn cut in. 'Can anyone imagine a motivation that would justify such a crime?'

Silence.

'Thank you Ifar,' Thorfinn said. 'You have revealed the ongoing deceits of Freydis Eiriksdottir. I will have her brought before me tomorrow. We'll see what she does with that tongue of hers after I've cut it out and boiled it.'

There were grunts and murmurs but no disapproval. Ifar sulked as though he'd been stung, but quietly retreated back to his place against the far wall, near Gottfried's arras.

'Now,' Thorfinn said. 'Which of you have the strongest and bravest warriors? Aside from myself. Who here will lead forces into Hop and bring back captives which will make you rich beyond your dreams?'

'I have the most axes,' Hrafn Onandarsson said.

'Mine are better with their atgiers than yours are with their axes,' Ceowulf the Galning said. Thorfinn smiled upon his champion and commander of his band.

'I will need five to send their bands,' Thorfinn said. 'Five, no less.'

There was silence.

'None of you?' Thorfinn half-whispered. But his words echoed through the Althing. In a rage, he stood upright. 'Shall my fighters go alone then?'

'We don't know what we're volunteering for, my Lord,' Ulfan said. 'Indeed no fires burn out there. The forests and the coast seem to have been evacuated. We don't know their number on Hop.'

'Freydis has your minds,' Thorfinn accused them with a swift wave of his hand.

'We have three times run afoul of the skraelingjar in battle,' Astrid said. 'Once they have defeated us. It was only because of your intervention we were saved. They know these lands. They could be watching us from a distance now, waiting to see our ships depart. If they could warn a large number of their own down on Hop of our coming five bands would find themselves in terrible danger.'

'She may be a deceiver, my Lord,' old Olfar Sigurdson said. 'Perhaps we could take caution enough just to ask her what she means by her warning. If there is lying in her, you will see it on her face. Won't you, my Lord?'

'What Norse people are these?' Thorfinn quietly asked Gottfried. 'Afraid of pygmies in the forest?'

'Norse people who think you are afraid of Freydis,' Gottfried whispered. 'They aren't your traders, these people. Words don't keep them alive. Bring her in here. Appease them. If she lies, slaughter her tonight.'

'Bring me Freydis Eiriksdottir,' Thorfinn ordered. Two sentries hurried out through the door.

* * *

'Hop will be safe to attack soon, my Lord,' Freydis said, softly. The Althing was forced to strain in order to hear her glassy, fragile voice. 'But not tomorrow. In a few days, skraelingjar will fill the forests and the coast and the lakes again. Their number on Hop will be reduced.'

'Then they'll be back here,' Thorfinn reasoned.

'Here is not where we must focus for now,' Freydis said. 'Hop is.'

The silence felt heavy. It seemed to choke every one of the Althing, and its grip tightened when they heard Freydis almost recite Thorfinn's own plan back at him.

'What if we don't believe you?' Gottfried said.

'Then I make no further discussion,' Freydis said. 'After all, my Lord is the appointed Chieftain of the Althing and of the Markland. If his judgement is to go to Hop at dawn, then so be it. I wish only luck to those who go.'

'Why do you say we need luck?' Thorfinn asked. 'You saw what we did to their number here.'

'Their number here is not their number on Hop,' Freydis said with her thick eyebrows raised.

'Tell us why they would fracture their number by returning, then?' Gottfried requested.

'I can offer you no more,' Freydis said. 'Only what I know. Their behaviours, their psychology, is quite beyond my understanding. But I know they will, if not why. And Hop will be yours for the taking, my Lord.'

'Your word is not good enough for us, Freydis,' young Asny Admundsdottir said. 'If the Chieftain's are not, nor should yours be.'

Freydis looked at Torvard, who lingered near the door.

'Why did you interrupt my night with my husband to accuse me of lying when it is nothing to any of you whether I tell the truth or not?' she complained. 'You can leave in a few days, when it is safe, or you can leave tomorrow. *Odin* be with you.'

'When will it be safe?' Ulfan asked.

'It is not for a simple karl to give orders,' Freydis said. 'That would be treasonous. And contradictory to the decision of the Althing. Only a chieftain or a king can send bands off to battle.'

'We are not asking you to send anyone to battle,' Thorfinn said. 'We are asking you if it is safe.'

'If you act on my advice, then it is the same thing.'

She turned to leave.

'How do you know?' Thorfinn demanded as he shot up to his feet and held Gunnlogi by his side. 'How do you know?'

Freydis stopped mid step and stared at him.

[117]

'You've told the Althing there is danger,' Thorfinn shouted. 'Would you let them go towards danger?' he turned to the Althing. 'This is what Freydis thinks of us. This is the true Freydis. She'd send us into danger she knows about...'

'I told you there was danger, didn't I?'

'So prove it!'

'I told you. I warned you. If you don't believe me then my conscience is clear.'

'We could torture it out of you,' Astrid said.

'Could you?' Freydis snapped back without missing a beat.

'Yes, I think we could,' Astrid said.

'In a few days you will see how I know what I know. Unless you move on Hop at dawn. In which case... as I said. *Odin* be with you.'

'Curse you!' Thorfinn screamed and before anyone could stop him, he'd stomped over the table and right up to Freydis and thrust the point of the sword at her throat.

She stood still. Even as the tip let a small red line of blood run down her neck.

'You see?' she said, softly.

'Gottfried,' Thorfinn called. 'Gottfried!'

'My Lord?'

'Will you take a band to Hop at dawn?'

'Not alone, my Lord.'

The Althing was silent.

'This Chieftain has heard a dire warning and wishes to send a band into Hop anyway,' Freydis said. 'He doesn't know when it will be safe. I do.'

'Then tell me.'

'First we find out how badly everyone wants to know,' she said. 'Thorfinn the Karlsefini has been voted by the Althing to be the Chieftain of Markland. I motion to challenge him.'

'I second,' Ifar shouted.

'You cannot challenge an elected chieftain!' Thorfinn shouted.

'She can,' Gottfried said. 'But only by combat.'

'Elect your champion, Thorfinn,' Freydis said. 'We decide at midnight.'

In the stunned silence, Freydis turned and walked with Torvard out of the longhouse.

* * *

Gottfried drove Gunnlogi into the snow-covered earth in the centre of Straumfjord while spot fires burned all around. Each jarl of the Althing elected a champion. They held their spears into a circle that surrounded the sword, with a small clearing between them and it.

Tall, broad shouldered and narrow hipped and with long hair and a strong, angular face, the mighty Ceowulf stepped into the circle. He slipped his helmet onto his head. In one hand a spear and in the other an axe. Ceowulf had no shield. Even the mountainous Gottfried came barely midway up Ceowulf's chest. The audience watched in silent awe. Tales of Ceowulf's fury were legion far and wide and all of the Althing wanted to see him in battle.

Gottfried turned to see Freydis' champion and his mouth fell open to see Freydis step into the circle herself. A small battle axe in one hand. A shield in the other. He turned and stepped out of the circle where Thorfinn waited.

'Kill her and be done with this,' Gottfried whispered to Thorfinn. 'Think nothing of rumours. You are Chieftain.'

Thorfinn nodded. He signalled to Ceowulf's lieutenants Halfdan Larsson and Olaf the Tree-Legged and both stepped into the ring with the giant captain. A hushed murmur of anger and disapproval issued in the firelit night.

Freydis seemed to smile.

Gottfried blew on a horn and the three fighters leaped upon Freydis. She stepped towards Ceowulf. His spear thrust forward and she caught her shield underneath it and forced, then heaved it aside as he brought his axe towards her. She leaped and slammed her shield into his shoulder to knock him aside. Olaf was just behind him. Freydis brought the edge of her shield down onto his face then threw her shield at Ceowulf. She turned and beat Halfdan's coming atgier from its path and split the blade off its pole.

Freydis ducked beneath a thrust from Ceowulf's spear, picked up the head of the atgier, rolled forward and rammed it through the soft flesh of Olaf's thigh. He screamed and fell on his back. Freydis spun and sidestepped a swing from Halfdan's axe, then chopped hard into his shoulder before he could recover. He screamed and fell. Blood ran from the wound and beneath his split leather. Ceowulf did not pause. He thrust his spear but Freydis rolled with the blow she'd dealt Halfdan and ducked down and picked up his dropped axe.

Freydis was dwarfed by Ceowulf, but as two men lay screaming on the ground he hesitated. They circled each other. Gunnlogi was between them. Sharp spear heads scraped against their backs. Freydis doubled her stride and stepped in the other direction. The sleight of step was enough to enrage Ceowulf, who raised his spear and thrust with all his might. With one axe head Freydis deflected, with the other she cut the polearm in two. And with a step she threw the other axe at Ceowulf. As he chopped it from his path Freydis took Gunnlogi from the dirt and thrust it into his side. Ceowulf swung at her. But she pulled away, spun on the spot and slashed Halfdan through the neck as he came up behind her with the axe she'd thrown. He fell, choking and dying.

Ceowulf seized his chance and swung his axe low. But Freydis didn't stall in her motion. She turned a full spin, caught the axe with hers and chopped Ceowulf deeply into his shoulder at the base of his neck with the sword. Blood ran through his long hair. Wide-eyed, he dropped to one knee. Freydis raised the sword high and hacked midway through his neck. The great body collapsed into the dirt. In two more swings, she cut the head from its body.

Olaf lay in convulsions as blood coursed from his leg. Freydis turned and buried her axe in his head and all three men were dead. Blood-spattered Freydis stood in the centre.

She removed her helmet and looked at Thorfinn, who watched as his jaw hung loose. The spears raised from around Freydis. The bearers kneeled.

10

Trusted Mooaumook

Gatherers sprung up from the grass as he huffed like he breathed fire and dragged his aching body back to the village of Gobidin. They came running towards him. Women, old and young, with their hands outstretched, their eyes full of tears and the air full of wailing.

'Mooaumook,' they cried. 'Oh, Mooaumook!'

'Are you hurt?'

'Did they find you?'

They braced his arms and lifted some weight off him. Mooaumook was almost carried back towards the enormous village that hosted all the families of the Forests, the Lakes, the Rivers and the Mountains.

Fear spun through Mooaumook's fatigue and alarmed him back to life. They would bring him to Gobidin. To Oonban. To his father. He wasn't ready to see them... to look at them... not ready to say her words to their ears as though they were his own... to communicate her poison to them.

'Demasduit!' he cried. 'Where is my Demasduit?'

'Demasduit!' the women repeated. 'He wants to see his Demasduit!'

The flock separated and Mooaumook saw Shendeek and Imamus on the edge of the village where they watched his approach. With them, appeared Gobidin. But the women hurried in front of them and called to Demasduit. Gobidin joined in the search for her. With only a few gatherers left to carry him, Mooaumook limped from the grass into the village and Shendeek cast his watchful eyes up and down his slumped and exhausted body.

'Let him rest a while.'

They took him to his host family's mamateek and he staggered inside. One of the young women broke away from the others and forced her way in behind him. She took some weeds and grains from her pouch. Mooaumook staggered to his bed. The young women ground the weed and grains and mixed them with water, then scooped up hot rocks from the fire and dropped them into the birchbark pot. Mooaumook watched sleepily. Little tongues of steam lapped and danced up from the mixture and the young woman brought it to his side.

As he laid there, Mooaumook's skin felt so cold it might crack. He could barely move his tongue it was so dry and his stomach ached like a stab wound. The woman dipped a birchbark cup to fill it and held it up to his lips.

'Son,' Makdaachk's voice froze him as he lifted his head up towards it.

Mooaumook looked towards his father. The great old man stood upright as the curtain flapped down behind him.

'She is here,' he said. 'Do you want her now?'

'Demasduit!' Mooaumook gasped. He sat upright and left the woman and her tea behind him. 'Demasduit!'

Makdaachk pushed the curtain aside and gestured. Demasduit stepped in. She moaned sharply and hurried into his arms where she curled up beside him and he held her tightly. Their lips met. They kissed hungrily and deeply and tasted and felt each other's warmth.

'We will come back later,' Makdaachk looked at the young woman.

She held the tea close to her chest, stood up and bowed her head as she followed the old warrior out of the mamateek. At last, they were alone.

'Mooaumook...' Demasduit began.

He silenced her with another long, deep kiss. Mooaumook lifted her up on top of him and braced her legs at his sides, though his arms throbbed with tired pain, and held her there and kept kissing her until the thoughts in his head aligned. Thoughts of iron winking in the sun... and from the weapons they wielded...

[123]

Thoughts of his people as well and how he could save them all now. Freydis would not want them all gone if she didn't think they could defeat whatever force she sent to them. But with them would die the caution she'd ascribed them. And the secret of iron. His people called it shining stone. How little they knew! How much he could teach them. What could it be, but a message from the God Spirits?

Freydis could speak their language. The language of the God Spirit's people. She spoke it as cleanly and purely as his own mother had. And she could teach him the secret of iron.

What did it matter, Mooaumook thought, *if a few had to die? They would have their chance to leave as well. If it is not the will of nature that I learn the secret of the iron and be the one to teach it to my people,* Mooaumook reasoned, *then Freydis would never have been allowed to come to us. She would not be able to speak our language. It was God Spirits that brought their great canoes to the shores of our country. Not Aich-mud-Yim or the Black Devils, as the shamans said. They are mistaken. They have to be. Aich-mud-Yim could not utter the language of the God Spirits as freely as Freydis could. My people have it wrong.*

I have to save those that will listen from displeasing the God Spirits. I have a chance to save them.

With that, Mooaumook took Demasduit gently by the head and lifted her so he could look into her brown eyes. Like the bark of an old pine. *How Freydis' eyes shone,* he thought. Greener than the pine's needles. Greener than the grass. And the other Pale Ones, with eyes like the ice. He desired them. As Demasduit's eyes flickered around before his, searching them, he felt nothing. Only thoughts of Freydis. Of her immense body and her eyes that could doubtless see the spirit that lived inside him.

And pluck the thoughts out of his head.

'What is it, Mooaumook?' Demasduit asked as she tensed her body against his lustfully. 'What have you seen?'

As he slid his hands down her sides, he could feel the patches of her skin that were hardened by the scars left by the bear. He hadn't seen them yet. The thought of her ravaged skin, bumpy and coarse like the very bark her eyes resembled, cooled him more still. *This is not the broad, muscular body of a true warrior,* he thought. *This is damaged.*

'They are coming,' he whispered. 'An unstoppable force larger than any number I have ever counted. Their canoes reached the horizon and they are headed in this direction. We don't have much time.'

Demasduit's breaths grew shallow and her eyes widened.

'Don't tell them,' she whispered back.

'What?' Mooaumook sat upright and forced her off him. 'Why?'

'Such a force would destroy us all,' she said. 'One way or another. But I fear they have something in mind that would be worse than death for us. The way they capture animals and keep them captive. Even force them to breed. And they live their whole lives inside their barriers. If we scatter, they will do that to us.'

'If we stay here, we will be destroyed entirely.'

'That is better,' Demasduit closed her eyes. 'Better we die fighting and never know captivity with them. Better none of us do.'

Mooaumook stared at her and saw the conviction in her pinched expression. It chilled him. The way she stared at him now. Just watching to see if she'd convinced him.

'It is not for you to decide,' he said. 'The Fathers must decide.'

'I am one of the Fathers.'

'You are not all of them.'

Mooaumook staggered to his feet and overcame the wave of dizziness as he stumbled towards the curtain. Outside stood Makdaachk, Oonban, Wobee, Shendeek, Keathut, Ninejeek and Gobidin and many others he didn't yet know the names of. They turned and looked at him. He blinked and took a deep breath of the icy air. Demasduit... he knew she would never give up. Never submit. Never accept the gift of iron even if he gave it to her. His eyes found Oonban.

'I reject your daughter,' he shouted before the fear could inhibit him. 'She is poison!'

Oonban's eyes, widened by the shock, fell upon Demasduit as she emerged from the mamateek behind Mooaumook.

Little Madawaak watched from a distance. Mooaumook saw him and ignored him, though the thought of him stayed in Mooaumook's mind.

'What has caused this?' Oonban asked, breathless.

'You are impassioned my son...' Makdaachk began.

'I know what I'm saying!'

'You must say it to the council.'

* * *

Mooaumook drank the young woman's tea and life coursed through him with its warmth. He ate of their smoked great auk while he told them what he had to tell them while Demasduit watched on from outside the circle.

'She,' he pointed a small portion of auk bone at her, 'wanted to stay.'

'I want to stay as well,' Keathut quickly said.

'She would have had me keep what I saw a secret!' Mooaumook roared. 'To let them sneak up and surprise you all with an attack.'

'Is this true?' Oonban asked her.

'Of course it is true!' Makdaachk interrupted. 'My son does not lie. He is the one brave enough to go back, even after he was captured! I didn't see any of you go with him. I did not see this brave bear-slayer go with him. If he says the Farther People have not come to our lands for the winter, then so it is. So we must go there to evade this attack. This Demasduit would have us slain in our sleep!'

'There are worse fates,' she half whispered.

Oonban's face fell and his body slumped as soon as she spoke the words.

'She is right,' Keathut said. 'Even if we are killed in our sleep, here they would have to kill us. Or we go home and we scatter. They will be able to overpower us and capture our women and children. Their lives won't be worth living. Death is better. We stay!'

'It was for all of us to decide, not her alone,' Oonban said, heavily.

'If it is the will of the council that we make our final stand here, then we need to know regardless,' Makdaachk said. 'We need to know so we can prepare ourselves and die fighting! This girl would have denied us all chance.'

'You would have seen them coming,' Demasduit, half whispered, though she looked down at her feet.

'Not with enough time,' Makdaachk said.

'If they are a force as big as Mooaumook says...'

'They are a force as big as Mooaumook says!' Makdaachk shouted as he slammed his fist into the dirt. 'Doubt him, and you should elect to go and see for yourself. As my son did.'

Demasduit said nothing more.

'Go, Demasduit,' Oonban said as the eyes of all the council pierced him. 'You are no longer welcome here amongst us. Go to your mother. We will decide what we will do with you later.'

Demasduit stood still and quiet for a moment. Then she turned and hurried out of the mamateek.

Ninejeek's face was the only one not full of dread.

'We make our stand here,' Keathut said. 'Arm our women and children and have them fight alongside us. Give them sights they will never forget, so they tell stories of us for all time. And slay as many of theirs as have ever been slain. Leave them with nightmares so terrible, they will never attack another people on this earth.'

'If we have the advantage of our summer grounds,' Ninejeek said slowly and thoughtfully, 'we should use it. If we are wise and careful, they will not systematically destroy us, but enter trap after trap until they are all destroyed.'

'It would take lifetimes,' Wobee said. 'And destroy an unknowable number of lives.'

'It would,' Ninejeek agreed. 'But as many of theirs. And we would live longer than we would if we stayed here and waited. I think we are too quick to assume going home would mean certain death.'

'Of course you would say that,' Keathut said. 'Going home would bring you closer to your friends the Farther People. Why do they hide?'

'They must be afraid of the Pale Ones,' Ninejeek said. 'They have seen this great force and they are afraid.

'If they are afraid,' Shendeek said. 'They could be turned.'

'I would not fight alongside them,' Keathut said. 'I would give my last drop of blood to the sea before I fight alongside them.'

'Think of what you say,' Douajavik urged. 'Death now and the murder of your own. Or death later. And the murder of only more of them. The Farther People may be of the Demon Spirits but they are not these Pale Ones. They respect the rule of law. We can go back to fighting them when our common enemy is defeated.'

'They survive the winter in our lands while we flee down here to Gobidin,' Ninejeek said. 'They can help us sustain ourselves for many more winters. All of the winters it takes.'

'How would we know they would make peace with us?' Makdaachk said. 'How would we trust them?

'They have made the terms of their peace clear,' Ninejeek said, and he turned his eyes slowly to Oonban.

'How many of their number remain behind in the cove?' Oonban asked Mooaumook.

'Not a shadow of the force that comes towards us,' he answered. 'I will go back there and see.'

'By that time, we will be tied to whatever decision we have made,' Oonban said. 'It won't matter.'

'It must be known,' Mooaumook said. He felt safer. 'We must know what Oonban makes the great sacrifice of his daughter for.'

The council looked at each other and murmured. Mooaumook felt a prickle of fear but he knew he'd won.

'Then you will marry Demasduit to the Farther People?' Makdaachk asked Oonban.

'I want to know first,' he muttered.

'We could die while we wait...'

'You were more than happy to die tomorrow a moment ago!' Oonban snapped.

'Grant him time,' Ninejeek said. 'I propose Oonban waits for Mooaumook's word to make his decision.'

The council nodded in the affirmative. Only Keathut did not break his deathly gaze at Ninejeek.

'You are a coward,' he seethed. 'Even if I am the only one who sees it.'

'I am not keen to die,' Ninejeek said. 'I want us to have a fighting chance. But I do not lightly ask that Oonban give his daughter to his enemies. We should know first. The Pale Ones will waste much time here. They will be expecting many more of us than they will find.'

'I wonder if they will be expecting the caribou and the fertile earth they find as well,' Keathut said. 'Enough to feed and grow an army that could cover the mainland.'

'All the more reason that we must do all we can to stop them,' Wobee said, flatly. 'Nobody ever won a war by dying, Keathut.'

'I agree with Ninejeek,' Shendeek said.

'And I,' Eendosha said.

'And I,' this time it was Douajavik who spoke.

'And I,' came the chorus from the council, until only four remained.

'And I,' Makdaachk said, as he stared at Oonban.

'And I,' Oonban said, softly.

'What did you say?'

'And I!'

'Then it is decided,' Keathut said. 'We cower. We surrender to enemies that might already have sold themselves to the Pale Ones.'

'They have not,' Shendeek said. 'Or they would have come to our lands and never given them up.'

'And I,' Keathut spat with a snarl. 'That leaves our host the mighty Gobidin.'

'I do not leave the Broken Lands,' Gobidin rushed, quietly but firmly.

'As is the wish of Gobidin,' Oonban said.

'Madawaak shall stay with you,' Eendosha said and immediately drew the surprised eyes of the entire council. 'Not to fight but to see. See this great force for what it truly is worth. I do not say Mooaumook would lie. Merely that the Pale Ones are deceivers. There may be empty canoes. Trickery to scatter us. We must know for sure.'

Mooaumook hid his shudder.

Outside were the sounds of small bodies in a scuffle.

'I offer my son,' Eendosha said. 'He is the only one fast enough to outrun them.'

'Demasduit could,' Makdaachk said.

'That would spoil the Farther People's prize,' Keathut seethed spitefully.

'Then it is decided,' Oonban said. 'We leave today.'

Suddenly, a small boy fell through the curtain of the mamateek and dragged another boy down with him. The two looked awkwardly at the gathered fathers. Silently, they slipped back out through the curtain.

'Leaving today would put many in danger,' Keathut argued. 'The winter is savage.'

'The snow will cover their trail,' Oonban said. 'Bring us Madawaak.'

'I will go now,' Mooaumook said. 'I will make a strong start to report back to you their numbers in the mainland. And if any of the Farther People have come, I will tell Madawaak on the way.'

Gobidin slowly nodded his head and that was all the approval Mooaumook needed.

* * *

Demasduit sat sobbing by the fire in their host family's mamateek while Chipchowinech and Bidesuk brewed root water. Shanawdithit kneeled behind her sister and braided her hair. Oonban stepped through the curtain and the heaviest weight he had ever carried in all his many years grew heavier. His eldest daughter slowly looked up at him with her teary eyes.

[130]

'I'm sorry Papa,' she said, in a weak, trembling voice he'd not heard since she was her sister's age. 'I wanted to catch him out... I didn't believe him.'

'You are brave,' he said. He wanted to step closer to her but found he couldn't. Only stand there and look down on her with more than an arm's reach between them. 'You have courage worthy of Gobidin. He is staying here. But the council has decided that we of the forests, rivers, lakes and mountains have a better chance if we go home. There is talk of making peace with the Farther People.'

The mamateek fell silent. Chipchowinech and Immamus both stared at Oonban. Only Shanawdithit innocently kept braiding her sister's hair.

'See,' she said as she stroked Demasduit's braids affectionately. 'There is nothing to cry about.'

'Gobidin and all of us will stay behind?' Bidesuk said.

'That is what is decided.'

Bidesuk nodded her head solemnly. 'I have to go see my children.'

She got up. Oonban stepped aside, further still from Demasduit, and let her pass between them as she left.

'How will peace be made with the Farther People?' Chipchowinech asked as she slowly rose to stand.

'Something more has been asked of us by the council,' he said as he looked down at Demasduit's big, frightened, teary eyes. 'Something I could never have done before today.'

'No!' Chipchowinech roared. She stood a step towards him, her fists balled. 'No.'

'It is the will of the council,' Oonban said. 'Mooaumook goes back to the cove now to see their numbers there. If enough of them have gone to invade this land, as Mooaumook says, then we can delay the offering...'

'You will not,' Chipchowinech said. 'You will go back to that council and demand that they change their decision! You will not!'

She was crying.

'I cannot change the will of the council,' Oonban said.

[131]

'Did you even try?'

Shanawdithit started to cry. Demasduit quickly took her in her arms and sat her in her lap so she could hold her and form a shield around her.

'I tried.'

'Aren't you their leader?'

'Gobidin is their leader.'

'And what was his decision?' Chipchowinech shouted. 'To stay here and die? Does that make him a traitor? Shall we offer him to the Farther People?'

'You are hysterical...'

'Do not call me hysterical!' Chipchowinech took another firm step towards her husband. Demasduit stood upright. She still held Shanawdithit across her chest with her head over her shoulder and turned away from them both.

'Stop!' Demasduit cried.

Chipchowinech stared at Oonban and spluttered as her cheeks shined with tears in the firelight. Oonban stared back at her. A single tear twinkled beneath his left eye. But they were silent. Shanawdithit cried and sobbed into Demasduit's shoulder.

'I will offer myself to the Farther People,' she breathed, though her body recoiled and her heart ached in fury at the very thought. 'I offer myself.'

Demasduit's stomach tensed but she caught the dry wretch before it showed.

'Dema...' Chipchowinech moaned. 'Dema, no...'

'I undermined the council,' Demasduit said. 'I undermined a hero of our people.'

She held her sister close so she could feel Shanawdithit's hot little face against her cheek and her soft hair and little body as it tensed with each sob in Demasduit's arms.

'I was wrong,' Demasduit said. 'This... in my arms... is all that matters. If she has a chance... and that is what it takes... then I offer myself as peace with the Farther People.'

'What have you done?' Chipchowinech breathed towards Oonban.

Oonban wiped the tears from his eyes.

'I will tell the council. They are still gathered. You all will leave here before noon.'

'And you?' Chipchowinech snarled.

'I will not leave here at all,' he said.

He turned to go.

'Papa,' Demasduit hurried towards him but he turned his back. 'Papa, why?'

'You will have new families with the Farther People,' he said, without looking back at her. 'And I am unworthy of your courage.'

'Stay with us,' Demasduit ordered, breathlessly. 'Come with us!'

But he was gone through the curtain. The powerful hands of Chipchowinech clasped over Demasduit's shoulders and stopped her from chasing after her father. She turned to her mother, Shanawdithit still in her arms.

'Why?'

'Dema,' Chipchowinech sighed. 'You have chosen to leave all of this life behind. Shanawdithit will go with you, when the time comes, but they will not take Oonban.'

'I want to know he's alive...' Demasduit sobbed. 'I'm not ready...'

'There is much more left to lose,' Chipchowinech said as she bound her daughter tightly in her arms and the three of them cried together.

* * *

Demasduit was weak but she carried her share as she, Shanawdithit, Odensook and Chipchowinech set out again with the column of families for another long migration. It was still winter. They'd never left the Broken Lands so soon after arriving. Most of the bodies in the groups were still bent double beneath the weight of their provisions and their necessities. Oonban was not with any of them. Even as all of Gobidin's people gathered in the grasslands to wave them goodbye, Demasduit did not see the shape of her father nor feel his presence anywhere. Her heart ached and she could not stop the tears.

It was like he was already gone. The world felt big and dark and empty. Every danger was just beyond the shadows. The precipice was so big it felt as though it might swallow her in every step. The journey ahead raged in her mind like fire. Roared with brutal anger. Every gust of wind carried a million arrows for her flesh and nobody was there to protect her anymore. Every thought felt rogue. Dangerous. Because Oonban was not there to give them perspective.

Demasduit held Shanawdithit's hand to keep her up with them. She looked around for something stable, anything to reassure her. Someone strong she could trust in this world.

Madawaak watched them from atop a boulder where he sat.

Demasduit looked around and saw Eendosha, Debseek and their daughter Ebauthoo amongst the migration.

'Madawaak,' she called. 'Madawaak!'

He saw her and slipped down from the boulder and disappeared into the grass.

'I will catch up,' Demasduit said as she slipped Shanawdithit's hand into Odensook's.

'Me too!' Shanawdithit cried, but a firm tug from Odensook kept her by her grandmother's side.

Demasduit took her chance to slip away as new energy flowed through her. Energy to carry her to Madawaak. She moved away from the migration into the grass and the two found each other and almost collided.

The near miss made her smile.

'You'll be late,' she warned him.

Madawaak just looked at her. His dark, haunted eyes fell down to the ground, then up at hers again and Demasduit chilled to look into them. There was a change in them. Something she'd noticed since they found each other here on the grasslands, but which had grown with his isolation. He'd pushed her away when normally she'd have to insist he leave her. Something was not right with him. *Perhaps he is sad to have seen so much death,* she thought, *or perhaps he is wounded by the loss of loved ones.* But now she saw something else. Something that made her flesh crawl.

For Madawaak to have no expression in his eyes at all was unheard of. But there it was. Nothingness.

'You're not coming,' she stated, as her lips contorted and her mouth dried. Her eyes stung but there were no more tears in her weary, heavy body.

Madawaak shook his head no.

'Does everyone I love insist on dying?' she stammered.

'Mooaumook will live.'

'I don't love him.'

'I will not die,' he said. 'I'm not staying to fight. I'm staying to watch.'

Demasduit didn't even know what to ask.

Madawaak was already backing away into the grass. 'To see if Mooaumook was even telling the truth.'

Demasduit followed him. She reached through the grass to part it to keep him in her vision. 'Why? Why do you think he'd lie?'

'It is nature,' his voice said.

As Demasduit grappled and peered through the grass she saw that he was gone.

11

Come Night

Stars shone brightly and filled the velvety night sky with glittering light while shafts of colour danced high above the still treetops that brooded over the pure white mantle. Mooaumook trudged alone through the stillness and the silence. Soon he would hear their din as it arose from the cove they called Straumfjord and soon he'd smell the smog of their industry. Their iron-makers. But, for now, all was silent. It was like no soul lived in this melancholy world at all.

But they did. And Mooaumook's heart pounded, for in this stillness no trail would be lost, and one would surely be left by morning for the Pale Ones to find. He knew that Freydis would not allow it. But would the migration go on? Or would Freydis' forces find them still there... she'd kill them all. Or they would fight back and kill hers. And then they would know Mooaumook's deception and the secret of iron would be lost to them forever.

No, he thought. *They would continue.* He saw how frightened the council were. Enough to turn Oonban against his daughter and Keathut against his long-held convictions about the Farther People. Freydis' deception had worked, even with Mooaumook as a conduit.

He sighed with admiration for her.

There is just Madawaak, he thought as the icy stillness numbed his face. Madawaak could escape them with news of their true number. Mooaumook had to make sure it didn't happen. He knew the way Madawaak took to get to Oonban's village...

Soon he was looking across a sea of descending pine treetops that swept down in a great bowl to one point from which firelight and smoke incessantly issued. Straumfjord. He diverted and moved across the top. towards the peninsula and the destroyed village. His eyes widened and his senses sharpened as he sought any sign of a sentry in the trees or patrolling the undergrowth.

All there was to hear was the heaving and sighing of the ocean, the rhythmic clanging that always seemed to ring out from Straumfjord, and Mooaumook's own pulse. His moccasins scrunched in the snow. He had done this many times. Mooaumook started to relax...

Mooaumook moved onto the slight incline that led him up to the destroyed village. He froze. A coldness not of the air gripped him and held him absolutely still. He grabbed for his dagger. But the weight of a net came crushing down on his head and a blunt force from the side knocked the senses from his head. The ground hit him. Then the throbbing pain in his skull that made his eyes feel like they'd explode.

By the time Mooaumook could regather his senses, the ground was scraping underneath him. They were dragging him downhill. Down towards Freydis.

* * *

'We saved a table for you,' Freydis said as she gestured to an empty rectangle right near her own, while other jarls were forced to stand there was so little room in the longhouse. 'Over here.'

Thorfinn, his shoulders slackened by fatigue, dragged himself over to it and took a seat. His merchants followed him. None of his armed men remained as his karls. The thralls still served them their platters and their ales and wines. But the men even seemed reluctant to accept this much.

'Now, don't insult me,' Freydis said. 'Smile. Be glad. You live. And you have a territory all to yourself.'

She pointed out to sea, meaning Helluland. Still she got no swell of enthusiasm from the Althing. Instead a heavy, awkward silence pressed down over the room. But Freydis had the sword. And Gottfried sat by her side.

'How much longer?' Astrid asked. 'I want to go home to my family tonight.'

'You shall,' Freydis said. She tapped the sword that leaned against her seat. 'Or I'll give this back to Thorfinn.'

Gottfried saw the Karlsefini lick his lips as he stared at Gunnlogi.

'Some of you still have families to go home to,' Freydis said. 'And still are here to enjoy my company. As much could not be said had this man's plans gone ahead. None would be alive tonight.'

Thorfinn's fists balled against his knees but his eyes remained fixed upon the sword.

The door opened and Sven Gigurdsson stepped out of the still night. He waited respectfully. Freydis gestured and he marched into the centre of the Althing where he bowed to the Chieftain.

'As you predicted, my Lord.'

'Bring him in,' Freydis stood up.

Sven marched back to the door, opened it and waved his hand outside. For the second time in just a few days, Gottfried watched as that same skraeling was dragged in before him and held by hunters in the centre of the longhouse. Freydis prowled around the table. She was holding the sword and, on the way, picked up a quiver of arrows and a bow. She slung them around her shoulder. The skraeling climbed to its knees. Gottfried watched in wonder while other members recoiled in horror and remarked in hushed tones to each other.

A sickening unease rolled over all of them like a wave from the bay.

'What is this?' Freydis smiled as she asked Thorfinn.

'A fine specimen,' he croaked. 'He would fetch a good price from Christians or Romans.'

Freydis jabbed him and giggled. The skraeling watched her but there was no fear in his eyes. Betrayal, perhaps. But no white terror that Gottfried would imagine...

...and then Freydis started talking to him.

The gasp that issued from the Althing made Gottfried jump. The skraeling spoke back to her from within his net.

[138]

'One family of skraelingjar remains on Hop,' Freydis translated to the Althing. 'One family. The rest are migrating back up into Markland.'

'What is this?' Thorfinn snarled.

'When did you learn to talk to them?' Gottfried demanded.

'It's a lie!' Hrafn shouted out.

'What have you offered this creature in exchange for his help?' Asny asked.

Freydis stopped in front of the skraeling and looked slowly around the longhouse.

'You don't like it?' Freydis asked. 'Don't like information that comes from one of them? Think I'm lying? That's alright...'

She pulled out her bow and primed an arrow and pointed it at the skraeling's head. His eyes filled with horror. And fury. He raised himself up and showed Freydis his chest, as though to welcome her death blow.

'See? He's not afraid,' Freydis said as she readied to draw back the arrow. 'I'm not afraid. But if you all are, I'll end his allegiance right here. We can outlast another winter in Straumfjord.'

'We captured this skraeling the day that Thorvald died,' Gottfried said to her back, slowly and steadily while Freydis still held the arrow ready. 'You knew him before then. You spoke to him. You'd learned his language and you'd made contact. And you kept it to yourself. You kept all this a secret. We had this skraeling locked in the privy. You could have saved your brother's life had you not kept what you knew secret.'

Freydis relaxed the bow and held the weapon by her side where the sword hung from her belt.

'Unfortunately, my brother and his advisors saw fit to send me back to Greenland,' Freydis said.

'You kept this secret until it suited you,' Gottfried accused her.

'What would you have had me do?' she posed, without turning to look at her advisor. 'Tell you everything? You'd have left me to freeze up there in Helluland. You'd never have let me claim my birth right. Never have let me stay here. Thorfinn would have my brother's sword and where would you be? Getting killed on Hop. With clubs and bone spears.'

'Do not insult us by pretending this was done for anything but to benefit yourself,' Gottfried rose to his feet.

'Do we not have clear passage to Hop?' Freydis said. 'Are the skraelingjar that were defending it not now spreading back across Markland?'

'How do we believe this?' Hrafn insisted. 'How do we believe that there were any skraelingjar on Hop at all? This is all rehearsed.'

'Delay going to Hop by one more day then,' Freydis said. 'In that time you will see their fires burning again. How long shall we wait to appease Lord Hrafn?'

'Not at all then.'

'Asmundsdottir asked a question as well,' Ulfan said. 'What have you offered in exchange for help?'

Freydis prowled again. She stood behind the skraeling and reached through the net to brush her fingers through his hair. Then she grabbed a fistful of his hair, pulled him back and held the sword in front of his eyes.

'The gift of the Gods,' she replied.

Freydis released him and moved back to his front. Now she stared at Gottfried, who stared back with his brow furrowed. Slowly it smoothed. He knew what she meant.

'You'll teach them iron.'

Now there was uproar. An unintelligible rabble of growled and shouted objection as arms waved and horns spilled their contents all over the desecrated platters. Freydis stood in the center and smirked.

She spoke to the skraeling. He answered in a fury and pounded his fists against the ground. Freydis said more and shook her head.

'What are you saying?' Olfar shouted.

'I am promising him he will possess iron,' she said to the whole Althing. 'He will know its secrets. But I require something more...'

'This is idiocy!' Thorfinn leaped to his feet. 'To give them iron. To live in peace with them! What delusion! What an idiot this Freydis is. Surely she knows they will betray us. And with weapons we gifted them turn against us. I could have offered you untold riches. Roman gold from the slave trade I'd have made from skraelingjar. Instead you get allegiance with them. And trust? You're all insane. You'll all have your throats cut with the iron you give them.'

He was finished. Freydis waited. There was no response.

'I was telling him that before he can possess iron, he must make us an offering of thrall slaves. One. To show his dedication to us.'

Gottfried watched the skraeling as his eyes flickered about at the dirt while he thought. He saw the conflict in the creature. The confusion. The frustration. Though he hated her so bitterly he could taste her blood on his tongue, Freydis had not deceived them this time.

'And what after that one?' Thorfinn asked. 'As many as he is happy to give us?'

'These skraelingjar have enemies on the mainland,' Freydis said. 'They are called Mi'kmaq and they grow to full height. Imagine this,' she pointed at the skraeling, 'but the full size of a man. Before then, his enemies on Vinland shall be our enemies and we shall take them for our own. You, Thorfinn. You shall receive a tribute from Straumfjord and Hop of two skraelingjar every month to take back to King Lief. If you do not, I shall stand down.'

'By then they'll have iron.'

'Let's hear him first,' Freydis said, and then she spoke to the skraeling with force.

He half-whispered back at her. Gottfried saw the beads of sweat form on his skin and the tremors break out in his hands and on his lips. As she listened, Freydis changed as well. Her back seemed to arch. Though Gottfried couldn't see her eyes, he knew the expression in them now. That sharp, piercing green that could slice flesh like a thin blade. That narrow, absolute focus. Her shoulders started to heave.

[141]

'What is he saying?' Thorfinn asked when the skraeling finished.

'You will go back to Helluland tonight,' Freydis said softly as she slowly turned to Thorfinn. 'You and your men. Leave now. Now. Go.'

'I will not. Not without Althing consensus.'

'You'll get your slaves to trade in one month.'

'I want to know what he said,' Thorfinn hissed through his teeth.

'Thorfinn leaves,' Freydis said to the Althing. 'Thorfinn leaves with his merchants and stays at Helluland until I send him slaves. If I fail, I will go to Helluland as a slave.'

Gottfried shuffled uncomfortably. She had something good. Something Vinland couldn't afford to miss out on. But she wasn't going to just hand it over. As he looked across the faces of the Althing, he knew everyone was thinking the same thing he was.

'Motion that Thorfinn Thorsson set sail to return to Helluland tonight with his merchants,' Gottfried said, though every word pierced him like a dagger. 'Now.'

The Althing raised their horns in approval.

Thorfinn looked around, as the colour drained from his face.

'Off you go,' Gottfried ordered.

Thorfinn turned to his merchants, still open-mouthed, and gestured them ever so slightly. They flocked around him. Though they walked quickly out the door, it was the longest few paces Gottfried had ever witnessed in his life. Men who went to be hanged didn't walk so painfully.

Once they were gone, attention was back on Freydis. She held the tip of the sword to the skraeling's throat and spoke very calmly and clearly to it. Gottfried didn't need any translation for it.

'What did he offer?' Gottfried questioned.

'A slave,' Freydis answered as she slowly withdrew the sword and slipped it back in her belt. She was dry mouthed with lust. 'A captive.'

'An important one?' Gottfried said, though he needn't have asked.

'We will go about it once there are settlements on Hop,' Freydis said. She snapped out of her trance and addressed the Althing again. 'One Knarr will sail with five bands aboard for Hop at first light. No prisoners. The family that lives there are the most hostile we will encounter. Kill them all. They will never submit to us. There is a passage from the south that the skraelingjar keep secret. I will draw it on a map.'

'What about this slave?' Gottfried asked.

'That will be another advisor's task,' Freydis said as she turned to face Gottfried. 'You will lead the colonization of Hop. You, Hrafn and Asny will take your clans. Pick two more. Not Ulfan, Astrid or Olfar. Any other two. You will all send us monthly tribute or wheat, barley, grapes and meats. Whatever else you can cultivate we will work out later. That will be all you have to concern yourself with regarding Markland from now on.'

'Tell us what he said...' Gottfried asked as he rose.

'You are not of this Althing anymore,' Freydis said. 'You are Chieftain of your own. Good luck. *Njord* grant you safe passage. *Odin* be with you.'

'Freydis...'

'This Althing is dismissed.'

* * *

The Broken Lands had far more vast areas of unbroken land than Madawaak remembered. They got their name because of the way the ocean jutted into them. Cut deep swathes of churning brine into the open grassy plains and craggy hilltops. But as Gobidin and his high council marched his entire village farther and farther across the grasslands until Madawaak's legs ached and his back became heavy as rock, he found himself almost forgetting the sea.

Pine trees stood around them in small stands or alone on silvery rocks capped with patches of greenery. The sky was a great, open dome of azure. The sun rolled across it for the second time since their walk began. Caribou roamed everywhere and great seabirds glided overhead. Light shone unbroken even by clouds. Everything was visible all the way to the point where the grass and the trees met the sky and the curve of the earth stole them away.

Madawaak wondered where anyone would go to hide in this land.

As though to answer him, the land ahead rose in jutted rock formations like grey jaws caught open and waiting to swallow them. As they drew nearer and the maze of rock grew larger, Madawaak began to realize that this was the intention. To be as far from any coast as possible. To hide in the only hiding place the Broken Lands afforded.

There was never any conflict here. Such things were never needed. Until the Pale Ones came.

'Gobidin knows that the Pale Ones who slew Mammasamit and his family came from the sea,' Oonban explained as he walked beside the confused boy. 'Since they will come from the sea again, we will hide the vulnerable ones where the sea cannot carry Pale One canoes to them.'

'Will we hide?' he asked and wondered how long it would be before the Pale Ones found them. How long they would have to sustain themselves.

'We will not hide,' Oonban said, gravely as his weary eyes watched the rock maze grow up higher and higher from the horizon ahead. Yellow evening light shone directly in his squinted eyes. 'Only those of us who cannot fight.'

All of the migration bent in their strides and hobbled painfully from the length of the walk. All but tall, upright Gobidin in the lead. Madawaak wondered if Pale Ones already walked this land, coming to harm them. Coming to kill them. The sun sunk beneath the rock formations which now showed their full height and plunged them into shadowy darkness.

Then, they started to climb.

Gobidin led them up the narrow passages higher and higher. *The beings upon which the Pale Ones rode will break their skinny legs if they try to climb,* Madawaak thought as the loose rocks slipped and buckled beneath him. When they reached the top, dry-mouthed and with stomachs aching, the women brought out their stores of sundried meat and pudding and water satchels made of birchbark and the migration began to eat.

'Go easy,' Oonban warned Madawaak. His huge, calloused hand felt rough upon Madawaak's shoulder. 'They will need as much as we can leave them. And we still have the grasslands to hunt upon.'

All was lone pines or bare rock caught in the deep shadows and brilliant golden highlights of deep, clear-skied dusk. The wintery winds cut like blades. Gobidin presided over the fathers of his people but said very little. Each one knew where his hunting party would go to seek out the Pale Ones' force. And what to do once they found it. After everyone settled, he came still light footed and upright over to Oonban, who sat stopped upon a rock beside Madawaak.

'You will both go back the way we came,' Gobidin said. 'Follow our own trail.'

'They aren't trackers,' Oonban said. 'They will not be able to see where we went.'

'They are not,' Gobidin affirmed, but he seemed grave in the dying light. As though he meant to imply something more that was unthinkable to Oonban and Madawaak. But he left them to their rations without another word.

Madawaak sat in the cold, dewy grass until he felt life pulse through his aching legs again and the pain let go of his lower back and shoulders. He could breathe again. The cold night air caressed his face under the stars and he managed to fall asleep.

Deep, panicked cries ripped him from his dreams.

Stars glittered above Madawaak in the moment's hazy peace before he realized that the hollering was coming from all around him and was not a phantom of his mind. He shot upright. In the silvery light, the lithe bodies of the hunters ran with their bows and tomahawks to the edges of their cradle and shot desperately down into the shadowy grassland below.

Oonban was gone from his side. Madawaak crawled on his hands and knees to a rocky outcropping and craned his neck to see over the edge. Below, the grassland glowed in ghostly turquoise under the moonlight. The hulking bodies of the invaders moved through it and left tracks behind them where they went. Fires alighted and drew the arrows. But Madawaak could see that they were unattended. With each whistle, a wooden shaft shot down into the burning pines of a lone tree or stand of shrubs.

Then the arrows came back up. But they were not like his people's arrows. They flew like meteors led by balls of flame into the air, leaving trails of vibrant light behind them as they arched down over the encampment and smacked into flesh and ground and bone and cloth with breathless thuds. The cries of women and children and elderly, those in the centre of the refuge, came to crescendo in a blood-curdling cacophony.

Madawaak dared not look behind him. Sweat coated his body. He gripped a tomahawk and looked along the ridges of the cradle where the hunters fired their arrows now in all directions. Blinded by the light. Heat radiated and an orange glow began to throb from behind Madawaak and compelled him to look over his shoulder.

As he did, and the flaming bodies of those they protected writhed around in screaming agony or kicked and flailed on the grass while the fire swelled and grew and consumed their entire forms, another hail of arrows came slamming down. Men ran towards the loved ones they'd tried to protect. They were run through midstride. Their senseless figures stumbled and fell and curled around the shafts that pierced their shoulders, their stomachs and their groins. Some hit in the legs crawled and screamed even as the fires billowed up in the grass around them. They disappeared in a din of screams.

'Hold the trail!' Gobidin's mighty voice shouted above the madness.

But as he did, the giant Pale Ones came charging on foot, their spears held out before them. In the confusion and the darkness, hunters charged them and by the strength of their own strides rammed their own bodies into the sharp points of the spears. The Pale Ones aimed low. The men coughed loudly or huffed as the air left them and the thick spears slid through their abdomens. With terror and pain smeared across their bulging eyes, their gaping mouths and their exploding veins, they crumpled and fell while the Pale Ones ripped their weapons out of their bodies. The pierced hunters clutched at them as they crashed helpless and dying into the grass.

The other hunters swarmed the Pale Ones from the sides.

Giant axes met their bodies with heavy thrusts that cleaved them down their shoulders and split their necks or their chests. Others were slammed in their guts or their ribs and they fell open as they collapsed. Madawaak saw Gobidin come charging to the fore. An axe met his face and bore halfway through his head. The Pale One left it there as the attack closed in.

Rage pulsed through his body and with a mighty cry, Madawaak charged the invaders even as they spread out around the fire and hacked and reaped their way through the confused and injured hunters who tried to fend them off with feeble hands and broken weapons. But a force seized him around the shoulders and held him.

'No!' boomed Oonban's voice.

The force of his body being turned away knocked Madawaak into a spin. Spasms erupted through Oonban's body and Madawaak looked up to see the three spearheads burst through his chest and push blood and viscera out through his skin so it showered warmly down over Madawaak's face. The body collapsed forward as the spearheads receded and Madawaak felt his immense weight fell over him.

He was pinned. Couldn't move.

As the heat from the grassfire spread, he could only lie in the dark and listen to the sounds of screams and choking and cries shredded by torn gullets or gurgled as they drowned in blood.

He closed his eyes and cried and waited for it to be over.

* * *

Silence.

Madawaak couldn't remember or figure out when the nightmare sounds finally ceased. The silence had been horrifying of itself. But he knew it meant that the slaughter had ended and Oonban's weight was becoming unbearable. He couldn't breathe. When he did, his lungs filled with ash and the grassy smell of burned corpses. The fire still crackled. But its light had dimmed beneath the morning twilight that was sickeningly peaceful upon Madawaak's tired eyes.

A V of geese passed slowly between the cotton clouds above.

Madawaak took a deep breath in and felt the dried blood crack on his face and neck. He pushed and wrestled with all his withered might but Oonban was flaccid, everywhere he pushed only seemed to cause his weight to press harder down on Madawaak somewhere else. But this was enough people's grave. It would not be his as well. He screamed out and pushed and fought and finally, exhausted, he wriggled himself free.

Oonban's eyes had turned white and his skin was waxy and hung loose from the bones of his face. Madawaak looked away. He knew that image would stay with him forever even if he never looked at it again. He staggered to his trembling feet.

Small, near transparent tongues of flame still lapped and crackled around the borders. The cradle was a scorched patch of blackness streaked with the twisted, skeletal bodies of his people. Some reached up with bent and broken fingers while others curled up into balls. Some still seemed to be moving. But Madawaak knew it was his fatigue and his hunger that played tricks on him. The bones showed through the flaking, blackened skin of these bodies. There was no life left in any of them.

Many that curled up did so around smaller figures that Madawaak couldn't bear to look at. He focused instead on the trails. Everything that moved upon the earth left its story written where its paces carried it. Madawaak could read them as easily as though he listened to the earth itself speak of what happened while he was pinned under Oonban.

None of the beings they rode upon carried them up here. As Madawaak had predicted. Their huge, flat feet moved in a circle around the central fire. Boxed everyone in. They fought their way around the edges of the cradle. The unburned but massacred bodies of the hunters littered their path. Gobidin was among the many. His head opened and his brains grey and rotting under the morning sun.

Some women had run. They didn't get far. The Pale Ones' feet closed in around their trail after only a few paces, yet there was no sign of them then. But Madawaak could see what happened. The feet of the Pale Ones sunk. Their strides became erratic. They carried the women, probably with babies in their arms, to the edge.

Madawaak took a deep breath and looked over the side. He shuddered as the hot terror ran through his flesh.

The women laid naked and dashed on the rocks. Their infants were scattered about further from them, bodies limp atop spattered bloodstains on the white surface. They threw the infants. Then they dropped the mothers.

But there weren't many of them. Madawaak looked back at the number who'd climbed up into the cradle. Barely more than they'd had victims. He followed their path backward to where they'd ascended... they'd known exactly where to climb.

Madawaak lost his footing and pitched into the dirt. He looked behind him. Gobidin's outstretched hand still held his tomahawk. Its stone blade was half buried in the dirt with the force he'd fallen. Its handle now leaned towards Madawaak.

His own weapons were gone.

Madawaak reached back with his shaky hand and took the wooden handle. Gobidin seemed to hold it tightly. But when Madawaak drew the weapon towards him, the fingers parted as though life flowed through them again. He held the tomahawk close to his chest and heaved up to his feet again and looked at Gobidin one last time. His great body sprawled out on the dirt. Not one drop of blood was drawn by his hand before he fell.

'I'll find them for you, Gobidin,' Madawaak said. The desire to seek out those who did this thumped through his veins and kept him standing. Kept him alive. He gritted his teeth and clutched the tomahawk so close the stone blade cut the skin on his breast and fresh blood spilled out over the blackened stains from the previous night. 'I'll find them for all of you.'

Buzzing in Madawaak's mind almost drove him into a frenzy as he carefully climbed back down. In the grass he found the trail they left. All around the hillside they'd come, from both sides. In such silence that even Gobidin's sentries couldn't hear? It seemed impossible. Madawaak followed them. Still there seemed only a few. Fifty to a hundred. No more. He followed one of the trails around until he got to the spot where the infants laid smashed on the stone. He tried to ignore them as he passed. Then, around the other side...

Flat dirt. They'd been here for some time. Many feet. A hundred. But no more. All walking. Moving about. Bodies lying down in the dirt.

A cold shiver shot through Madawaak. On the strength of his rage, he climbed up the incline and looked out over the grassland whence they'd come.

Gobidin had spoken of a landing on the far side of the Broken Lands once. When Madawaak was little and his people were at war with the Farther People and the winter had come and the families had sought refuge with the great Father.

'It is near to where we'll hide,' he'd said, and Madawaak had always remembered because of the fears and the nightmares he'd known at that time. All was dark flashes and objects and sounds. Nothing coherent. But Gobidin's words were as clear as though they were spoken today. Madawaak hadn't known what they'd meant. But now it made sense. *If they ever found it, we would lose the Broken Lands forever.'*

The trail led off towards the landing far from where the Pale Ones' canoes had ever travelled. They'd found it. Somehow, they'd known. A nameless suspicion prickled in Madawaak's skin but his mind could not grasp it. He was too sick. His insides were heavy with sorrow and horror at the thought of them waiting there while Gobidin had led them up to the cradle. Waiting for them because they knew that's where they'd go.

Pale Ones could only know such a thing if someone told them.

Faces flashed through Madawaak's mind. Makdaachk. The cruel face he'd seen wielding Pale One babies against walls and rocks to break their heads apart. Shendeek. Wobee. Those who'd massacred the chained ones and the helpless. Surely betrayal though...

Still there were only a hundred in the earth. Maybe ten to twenty more or less, but certainly not more than Madawaak had ever seen five of their biggest canoes carry. Canoes that filled the ocean...

Madawaak stopped as the horror flooded him. Propelled by a new energy, he turned towards the north and ran through the dewy grass.

12

The Journey Far

The other families broke off from the village of Oonban which stood as it had before they'd left, even without its father. They disappeared one migration at a time. Only then was it obvious how much smaller all of the families who'd converged in the cliffside village were. The groups looked so tiny. So vulnerable as Demasduit watched them go. One at a time. Some at dusk. Others at dawn.

'Where is everybody?' Shanawdithit asked Demasduit as her little hands crept under Demasduit's blankets in the night and woke her.

'They're going home.'

'But what about all the others?'

Demasduit closed her eyes and felt the sting of tears in the darkness of their mamateek while she thought up an answer. Darkness which felt so complete and so eternal. Never again to be filled by the protective sentinel that was their Oonban.

'They went to the spirit world, Shanawdithit,' Demasduit finally whispered. She heard how shaky her voice was.

'Is Papa with them?'

'Yes.'

'Oh.'

Shanawdithit eventually slept. A warm little body beside Demasduit that moved now and then. Demasduit heard Chipchowinech cry softly. She didn't know why. Perhaps their mother knew her husband was either dead or doomed. Perhaps she felt the precipice of unknowable change the three women blindly ran towards. Perhaps she'd been listening.

When the last of those families had departed, Demasduit would go with them. Her mother and little Shanawdithit would come too. Demasduit wanted to wake Shanawdithit and explain to her. Tell her that there was greater significance to the families leaving them than merely their unseasonable return home. That they were as the evening sun. They were taking the last breaths they would as the women of Oonban.

But she couldn't.

Demasduit just laid there in frustration that she'd not told Shanawdithit everything while her little sister was awake and asking.

Sleep must have come, for Demasduit woke with a shudder and found herself in a pool of sweat. Sickly feelings churned in her stomach like weeds in the changing tide. She reached out for Shanawdithit to see if her dreams had awoken her little sister but felt only empty furs. Demasduit sat up and peered around. In the dim light, she saw Chipchowinech curled on her side with a tuft of brown hair spilled out from between her arms and splayed out on the mamateek floor. On the far wall, Odensook sat upright and stared into the darkness, knowingly. She looked at Demasduit. Demasduit looked back.

The dense air of the room choked her.

Demasduit turned and scurried out from the mamateek as the sun peeked above the rolling ocean and spilled its maple-tinted light over the snow-blanketed hillside. The pines below were a sparkling sea of white peaks. The sky was still clear. The ocean heaved and sighed heavily on the rocks below.

That spot.

Breathless, Demasduit hurried to the cliffside and climbed down on the same rocks she'd climbed upon since she first could take her own steps. The white caps shone deep crimson in the waves and the sunrise and even the chalky cliffside seemed bloodstained as Demasduit eased herself down onto her rock and sat there. The penguins chipped and fluttered below. The sea was rich and bleak. Demasduit watched and tried to match her breaths to its rolling thunder. The updraft chilled the sweat against her skin.

Oonban was dead.

* * *

'I could take you for my daughter,' Keathut said to Demasduit after she'd emerged. His family heaved the last of their travelling goods onto their shoulders and waited for him to lead them into the forest. 'Your mother and sister would be safe with us. You haven't seen our home amongst the lakes. They are far from Pale Ones. Farther People know never to go there.'

Demasduit looked at his intense eyes and pursed lips. She looked again down at the untouched strips of cormorant meat that Imamus had pulled up from the fire ash. Then around at the village. Of the guest families, only Keathut's, Ninejeek's, Eenodsha's and Douajavik's remained. Eenodsha's would stay. Keathut's would be the last to leave without taking Demasduit with them. Still, when Demasduit looked back up at him and those fierce eyes and that sturdy face that made absolute truth of his promise, she knew she couldn't. Demasduit's heart sank. Her stomach already numb and sickly churned yet again.

'How *long* will we be far from Pale Ones?' she asked. 'How long before the Pale Ones join with the Farther People?'

'We can reason with them some other way,' Keathut half-whispered.

'They have stated their terms.'

Keathut looked down at the ground and his shoulders slumped. A long breath hissed out of his nose and he looked at her for the first time with eyes that weren't fierce or hard but softened and weak with sorrow.

'Let no Father of any land say ever that Demasduit of Oonban was not the bravest of us all.'

When Demasduit finally emptied her breakfast into Shanawdithit's birchbark, Keathut and his family were gone.

* * *

'Get whatever you want to bring with you into the Farther Lands,' Chipchowinech said once she'd seen Douajavik and Ninejeek and their families pack down their mamateeks.

Just like that, it was time. Demasduit had slept her last night in the place of her childhood's summers. Shanawdithit bounced around excitedly. Demasduit stood over her bed and looked at all the useless nothings; the trinkets, the beaks, the carvings and the necklace of polar bear teeth... and felt revulsion. Such useless, petty things. Why take teeth and pieces of chert when she'd already lost her father, her home and her life?

And Madawaak.

Demasduit hadn't been able to hold onto a thought all morning. All day emotions had sprung upon her and filtered through her like warm water in her cupped hands. But now she felt Madawaak. A great, grinding sorrow that turned slowly inside her. She cried so hard she fell to her knees. Shanawdithit was first upon her.

'It's okay Dema,' she consoled her sister. 'I'll carry some of it for you.'

Demasduit wanted to reach up and grab her. To hold her and tell her everything she thought was wrong and everything she'd loved was gone. But she couldn't move. She could only sit there and cry.

'Come on, Shana,' Odensook said as she led Shanawdithit away.

'Does she miss Papa?'

'Very much.'

'I miss Papa too.'

Shanawdithit started to cry.

Good, thought Demasduit. *She should cry. She should be howling into the sea. Why me? Why my father? Why my family? Why, of all the lifetimes there have been, did they have to come here in mine? Why did I have to be so important?*

Through the blur of her tears, she caught sight of the bear teeth necklace she'd been gifted. In a fury, Demasduit seized it in her hands. Before anyone could blink, she was upright and storming across the village to the cliffside. Chipchowinech came running after her.

'No! Demasduit!'

But her daughter couldn't hear her. Demasduit ran up to the edge. How she stopped in time, nobody could know. But, with all her strength and a mighty howl, she hurled the necklace out over the cliff. It flew out before her just as Chipchowinech seized

her arms strengthened by panic and dragged her down to the
snow where they lay side by side.

'I wish it had killed me,' Demasduit sobbed. 'Why couldn't it
have killed me?'

'Because you are too strong,' Chipchowinech roared as she
rained fists weakly down onto Demasduit's shoulder. 'Stop this!'

'I don't want to be strong! I want my father! I want my life
back!'

'This is your life!' Chipchowinech screamed. She'd taken her
daughter's face in her strong hands and held her head upright
so she could stare down into those tear-flooded eyes and dry
them with her fury. 'There was never any other life. You were
born into this and this is now your purpose.'

'I don't want it to be,' Demasduit blubbered.

'Nobody wants it to be,' Chipchowinech said. 'It isn't too late
to give up.'

'I can't give up.'

'Then do not despair. Despair will kill you and you know it
will. Despair is just the same as giving up. It's the same thing.'

Demasduit was silent. Chipchowinech held her daughter in
her arms and quietly cursed the spirits that this child should be
the one who was burdened with marrying to the Farther People.
That this child should have lived to see these times at all. It felt
like if she thought these things, Demasduit wouldn't have to.

Hands rested on them. The village, and the three remaining
guest families, gathered around. They put their hands on the
mother and daughter.

And bowed their heads.

* * *

'My son... when he comes,' Eenodsha said in a sleepy tone.
'When he comes, he will be looking for you.'

Demasduit was numb again with Chipchowinech and
Shanawdithit at her sides and Ninejeek and Douajavik's families
waiting for them at the base of the hillside. All over. Even the
cold couldn't penetrate the nothingness she felt. But she
reached out and touched a hand to the sad old man's chest.

'I will tell him you're alive,' he finished.

'And well,' Demasduit said. 'And waiting for the day I can see him again.'

Eenodsha opened his mouth. Demasduit knew what was coming. Even if her Farther People husband did allow an allegiance with the Fathers, they would never allow Demasduit to enjoy any trace of her old life again. But he closed his mouth without saying it. Instead, Eenodsha nodded his head and touched her shoulder and with that, they parted.

Just as the snow-capped pines enclosed around them and the frozen ferns began to lick at Demasduit's knees like they did so many times before, she turned and looked back.

Eenodsha was still standing there. Watching them.

'Shana, keep up!' Chipchowinech called.

Demasduit saw her little sister running amongst the ferns like she always did. Her head was higher than the frost-covered fronds now and she laughed as they swept against her neck and little shards of ice fell away.

'I get to go with you,' she called to Demasduit.

'Well... I think you're big enough now.'

* * *

'What I propose is that we come upon her while she sits in Thorfinn's seat and spill her throat all over Gunnlogi in front of the Althing!' Jannik snapped. Still, he calmly and rhythmically stuck his curved dagger into the top of the wheat barrel, pulled it out, and dug it in again.

Goran the Hairless looked at the hard faces that sat around the barrel in the smelly little stable. He saw not one that seemed to understand what was being proposed. Last he looked at Kaia Svenungursdottir, who'd brought him there to meet these karls, and she too looked at him as blankly as had they proposed going fishing. When he spoke, he spoke to her.

'It is treason.'

'Under Eirik the Red's law,' Jannik said. 'We are far from the land of Eirik the Red.'

'King Lief said himself that if he heard nothing from Freydis after ten years, he'd take no more interest in Vinland,' Kaia said. 'He need never know.'

'We still have to trade with him.'

'Not if no more people come,' Otto said.

'There is more than enough food here for what there is,' Jannik pointed out. 'Gottfried is down on Hop to trade with come the wintertime. Baldar will remain Chieftain on Helluland. Thorfinn will conduct his trade directly with his contacts in the Mediterranean. We need never come in contact with any of Lief Eiriksson's camp again.'

Goran heard them but couldn't grasp it. Perhaps if they'd merely been a rabble of karls it would all seem simple and he'd only have to report it to Torvard or directly to Freydis. But with Kaia there...a jarl of the Straumfjord Althing... for her to agree with them!

'She's mad, Goran,' Kaia said, having read the confusion on Goran's darting eyes and furrowed brow. 'It is one thing to trade with skraelingjar but to be seen flirting and playing with them and deceiving us into thinking she has some kind of accord with one of them...'

'What if she's telling the truth?'

'All the more reason to end her time here,' Kaia said.

Goran could see meaning. Nepotism was all that kept Freydis alive, and where was nepotism excused in the court of Eirik the Red? For her then to abuse her standing. To challenge their elected chieftain and seize control and then play allies with the skraelingjar... it was too much. These people spoke of murder. Of becoming refugees from their own people and exiles from their own world by their own hands. But Freydis would push them to the mainland. She would never stop until all the worlds were conquered. They all knew she meant to create no simple sanctuary of Norse here in the New World, but to establish a stronghold from which Europe and Nubia could be besieged into destruction. She had an Empire in mind. And she was its Empress.

It was known. Unspoken. Barely thought. But known. Even in the total silence the subject was treated as though every man and woman of Straumfjord knew that those who followed and supported her only did so because they also favoured a crusade against the world. An expedition of conquest that would make Alexander the Great seem incapable. Goran wanted to have his land and his life and that was it. The New World might be conquered. All the better. But no more. The world was too big for him.

Not for Freydis.

'How would you convince the others?' Goran asked. 'Ulfan will never agree to this. Nor Astrid nor Olfar. And if any of them hears a whisper of it they'll order our hides before word ever gets near Freydis.'

'You see? Hrafn and Asny would agree with us. That's why they're on Hop with Gottfried. So we bide our time,' Kaia said. 'They'll turn against her the more they see her ploy. She's played well thus far. Perhaps she learned their migration patterns. Or perhaps her skraeling told her something we don't know, but she has played well. It can't last. Sooner or later she'll make a mistake, just like last time. Until then we needn't advertise anything. Just plant seeds. Just wait.'

'Just wait,' Jannik echoed. Goran knew by his tense energy that he was the one behind it all. Since Goran came to this rudimentary council, the butcher had not blinked. 'But comment on her. Everything she does. Every wrong. Every time she speaks with the skraeling behind a closed arras or maybe invites him into her bed at night. Every time. It needs only be spoken.'

'I've lived to see chieftains overthrown,' Kaia said. 'We can stop thi...'

'Hello!' the sharp bark of Olfar cut through the still evening. Goran suppressed the shuddering horror that they might have been caught.

Olfar was vacuous-looking as usual.

'She wants an Althing.'

'We're on our way,' Kaia said.

'Just as soon as we're done trading with these karls...' Goran tried to stop himself mid-sentence. Too much. Too much covering. Had he said nothing, Olfar might have made his own assumptions. Now as they walked towards him, suspicion played in his normally empty eyes.

But he led them without a word towards the Chieftain's lodge.

* * *

The chains around Mooaumook's neck and ankles dug into his skin and itched relentlessly. On the other side of the arras, the Pale Ones gathered for yet another of their councils. The air was dense and heavy with their heat. On this side, Freydis.

'I want to know what she looks like,' Freydis said in his language. Softly.

'Very small,' he answered, hiding his rage at this treatment he'd endured for too long now. 'Even for one of us. Short and thin.'

'Is her skin like yours?'

'She is not pale.'

'Her hair?'

Mooaumook touched his own hair. Afraid that if he spoke, he might give Freydis a hint at his anger and deny himself a chance he knew was close now.

'But you said she has...' Freydis stood up from her bed and touched her hips through her pleated leather tunic.

Mooaumook nodded.

Freydis sighed and looked at the curtain.

'You have the Broken Lands,' Mooaumook said. He felt his voice thicken and tremble and his lips twitched in a snarl but he controlled himself. 'And my people where you want them. When do I know the secret of iron?'

'Soon.'

'You said when you have the Broken Lands and when...'

'That was before you told me about Demasduit,' Freydis said with a wave of her finger. 'Now our deal changes. To make room for new information that you provided me. You will have the secret of iron and be a God amongst your people when I have Demasduit.'

Freydis moved towards the curtain...

'Why do you want her?' Mooaumook interrupted. Freydis looked at him with a smirk. 'Will you kill her?'

'I wouldn't dare.'

'If you bring her here...'

'She'll see you,' Freydis cooed. 'And she'll know exactly what you did.'

Mooaumook swallowed dryly.

Freydis just smirked again and threw the curtain aside. Two men stepped in to replace her. They watched Mooaumook and waited.

* * *

Goran sat at his table near Kaia's and watched Freydis take Thorfinn's seat with Torvard of all people by her side. He felt Kaia's eyes burning him and granted her a look back.

Rolf the messenger stepped forward.

'Gottfried is overseeing the building of the settlements on Hop,' he said. 'There are farms on workable land and hunters gather caribou for breeding as we speak.'

The cheers for Freydis' accomplishment were hollow and weak. Goran looked around and saw at least a quarter of the Althing stayed completely silent. He took stock of the sullen faces he saw. Karls amongst the jarls. Kaia looked at him again.

'Go on,' Freydis said. 'What of the skraelingjar there?'

'Dead to their last,' Rolf said, grimly. 'The trap worked.'

'The directions provided by my skraeling were accurate, then?' Freydis questioned with affected surprise.

'They were.'

A murmur arose. Faces once sullen turned to others at their tables and said a few words and turned back both surprised and alighted. Kaia did not look at Goran.

'Thank you, Rolf,' Freydis said. 'Go back to Hop. I'm sure you and your families are eager to settle.'

Rolf bowed deeply and hurried out of the longhouse.

'Everything seems to have happened as I said it would then,' Freydis said. She spoke to the lodge. 'But still my Althing does not entirely trust me. They think that my giving the skraeling iron will cause an uprising against us. I will give my skraeling iron for what he has done to help us. I will. But there are stronger things in this world than iron. There are ideas. There are spirits. And without ideas or spirits, all the steel in the world cannot make a strong enemy.'

She signalled her arras and two men dragged the chained skraeling out into the centre of the lodge. He lay there under their weight and writhed.

'Amongst the Markland skraelingjar there is a girl who is seen as a great icon of power,' Freydis said. 'Their females are not respected as ours are. They are commodities. More like Christian women than Norse. But if one should happen to distinguish herself, she becomes more valuable to her people than gold to Thorfinn the Karlsefini.'

There was murmured, nervous laughter from some.

'My messenger here tells me one such female exists in Markland,' Freydis said. 'She's being taken north. The skraelingjar fear and hate the skraelingjar in Helluland. But none of them hate or fear anything now as much as they do us. Right now this female is being taken to Helluland to be offered to these northland tribes as a bride. In exchange, they will forge an allegiance against us.'

'How many?' Ulfan asked.

'It doesn't matter,' Freydis said. 'The bride will never arrive. I have asked my skraeling for more in exchange for iron and he has given it to me.'

Quiet chuckles then.

'I have taught him maps and he has shown me their passage to their enemies in Helluland,' Freydis explained. 'We will stop them. We will bring her back here. She will not be theirs. She will be ours.'

Goran and Kaia again looked at each other. Kaia grinned. Goran knew what she was thinking; Freydis would be alone without some key guardians if...

[162]

'Do you think they will respect us then?' Astrid asked. 'Or will both turn against us for an insult?'

'They will respect us.'

'How can you know that?' Olfar asked.

'I will make sure of it,' Freydis said. 'In fact, I will wager my life on it.'

Goran shivered. For a moment, she seemed to be speaking to him and only him.

'I will take my finest champions along this passage and we will bring this girl back here ourselves,' Freydis said.

Kaia's mouth fell open.

'You wager all our lives on it,' Ulfan said.

'Ulfan, Astrid and Goran, you will muster all your warriors,' Freydis ordered. 'The lights that burn close enough to see are too close for my comfort. And I'm sure many of you feel the same way,' she looked at the captive skraeling. He looked back uncomprehendingly. 'Lead raids on those villages. Leave none alive. *Only* the villages you can see from here.'

Kaia turned and looked at Goran, her face so suddenly ashen and her eyes so wide and full of worry that he shuddered hotly. Ulfan and Astrid stood and bowed to Freydis. Goran quickly gathered himself and did the same, careful not to look at Kaia as he did.

'Dismissed, Althing,' Freydis said, so softly Goran could hardly hear her. 'We depart tonight at sunset. The first skraelingjar village,' she nodded in the direction of the large settlement that looked over them from the high cliffs. 'Burns by morning.'

Strong fighters stood from the tables of Ulfan and Astrid and joined them as they made for the front door. Goran had brought nobody else with him. He saw Ifar was standing near and pointed him out. He looked at Kaia one more time as he led his karl out through the door, where the other two Jarls and their champions were waiting.

'We meet back here, I suppose,' Ulfan said. 'At midnight we ride.'

13

The Storm

Clouds covered the sky before the sun could reach beyond noon. Beneath the thick, creamy white, Demasduit followed the migration of Ninejeek's and Douajavik's families along the first and smaller of the two rivers that cut through their country and blocked the way to the Farther People. They walked along the banks with the deep forests of Ninejeek far ahead. They would follow the forests into the mountains where the Great River collected and where the family of Douajavik would be told that their Father Moisammadrook died a noble death and would never be coming home.

From there, it was on to lands unknown and a fate that haunted Demasduit's mind. She knew of the Farther Lands. Somewhere there was a lake so big nobody could see across it. The forests stretched so far they almost touched the Big Country where the Mi'Kmaq people lived. But such images could not dull the pain that throbbed and roiled inside her and the uncertainty that tensed her flesh and shortened her breath. Even as they walked along the brooks and hollows of the Forest River, where snowflakes fluttered down through the thin canopies of the evergreens and settled in the tufts of grass and dried twigs, or coated the river in white specks, washed away or gathered in the pools made by beaver dams, she found her teeth grinding. Her mind ached with unknown fears. Shapeless horrors of what her life would become.

Deep shadows fell over the migration. Adieich, son of Ninejeek, carried Shanawdithit on his chest while her legs dangled by his sides and her arms draped over his shoulders. Demasduit walked behind. She saw Shanawdithit was sleeping. Demasduit's face stung in the biting cold and she wanted to pitch herself into the water and stay under until the forever sleep took her and she'd never have to feel so much again.

Instead, she cried as she walked as softly and quietly as she could. Demasduit watched as the tears rolled off her cheeks and landed amongst the gathering snowflakes that slowly covered the muddy fallen leaves at the riverside. She felt a hand at her shoulder. Either Chipchowinech or Odensook. They were the only ones behind her. She didn't care to look and either woman couldn't do any more to comfort Demasduit. They felt no comfort themselves.

The deep grey day became a bleak night and the migration settled around fires where they opened their birchbark bags for the cold pudding fudge and smoked meat inside.

'I don't want to eat,' Shanawdithit complained while Chipchowinech tried to give her a portion. 'I'm too tired.'

'Oh, please,' Chipchowinech whispered. 'I don't have the strength for this now...'

'You've always wanted to adventure with your big sister,' Odensook said. 'Your big sister knows how important it is to eat.'

'She never went this far away,' Shanawdithit said.

'I did,' Demasduit said. 'Even further.'

'I'm cold.'

'If you eat, you'll be less cold,' Chipchowinech tried to convince. 'You'll feel less tired. We'll sleep soon and you'll have your energy back in the morning.'

'I can't,' Shanawdithit curled up against her mother. 'I'm too tired.'

'You have to.'

'Demasduit hasn't eaten for days.'

Demasduit felt a sting of guilt. Her stomach was painfully empty and her hands shook, but her heart had not been able to muster the courage to feed herself. It had felt too much like life.

'I'm eating,' Demasduit said as she took a scoop and put it in her mouth. It stung her tongue. Flavour had become alien to her. 'See?'

Shanawdithit lay there for a while longer while they heard only the crackle of the fire and the babbling of the river. Then, finally, she picked up some fudge and ate. Demasduit felt some strength course through her again but it only made her feel worse. If there were tears left in her body, she'd have cried again. But all she could do was sit there in her cloud of misery.

Odensook curled up with Shanawdithit and Chipchowinech was left with Demasduit. Neither one knew what to say. Demasduit could not form a coherent thought and neither could Chipchowinech, judging by the way she seemed to look longingly upon a gentler shore somewhere nobody else could see.

Demasduit couldn't stop herself from speaking.

'You didn't have to send him away.'

Chipchowinech looked at her daughter.

'I didn't send him anywhere.'

'You did. He stayed behind because of you.'

'He stayed behind because of shame,' Chipchowinech hissed, too weak to shout. 'For siding with the council over his family.'

'The council was right.'

'It wasn't his decision.'

'He was righ...'

'I don't want to hear that anymore!' Chipchowinech suddenly barked. 'You volunteered to go to another family. To the Farther People. They'd have killed him if he'd not stayed behind. That is their way. They would not take you and allow his life to influence you as well. He knew that. Whether by his decision or yours, he'd have had to say behind.'

'Then it's my fault.'

'It's his fault,' Chipchowinech said, her voice softened. 'It was his idea.'

'It was my idea,' Demasduit said.

'He guilted you into it.'

'No,' Demasduit argued, as firmly as she could manage. 'I could not save my people and him, if that's true what you say. I chose my people. It's my fault.'

There was silence.

'You are brave,' Chipchowinech said. 'I am proud of you. So is Oonban.'

'I have done exactly as he did,' Demasduit said. 'Be proud of him as well.'

Demasduit got up and staggered away from her mother as she buried her head in her hands and moaned. Demasduit sat down by the beaver dam. The wet snow seeped up through her skins and bit at her flesh. But the water was calming. The sheets of melting snow shone in the firelight as they raced upon the water down towards the sea.

'Don't be afraid.' Ninejeek's voice startled her. He was sitting on a large root under a tree, watching the water as well. 'I know you're afraid.'

'I don't know what's going to happen,' Demasduit admitted.

'You're going to forge the first alliance between our people and the Farther People that has ever existed,' he said. 'Since our time began. You are going to save both our worlds from the Pale Ones.'

Demasduit took a deep, shaky breath of the fresh, icy air.

'They are our enemies.'

'Hmm,' Ninejeek said. 'They always have been. For so long now, nobody could tell you why. Not even Keathut. They live across a Great River, in colder weather than us. That's all we know. Is that enough to fear them?'

Demasduit looked at him. There had been a sadness to Ninejeek as long as she'd known him. A thoughtful silence that hung over him, even when he spoke and it seemed to stop him saying everything he wanted to. Now was no different. He took another deep breath and looked at the river, as though it was a great burden to talk any more.

'If not for the fear,' he said. 'Well, if not the fear we wouldn't be in this situation. We'd already be friends with the Farther People.'

* * *

At midnight five horses and four riders set out from Straumfjord. They rode through the village, up the hills out of

[167]

the glow of the firelights, and beyond the veil of absolute darkness. Snow sprinkled behind the kicking hoofs. Freydis led them. Near the longhouse, in the center of town, Ulfan and his band waited for Astrid and Goran to join him.

* * *

Madawaak stood upon a hilltop and saw across the tundra the patches of dirt they'd exposed from beneath the grass while in the distance their growing settlement stood hazy in the snowy sunset.

He used the dying hours of day to walk to the coast.

There at the landing, he saw their giant canoes rested on their sides on the stony beach while the gentle evening tide lapped at their great hulls. He stole some eggs from the abandoned great auk nests beneath the snow. White petals fluttered down from the darkening sky until all the world was plunged into the depths of a deep night. In a cold that sliced into his flesh, Madawaak ate the near frozen eggs with the last of the baby caribou meat he'd kept in his woven birchbark satchel while the ocean thundered invisibly below.

Tiny specks of ice kissed his exposed face as he walked back to the hill and climbed it again. Nigh blind, he knew the land well enough from what he'd seen of it in day. Once at the top, he could see the thin strip of orange glow just below the black-on-black horizon. Their fires burned already. They skinned the earth like an animal and built their houses from its topsoil.

Madawaak moved along the far side of the hilltop to where the pine trees clustered, cut down some low-lying fronds and fashioned himself a bed. There he drew up the collar of his skins. Sleep brought him no respite. He teetered on the edge of consciousness while visions of blood and hacked flesh flashed before his mind and the shredded screams and moans of torment and death filled his head. The heat boiled up inside him. Skin flushed. Fists balled. Madawaak realized he was muttering unintelligibly to himself as the rage held him in a furious grip.

Then he'd relax. And it would start all over again.

When sleep finally did come, the images became more vivid. Skin was ripped open and stringy, bloody flesh burst from the wound. Eyes widened until they might have burst. Mouths screamed in horror. Women cried and wailed as their bodies were torn until their bones cracked and their limbs popped out.

Madawaak would wake. Then it would start again.

He saw his people in dirt. Great walls of dirt rose up around them. Madawaak saw a crack in one and looked through. On the other side were giant, hideously distorted human-like figures that roared and they burst through the crack and flooded his people's hiding place. Their legs were long and crooked like their arms. The beasts with huge heads and sharp teeth roared and set upon Madawaak's people. He saw Demasduit amongst them and yet he could not intervene, not help her, for he was a spectral presence. He could only watch. The monsters crushed his people between their giant bodies. They rammed members as long as spears into them and hollered. One of them laid the babies down in a circle. Then crouched down and plunged a long dagger through their bodies in turn with rhythmic stabs so deep that the dirt came up through their wounds as he withdrew.

Madawaak woke and raged until he thought his skull might burst. Daylight saved him. Daylight brought things to do. He crawled up from the snow and scavenged more caribou meat from the pothole of snow he'd preserved it in before he went back to the hilltop. Milky mist swallowed the distance in every direction. Only the odd pine peeked through it like a phantom watcher. The patches they'd dug from the earth were buried beneath the snow. The ghostly outline of their nearest structures were but shadows. The long grass of Mammasamit's prairies had been crushed beneath a blanket of snow so Madawaak went towards it.

In the grasslands, the snow swallowed his legs up to his knees with each laboured step. Madawaak kept a sense of where the Pale Ones' settlement was. One of their structures stood ahead amongst the flayed portion of earth, cut in a perfect square, where the mantle ceased. It was so close he could see the thin

[169]

column of wispy smoke that issued from its rooftop. Firelights glowed between the gaps in the doorway.

Breathless, Madawaak waded away from it deeper into the grass. Snow came up to his chest. It bit into his flesh. The cold air cut his gullet and lungs like shrapnel. He came upon a lone pine and reached into its needles to climb up out of the enveloping powder.

The cold air cut through his wet furs but he climbed until he had a vantage point to look over their settlement.

There, he waited until morning mists began to clear.

Before long, even the black waters of the ocean on either side of the land bridge that led to his home country were visible. Madawaak looked over their growing settlement. Like a toxic flower, it unfurled through the dying mists and revealed all the familiar structures he'd spotted in their other village in the cove. There was the one that burned brightly and always with the black smoke rising from it. There was the big lodge right in the middle. There was the way down to the coast and there were the fences they built around patches of grassland and held foreign beings captive. Fat, stocky things with their snouts forever buried in the hard, icy dirt. Or tall things not so different from the beings they rode upon, only fatter and less muscular.

A soft ocean breeze swept the last of the fog away and Madawaak could see the distance that their pastures had spread across. They blocked the passage back home.

Madawaak stared achingly at the structures and bare patches of dirt that barricaded him from the others. He couldn't warn them of Mooaumook's deceit. He couldn't stop those that were left there from hunting down and destroying his people. As sorrow overcame him, he accepted that Demasduit would die like those women and children in Gobidin's cradle. His mother. His father. His sister. Smashed and broken and burned by hideous creatures like those that haunted his nightmares and memories. Soon they would be bloated, rotting corpses like Gobidin, Oonban and the others. His heart felt as though it might explode. Little Ebauthoo and Shanawdithit would...

A large man emerged from a nearby house. Broad across the shoulders, his long golden hair tied back while his beard hung rugged over his chest. He carried some tool which he began to disturb the bare dirt with. A woman joined him. From a basket, she sprinkled seeds into the dirt. Children emerged from the house. Little ones like his and Demasduit's sisters. And a mother and father like Dabjeek, Eendosha, Chipchowinech or Oonban.

Oonban, he thought. Who'd given his home to him so many times. Given his food to Madawaak. Shared their warmth. And ended with sparing Madawaak's life in exchange for the boy's, all before Madawaak could even repay the smaller kindnesses given to him.

Madawaak clutched his tomahawk.

Heat bubbled up again. Memories of blood and screaming and hacking and bones cracking and skin ripping open and flesh and death.

His loved ones would not rest alone.

* * *

'My son will come home,' Eenodsha said again as Immamus joined him on the high cliffs that overlooked the country's rugged coast. Every sunrise Madawaak did not return, he thought, was another one closer to the sunrise that brought him. But today all was blanketed in thick mist. If Eenodsha looked inland, he could see down to where the forest edge brooded over the hillside and if he looked out, he could see where the cliffs peaked and dropped away into the churning waters below, but nothing more.

The village slowly awoke. Men set out for their day of cutting trees for hunting fences while women repaired damaged mamateeks and made garments and satchels and brought food down from the hung baskets or went picking for roots, auk or goose eggs.

'Your wife wants you,' Immamus said. 'She wants you to eat with her and Ebauthoo. She said that you haven't for too long and they miss you.'

'Madawaak got away,' Eenodsha said. He watched the mists as though, any moment, the shadow of Madawaak would emerge from them and bring word that the Pale Ones would not re-join their fellows here in the Forest Lands but would stay down there in the Broken Lands.

'He will come,' Immamus said as she stroked his shoulder. 'But you have family here who need you.'

'Where is Mooaumook?' he demanded. 'Mooaumook was always so much stronger and better and faster and smarter than my son, so where is he? What news does he bring of those Pale Ones who are still here? Why do we sit here and know nothing? Demasduit is giving up her life for us. Where are we?'

'Mooaumook...' Immamus began. She wanted to tell Eenodsha that the boy was probably caught and killed so he'd stop raging about it day after day. But he didn't need to hear such a thing. He needed nothing but his son back. 'Madawaak will come. Whether you neglect your family or not.'

Eenodsha looked at her as though he listened for the first time that morning. He turned his eyes back to the village.

'Madawaak will come,' he whispered. 'This fog has held him up, that's all. Mooaumook has abandoned us. I will send someone to the lakes to tell Makdaachk. His father should know.'

They started back up towards his mamateek. A soft rumble stopped them. It seemed to issue from the wall of white fog that surrounded them. Eenodsha stopped and looked back. Immamus stayed behind him, timid with fear. The rumble drew near and both knew what they heard. The ghostly silhouettes of the giant riders mounted upon their galloping beings emerged from the gloom and terror filled them both.

Eenodsha turned towards the village and ran, screaming.

'They're coming!' he screamed. 'Pale Ones!'

He did not even get to Immamus before an axe swung down as a horse passed by him and cracked his skull. Blood and matter burst from the wound as his body splattered limp in the snow and crimson patters dotted the white surface. Another swing chopped deep into Immamus' jaw and cheek and her neck cracked sharply backward as her body fell beneath the trampling hoofs.

Men charged up the hill and out of the village with their bows and arrows, spears and daggers and tomahawks and charged towards the wave of horses. But the riders formed a straight line. From their mounts, they lowered their spears. Men from the village hurled their spears and loosed their arrows. A Pale One amongst the charge fell here and there, or a horse crashed down and disappeared beneath the hail of snow and mud beneath their charge, but the line was unbroken when the spears came smashing into their pelvis and guts. The bodies snapped and distorted beneath the hoofs.

The riders breeched the village. A spear struck a Pale One in the head and knocked him from his mount. Another took his place. The horses charged the mamateeks and smashed and kicked their way through the walls to expose the vulnerable elders and children inside. Riders dismounted and hacked wildly into their soft bodies. With ragged cracks and thuds, they chopped and hacked and speared the life from them. Hunters with tomahawks hurled themselves onto the backs of the horses and cut into the shoulder blades of the Pale Ones. Two others attacked from the flanks and dragged them down. But the Pale Ones were too many. They spread quickly through the village and spread fire through the mamateeks. Hunters ducked and wove between the houses and tried to get a good shot at them with an arrow, but another was always just around the corner. With spears held high, they charged the men and rammed their spears through the hunters' bodies.

Inside Eenodsha's mamateek, a woman rounded the small children against a wall and huddled with them. A horse kicked through the wall. The low roof knocked the Pale One off as the animal charged inside and Ebauthoo and Memet saw a chance. As the Pale One quickly recovered, they ran past the riderless being while the Pale One shoved her atgier into the woman's neck at her shoulder. Blood erupted over the Pale One's arm and the other children swarmed her legs. She kicked them away.

Ebauthoo took Memet by the hand and led him through the break in the wall. Around them mamateeks burned. The black smoke lifted into the mist and created a swirling veil that billowed and blinded everyone. Ebauthoo led the younger Memet between the fires towards the edge of the village. Figures moved through smoke and mist. Horses galloped. Arrows and spears from both sides flew. A Pale One emerged flailing and screaming from a burning mamateek. Arrows pierced his body and he fell. Hunters ran past the body but arrows struck them as well. In the snow laid bodies. Cut open. Chopped. All around them the snow was red. The shuddering screams of horses filled the air. Memet's hand fell away from Ebauthoo's. She turned and looked back.

The boy stood terrified as he looked up at something. A rider mounted on its being thundered past and Memet's body crashed against the horse's galloping forelimbs and he fell beneath its hoofs without ever making a sound.

Ebauthoo did not go back for him. She kept running. Feeling nothing. Thinking nothing but of getting away from it. Soon the sound and the smoke were behind her. She ran down the incline. Down to the tall shadows of the trees. Between them, the mists were pierced by sunbeams and Ebauthoo kept running. She didn't know where. Anywhere.

Away from it.

The ferns covered her. Ebauthoo ran until she was so tired she almost collapsed. But still she was just amongst the ferns that brushed against her and surrounded her until every direction looked the same. *I'm lost,* Ebauthoo thought. Anywhere she ran might lead her back to them...

Ebauthoo cried. Quietly at first but as her immediate situation overcame her, she just wanted someone to hear and forget about Pale Ones. She wanted her mother to hear. Her father. For their strong hands to take her and lead her somewhere safe. With them.

'Papa,' she cried, yearning for him to carry her above these ferns.

She wandered and wandered. Ahead, dim daylight peeked through a break in the ferns and Ebauthoo forgot how tired she was and ran for it. Out in the open. Trees stood tall above her. Hills rolled up and down everywhere. Snow and pine needles covered the forest floor. She turned and saw someone standing there...

Gasped.

It was one of her people, but nobody she knew. He carried a bow and a quiver of arrows was at his hip. He stared at her, open mouthed. She sobbed as she stared back.

She saw a strange man out on the hunt.

He saw a little girl spattered with blood.

14

The Crossing

Madawaak left his hiding spot to find food and came upon lakes where he caught fish by spearing them with an arrow and ate them raw. All through the day the sky grew gayer and heavier. Not a wink of sunlight broke through its dense cover. By the time Madawaak returned to the tree and climbed it again the world was darkening and the Pale One family had settled in. Their fires glowed from inside their structure. Madawaak set his bow and arrows down on a thick branch in the pine and descended with his tomahawk.

He kept low as he ran across the pure white sheet in the night towards the house. The rhythmic thudding of one of their riders in flight stopped Madawaak and he pitched into the snow and lay still.

The rider came out of the wilderness and headed in the direction where the glowing beacons from their settlement's fires clustered at the horizon.

Madawaak got up and continued towards the home. When he reached it, he jumped into the exposed earth and found it was soft despite the cold. The Pale Ones had spent the day churning it. Planting their seeds. He crawled on his belly towards the domicile until he heard a wooden click. Madawaak froze. A rectangle of orange swept up at the front of the home as the door opened and allowed the firelight to spill outside. The large man stepped out. Closed the door behind him. Madawaak held his breath.

Might have been seen.

He heard the man's heavy footsteps move to the side of the house and then the splashing of water. Madawaak braced himself on his hands and feet. The man took a deep breath and exhaled through his nose. He turned back towards the door.

[176]

Madawaak shot up to his feet and ran on the tips of his toes, the tomahawk held high. The Pale One turned slightly. Madawaak leaped through the air and brought Gobidin's tomahawk hard to the man's jaw. He felt the chert blade crack through the bone. The Pale One snapped to his side and crashed down onto his knees with a loud scream. Madawaak seized his hair and chopped into the back of his neck, then drew out his tomahawk and leaped down to the side of the house as the door flew open and out stepped the woman, arrow already set in a bow.

Inside, the children were silent.

The woman kept the door open and the light spilled out across the front of the house. Madawaak peeked around the corner and saw her nudge her husband's foot with her shoe. Her breath quickened.

Madawaak found the edges of the house bricks. They were the turf cut in blocks out of the ground where the Pale Ones had sewn their seeds. Bricks made of earth and grass. He found he could get his feet atop them and quickly climbed.

The Pale One heard him and followed the aim of her arrow around. Madawaak quickly dropped back behind her and swung the tomahawk at her crown. The blade cracked through her skull and she dropped her weapons and her body crumpled and she fell. The Pale One's muscles spasmed. Her eyes were wide open and reflected the firelight from inside.

Madawaak pressed his foot into the back of her neck and wrenched out the tomahawk. He then moved to the front door and stepped inside. Beyond the fire, the two children quickly pulled their blankets over themselves and whimpered and sobbed. Madawaak felt the heat bubbling inside. The rage. The fury. He set upon the mounds beneath the blankets and beat down on them with the back of his tomahawk until blood seeped up through the fabric and spread to every corner.

He picked a block out of their fire and threw it onto the bed.

He ran into the night. The cold wind whipped against his face and his mouth dried. But the rage had died. Cold overcame him and he collapsed onto his hands and knees.

'You shouldn't run in the cold,' Demasduit's voice haunted his mind.

Distant voices shouted.

Madawaak pulled himself up and ran past his tree. They'd find his bow and arrow. He'd go back to the cradle, for now. Back there and find another one. Where the bodies of his own people's families and children lay dead by Pale One hands.

They'd come for him. He'd be waiting.

* * *

'Wolf scat,' said Adjieich as he inspected the foul-smelling pile they'd stumbled across. The rest of the migration formed a circle around him. Demasduit watched as he fiddled about and pulled something out. He held it up and some cousin of Douajavik moved her flame in closer. 'It's a vertebra. Polar bear. This is a large pack.'

Adjieich dropped the scat down, stood up and dusted off his fingers. His eyes did not leave the ground.

'They're moving along our path. Hunting. We must go another way.'

'We'll lose half a day,' Douajavik said.

Demasduit looked into the darkness ahead and chilled at the thought of the wolf pack just beyond its veil. Shanawdithit moved in closer to her and wrapped the hem of her tunic around her fingers the way she did when she wanted to be close as possible to her sister. Demasduit touched her hair.

'They have pups,' Adjieich said. 'Forty. Many more adults. Too many.'

'We will take the path home,' Ninejeek said as he pointed in the direction of the Great River. 'You go towards the mountains. If we are followed then maybe they will find only wolves...'

'Half a day!' Douajavik seethed.

'We aren't strong, Douajavik,' Odensook said. 'I fear for the children.'

'We could have reached home before sunrise.'

'Not with wolves in the way,' Ninejeek said as he moved towards Chipchowinech.

Douajavik huffed.

'Walk a few more hours,' he told his family and Demasduit's, as he indicated another passage more north-westerly than they had been travelling. 'Then we make camp at higher ground. Sentries will watch for these wolves.'

'This is where I leave you,' Ninejeek said to Chipchowinech. Demasduit looked over at him sadly. He looked back at her. 'I know we will see each other again. When the rift that exists between our worlds has healed. And we will always remember it was Demasduit who healed it.'

Douajavik impatiently led them on and Demasduit felt the smaller number in their migration as they moved on the coldness of the air and the darkness of the forest that surrounded and gradually enclosed upon them. The ground inclined up and stayed that way. Shanawdithit held her arms up but Demasduit had no hope of lifting her. She looked back at Chipchowinech who held her own mother's withered hand to guide her laborious steps behind her. There was nobody who could carry the little one.

Those of Douajavik's family passed by them until again they were the last in the migration. Soon, they couldn't see them ahead at all. Only little torchlights that flickered through the low foliage. Demasduit gritted her teeth and marched on. She held Shanawdithit's hand and ignored her pained complaints.

'Demasduit,' Chipchowinech said. 'Slow down!'

But Demasduit wouldn't. She set the pace and the others, huffing and whining through they did, managed to keep up. Finally, they entered the firelights of Douajavik's camp. Demasduit staggered right up to him and stared the young, hard-headed fool dead in the eyes.

'Do not leave us like that again,' she said.

'Keep up,' he answered.

'Slow down,' Demasduit demanded.

'I am in charge of this migration...'

'You are in charge of getting us to the Farther Lands. Without that, you have nothing to deliver your family but news that their father is dead.'

Douajavik looked around and saw that everyone was looking at him. He raised a fist.

'Do I listen to you?'

'I wonder how pleased the Farther People will be when they see you've gone and laid your hands on me.'

Douajavik lowered his fist and smirked.

'I wouldn't be the first.'

Demasduit's family had settled down by one of the campfires. She went to join them. The witnesses went back to their own warmth and Douajavik joined his brothers. Demasduit looked back over at him as she settled. He paid no attention. She looked into the fire. For some reason, she could only think of Madawaak.

Alive out there somewhere. She could feel it.

The wolves howled for the invisible moon.

* * *

When they woke, they were blanketed with powdery snow. Shana had huddled up in Demasduit's furs with her and Chipchowinech with Odensook and their bodies had kept them warm enough. They dusted themselves off and continued on the new path. When the sun rose, the daylight was barely different from the night such was the bleakness of the looming clouds above, but Douajavik led them without break. Up the mountainside they climbed with their feet numb and their legs shaky and their lips cracked and their eyes stinging in the cold. Gurgled coughs sounded out intermittently from all around the shrunken migration.

Douajavik led them on. Even as he limped and coughed himself.

The winds kicked up and cold air lashed against the trees. The snow blew from the pines and sprayed on the migration as they followed the narrow path that skirted the mountainside. Women clutched their young. Men carried the young that were too big for the women or the women themselves. Demasduit looked out into the sea of white. The battering swarm of snowflakes. Beyond it laid the Great River and the tribes which lived all along the high ridge that overlooked it. By now it would be carrying clumps of snow into the ocean. She couldn't see it. But migrants from Shendeek's, Keathut's and Ninejeek's families had told her about them and Moisamadrook's family had told her of the view from here.

Still the path led upward.

Then, from above, there came a roar. Right above Demasduit. The families ducked and almost scattered as though they forgot the edge and the sheer drop. Shanawdithit squealed. Chipchowinech held her and stopped Odensook from being pushed over the edge and into the clear white abyss.

Gusts of wind suddenly shifted direction and the mountain covered them. The hail of snow ceased and there above them, beside the mouth of its cave, stood a drooling black bear still caked in the mud of its hibernation. It roared and stomped its forelimbs on the icy rocks. The migration cowered.

Demasduit raised her hand to it.

'Stop, bear.'

The bear roared. Saliva dripped from its mottled fangs.

'Stop bear!' Demasduit cried. Everyone else cowered on the ground but Demasduit and Douajavik. He drew back his spear.

'No!' Odensook cried. It was enough to stall him.

'Do not bother with these people,' Demasduit said, softly. Below the howling wind and whimpers of the migration. 'They are weak and broken.'

The bear grunted and stomped its forepaw.

'Their enemies are your enemies.'

The bear looked them up and down as it barked and huffed. Douajavik again drew back his spear but Odensook stood and stepped towards him, both hands up.

'No!'

Demasduit lowered her hands and stared at the bear until it stared back at her. Douajavik held his spear in a tense arm, ready for the throw, but the old woman would not get out of his way. Shanawdithit buried her face in the hem of Chipchowinech's tunic.

Thoughts bombarded Demasduit. She'd thrown her necklace away and lost her place amongst the council and been disgraced by her people. Could she still talk to them? Would they still listen?

The bear coughed, turned and went back into the cave.

The migration rose all around her and breathed an audible sigh of relief. Hands touched Demasduit as they continued to walk quickly to pass the cave without getting too close to the ledge, now hyper-aware of the dangers around them.

Douajavik lowered his spear and turned to lead them on. A firm grip took his arm and turned him back and met Bidesook's piercing glare.

'You insulted her.'

Douajavik saw the firmness in his mother that swept him straight back to his childhood when he'd see this look right before her bow or spear was smacked against the bare skin of his back. He bit his cracked, dry lips and nodded. Bidesook led the migration on and Douajavik waited as the line ambled past him until Demasduit came along. He stopped her and her family there.

'I am sorry,' he said.

Demasduit nodded.

* * *

Night fell again with a blackness like a solid wall and only the lights of Moisamadrook's village could guide them into the nook in the mountainside where the willows and the rocks formed a natural fortress. Beside it was a waterfall that poured into one of the many streams and creeks that ran eventually into the Great River. Beyond the nook, a wall of snow-covered trees stood grey and stripped of greenery. Their spindly limbs reached up and caught bundles of snow like reaching talons and they formed the gateway into the unimaginable Farther Lands.

'Are we there?' Shanawdithit croaked from the breast of Yeothoduk, the hunter that carried her.

'We're home,' Yeothoduk answered as Chipchowinech reached across to stroke her younger daughter's hair.

[182]

A young woman walked up to the edge of the trees. With the fire glow behind her, she was but a silhouette, but there was tension around her shoulders and hands as she waited. Douajavik stepped ahead of the others and started up the slope towards her. She didn't relax.

'Shansee,' he called. He continued towards her and the migration followed. When he reached up, she seized his hand and he stepped up beside her. They kissed and held each other.

Demasduit looked away. She didn't want to be reminded of Mooaumook. Now or ever again.

'Where is Moisamadrook?' she heard the soft, tense voice hiss.

'We mourn him,' Douajavik answered. 'But we bring something that our ancestors will remember for all times. Your people and mine will never be divided again.'

'Our people?' Shansee said as she looked down into the migration. Demasduit could not help but look back up and see that the soft face and delicate brown eyes were directed at her. The tired, bent bodies shuffled past them into the warm firelight of the village. 'Then she is with you?'

Douajavik just looked at her.

'Run!' she suddenly screamed. 'Run away! Run away! Run away!'

As she cried out, arrows shot through her body and Douajavik's.

Demasduit stopped midstride as hands reached out and grabbed her. Riders charged on their mounts from the darkness that pooled between the trees and beyond the firelight in the surrounding forest. Demasduit stumbled into Chipchowinech's arms and looked for a place to run to.

The beasts reared up as the riders' spears thrust down into the flailing hands and fleeing bodies. They were surrounded. The riders moved through the migration and mowed them down with swings of their weapons or thrusts of their spears.

'Into the village!' Yeothoduk screamed as he carried Shanawdithit.

Demasduit took her mother by the arm but she couldn't pull her away. She looked back and saw Chipchowinech still held onto Odensook even as a spear rammed into the ancient woman's back.

'Mama!' Chipchowinech cried as the beast snorted steam and clacked its square teeth from just beyond the glow of the village fire.

Demasduit pulled her mother's arm with all her might and ripped her away. They ran after the pitchy squeals of Shanawdithit until they hit the steep embankment. Yeothoduk disappeared through the willow vines at the top. Demasduit roared and guided her mother but the weight was too much. Finally, a hand pressed against Demasduit's back. She looked down.

Chipchowinech's face was stern.

Shanawdithit's squeals filled Demasduit's heart and she cried out as she let go of her mother and charged up the embankment into the trees. She followed the light of the fire into the trees. Another person ran beside her. They hurried between the mamateeks as a huge weapon swung out from behind them and cracked the other runner across the chest.

Demasduit ducked away and ran through the screaming, panicked people who dashed back and forth while the two horses cut up and down between them and the riders swung their shining stone down into their bodies which broke under the force of the stone. They burst open with sickening howls and dull smacks. Blood and viscera flew from their shredded clothing as they crumpled and fell. Fire rose from the mamateeks. The riders moved with animal relentlessness. Giant figures bulging and faceless upon enslaved beasts.

A squeal. Shanawdithit. Demasduit followed the sound and saw tall Yeothoduk across the village. Demasduit screamed out and charged after him. Her feet slapped against a soft figure and she fell into the pool of blood beside the eviscerated body. A spear was still in its grip. She plucked it from the stiff fingers and leaped to her feet, roaring with rage.

Yeothoduk suddenly stopped and ducked down. Another horse reared right before him. It reared up and the rider thrust a weapon towards him that none of them had seen before. A shaft of shining stone, sharp on both sides. Yeothoduk dropped Shanawdithit down behind him and held up his tomahawk. With a single swing, the rider cut the chert and wooden handle in two and embedded the weapon midway through his skull. Shanawdithit was right behind him. Crimson beads spattered across her little face.

Demasduit screamed and charged with all her strength.

The rider dismounted and kicked Yeothoduk's writhing body off the end of her weapon. Demasduit could see from the way the hulking figure moved it was female. She thrust her spear forward and hunched down...

In a motion swift and fluid as water the woman swivelled to one side, cut through the spear and drove her elbow down into Demasduit's temple with a blinding crack. Demasduit hit the ground. She thought her eyes might have exploded. The world spun and blackened and Demasduit grappled and fought just to hold onto consciousness.

Shanawdithit didn't make a sound.

Nothing did. Demasduit could hear her own breath. Then, the crackle of fire. Suddenly the terror filled her again and she clutched the spear and turned it to them.

It was broken. Cut off clean. She remembered.

The Pale Ones stood in a circle around her. Their beasts stood obediently between the burning mamateeks and amongst the scattered bodies, of which none were their own.

'Where is my sister?' Demasduit spat, as she crawled to her knees and still wielded the broken spear. 'Where is my sister!'

'Here,' a melodious voice, like the winter tree sap, answered her. Between two of the giant Pale Ones stepped the woman, without her helmet, and Shanawdithit was at her side. Barely taller than her captor's leg, she stood with her hands by her side and her eyes wide with fear. The giant woman's hand rested on her tiny head.

[185]

'Get away from her!' Demasduit shrieked as she held up the spear.

The woman raised the strange weapon, coated in blood, and cocked an eyebrow.

'I knew it was you,' the woman answered. Demasduit chilled with horror as she realized the language was her own. 'The moment you came towards me with a spear I knew it was you.'

Demasduit could only stare, mouth agape. The woman wasn't as tall as the men, nor as broad, but there was a stoutness to her and a sureness in her smirk and a knowing in her otherworldly eyes that dominated Demasduit's attention. The woman kneeled beside Shanawdithit and gently touched her fingers to her bloodied little face.

'Don't touch her,' Demasduit snapped.

'Tell me who this is, little girl,' the woman asked.

'Demasduit,' Shanawdithit answered, breathlessly.

'Demasduit,' the woman repeated as she rose to her feet again. She picked Shanawdithit up and carried her from the circle.

'What are you doing?' Demasduit demanded. She leaped to her feet but two of the powerful men pinned her down. 'What are you doing to her?'

The woman put little Shanawdithit down against a charred post and another man tied her there. The woman turned back to Demasduit.

'You have come here, Demasduit, to meet your new family,' the woman said. 'Us.'

'Never!' Demasduit screeched. Her whole body tensed against her captors but their weight was moveable as a mountain. 'No!'

'No?' the woman said as she slipped her weapon into a loop in her belt. 'You've come to make an alliance with the people across the river. We are more dangerous than them. We are stronger than all of you. Your people would be better off with us. You will not survive a war with us. Not any number of you.'

'I am not afraid!' Demasduit screamed as she stared directly at the woman. 'I am not afraid of you!'

The woman was nodding her head.

'Oh, I know,' she said. She pulled a smaller weapon, a dagger, of shining stone from her belt. 'I know you're not.'

'I will die before I go with you.'

'You will come with us,' the woman said with a crooked smile. 'Your little sister will not. She will stay here. You can give her a good chance of surviving.'

Another of the men dragged Chipchowinech into the circle. Demasduit tried to leap on her but was restrained. The man pulled her to her knees. Held her by the hair.

'Will sister have her mother with her?'

'We will not go with you.'

'That's a no.'

The woman stepped over, dropped her hand down beside Chipchowinech's face and drew the dagger deep along her throat. Demasduit screamed. Her mother gargled as blood bubbled out of her mouth and her gullet spilled over her collar. The Pale One let her fell onto the ground where she writhed and clutched at her neck and bled and wheezed and gasped.

'Will she have her eyes?' the woman asked.

'Stop! Stop it!'

'That's not a yes...'

The woman kneeled and took Shanawdithit under the chin.

'Don't!'

'Look at your sister, little one,' the woman said. 'Look at her betraying you.'

With two quick motions the woman ran the dagger across Shanawdithit's eyes and slit them both. The child screamed. Blood ran down her cheeks. One of the Pale Ones took a step toward the child but those at his sides held him back in line.

'I'll go with you! I'll go with you!'

Shanawdithit kept screaming as the woman slipped the dagger back in her belt. She nodded to a man who cut Shanawdithit's bonds. The little girl fell on her face. Her hands clutched at her eyes but felt nothing but pulp and blood as she screamed and screamed.

'The farther people have seen this fire,' the woman said. 'Maybe they will save her.'

[187]

'Don't leave her!' Demasduit screamed as the men pulled her up to her feet. 'Don't leave her.'

The woman touched the bloodied dagger to Demasduit's face and looked at her closely with those monstrous eyes.

'Make another sound,' she warned. 'I will cut off her hands.'

Demasduit stared in disbelief at the demon before her. But she made no more sound. All her instincts focused on keeping Shanawdithit alive. There was no thought of the little girl's eyes or of her being alone in the forest amongst the bodies that would attract the wolves. Only of keeping her alive.

'Good,' the woman said, pertly. 'Come with us. I am Freydis. I am your family now.'

15

The Old World Crumbles

'Another one?' Asny asked as she shone the flame light around the little fisherman's hut on the far side of the settlement to where the family of Knut the Grower was found. Gottfried looked at the floor before he raised his eyes up to them.

Claus Finnson was wedged in a sickening angle against the corner. His fishing net was draped across his legs and his jaw hung ajar from the smashed skull which seemed but a mass of greying pulp and hair. One glassy eye looked out towards Gottfried. Gottfried pulled the door aside and found Lotta on her side, her head massacred much the same way. There was a deep cut into her shoulder that severed the shoulder blade where the assassin missed his blow while Claus' foot hung at a strange angle where he'd been hobbled.

Above his body on the wall was their shield and a fishing spear.

Nauseated by the putrid smell, Gottfried stepped back outside. Asny followed him while her champions and his stood waiting in the darkness. The lapping pebbly shore clacked and crackled under the heaving waves on the far side of the house and the night was deep and dark.

'The same one,' Gottfried said to Asny.

He looked at the young jarl as she held the torch beside him. Thin and wiry, she didn't seem capable of wielding the atgier she usually kept at her side. Her face was broad but delicate. High cheekbones and soft jawline that might have been fashioned of glass. Her hair was like spun gold. If these massacres had been done by a Norse, it would be a woman and it would be someone like young Asny Asmundsdottir.

'These are your karls, Lord Asny,' Gottfried said as he looked again at her champions. 'Find the skraeling. He is young, he is alone, and he is watching us. He watches us by day until night falls and then he strikes at an innocent family. We can consider ourselves lucky that this fishing couple were childless lest there be a find as gruesome as last night's. We won't be so lucky again. Find this skraeling. He is the only one, or he would have brought help this time.'

'Magnus,' Asny called. The powerful Magnus Bosson stepped forward with his double-sided battle axe held in one ropey arm. 'Take a patrol and find a trail to the north. See if this skraeling comes from Markland. The rest will come with me. We will find out if he remains on Hop...'

'Viveka,' Gottfried called. His own champion, Viveka Viggosdottir, stepped forward with her spear, her shield, and her bow across her back. A strong, withered looking skjoldmoy with skin like ashen granite. The perfect example for delicate for little Asny to learn from. 'You lead the inland search. You will answer to Lord Asny until the skraeling's head is mounted outside my longhouse.'

* * *

Madawaak watched the torches move out into the sea of blackness from the glow of the village like little flaming ants as they left their nest. He tensed. His body urged to gather his things, leap down from the pine tree and run off to safety immediately. But he had to stay. Madawaak held his breath as though that would defy the urge to run. They had to find his trail this time. This time they would follow him home.

He'd been careful. Found a couple without children. They were young, but the Pale Ones became warriors quickly and the women were no less fearsome than the men. Still, their screams lingered beyond the silence of night. Still, the sight of their bodies as they struggled against agony and death haunted the darkness behind Madawaak's eyelids and flashed before him every time he blinked. Sleep hung heavy over him.

What was it now? Two days? Three?

But sleep brought the sounds and the sights together in a phantasmagoria that bubbled and boiled to the point where he thought it might crack him open. He felt it even now. His fingers curled and trembled. His teeth ground as the little beacons of light dispersed and moved around. Some further away from the groups than others...

Madawaak slung his bow over his shoulder. Gobidin and the last stand his people took in the cradle were in his head and Madawaak forced his mind's grip on them so he'd think of nothing else. Not pity. Not fear. Not sadness. The screams of Pale One children died away. He heard only the screams of his people's children. Of the women who took the blows to their backs as they curled around the defenceless infants. The demons were looking for him.

Some of them would find him.

He climbed down from the tree. Eye level with the grass, some of the torches disappeared into the clustered glow of the village lights. But he could see the ones that strayed too far. Madawaak kept low and stepped briskly through the grass. The slither of the long blades sounded too loud against his body and sweat beaded on his brow as he began to hear their calls to each other. Short, swift barks. Orders.

They wouldn't find his trail. These Pale Ones could not track at all. Madawaak would have to show them...

He peeked above the grass and saw the group of three that were nearest to him. Madawaak could see the shapes of their arms under the torches and the soft light against their faces. The cumbersome weapons they carried. They moved their torches side to side and looked out into the night or felt their way around in the grass but none looked at the ground. Beyond the nearest three were others that were alone. But as he watched, the three grew further and further from each other. One of them called something to another. A woman's voice. The other two answered with the voices of men. Madawaak watched and stalked. Behind the shelter of complete darkness, he fixed on the man and followed him gently.

A cold breeze blew out of nowhere. The grass leaned. Madawaak leaned with it but his heart jumped. The tomahawk handle slipped in his sweaty palm. His every breath was like thunder.

The Pale One turned and exposed his back to Madawaak. The boy took his chance. He slunk through the grass and held his breath and raised his tomahawk. The Pale One turned and swung his axe but Madawaak ducked low beneath the rising shield and rammed his tomahawk into the Pale One. He felt the blade embed in the Pale One's hip bone and the man roared and fell. Madawaak jumped away from him as an arrow flew past him. In darkness again, he scurried while the female Pale One primed another arrow and Madawaak primed one of his own. Her light guided his aim. She screamed and dropped with his arrow stuck through her collar.

The third charged him with a spear. He threw his torch ahead of him. Madawaak watched it spin through the air and land in the grass. He hurried away from it, while the wounded Pale One rose and pulled the tomahawk from his hip and threw it aside. He staggered and held his axe and shield. Others called out and were quick towards them. Madawaak charged the wounded Pale One and leaped up and slammed against his shield. He drew back his axe but Madawaak evaded and ran through the grass.

Their lights pulsed and flickered behind him. Their arrows whizzed by overhead, some close to his ears and he zigzagged to avoid them. But it slowed him. Madawaak could not outrun the light of their torches.

Onward he went. He knew he couldn't outrun them, but he could outlast them. The cold burned his lungs and phlegm scored the back of his throat but he knew he could outlast them.

With a loud thwack, a hot pain streaked across his ear as the air off the side of an arrow hissed past his face. Too close. He broke his pattern and kept breaking it. Zig-zig-zag. Zag-zig-zig-zag. The arrows came thicker and harder. Madawaak ran harder. More were stopping to shoot at him.

Finally, the light behind him faded. Madawaak kept running. He kept crossing back and forth over his path and varying the distance and interval. He ran until the wet grass was over his head and he had to wade through it. Until he could look over his shoulder and see only the distant glimmer of orange against the velvet blackness. Until his chest ached so much that he had to stop. A hard surface hit Madawaak in the shoulder and he staggered a few steps and collapsed into the dirt.

* * *

Adjieich rolled over in his second night of sleeplessness and found his wife's still, warm figure beside him. She fidgeted and looked at him in the darkness.

'Something is wrong,' he said. 'We shouldn't have let them go.'

'Then you have to go to them,' she said, sleepily.

As soon as morning gave him enough light, Adjieich set off back along the path they'd come from the intersection where last he'd seen Douajavik and Demasduit. Snow still covered the pines but had cleared closer to the mountainsides. He looked once more at the mounds beneath the blankets. Then he followed the shadows back into the forest. Back up away from the Great River. Adjieich kicked the stones and twigs and barely looked up from the narrow path just as had been his way since he was a child. Having his head down helped his mind to wander. It passed the time. He knew the way by heart anyway. Even as the creamy morning light spilled beneath the rugged canopy and the birdsong filled the rustling leaves as though carried on it, he didn't look up. Adjieich thought he could walk these paths blind.

As the day wore on and the sun grew high and Adjieich kicked and wandered away from his family, he began to feel silly. Why was he doing this? Had he dreamed something and forgotten about it? What had disturbed him? A feeling? He and the migration had staggered home only the day before so deliriously tired he couldn't have told his wife which way the Great River flows. Now he followed a feeling.

Silly, he thought. *Turn back.* The next he'd hear of Demasduit is that she'd successfully married a Farther Person and, he could only hope, loved him as dearly as she loved Mooaumook....

A southerly breeze cut up through the trees and was dull against the cold on Adjieich's face, but it carried an unmistakable odour. *Death.* Adjieich looked up ahead and then turned his eyes skyward. Golden sunlight glittered through the leaves. It blocked his view. He walked on until he could climb to higher ground on the rising mountainside and from there, he looked out at the sky again.

Ahead, he could see the birds as they spiralled in the sky. All kinds flocked there. Circled as they did whenever they found food but were deterred from setting upon it because of predators or larger birds. It wasn't far. But it was off the trail that Douajavik had taken them.

Still, turkey vultures were down there making the best of some lucky find.

A moment of fury tensed Adjieich as he concluded that Douajavik had led them along the path to the wolves against his word, but the thought of turkey vultures feasting on the remains of those poor, weary travellers was too much. And the action too out of character, even for Douajavik. Adjieich watched the birds and wondered. It was certainly a big kill up there. It wasn't wolves that had brought it down either, otherwise there would be turkey vultures in the sky amongst the others. No, they were already on the ground.

Unnerving thoughts moved formless through Adjieich. He remembered what had woken him and set him off in the first place. With his spear clutched in his hand, he climbed down from the rocky outcropping and hurried along his path that was still flattened by his last migration. Closer. Urgency prickled up inside him and he didn't know why. He started to run.

Adjieich ran until he could hear a rumble on his heavy breaths. The scent hit him like a punch across his face and filled his mouth and nose with the stench of death. Nauseating and foul. He moved through it. Suddenly his mind was possessed. His body moved on its own. Nothing stole his attention but the thought of Demasduit and their safe passage north... nothing but the thought of their journey having led them here. This awful smell that maybe issued from their carcasses. Adjieich became so blinded by it he stopped looking where his feet landed for the first time in his life and slipped over. The ground was sticky with dried and blackened fluid. Chunks of rancid flesh...

[194]

The turkey vultures hopped aside but did not lift in fright of him. Adjieich stood and looked around the nightmare sight of the rotted-solid blood that streaked the still grey fur and the fangs that hung open through lips forever retracted or eaten off by the buzzards. Paws stuck in the air and were stripped to the bone. Their eyes were missing and their tongues. Many were opened across the chests, at the side behind their forelimbs or by a single cracking split across the top of their hard heads.

Wolves.

The pack of wolves that had brought down a polar bear and left scat on their trail were dead before him. By the looks of their deflated, eviscerated and stone-coloured carcasses, they had been there for a long while. Long enough for the vultures to have stripped much of them. There were no pups left. Not a trace of them but their little tracks towards the centre of the pack.

They'd tried to protect their young.

Though he could barely stay upright in the thick but invisible miasma, Adjieich knew he had to get closer. He had to see what did this. The nearest one was on its back with a long spear broken off through its ribs. Black blood ran frozen down the sides of its upturned jaw. The spear was long and thin. Not one of theirs. At the end was a head of shining stone.

Of course it was them. They had come through here. They were...

The realization hit Adjieich with a horror that made him forget the smell. His eyes widened and he gulped for the foul air.

They had come through. They had followed the path and cut in front of the migration on the way to Douajavik's village... which meant they got there first. Which meant that...

Without another moment's thought, Adjieich turned and ran back along the path away from the Great River and towards the lands of the Forest Fathers. The nearest of them was Keathut. Adjieich ran with all his might.

* * *

Around the lakeside village, they heard the pattering steps and
panicked cries of Gheegnyan and his cousin Adyouth long
before they saw them burst through the tree line and disturb the
colony of seals as they sprinted towards home. The air of unease
grew instantly. Anyone still outside slowly and inconspicuously
began their way back to the shelter of their mamateeks and the
security of the weapons they kept inside.

'Father!' yelled Gheegnyan.

'Uncle!' Adyouth cried.

Makdaachk turned his head and looked back inside his
mamateek where Wathik still comforted the child, Ebauthoo,
by their fire as she continued to relive what she said she saw
again and again in whispers as she stared into the glowing
embers and lapping flames.

It wasn't true, he thought as she looked back to his other son
and nephew run stupidly towards him. *They were idiots,
Gheegnyan and Adyouth. They were frightened when they left.*
He'd seen it in their wide eyes and darting sentences. They'd
have looked for anything to justify their fear and make the little
girl's story real.

The seals did little more than lift their heads and huff in the
wake of the two young men who then ran through the all but
empty village right up to Makdaachk's mamateek where he
greeted them, arms crossed defiantly.

'What the girl says is true,' Gheegnyan said. 'They have razed
the village of Oonban to the ground and the village of Eenodsha
lies smouldering by the sunrise. The village of Wobee is closest
to them. But they could be here next...'

'We must warn Wobee,' Adyouth said.

'Alright, quiet down,' Makdaachk spat and he stepped aside
and gestured the boys to enter his home.

'We shouldn't be quiet, father!' Gheegnyan whispered as they
both entered with their heads down. 'We should yell and
scream and warn everyone!'

'Sit down,' Makdaachk said as he drew the pelt back over his
doorway.

The little girl, Ebauthoo, watched with big, watery eyes. Gheegnyan did as he was told but Adyouth remained upright and his respectful gaze turned into a sharp glare towards Makdaachk.

'You don't mean to sit and talk while Wobee and his family are in such danger?' he said. 'Surely. If what this little girl says is true then they're slaughtering everyone. The families of Oonban and Eenodsha are dead to their last.'

'Wobee is a strong warrior,' Makdaachk said as he ambled over to the fire. With a wave of his hand, he sent Wathik and little Ebauthoo off into the shadows while he eased himself into their spot. 'Oonban was already dead. He stayed behind in the Broken Lands after he offered his daughter up to the Farther People. He died with Gobidin. Eenodsha was...' he trailed off and twirled his calloused old fingers in the air while he thought. '... more of a woman than a man. A caretaker and a nursemaid. He knew less about fighting than he did about tending to children. He should have had a husband rather than a wife.'

'You're talking about the dead,' Adyouth cautioned quietly.

'What will we do, father?'

'What did you boys see? Tell me.'

'We saw...' Gheegnyan looked at Adyouth...

'Don't look at him. Look at me.'

Gheegnyan turned his head back and thought hard.

'We saw Eenodsha's village,' Gheegnyan mumbled. 'They were there...'

'Pale Ones?'

'Yes,' Adyouth answered.

'I am asking my son.'

'Pale Ones,' Gheegnyan said. 'They were on their beasts and had the largest and strongest looking weapons I've ever seen them with.'

'Well, you haven't seen much of them. You didn't do your part in their village, as we discussed.'

'But I've heard...'

'Things we hear can be exaggerations. Especially if children said them.'

'Well, they had big weapons. Strong weapons. And they'd killed everyone. I could see the bodies smashed and cut open and thrown in a burning pile while the mamateeks burned and the Pale Ones were just watching.'

'How many?'

'Many. Enough to destroy two whole villages and...'

'Two weak villages. One without their father and one with a father worth less than his wife. How many?'

Gheegnyan looked down at his hands in silence.

'More than a hundred,' Adyouth finally said.

'For the last time. I am asking my son.'

'As he said. More than a hundred easily. And more were still arriving.'

'My son told me...'

'This is your son,' Adyouth gestured at Gheegnyan.

'My *son*,' Makdaachk repeated with a look at Adyouth as strong and blazing as the stone the Pale Ones' weapons were fashioned from. 'Told me that their entire force was on the Broken Lands. They did not have enough time to kill everyone there and come up here. And not enough of them could possibly have stayed in the Forest Lands to send a horde of over a hundred, as you say.'

'How do you know they went to the Broken Lands?'

'Because my son told me that's where they were going.'

Makdaachk now said 'son' with a sharp punch and looked at Gheegnyan every time he said it.

'How do you know they didn't come back?' Adyouth pressed. 'Maybe they gave up without fighting and just returned?'

'Because a thousand strong force don't go anywhere, they mean to just depart from a day or two later,' Makdaachk said. 'That is something our cultures have in common, theirs and ours. And because my son told me. And because Eenodsha's son stayed behind to report on what happened on the Broken Lands. He was to run away as soon as the attack started. Just what a son of Eenodsha would be good for. Madawaak has not reported to us yet. He wouldn't have waited this long with nothing. So he didn't escape in time. They got him. He's dead. With his father and his mother in the Spirit World.'

Makdaachk looked over at the little girl who sat half veiled in shadows and in his wife's arms.

'Now you dare to come here and contradict my son,' Makdaachk said to both of the boys. 'To make my son out to be a liar.'

'Gheegnyan is your son too...'

'Mooaumook did not lie to me!' Makdaachk suddenly roared and he slammed his fist down into the pelts he sat on. 'Mooaumook is no liar!'

'Where is Mooaumook?' Adyouth asked.

'He's watching them,' Makdaachk raved as he waved his arm around in a rage. 'Watching over their settlement in the cove. Watching in case he was wrong about the forces departing for the Broken Lands. And he hasn't come to report anything different to what he said before. So he's still there watching. And he hasn't come to tell me that any horde of Pale Ones left the cove...'

'Maybe he's dead?' Adyouth said. 'Maybe they got him before he could get away and he's dead.'

Makdaachk leaped to his feet and held his hands in tight fists. Both Adyouth and Gheegnyan flinched.

'You two can go to Wobee if it pleases you,' Makdaachk seethed through pursed lips. 'Take this lying spawn off with you as well,' he pointed at Ebauthoo. 'My son is no liar. My son does not lie! Keathut believed him enough. He will send fighters. Real fighters. And we will join with the Farther People and we will go to the land bridge to the Broken Lands and there we will fight this force of Pale Ones to their last to reclaim the lands of Gobidin. But we won't need weak, frightened little liars. You go to Wobee. You stay with that old pacifist fool. And when you see that no Pale Ones are in the Forest Lands now, or because of us will there ever be, you can ask him to take you as his son and nephew because I no longer have any use for either of you as mine!'

'Father...' Gheegnyan whispered.

'Go!' Makdaachk screamed. He turned to Ebauthoo. 'You go too. Let her go!'

Wathik withdrew her hands but Ebuthoo curled up in her lap. Makdaachk stormed over and seized the little girl by the hair and threw her at the boys. She screamed and fell at Adyouth's feet. There, she cried.

'Come on, little one,' Adyouth said as he kneeled to help her up. He looked at Gheegnyan. 'Come on.'

Gheegnyan still sat. He turned and looked with weepy eyes at his father.

'You think I lie?'

'You think Mooaumook does?'

'I think Mooaumook is...'

'Shut up!' Makdaachk said. 'You'll die long before him or me.'

Adyouth leaned over and took Gheegnyan by the arm, once he had Ebauthoo safely at his side. She still held her head and cried. Gheegnyan rose and nodded at his father.

'Alright,' he mumbled.

'Mak...'

'Shut up!' Makdaachk threw a foot backward into his wife's side to silence her.

'I will try to warn you, somehow,' Gheegnyan said as he backed away. 'I promise.'

'Don't bother. Just get out.'

The two brothers stepped out through the doorway and into the light and the pelt curtain fell and blocked Makdaachk's view of them.

16

A New Home

Shanawdithit.

Her little body curled over her knees amongst the burned mamateeks and slain corpses whose blood dried on the ground. Her own dropped into it. Like teardrops it fell from her eyes. She cried loudly. Her little hands felt their way through the blood, viscera and ash left on the ground. Away from her mother's corpse. Around her, the wolves had moved in. They were digging their noses into the open wounds on the corpses and dragging out the stringy flesh within. They didn't fight. They scattered quickly for there was more than enough for the entire pack.

Shanawdithit crawled and cried while they stalked around her. Their eyes caught the light off the embers and shone red in the darkness.

* * *

Demasduit tried to force the vision from her eyes. She didn't try to scream this time. The gag was tight in her mouth and dried her throat out. It was agony to utter so much as a whisper anyway. And her face was still swollen. Sense had to prevail. Shanawdithit couldn't hear her and couldn't see her and these monstrous Pale Ones were never going to take her back to her sister anyway.

She's dead, Demasduit told herself. *It was quick.*

Tears flowed from her eyes the moment the thought came to her. The soft starlight that rippled on the brook's surfaces blurred and sparkled through her tears. They slept on the ground all around her, except Freydis, who watched her all the time. Demasduit could feel her serpent's eyes even now as she wept helplessly. Demasduit forced her sorrow into rage. Her bonds dug at her skin as she pressed her flesh harder against them and her vision became clear. Freydis sat against a tree root by the brook while their horses scraped around and snorted in the brushes above them. The other Pale Ones were asleep. Their enormous bodies heaved up and down deeply and rhythmically. Demasduit looked at Freydis.

Freydis stared right back.

'There it is,' Freydis said in Demasduit's language. 'There's that strength.'

The demon climbed to her feet and Demasduit's whole body ached to lunge at her and rend her face from her skull with nothing but bare fingernails, but the bonds held tight. Freydis slowly moved closer.

Then Demasduit heard it. A sound almost undetectable to human ears. A scamper in the dry leaves above the little ravine. Human feet. She forced herself not to look. Not to give it away. Even forced away the rage that kept pounding out of her and summoned the thought of Shanawdithit to stay in the fore of her mind. But her people were here.

'I don't see your women in battle,' Freydis said. She stopped short of wetting her boots in the brook and turned and crossed the bank to her horse which was tied to a fern trunk. 'But I know you'd make fine warriors.'

The Pale One slipped a long spear from her horse's saddle. Demasduit's blood ran cold. *But there is help here,* she thought. *There is help. Stay angry,* she mused. *Hold on to the fury.*

'I'll bet that's what you always wanted,' Freydis said as she turned back to Demasduit and again walked towards her. That smirk was on her face again. 'To be a warrior like the men.'

She was talking loudly. The Pale Ones she'd brought with her stirred and some even lifted their heads.

'I'll count you amongst the finest men,' Freydis said as she raised the spear and stepped through the shallow brook. 'The finest men stand beside the finest women, in our society. I will make you a...'

She stopped. A word she didn't know.

'I will make you honoured as highly as any person can be,' Freydis continued. She stood right in front of Demasduit. The spear was long enough to push right through her if Freydis thrust it from where she stood. 'You will bring peace between us. And prosperity to your people. Why, after all, would you sell yourself to a people you hate? Why do that when you can become a great honoured woman amongst my people and then your enemies will be our enemies and it will be the Farther People who must live in fear. And... and you won't even have to marry anybody. No. If you marry it will be for love. Not for a treaty with an even weaker people than you already are.'

Freydis kneeled in front of Demasduit and held the spear at her side.

'We will honour you forever for making peace between our people,' Freydis said. 'I have gone to such lengths. Do you see that I speak your language? I learned from the Farther People. I know them. I know how weak they are. They will make no worthy allies. Not against us. But with us...' she grinned. 'With us they will fear you. With us the Mi'kmaq will fear you. The Algonquin will fear your people. Your people will prosper on whatever land they chose and will never be bothered by any others ever again.'

Freydis allowed for a moment's silence. The sounds around them had stopped. Demasduit waited for the death blow to come to Freydis from above. For her saviours to set her free and run with her back to save Shanawdithit. It wasn't too late.

'All I ask is that you come with me,' Freydis said. 'Join us for a feast and see how honest we are. No more fighting. Not between us. We've too much in common.'

Freydis bowed deeply. Then, she lifted her head with a broad smile she held low in the shadows. She whispered, 'I see them.'

It happened so fast. Demasduit never even had time to scream out and warn them. Freydis leaped to her feet and spun and hurled the spear up the embankment where it ran through Adjieich's breast and pinned him to the tree he had been sheltering under. He never made a sound.

[203]

The Pale Ones reached for their weapons, woken by Freydis' loud talking, and sheltered from the volley of spears and arrows that showered down over them. Freydis drew her sword.

'Demasduit!' cried the voice of Keathut from behind her. 'Run!'

The Pale Ones rose behind their shields. One fell with a scream while his hands clutched an arrow in his knee. The rest of his body was open for piercing. But no sooner did he fall than did the Pale Ones return the volley while others charged up the embankment with their axes and their atgiers thrust forward.

Demasduit kicked her feet up and rolled over. She crawled towards the embankment amidst the confusion and started up, while Keathut ran down towards her with his spear ready. He looked behind Demasduit. She didn't look. She knew Freydis was coming after her. Screams began to issue from the bushes all around them. Keathut threw his spear. He reached down for Demasduit.

A great force from behind ripped Demasduit away from Keathut. She felt herself become bound in Freydis' great and powerful flesh while the long shaft of shining stone, the sword she carried, swung over Demasduit's head and cut through Keathut's outstretched hand. He cried out and withdrew. His face was spattered in his blood. Behind Keathut, his brothers and sons and nephews came running but the sword was quickly across Demasduit's chest. Freydis ripped open the girl's clothes and exposed her breasts. Then she held the sharp side of the sword to Demasduit's chest and used her captive as a shield.

The oncoming hunters stopped. Their spears and arrows were primed.

Behind Freydis, the Pale Ones had mounted their horses and formed a line. Three were now without riders. Freydis backed towards them and held Demasduit to her front where the hunters saw that if they fired, she'd cut through Demasduit's breast.

'See?' Freydis cried to Keathut.

Keathut held his mangled hand in front of him and sat there on his knees in front of his frozen line of hunters, his face full of horror.

'See,' Freydis said. 'See which one is faster. Your arrows and spears or my blade.'

Demasduit managed to push the loosened gag from her mouth.

'Do it Keathut!' she screamed. 'Kill us both! Kill us! You won't get another chance.'

'Go on, do that. Kill us both,' Freydis mocked. 'I take her to my village. My village Straumfjord. Straumfjord! Remember that name! It is the name for my village. It is the name for your village. The centre of our people.'

'We are not one people!' Keathut cried.

'You heard me,' Freydis said. She was arm's reach from her horse now. 'We will be.'

'Kill us Keathut!'

'Keathut!' Freydis cried. 'This is my daughter now. She has no family elsewhere.'

'She will never be your daughter.'

'We are the same flesh and the same blood!' Freydis shouted.

'Kill us Keathut, please!' Demasduit cried sorrowfully. Her voice pierced the heart of every man there and the arrows trembled and the spears wavered.

'Go on Keathut, kill us both,' Freydis said.

Keathut's face rippled with emotions too quickly for anyone to read but no words came from his mouth. Nor did any arrow or spear fly from his hunters. Freydis giggled mockingly, mounted her horse and the Pale Ones turned and rode off into the darkness beyond the shafts of starlight that shone down through the forest canopy.

A mighty war cry followed them through the night.

* * *

'When did they come?' Wobee asked the little girl as she ate her broth by his fire.

Her sleepy eyes trailed up to him.

'As the sun rose.'

'You are sure they're coming this way?' he asked the two young men. 'Not to your father's village?'

'Eenodsha's village is back towards their stronghold,' Adyouth said. 'They aren't moving outward; they are moving around.'

'Clearing the area around them,' Wobee nodded.

'Makdaachk did not want to warn you,' Adyouth said.

'He didn't believe us,' Gheegnyan muttered from where he curled up beside the modest fire in Wobee's mamateek. 'Otherwise he would have.'

'Then he will not come to help us,' Wobee said.

'You don't need his help,' Adyouth offered.

'Their weapons are strong. The beings they ride on are fast,' Wobee said. 'And if their force is as great as you say then there are too many of them for us to fight and kill them all.'

'We don't need to kill them all at once,' Adyouth protested. 'Just enough.'

'A strong fight is not as simple as clashing with your enemy,' Wobee said. 'You have to outthink them. They are killing everyone in these villages. We only know what is happening because this little girl escaped,' he touched Ebauthoo's shoulders with his fingertips, 'that means that the surprise is important to them. But it could mean there is another aspect to their plan that we are not meant to see.'

'More could be coming,' Adyouth said.

Ebauthoo had curled over and fallen asleep. She lay with her little hand draped over her eyes and snored softly while the birchbark bowl she'd eaten from spilled its remaining contents silently into the dirt.

'We will only find out if we are alive to see something of it,' Wobee said. 'We will only stop it if there are enough of us left to fight.'

'What are you saying?' Gheegnyan asked.

'Go back to your father and warn him of the coming danger,' Wobee said. He looked up at Adyouth, who stood rigid the entire conversation. 'You stay with me. So will the girl. It is time now to let the Pale Ones think they have won a victory.'

'They won't stop until we're all dead,' Adyouth protested. Ebauthoo stirred.

'You said yourself they are clearing the area around them,' Wobee said. 'Think about that. They don't want us all dead yet. We can use this to our advantage. We can survive.'

'What will you do?'

'I will send your cousin back to his father to warn him that Wobee has failed to stop the coming tide of Pale Riders. When that is done, we will talk.'

Wobee stared at Gheegnyan.

'You want me to leave now?'

'If you aren't afraid to walk in the night,' Wobee said. 'Yes.'

* * *

Goran led his horde between Ulfan and Astrid's as they followed the long shadows cast by the morning sun deeper into the forest. He looked to the right and left of him often. Too often and he knew it.

Freydis, he kept thinking. She didn't send him with these two who were so loyal to her because she didn't know something was going on. He tensed beneath his leather. He'd given it away and he knew it. Bolts of panic shot through his body and he looked at them in turn again.

Ulfan watched the trees as they thickened ahead.

Astrid led her horse and her riders with that steely, ice-blue gaze.

Ulfan was a short man. Stocky and broad with watchful grey eyes that flickered from side to side as he spoke.

Astrid was thickset and fleshy, with a face reddened and pitted by years she'd not yet lived...

'Are you afraid, Goran?' Ulfan asked in his high-pitched but gravelly voice. Goran looked at him again.

'No,' Goran said. He looked back at Astrid. Now she was staring at him as well. Had Freydis said something to them on the night they'd prepared? Had she taken them aside while he saw to his duties? How he wished he could ask the birds if they'd seen Kaia alive at Straumfjord since the raids began. For all he knew, her head was amongst the skraelingjar's that hung rotting from the trees around the forest edge.

'Their fires burn ahead,' Astrid said. Her voice was deceptively serene and melodious.

'Goran... are you with us?'

'Yes!' he gasped, quickly.

They were already galloping ahead. Their hordes followed and Goran hurried to keep up. The trees closed in around them and the horses crisscrossed through the low fern gully until they came up the snowy hillside and thundered towards the village. The hordes split up again. Astrid took one flank. Ulfan the other. This time, Goran led the headlong charge into the village and their horses thundered through it. Their axes, atgiers and spearheads gleamed and winked in the sun. The hordes spread through the cluster of homesteads like a flood of flesh and steel.

But there were no skraelingjar.

'Burn the homes!' Goran roared and his horde quickly plucked torches from their glowing spot fires and held them to the dry bark and mud of the huts. The structures lit up and burned. The snow melted away around them and left patches of dry earth. But even as the supporting pillars cracked and the roofs caved in and the homes collapsed, there emerged not one skraeling.

Silence, but for the snorting horses, their thudding hoofs as they stamped around in nervous confusion, and the crackle of the fires. Then, Goran felt the cold shudder.

'Ambush!' he screamed.

Just then, the arrows flew out from the trees. A chorus of screams erupted as they hammered down on the unsuspecting horde. Ravaged, panicked, high pitched screams. The screams of horses. Men and women as well. But the horses took on a volume and fevered timbre that curdled the blood. The riders held up their shields but it wasn't their bodies the arrows were aimed at.

The horses fell. Some with their riders' legs nailed to their sides by the volley of arrows that relentlessly arched out from the treetops and forest depths like an attacking swarm.

'Archers!' Goran heard Astrid scream, faintly. 'Archers!'

The sheltering warriors returned arrows towards the trees but already the volleys had thinned. The skraelingjar were retreating. Goran's horse lolled to one side and collapsed and crushed his leg beneath it. He cried out as he felt the bone crack and shatter. A series of pops and snaps inside his leg. Ulfan rode past him towards the trees, still with a large horde behind him, and they charged onward in pursuit of the skraelingjar. Then the pain hit Goran and stole his senses away. He screamed and pushed at the dead body of his horse but all his strength could not move it.

* * *

Goran finally collapsed into trembling exhaustion. Astrid stood over him. A large axe was in her hands. A few screams rang out from the silence that surrounded Goran, as always, in the aftermath of a battle. Without saying a word, Astrid swung the axe high and brought it down on the spine of Goran's horse. Pink flesh peeked out as the wound opened like butterfly wings. She hacked again and again. Two of Goran's horde took him by the arms and dragged him. The pain seized him in a crushing grip and he screamed out.

'Quiet!' Astrid shouted.

One by one, the ravaged cries of injured warriors fell silent with the thud of a spearhead and a brief gurgle or ragged croak. The injured horses had already been silenced. Goran looked around and saw the dead. Many still stood on two legs and some even still on four. His horde, as well as Astrid's and Ulfan's. The arrows that still stood upright from the corpses of horses and warriors stood higher than the tallest head.

'A trap,' Goran wheezed as another wave of agony rolled up from his leg and through his body. Sweat poured from him.

'Someone got away from one of the villages and warned them. Maybe they warned all the others, who knows?' Astrid said.

Goran saw Ulfan's horde joining up with Astrid's beyond the village edges while his champions remained amongst the burning structures.

'I have to go back to Straumfjord,' he said.

'It was two traps, hairless one,' Astrid said. 'Ulfan never came back. I will take his champions back to Straumfjord. You will stay here in case the skraelingjar of this village return.'

'No!' Goran cried. 'No, you can't leave me! Not like thi...'

The pain stole his words and senses again and he screamed out. But ever in his mind there lingered the horrifying thought that Freydis knew. Even somehow planned this. She could talk to the skraelingjar. She knew. She warned them...

Astrid was gone. Already she led the two hordes back into the fern forest. Slowly the presence of a strong number faded and dwindled around Goran while he screamed and cried his insensible objections.

When all that were left were his own, they limped over and surrounded him.

'We have come to a decision,' said Jen the Many-Times-Broken as he stepped forward with his spear at his side. 'We need a new jarl.'

Casually, with the slow motions of battle fatigue, Jen lowered the spear and drove it into Goran's throat. He clutched at it. Warm blood exploded out of his hand from his mouth and his wound. Goran felt it rammed through his gullet. That was the last thing he ever felt.

* * *

'No!' Makdaachk delivered another kick to Gheegnyan's side as he cowered in the corner. Wathik whimpered. 'There is no force!'

'Please father!' Gheegnyan wheezed.

Rage so filled Makdaachk that he thought his skin might melt off. Hot in fury, he stomped towards the pathetic child again...

Suddenly the curtain of his mamateek was flung aside and Adyouth stepped through, streaked with fresh blood. He carried something heavy in his hand. Threw it at Makdaachk's feet where it landed and dabbed blood on the furs of his floor.

A head. A Pale One. Wide, grey eyes stared blankly and mouth hung open and twisted in silent horror.

'There are more,' Adyouth warned. 'But the most have turned towards the cove. Wobee evaded them. We killed this one that came after us.'

Makdaachk's knees buckled.

'Wobee needs the shelter of the wood's depths in your country for what must be done next,' Adyouth said. 'He will make his hideout there whether you allow him or not. He asks that you allow him.'

'Uh... I...' Makdaachk gasped breathlessly as his trembling hands lifted up to his face and covered his eyes. 'My son. My son is dead, then.'

'You still have one,' Adyouth said as he looked pitifully at the beat-up form of Gheegnyan on the floor.

Makdaachk suddenly exploded with rage and charged at his younger son again.

'It should have been you!'

Adyouth caught him with his forearm and drove the elder man back. He stood between them. Firm and ready.

Makdaachk glared at him, out of breath, as tears ran from his eyes.

'I will take that as consent to Wobee,' Adyouth said. He helped the trembling, frightened Gheegnyan from the floor and led him slowly out of the mamateek. Makdaachk never moved. He didn't even watch them go. He just stared at the floor, open-mouthed, not unlike the head that lay severed near his feet.

* * *

Torvard stared wide-eyed at the skraeling that was tied spread-eagle upon their bed. She seemed painfully small. Her limbs were narrow and bony and her ribs showed through between her exposed little breasts. Her hips were barely the breadth of Torvard's hand. Yet, as exposed as she was, she never took her eyes off the captive male skraeling. Mooaumook. Her head was lifted so she could look down along her own open and vulnerable body, covered only by the soft shadows that the firelight could not reach as it glowed through the arras, right at Mooaumook, who was caged in the corner.

He had curled tightly into a ball the second Freydis had dragged the poor skraeling woman in and with two of her biggest champions, Gustav and Casper, tied the tiny girl down. As the captive continued to stare, Mooaumook seemed only to curl up tighter. He never looked back at her. Only evaded first with just his eyes, then by covering his face and turning away from her.

'Her name is Demasduit,' Freydis said as she gently ran her fingertips across Torvard's exposed back and shoulders. 'She is going to make us lords of this land. And you are going to help her my love. And you are both going to give me what you and I alone could never.'

Beyond the arras, the longhouse murmured and bumped with the sound of the Althing that gathered. The two champions departed through the arras. Freydis moved to Torvard's side. She touched her finger to his chin and turned his head to look into the green infernos that were her eyes. He saw tears wet them slowly. They flickered back and forth between his, both focused on one of his at a time.

'A baby,' she whispered, shakily.

The old shame kicked Torvard in the guts.

'I can't. You know I can't.'

'You can,' Freydis breathed as her eyes suddenly fell to the floor. She stepped away from Torvard. 'It's not you who has the problem. It's me. *Freyr* has seen fit to grant me every maternal instinct and desire a woman can hold in her body and yet deny me the proper mechanics to make it happen. But for my desire I am an empty shell.'

'Are you sure?'

'Yes, I'm sure!' she snapped and turned away from him, then moved over to their bed where she stared down at the girl Demasduit. Stared with wide-eyed malice. Or envy. Or admiration. Torvard hated that he could never properly read her. 'I'm sure. I know my body. Not like this one. Small but capable. All there. Like an apple tree bursting with fruits.'

Freydis' hand hovered between Demasduit's legs.

'You always said... such cruel things.'

'I know I did,' Freydis said. 'You must understand Torvard. I hurt. I am a mother without a womb. *Loki* looks on me and laughs,' she looked at Torvard again. 'I can birth nations but my body can't make life like any other woman's. I would give nations for the right pieces.'

'What would you have done...' Torvard's mind wandered with his gaze over to Mooaumook...

'It doesn't matter,' Freydis raised her voice and startled Torvard. 'This is how it is. This way and not any other way.'

Torvard looked at the tiny Demasduit and felt no desire. Pity bit inside him. But he knew this was the child in him that refused to die. So his father had always said and so Freydis had said ever since his father had died.

Demasduit was like a child. He couldn't imagine desiring such a tiny figure. Couldn't even imagine how he could physically come into her. She looked so fragile. So young. *Even for one of them, small as they are,* he thought, *she can't be old enough.*

'I still don't think I can...'

'Think of me, love,' Freydis coaxed. 'Think of whoever you want. Whoever might help you get there, but make it happen. Make this happen for me. I am shield-maiden. I am warrior. I rule Vinland and go to war and provide this province for you in place of your weakness. I have been enough to compensate for your shortcomings. But I cannot do this. I need you for this. This is the last duty I ask of you, my love, Torvard. My love.'

Torvard looked at the tied-up body and felt only revulsion. While Freydis stood between Demasduit and Mooaumook, Demasduit focused on her captor and the fury that radiated from her face weakened Torvard's resolve only more.

'I don't understand...'

'Alright,' Freydis said. 'Alright, Torvard. I'll find someone to do it. Perhaps Ulfan will...'

'Ulfan is dead. Goran as well. They were ambushed at the third village. I didn't have time to tell you.'

Freydis licked her lips. Torvard could only hide the spring of delight that flowed through him at having once in every brief while the upper hand.

'Astrid brought Ulfan's champions back. And her own. Goran's remain in the camp.'

'Then they weren't defeated.'

'Not unless more news comes.'

'Then it doesn't matter,' Freydis said. 'Soon there won't be any ambushes or skirmishes or battles or any more dead of us. But I don't have a man around who can do it.'

She clicked her fingers mockingly.

'Ifar,' she said. 'Now I know what a man he is.'

'The things you say...'

'Watch what he'll do to me, if you won't.'

'I'll do it!' Torvard snapped. He felt his inside cool as the words leaped unconsciously from his mouth. 'Ifar can have his deer.'

Freydis looked at him. For a moment, a brief glimmer of affection seemed to shine from her, but her smile quickly veered into that smirk.

'Good,' she replied.

Freydis knocked twice against the arras. Casper and Gustav returned and followed her gesture to Mooaumook, whose iron clasps rattled as they raised him off the ground. Demasduit watched Mooaumook's bloody, maggot-infested wounds where the cuffs were pinched around his wrists and ankles, but her expression didn't change at all.

'You're excused from today's Althing,' Freydis said. Then she kneeled and caressed Demasduit's face. The girl recoiled. The hand that touched her might as well have been aflame. Freydis spoke to her in their language. Then she stood and opened the arras.

'What did you say to her?' Torvard asked.

Freydis smirked and left.

* * *

The Althing sat in silence as Mooaumook was thrown into the center yet again and Freydis stood in front of her table. Torvard did not show himself. Kaia looked frantically around for Goran. She could see Astrid a few tables away, ever pale but this time ashen and sullen where normally she'd wear the expression of stone. Kaia's heart started to thump.

Ulfan, she thought. *There is no Ulfan either. Wherever Goran is, he is with Ulfan. Yes... there is no way Freydis know or even suspects our meeting with Jannik. No way. It is mere misfortune that Goran has been sent,* she told herself. *It's just a coincidence that Freydis has sent Goran with her two favourites. No... nothing to worry about.*

Kaia caught herself looking around too obviously. Freydis was looking at her.

'Word has come to me,' Freydis began. 'Ulfan and Goran are both lost. May the Valkyries carry them to Valhalla to feast with Odin for all eternity. They have earned it many times over.'

Astrid covered her eyes. Kaia's blood rushed from her face and she felt cold.

'But they fulfilled their duty,' Freydis said. 'The near villages are gone. Nobody will come to save my captive princess. The next nearest is the village of one named Makdaachk. The father of our friend here.'

Mooaumook eased up on his knees at the mention of his father's name.

'We can expect a few insurgencies,' Freydis said. 'And Astrid will have her chance for revenge against the skraelingjar that ambushed her. But they aren't many. And the rest will follow Makdaachk once he receives Demasduit with our peace offering.'

'How can you be sure?'

'Because we will give Demasduit what Makdaachk wanted their enemies across the river to give her,' Freydis said. 'A child. Half theirs, half their enemy's. A way of showing these skraelingjar that their superstition of spiritual superiority over us is false. They are weakened enough when I speak to them. When they see their most respected daughter impregnated by us, they will bow at our feet.'

'Skraelingjar are skraelingjar. They can never be trusted.'

'I'll show you,' Freydis said. 'We'll need them. We'll need their gifts for reading tracks off the ground and their knowledge

[215]

of their fellows. These skraelingjar of Markland have many enemies. Not just more of their own in the north, but on the mainland. Many wars have been fought before our coming. We will need their assistance. The Karlsefini will have to start shipping thrall skraelingjar back to my brother the King before this winter ends. I have chosen our alliance carefully.'

'Are you sure?' Astrid asked. 'Can we really make babies with their kind?'

'They're human,' Freydis said with a smirk. 'No different inside to us. Just smaller.'

'Who will impregnate this Demadammit?'

'My Torvard,' Freydis answered. 'The Chieftain of Markland's husband and the princess of the Markland skraelingjar will make a child that will be worshipped amongst them. Godlike. When we use them to lead our forces on the skraelingjar across the river, they will worship us as Gods as well. Their enemies will become our slaves.'

Nobody could argue.

Kaia started to wonder if her chance would come yet...

'But first we have a promise to keep,' Freydis said as she leaned back on the table and clapped her hands. 'Mooaumook has earned his iron. I want us all to move to the Straumfjord forge.'

Kaia followed the dense crowd out into the icy air. Their feet crunched through the snow as they shuffled in a thick line to the forge near Rolf's boatyard. There the fires burned hot and the smoke was black. The blacksmiths worked every hour of sunlight.

By the time everyone had gathered, Casper and Gustav had dragged Mooaumook to the forge and put him down at the blacksmith's anvil. He rose to his knees. Freydis spoke his language and pointed to the molten steel in the ladles and the Nubian thralls who pumped the bellows and the Kurdish thralls who extracted the raw iron and the blacksmith Viggo who beat the iron alongside his two young apprentices. Freydis carefully talked in the skraelingjar tongue. The blacksmiths looked up and acknowledged her but kept working.

The unease that Kaia felt from everybody that stood around her became so dense she had to fight against her smile. This would be Freydis' undoing. The gift of iron for their enemies. This would backfire and the Althing would...

Freydis put on one of the blacksmith's heavy gloves and picked a ladle out of the fire pit. In the smoky air it steamed. She still spoke the skraelingjar language, but her voice grew louder and her eyes blazed. Gustav and Casper seized Mooaumook and held out his arms. Freydis stood over him with the ladle.

Kaia dry-wretched while her hopes went up with the smoke of the forge.

Casper held back the skraeling's head by the hair and he screamed as Freydis poured the iron into his mouth. The scream gargled and sizzled. Molten steel burned through his flesh instantly and poured from his throat. His eyes bulged. They rolled backward as the steel ran over his chest and stripped the flesh off his bones and hardened there like a breastplate. He shuddered and died. The sizzling sound, the cooking meat, persisted as the steam billowed from his corpse. Casper and Gustav let the body fall and it clunked in the exposed clay.

Freydis handed back the ladle. She turned to the ghostly faces of the Althing.

'I promised him the gift of iron and he got it,' Freydis said. 'In exactly the way anyone who betrays their own people deserves it. This is my land. This is my law. You are my people.'

Casper and Gustav parted the crowd and Freydis walked away with them. The Althing said nothing. Slowly, they began to disperse. Sullen eyes and shocked faces held firmly towards the ground. Kaia remained with the mangled corpse.

She shivered in the cold.

17

Revenge

Exhausted, Madawaak sat on the edge of the cradle and looked at the bloated, snow-blanketed bodies. Vultures pecked at their naked limbs where they peeked up from beneath the sheet of snow. They pulled strips of the greyed, rotten flesh out. Gulped them down with a few snaps of their thick beaks. A few eagles moved around amongst them. Up close, the little white maggots could be seen crawling around in the meat and the droning of flies hummed loudly.

Before Madawaak were two piles of clothes. Those that were infested by blood or dried clumps of viscera and those that were clean. One swarmed with flies. Vultures pecked at it as well and smaller birds which came for the maggots and the flies. The other stayed untouched. He'd had to pull a few garments out of the clean pile and throw them in the infested pile. The flies had shown him the way. But now he had it right. Clothes to wear and clothes to burn once nature had done with them.

A grouse waddled close to Madawaak's numb feet.

'Bring me news,' Madawaak demanded of it. 'What happens in the Forest Lands where my people still exist?'

The little grouse pecked at the clean clothes.

'Leave that for a moment, will you? Tell me something.'

None of it matters anymore.

'I still want to know. I want to feel something again.'

The grouse cocked its head and looked at him with one eye. Madawaak imagined the dismembered corpses of those who'd died in the battle at the cove hung from trees and decomposing there. He balled his fists.

Demasduit was their captive. Chained. He saw one of them on top of her exposed body. Penetrated. She wept as the hulking figure thrust into her and made her bleed and cry.

'Go on and eat your maggots grouse,' Madawaak said as a tear warmed the skin beneath his eye. He looked out across the white desert. Across it, the Pale Ones searched for him and Madawaak knew it was only so long before they would think to check this place.

'They think I'm afraid of the bodies,' Madawaak said aloud. A way of filling the sparseness that surrounded him. A human sound amidst the whisper of winds through the scattered stands of snow-capped trees, the crunch of snow and the symphony of decay in the hilltop. He stood up. Heat moved through his legs and arms again and he staggered a few steps before he could walk to the edge and look out at the vastness he'd crossed to get away from them. An icy updraft covered his face.

Pale Ones were out there looking for him.

A tingle ran through him at the thought of it. They'd find him. Eventually. Soon. They would remember the day.

He looked at the half-covered bodies as the buzzards fluttered around them with their heads ducking and popping back up again. The grouse moved amongst them.

'Give me bones, my friends,' he said. 'Give me spare bones.'

* * *

'We'll never find him out here,' Asny said as she wiped the grease from the caribou meat through her hair and then settled on one elbow beside the fire.

'Give up then?' Viveka asked. She played with some rune tablets that hung around her neck.

Asny looked into the inky darkness that stared at them beyond the throbbing glow of the fire and imagined the tundra of white wasteland it had been under the sunlight. They'd lost the trail when the snow had come down. Since then, they had wandered in the general direction the skraeling boy had taken off in but come across no other trail nor encountered anything left behind by him. A hunt. A fire. Nothing. The horde had taken their share of the caribou and retired to their robes. Aside from the rise and fall of their chests beneath the robes, thick with polar bear fur, they had not moved since. Asny heard their snoring in the darkness. It was hypnotic. Dizzying fatigue rested heavy on her flesh. Two days they'd ridden slowly and searched through flat snow across endless icy plains with nothing to see but snowy caribou, wandering birds and the odd pine tree or rock outcropping.

The sudden thwack of a bone breaking startled Asny out of her sleepy trance. It was Magnus. With the back of his axe, he broke off a hock and picked up the hot bone while the marrow steamed and gurgled inside it.

A horse snorted.

'We've lost him,' Asny said. 'He isn't here.'

'Do we go back or not?' Viveka asked. She got up and dusted her pants off and moved over to her robe.

The thought of going back daunted Asny. She watched as Magnus casually sunk his front teeth into a clump of fat in the hock and tore it free. Viveka nestled into her robe and sighed. Magnus was Asny's champion. Viveka was Gottfried's. Around them were warriors loyal to both Asny and Gottfried and the thought of admitting defeat to them was enough to make Asny feel sick in her stomach.

'I don't think we should go back,' Asny half-whispered.

'You need to make a decision,' Viveka said. 'Your horde will walk with you until they die of exhaustion or exposure. Or they will give up and go home to their families. But they will not tolerate indecisiveness.'

Magnus looked at Viveka and Asny caught him. He looked down at his hock. He'd served her father and now he served Asny but she'd never had a fight before her until now. No chieftain had ever bestowed such a duty upon her. The thought of him turning on her haunted her. Made her feel cold. But she thought it could happen. It would if he saw weakness. Viveka already snored away in her robe.

'I wonder about the place where Freydis' skraeling told us his people would be hiding,' Asny said. 'Where we found them.'

No answer. Another horse snorted and Magnus chewed loudly.

'Could he have gone back there?'

Magnus threw the bone into the embers and sparks flew up and twirled into the black sky.

'Magnus, take a detachment and go there,' Asny said. 'Take twelve men and look for a sign of life. Nothing else.'

'He would not have gone back there,' Magnus said with a wave of his huge hand. He lay back into his robe.

'So Viveka said. But I am telling you. Take twelve and go back there. Check for a living skraeling.'

'Yes, my lord,' he half-muttered and then he was asleep.

The horses' big eyes glinted as they caught the light of the dying fire. The night was deeper than the ocean. They would keep watch. She rolled up into her robe and waited for a sleep that wouldn't come.

* * *

Magnus and his crew rode at speed from the ponderous horde back to the junction where they'd moved northwest to sweep towards the peninsula. The sky again gave them nothing but white clouds. So Magnus led from memory back towards the rocky badlands where the skraelingjar had been slaughtered.

At high noon they rested and chewed some of the salted, sun-dried provisions they kept with them. When they rode again the sky had cleared. Soft blue peeked through at them from the sweeping clouds.

'Hold!' Magnus shouted when he saw the strange black object in the distance. Beyond it was a pine forest that enshrouded the earth beneath it all the way to the horizon. The twelve riders stopped.

The black object was moving.

Magnus led them towards it over the slight hills and past the lone trees and boulders. As they got closer, they realized it was a predator. A bear. It growled and grunted as it wrestled with something in the snow. Magnus stopped when it raised its off-brown face and looked at them as they approached. He raised his spear.

The bear growled as the other horses continued their approach.

Magnus charged through the twelve and hurled a spear. The bear howled. Struck through the shoulder at the base of the neck. The others threw their spears. The bear growled and swiped its paws in the direction of the riders. It bit at the shafts that stuck in its body. Blood gurgled up from its mouth and it kept moving around. Soon red streams ran from the spears stuck in its skin. Magnus got close, dismounted and unstrapped his huge double-edged battle axe. With it he struck the bear once behind the ear. It collapsed into the snow and curled up into a ball. Magnus struck it again in the same spot. The head opened and red blood and meat raised up and the bear's body slackened and rolled onto its side.

He hit it one more time but it did not react.

Thor and Carl dismounted and joined Magnus at the mound the bear had been tugging. There was the hardened pelt of a deer. Beneath it the bones. Magnus dug at the snow and brought up a partial rib cage with the flesh rotted down and the skin peeled back. It had been cut with a blade.

Even a hibernating bear wouldn't have left such a scent unchecked for so long as had passed since the battle in the badlands. Magnus rose and turned to his men.

'Three of you go on,' he ordered. 'We will search this forest.'

'That will take weeks!' Carl said.

'You go to Lord Asny,' Magnus said. 'Tell her to turn the horde around and meet us here.'

'We should go to the village and alert Gottfried,' Carl said as three of their company quietly rode off in the direction they'd been headed. 'We will need more fighters.'

'If you want to rouse Gottfried for everything we find go ahead, but do it on your own,' Magnus said. 'I would rather bring him the head of the skraeling.'

The other riders had already started towards the forest edge.

'Are you going?' Thor asked Carl.

'Where?'

'Gottfried, if you like,' Magnus said. 'But alert Lord Asny on the way before you waste the Chieftain's time.'

Carl huffed and mounted his horse.

* * *

Magnus and his men tied their horses to some pines in a clearing before the forest grew denser. They searched on foot while branches and rocks snatched at their feet. Fern fronds and brushes wet their flanks as they looked.

'The den!' Thor cried.

The others hurried to Thor as he unearthed the den the bear had been sleeping in. Three little cubs raised their sleepy eyes and mewled in protest but the warriors bashed their heads in with the backs of their axes and quickly stripped their pelts to tan in the afternoon air. Two remained to wash, defat and bag the meat. The others spread back out and searched. Every hunter could hear the taps and plops of melting snow that dripped down from the canopy sent a jolt through them.

Night began to fall and they reconvened at the den. In the distance, wolves howled.

'He isn't in the forest,' Gerda said with a shaky voice.

Visible breath that billowed from the hunters' mouths thickened and grew more frequent.

'Out to the horses,' Magnus ordered.

The hunters hurried to their horses and led them back out into the snowy tundra. A scant scattering of stars twinkled above them in the misty sky and gave them just enough light to see their footsteps against the slushy mantle. They gathered a distance from the trees.

'They'll come looking for that,' Thor said. He nodded towards the dead black bear.

The warriors moved further out again.

'I've heard they can talk to beasts,' Hans said. 'Even convince bears and wolves not to harm them.'

'Nonsense,' Gerda breathed. She spat into the snow. 'Rumours. No man would be stupid enough to camp in forests patrolled by wolves, even if wolves could be reasoned with.'

A voice cried out in the night.

'A flame!'

It was the detachment Magnus had sent to the rocky hills. They rode back at full gallop. The spray of snow in their hoofs' wake glittered in the night. The others quickly mounted as they approached.

'A fire! Atop the hill where the dead lay.'

'Then he is there,' Magnus said.

'Shall we wait for Lord Asny?' Thor asked.

'Of course not!' Magnus roared with his battle axe already in his hand. He kicked his horse into a strong gallop.

The rest of the eleven galloped off to follow him.

* * *

Sunrise showed its first signs over the horizon. Madawaak finished affixing the bone tip to another wooden spear with his bleeding hands and set it aside with the others. More were set up on the path up. Brushes there were cleared of snow as well. His clothing fire still spewed its black smoke in a long column that leaned towards the north as it smouldered.

Madawaak touched the tomahawk at his side. His arrows and bow. Spears. Sharpened sticks. In his mind, he took stock of where he'd hidden them. They were there. They had not moved since last he'd checked them.

There was nothing left to do but wait.

The band crept along the white sheet of landscape towards him and Madawaak saw there were only a few. An escalating heartbeat quickened his breath. The air that hovered above the ice stung his throat but Madawaak stayed firm and watched their approach. They grew near enough for him to see the colours of their beasts' fur. The shape of their garments. The shining domes of their helmets. The wink of their shining stone as it caught the rising sun.

Eleven.

Soon they disappeared behind the rocks, headed for the pathway up. Madawaak kept time of their pace as he hurried to the smouldering clothing pile and dipped the shredded end of his arrow into it. Blew until it caught fire. Hurried to shelter by the top of the path. The hoofs of the creatures drew nearer...

They were riding up! Surely their beasts wouldn't make it... they knew better last time than to...

[224]

Now wasn't the time. Madawaak held his breath and leaned out over the path. The lead Pale One roared and raised his great axe but Madawaak fired the burning arrow into the dried piles of thickets he'd left clustered on the path. The animals screamed and reared up on their hindlimbs. Two of the riders fell and the animals behind them panicked and stomped their hooves and trampled their bodies. Madawaak stood and quickly fired off three arrows. Aimed for the animals' heads. They screamed as one of their arrows buzzed by Madawaak and he retreated into the cradle.

* * *

One of the riders broke through and gave chase up to the top. The horse struggled but she pushed and pushed. Every stride felt like it might have toppled over but she forced its shaky legs and finally it carried her to level ground. Gerda found nobody but corpses half buried in the snow and stripped to their bones by birds. The vultures still covered much of the ground. She rode to the passage she could see across the top. Where the women had tried to run. The vultures flapped their wings and moved away as she passed by them.

The Skraeling shot up and chopped into her side. Air burst out of Gerda's mouth and she raised her axe high to chop at her assailant but Madawaak dropped down. He pulled the handle of the tomahawk and dragged her off the horse with him. He slammed another tomahawk into the base of her skull, beneath her helmet, so blood ran over his hand and painted it red. He ducked between the horse's legs as arrows flew at him. From there, he grabbed a spear and threw it at the first of the two other Pale Ones who had climbed up.

* * *

The man he hit in the chest grabbed the spear and cried out. Madawaak fired an arrow as his fellow fired another of his and the two shafts of death crossed mid-air. A streak of hot pain shot across Madawaak's hip. The horse, littered with arrows, laboured down onto its haunches and then collapsed in the dirt with a painful howl where it kicked into the air. Madawaak sheltered behind it and returned two of his own arrows. He hit their horses in the neck.

The animals screamed and bucked and turned. Their rides fell. The one run through with the spear fell heavy and still while the other quickly crawled for cover on the pathway.

Madawaak scampered away from behind the horse along the trail. He passed where the Pale Ones had thrown the women and children off the cliff and found the precipitous rocky ledges they would have climbed down.

* * *

Magnus and Hans passed through the growing fire on foot with their heads ducked low. Thor led the others back down the path on horseback. Magnus and Hans emerged from the fire with embers in their beards that singed away the hair. They coughed and staggered.

'That way! That way!'

Magnus grabbed Axel by the arm and lifted him. The three of them got to the top and Hans shot two arrows through the belly of the dead horse as they approached it. Magnus stormed up and swung his axe. The steel buried into the back of the horse. Magnus roared and followed the footprints in the snow with the two others behind him.

Suddenly, Hans screamed.

Magnus turned and saw him topple over the side off the hill, a sharp stick stuck through his foot that was buried in the snow. He crashed and rolled over the side. Magnus looked over just as he landed with a smack amongst the decimated bones of the skraelingjar they'd thrown down there. Mangled and twisted and still.

* * *

Thor led the six riders to a steeper, narrower way up on the other side of the hill. It too was covered in thickets that had dried and seemed to have been placed. Nothing was burning yet. He saw no flame. But he held the others anyway and they looked all over the rocky face for...

An arrow seemed to fly right out from the rocks and slam through the shoulders of Cilla's horse. It screamed and she leaped clear as it fell and started to kick its feet in the air. But the arrow was not burning.

'Go!' Thor screamed as arrows were flung back towards the spot whence the skraeling's had come. He charged up the passage with three others around him. They rode hard into the thickets and suddenly the horses screamed and came to a halt. The riders' bodies pitched forward. They rolled over the horses' necks and into the sharpened sticks that laid hidden in the thickets where their bodies were pierced; their bones cracked and they screamed as blood gurgled up into their gullets.

* * *

Magnus and Axel followed the sounds of the screams along the edge and found the narrow path down. Below them, Thor and the others lay screaming. Sticks rammed through their mangled bodies.

'Get up here!' Magnus screamed down at Cilla and Ari as she climbed up onto his horse. He turned to continue along the top. Axel's arm suddenly reached out and seized him across the chest.

At Magnus' foot, another sharpened stick peeked out from the snow.

Carefully, he stepped over it and the two continued to prowl along. Magnus leaned close to Axel.

'He'll come up behind us,' he whispered. Axel primed his bow. The screaming of the men in the thickets was slowly dying down. 'Now!'

They both turned quickly and Axel drew back the bow. The skraeling's hand grabbed the top of the bow and turned it skyward just as his tomahawk slammed into the back of Axel's helmet. The iron sheared in two. The body crumpled and fell away. Magnus swung his giant axe but Madawaak dropped down, rolled and threw a spear.

The spear stopped in Magnus' grip. He spun it about in his hand and threw it back at Madawaak, who quickly rolled right over the edge and disappeared. Magnus chased after him. He looked over the edge. Battle axe ready. But the skraeling slid down on his hands and knees, backwards, and jumped into the snow-covered bushes below.

'Ari!' he screamed as he hurried back to the pathway.

Ari emerged mounted as the horse struggled on the last leg. Magnus watched its bulging eyes and bursting veins as it scampered but suddenly gave up and fell. Ari jumped clear. Cilla hurried out of the way as the animal crashed onto its rump and then toppled backwards with a scream. It smacked into the rocky path with a loud snap and rolled a few feet limply. Then it came to a rest just below them, head at a sickening angle and tongue flopped out of its mouth.

'Are you alright?' Ari asked Cilla just as a spear crashed into his shoulder blade and burst through his chest in a fountain of blood. He fell into the ashy cinders of the thickets that had burned away. Cilla ducked low and ran up to the top of the hill.

There Magnus stood with his axe braced. His teeth shone through his singed beard.

Still the hunters in the thickets were screaming.

'What now?' Cilla breathed. She had her spear drawn and ready to hurl.

'Arouse that fire,' Magnus said. 'We can stall him until Lord Asny comes.'

Cilla kept the spear ready and edged over to the fire. Her knees trembled. With her gloved hand, she reached into the smouldering pyre for the topmost garments and...

The top garments flew up with a massive eruption of flame and enclosed her. She screamed as the burning skins draped over her face and shoulders.

* * *

Madawaak rammed his dagger into her face. Blood seeped through the fire. The scream stopped. He picked up a burning stick and charged at the giant. The Pale One received him with a swing from his axe that swept and then followed through with a chop but Madawaak ducked around him. He rammed the burning stake into Magnus' gut. Magnus cried out and swung his axe again as Madawaak rammed his dagger into the giant's neck. He then turned and ran along the top.

The giant chased him. Blood haemorrhaged from his neck and mouth but he chased with that axe clutched in his hands. The fire from the stake spread across his side. It caught the furs of his leathers and flared up like a coat of flame but still he kept coming. Madawaak stopped and turned to face him with a spear he'd had buried in the snow.

The giant swung the axe high and took a final step to lead into his blow. Right on top of the sharpened stake. He screamed out and buckled and Madawaak rammed the spear into his collar and the mighty Pale One reeled backward and fell down the narrow path into the thickets. The Pale Ones on the stakes could only watch in terror and agony as the flames spread from the giant's body out into the thickets and came towards them.

Madawaak stood at the top. Breathless. His flesh tender and weak and ready to let him collapse. But alive. He blinked hard as the fire consumed the thickets and the screams hit a new frantic pitch. Not time for collapsing yet.

He needed a tomahawk.

* * *

Asny rode hard across the waste with Viveka and Carl at her sides. Evening mists rose and consumed the landscape but ahead the black smoke had plumed and spread across the portion of the sky so they followed that. The horses were breathless. They wheezed and veered side to side. But Asny pushed on.

She couldn't let Magnus get in first.

The horde rode behind her and the thunder of their hoofs kept her central and focused as the snowy plain plunged into deep blue twilight. The rocky hills were near.

Ahead, from the mists, things started to emerge. Amidst the gloom, they looked like tall, thin mushrooms. Asny led them on closer. She turned to get a closer look at one...

Details emerged in the gloom. The hanging hair. The blood and pulped flesh that hung dry and rotting from the neck. The mouths. The eyes. Asny pulled up the horses as the great rocky outcropping loomed above them in the fog and the horde came to a halt.

The heads of Magnus' detachment led the way to the passage up.

'We go back,' she whispered.

'My Lord?' Viveka asked.

'Back! Back to the Chieftain!' Asny cried as she turned her horse about. They wouldn't make it tonight. But they rode behind their fevered leader in the dying traces of day that were left.

18

The Life of Demasduit

The chains came off once she was in the cage behind Freydis' arras. Demasduit checked the deep, red wounds around her wrists and ankles. She was lucky. Nothing crawling in them. But a pungent odour rose from them that unnerved her and the flesh turned jaundice around the edges of her ripped skin.

The cage did nothing to change the routine. That night, she was brought out by the two enormous men and tied across Freydis' bed. Freydis took off Demasduit's clothes.

'Make noise,' she whispered in Demasduit's language. Just as she did every night. 'Try. My mother always told me it would hurt less and pass quicker than if you resist.'

Then Torvard took his clothes off. His huge, white body with patches of red hair was so enormous, rounded and fleshy that Demasduit could not but recoil in horror. He was nothing that reminded her of pleasure. He climbed onto her like a huge mound. Didn't try to kiss or touch her. Just pushed into her. It was dry and painful in a way that pierced deeply into her and crushed and bruised her heart at the same time. All her spirit wanted to scream. But her voice was gone the moment he'd started. All her flesh ached and burned to struggle and fight but she could not move even with the range of play her bonds allowed her. Frozen and mute. The pain was more than physical. It repulsed her and roiled inside her gut and burned inside her skull and yet all she could do was lay there.

Freydis always watched. Sometimes she'd say little things in their tongue, of which Demasduit only knew their two names. But mostly she was silent.

When it was over, as with the last time and the time before that, Torvard would rear up, look into her eyes and she would feel his tears splash down on her neck and chest. He'd whisper something in a mournful tone. Then climb off her and retreat to the corner. Freydis then climbed on top of her. The two men entered and untied Demasduit's legs and Freydis pushed her knees up into her chest. Demasduit could feel the ooze seep inside her.

Then she cried. Heavily and deeply and mournfully enough that her father might have heard her. Madawaak. Chipchowinech. Even Mooaumook, so he would hear the suffering he had caused her.

When the fires that glowed red against the arras died down, it all went quiet. Torvard climbed into his bed. Demasduit watched him in the dark as he lay there. Freydis had gone beyond the arras and they were alone together. Desperation arose inside Demasduit. She hated that giant body there and wanted to cut it into pieces and burn it. But she wanted more to get out. To run through the icy night and back into the arms of family or someone she knew. Then go find Shanawdithit.

'Please,' Demasduit muttered in her own tongue. She watched as the body stirred. Went rigid. As though frightened by some alien sound in the night. 'Please.'

He whispered something. His tone was vulnerable and meek. Demasduit could have plunged her fingers through his eyes and pulled them out of his head. Her hatred was hot. She could taste it. But he was weak and Demasduit knew he didn't want to do what Freydis had him do night after night.

'Let me out,' she pleaded. 'Let me go.'

He said something, then pulled the furs up over his head.

Demasduit sobbed.

Shanawdithit. No matter what she endured there was a portion of her mind, some corner detached from all her suffering, that kept her sister in her thoughts. It was like a spring that fed her spirit. Kept her alive. When all the rest of her wanted to cease to exist or fall into the earth or collapse into dust and blow away into the wind and high into the air where not even the hands of the Pale Ones could seize her, Shanawdithit kept her whole. Her sister was alive.

The very promise that Shanawdithit would visit Demasduit in her dreams welcomed her into sleep when her flesh quivered and her heart ached so much that she'd never have otherwise found the peace. In the night she woke. Many times in deep darkness with no sound but the heavy breathing of the sleeping Pale Ones. Demasduit would find herself trying to dig through her own flesh into her womb with her fingers. Or to reach into herself. Pull him out. Rip out whatever he'd spit up inside her.

Futility dawned on her and the world was a dark nightmare again and Demasduit would fall back to sleep to escape into her dreams. There Shanawdithit waited for her.

The little girl moved amongst the ferns.

'Are you alive, my Shanawdithit?' Demasduit called.

The little girl emerged, her hair messy and her clothes tattered, but alive.

'Come find me.'

'I'm stuck, my Shana,' Demasduit said. 'Just know, wherever you are, that I love you and I want nothing but to see that you are safe somewhere. That alone keeps me alive.'

She turned and looked at Demasduit. Looked with empty eye sockets. Raw flesh peeked out from behind her eyelids.

'I dream of you too.'

Demasduit awoke. Daylight shone through the chimney flues. Freydis sat at the bars of her cage and stared at her. The sight sent a shudder through Demasduit.

'It hasn't worked yet,' Freydis bit.

'It's too early to tell,' Torvard said. Though he prayed to *Freyja* that soon she would bless this poor skraeling. Then his ordeal, at least, would be over.

'I know,' Freydis said. 'I can tell. I know a pregnant woman when I see one. This woman is without child.'

'She's still a girl,' Torvard said. 'Maybe she can't...'

'She can,' Freydis snapped and turned her head towards him but did not look at him. 'It just isn't working.'

'It never does. Not the first time,' Torvard answered as he sat on the edge of the bed and let his senses slowly gather. He ignored the guilt and self-disgust that stabbed him in the gut. 'It will take time.'

Freydis looked back at Demasduit and sighed. The skraeling had curled up in the back of the cage, away from her and held up her blankets like a frightened child.

'Perhaps there is another man who could do this job for me,' Freydis said. 'And occupy my bed while he's at it.'

'Freydis,' Torvard stood. 'I am trying.'

'You're not trying hard enough,' Freydis looked over her shoulder but again not at him. 'You're crying like a girl every time. Enjoy it! Be a man and pierce her cleft with passion! It won't work otherwise.'

'It will work,' Torvard argued, though the shake in his voice was obvious.

Freydis stood up and turned away from Demasduit.

'It had better.'

Then she was gone. Torvard dressed himself slowly and Demasduit did not move. He stopped as he passed by her cage.

'Please fall pregnant soon,' he said to her uncomprehending face. 'Pray to your gods as I do to mine. End this.'

Then he went to tend to his wife.

* * *

Outside the arras, Demasduit could hear the murmur of voices and shuffle and bustle of movement. Inside she felt like an endless void. A night sky that her spirit had fallen into and got lost in and where only one little star twinkled. Distant. Probably imaginary. Or already dead somewhere an unknowable distance away.

Shanawdithit.

The arras parted and the woman with the cuffs walked in with a large platter. One of the giant men who handled Demasduit for Freydis followed her and lifted her door from its hinges so the woman could step in. The woman had paler skin than Demasduit but she wasn't one of them. Her ankles were chained together, there were cuffs around her wrists and her hair was darker than theirs. The colour of raw ochre or tree sap. And her eyes were darker. The colour of the maple leaves in the Fall. She placed the platter down and looked at Demasduit as Demasduit looked back at her. In that moment, real life coursed through Demasduit again. Then the woman stepped backward out of the cage and the huge man closed the bars over the front of it and slid the hinges home and they both left her alone again.

Demasduit didn't want to eat. She wanted to vomit up all her insides and clean them off and then put them all back fresh and new. Then go find Shanawdithit. But she knew her sister was alive and therefore Demasduit had to stay alive. Somehow the two were giving each other strength simply by being. Demasduit felt it when she felt nothing else but pain. So she ate. Choked down the meal as she did the meal at sunset and the meal they brought her at noon.

When she was finished, the big man came back and he had a big woman with him. Both of them were Pale Ones. The big man unhinged her cage and the woman put a single cuff around Demasduit's neck connected to a chain that she held the other end of. Then she gave it a firm tug. The cuff dug into Demasduit's neck and jerked her head. She got upright and they walked her out from behind the arras.

Freydis sat at the table but ignored her. A small group of lesser Pale Ones gathered before her and spoke and she listened while she drank from a horn. Torvard sat at her side. The woman walked her out through the door, escorted by the giant man, and Demasduit saw the line of Pale Ones continued outside. Some were alone. Others were in groups. Demasduit could see how their hierarchies took form.

Freydis was their leader. Of this there was no doubt. Torvard sat beside her. Then there were the ones like this giant man and the woman he escorted. They had power but not as much as Freydis. Then there were those below them. Demasduit could see them working on their huts or building things. As they walked, she saw different huts had different Pale Ones in them and they all performed some task or another. They carved wood. They fashioned objects. Down by the water they built their giant canoes. One of them, in the hut that spewed the heavy smoke and smelled awful, made their weapons of shining stone. Demasduit could see it at a distance. They never walked her close enough to see how it was done.

Below, the workers were others. They were not true Pale Ones. Like the woman who brought her meals, they were all different. Some were brown and almost like Demasduit's people, but still bigger. Some towered and their skin was black as the night. Some were darker brown but not so black. Some were pale but with black hair. Some even wanted arms or legs. They all wore cuffs on their wrists and chains at their feet and that distinguished them.

Kept like the beasts in their pens, Demasduit thought. She wondered if Freydis had plans to keep her people the way she did these other people from distant worlds beyond the big water. Freydis had some plan for her.

A sickly feeling made Demasduit want to stop.

The Pale One woman tugged on the chain. Demasduit had to keep walking.

They walked over the crunchy, ash-stained snow and the structures thinned and soon they crossed the clearing. They went up the incline. Out of the cove. Trees surrounded them and the air smelled fresh with pine and Demasduit's eyes filled with tears. How she wished this freshness in the air, this stillness and purity, would take her body like an embrace and carry her spirit from her. Up into the clouds. Up away from all this. Into the nothing.

She would find Shanawdithit from anywhere in the sky.

At the top of the hill the trees cleared again and there were the ruins of the other Pale One village. The earth had reclaimed much of them. Now only the outlines of structures remained or the broken fragments of their turf walls or a rotten log half consumed by the snow and the clay. Demasduit felt deep sickness in her stomach. Like the spirits of those dead there churned inside her and worked Torvard's poison through her veins.

They kept walking along the coast. Followed along the bite that led them back towards the heart of the Forest Lands and

[236]

then across the river and back out towards the sea again. Then up along the cliffs. towards her old village. Demasduit stared out at the water and thought of all the years she'd spent idly staring out into it as though it went on forever and there were no worlds beyond it to know but whatever her imagination could put there.

But there were worlds. Worlds of Pale Ones. Worlds of cruel beasts that drove Pale Ones from their homes and to hers. What did compel them?

As they drew nearer to her village, Demasduit began to tremble. They were getting close. Surely Eenodsha's sentries would see them? Did the Pale Ones no longer fear her people, because they had her?

But no streams of smoke rose from the clifftop as they approached from below. No sounds. No songs. No smells of food and life. There was just one column of thick, black smoke and a foul odour of decay.

'No, no, no,' she began to whisper. And then as the truth gripped her and crushed her heart and everything inside her, Demasduit's knees buckled. She fell to the ground. The Pale One woman yanked at her collar but there was no pain. Nothing felt stronger than the ruin inside her. She cried and wept and wailed.

The giant man scooped her little body up in his arms and carried her the rest of the way. When they reached the smouldering ruin of her village, he threw her on the grass beside the pyre upon which twisted carcasses lay blackened, ruined and broken. Only the odd grasping hand with fingers curled sickeningly, half exposed skull with its mouth agape in mute agony, or rib cage exposed from beneath charred and flaked skin suggested that these were once men, women and children.

Demasduit screamed and howled until she found herself possessed of a sudden rush of energy. A despair so great it whipped up like a storm and lifted her to her feet. She leaped up and hurled herself towards the white ash and embers to be with her village.

The jerk at her chain punched the breath out of her lungs. The dry grass slammed against her back and Demasduit laid there. Her tears were blackened with ashy smoke.

Both the woman and giant man Pale Ones sat down. The woman was just far enough that the chain didn't allow Demasduit any movement beyond sitting upright. They spoke to each other. Words Demasduit couldn't comprehend. She laid there by the pyre of her entire world and the horrifying reality washed over her deeper and deeper like a rising tide.

Everyone was dead. Everyone.

Nobody would or could come to save her. Nothing would restore what was lost. She saw the faces of Shanawdithit, Chipchowinech, Madawaak, Oonban and everyone else. Even people she couldn't recall the names of. Gone. Gone forever.

Despair rose like the moon and Demasduit found herself still and calm. Everything detached. They'd use her, like they did Mooaumook, and then they'd dispose of her. She knew it. The only thing she could do now, Demasduit decided, was pray to the god spirits that she was infertile. That their plans for her would fail. Then Freydis would simply give up and kill her and move on to another plan and that would be the end.

The end would be like a sunrise, Demasduit thought. *The dawn of acceptance. Of no more conflict. No more learning. No more fighting.* As surely as if her world was cracked to pieces and sinking into the ocean, she felt the deep abyss of doom. There was nothing left to fight for. Nothing left to resist.

Kill the baby, she thought. *If it happens, that's what I'll do, kill the baby. That would be it.*

After a short while of silence, the Pale One woman stood and gave a painful tug at Demasduit's collar. The giant man groaned as he heaved himself to his feet. Together, they walked back to Straumfjord.

Demasduit was put back in her cage. The enslaved woman, whom Demasduit would come to know as The Venetian though she knew nothing of what that meant, brought her lunch. Then she was taken for another walk around the village. The Pale One woman, without speaking, showed her where they put grains in barrels and let it go mouldy to be turned into a foamy drink; where they crushed grapes to make another drink; where the women in cuffs and chains bathed the Pale One men and women alike in tubs of steaming warm water; and finally, the smelly little house at the side of the longhouse where women, all with cuffs and chains, prepared food for smoking or drying and salting. Demasduit saw The Venetian amongst them. The Venetian did not look at her.

Then at night she was tied to the bed. Torvard entered her and exploded into her and cried and then went to bed. Demasduit was thrown back in her cage. So it went. Over and over. Days changed to nights. Nights into days. The snow melted away and the grass rose from the hardened earth. Colour sprung up in the forests and the sunlight warmed with each new dawn. On and on the routine went. Demasduit lost the will to think. Daydreams left her. She spent one night trying to remember her name.

Then, one morning, her body felt different.

* * *

Freydis tensed with silent excitement as she watched Demasduit vomit up the rest of her breakfast. She turned to Torvard.

'It's happened,' she said, breathless. 'It worked.'

19

Terms of Surrender

'Is this all? This *can't* be all,' Makdaachk said as he looked over the last of his visiting guests.

They gathered outside his mamateek. The host families who stood on the sides, waiting to receive them, outnumbered the guests so much that each host family might only have had to welcome one member of each visiting family.

'You didn't see them all!' Makdaachk screamed at Mekwek, the young nephew he'd sent on the gathering errand.

'Shendeek is old and frail,' Mekwek excused. 'He said he can spare nobody after the intensity and all the migrating of the winter. Wobee is still nowhere to be found.'

'Forget Wobee,' Makdaachk slapped Mekwek on the back of his head. 'He is not one of us anymore. What of Douajavik? Where is Douajavik?'

'There is nothing left up there,' Ninejeek reported. He seemed smaller, greyer of colour since last anyone outside his family had seen him. A light inside him had dimmed and left him hollower and weaker. 'There is no Douajavik. There is no Mountain Father anymore.'

'They have gone to the Farther People!' Makdaachk spat.

'They are dead, Makdaachk,' Keathut said. His mangled arm was bandaged in skins as though it were only a stump. 'Slaughtered to their last. We are all there is left.'

Makdaachk looked over them sombrely. He nodded his head.

'Then we will do. Make yourselves comfortable. We will sit together at nightfall.'

* * *

'Where are your sons?' Keathut asked Makdaachk when everyone had settled and joined him around his fire in his mamateek. Wathik and other women of her village moved around the circle and portioned out platters of meat, water and pudding for them, but otherwise kept their distance.

'My son?' Makdaachk murmured. 'My son is why I have called you here.'

Tears flooded his eyes and his voice became choked.

'My son is dead. Mooaumook is slain by them...'

'But your oth...'

'I have called you here to mount another attack on the cove,' Makdaachk declared as he suddenly swallowed his tears and composed himself beneath a veil of maniacal determination. 'Not to talk. Not to ponder. Not to prepare. But to form the strongest hunting party we can and lead a second raid of their village. To do as we did the first time. Before the winter. Before we knew we were doomed.'

'Where is your other son, Makdaachk?' Keathut pressed. 'Where is Gheegnyan?'

'Dead to me!' Makdaachk cried with a wave of his hand. 'I have no other son.'

'Regardless of whom his father is,' Ninejeek said. 'Keathut has asked you where Gheegnyan is.'

'He ran off with the coward Wobee,' Makdaachk said. 'Hiding in the depths of the forest beyond the lakes. He is not one of us.'

'What you propose,' Ninejeek started slowly, 'would kill us all.'

'Of course the half-Farther One says that,' Makdaachk said.

'He is right,' Keathut said.

'Well of course it will!' Makdaachk retorted. 'Are you in denial? There is no victory against the Pale Ones. Our world is ended. No force can defeat them. They have massacred Gobidin and Oonban, they have killed my son. There is no future for us. But we can leave something in their memories. We can leave scars on their bodies. We can be remembered as people who did not die off quietly or in fear as Wobee chooses to.'

Silence hung over the council.

'What happened to Demasduit?' Kukuwes of the Great River questioned. 'Why have we heard nothing of Douajavik but that they are gone? Where are they?'

'We failed Demasduit,' Ninejeek said. 'They knew where she was going somehow... somehow... I don't know how. Nobody knows how but they... there is nothing left of Douajavik and the people of Moisammadrook. Nothing but bones and ashes. They were slaughtered and Demasduit was taken.'

'It is true,' Keathut confirmed. 'I tried to stop them.'

He held his bandaged hand close to his chest.

'I have seen the one that leads them. She is woman, of their kind. But fiercer than all of them. It is like she can see in the dark. Her hair is like flame and her eyes can see through flesh. She left me this,' Keathut held up his hand. 'And she spoke to me.'

'She spoke to you?' Kukuwes quickened.

'In our language. As purely and clearly as I speak to you now.'

'Our language?' Ninejeek asked, breathless. 'Only the children of the God Spirits may speak our language, otherwise Mi'kmaq would...'

'I tell you she spoke to me and said my name!' Keathut snapped as his lip began to tremble.

'You lie,' Makdaachk said slowly. 'You lie!'

'I do not lie Makdaachk,' Keathut said. 'But I can see that grief has stolen the senses from you. Do not accuse me again. She spoke. Their leader spoke.'

'It is lie...'

'What did she say?'

'A lie...'

'She said... shut up Makdaachk!'

'You lie.'

'She said she means to make a child with Demasduit,' Keathut said. 'She means to impregnate her with the seed of one of her men.'

'It can't be done,' Ninejeek said.

'If it can...' Kukuwes began.

'It can't...'

'If it can... then they are of the god spirits.'

'It can't be done.'

'Wouldn't you have said the same of a Pale One speaking our language if you didn't know better?' Kukuwes asked. 'We may be wrong.'

Makdaachk sat quietly. His eyes hung wide and his mouth was distorted in a sour twist. He stared at Kukuwes.

'It is true,' Ninejeek said. 'We were promised only the god spirits can speak our tongue. That is enough. But if the strongest spirit that walks amongst us now can bear a child with one of them then we must accept them as our own.'

'But they kill us. They murder us!' Makdaachk said. 'They are our enemies! The Farther People speak our tongue and make children with us. That gives them no privileges!'

'The Farther Ones were kin to us and they broke with us,' Keathut said. 'It is different. The Pale Ones have no history with us. They are not of our kin. If they are of the God Spirits then we must accept that we are not.'

'We are promised that we are,' Makdaachk said.

'We were promised many things,' Ninejeek said.

'We do not know it can be done yet,' Makdaachk noted. 'And I do not believe the words of Keathut. I think he has lost his mind. From grief. Or wounded pride. I don't know. My mind is sound. A sane man would see that...'

'A sane man would have stopped the Pale Ones and rescued Demasduit or died trying!' Mekwek said. Makdaachk gently touched his arm.

'A sane man would have come to the aid of the other Forest Fathers,' Keathut said. 'Instead of waiting for *us* to come and for *them* to all be dead.'

A long uncomfortable silence.

Suddenly, Mekwek prickled up. He cocked his head. Others listened as well and heard the dull rumble like a small stampede of caribou. But the beasts were bigger.

[243]

Pale One riders.

'You didn't post sentries!' Keathut spat at Makdaachk as they all jumped to their feet and hurried outside the mamateek.

The night was crisp and clear. A few men had charged from their mamateeks in excited haste, bows and arrows ready, but froze upon seeing what the council saw.

The village was surrounded by a sparse line of them. Pale Ones atop their beasts with their spears held ready and arrows set in their bows. Just beyond the edge of their village, by the shores of the lake and facing Makdaachk's mamateek, was the demon-woman herself. The village was gripped in a tense silence. Flesh braced for Pale One arrows and spears to burst through it.

'Makdaachk,' the demon called. 'I have come to sit on your council.'

Makdaachk buckled and almost fell. Mekwek quickly gripped him under the arms and propped him up. He looked at the other fathers of his council.

They stared back at him. Stern. But the fear in their eyes could not be contained.

Makdaachk looked back at the demon as her beast carried her slowly closer to them.

'I did not come to kill anyone,' she said. 'My name is Freydis. I am the Chieftain of the Pale Ones. Demasduit carries my husband's child.'

'Don't speak to her,' Mekwek whispered into Makdaachk's ear. 'Say nothing.'

'We are kin,' Freydis said.

'You killed our people,' Keathut shouted.

'Keathut,' Freydis said with a grin. She was close enough now that they could make out her face in the dim starlight. 'I had to show you our strength so you would no longer want for the Farther People's. You have seen now that no enemy can stand before us. But with our people united we will rule this world.'

'We have no desire to rule this world,' Ninejeek said.

'Then *we* shall,' Freydis said. 'But you will forever have our kinship and protection. It is the least we can do for the gift you have given my people. A child. Half-bred between our bloods. Your mightiest and my greatest. The child shall unite us. Then your enemies will become our enemies. You will fear nothing. Never again.'

'Demasduit will not carry your child to birth,' Keathut said. 'She will never allow it.'

'I know you believe so,' Freydis said. 'At the end of her pregnancy, I shall return here with them both. Until then you will live your lives. My people will live ours. We shall be as separate as we can be on this little portion of the world until my child is born. Then I will come back with Demasduit and the child. Both of them. You will see she is willing. You will see she is with me. And then we shall discuss the terms of your surrender to me. They will be greatly in your favour.'

There was silence.

'I have corrected a mistake you were about to make,' Freydis said. 'The Farther People would never have stood a chance against me. Now they will never stand a chance against us.'

She gave a nod, turned her beast and rode back off into the forest. Around them, the Pale Ones receded from the pool of starlight by the shimmering lake and followed her into the surrounding darkness.

* * *

Her body changed.

Demasduit watched it and felt it. But she could conjure no thoughts of it. Nothing stuck. Only fleeting fancies. What was this thing that grew inside her? Would it stretch her out until she burst open? Kill it, she'd think. Roll over in the night and lay on top of it. But when the nights fell Demasduit found that she couldn't physically get herself over. Her legs thinned. Her arms were bony and narrow. Even the skin around Demasduit's face felt thin and as though it stretched every time she wept or opened her mouth to drink or eat. All her energy seemed to be sucked into her swelling abdomen. The thing that grew inside her.

[245]

Momentary lapses would have Demasduit feel affection for Freydis now and then. Someone who cared in a cruel world that had abandoned her. That was all it was. Whenever the truth of how Demasduit had got here, who had done this to her, and the reason why she was here faded from her mind there was only caring, concerned Freydis. When Demasduit would catch them, the guilt would stab her like a dagger to the gut.

But there were other pains in there now.

They brought her more food. More water. Demasduit knew it was all they could think to do. Freydis watched always, awash with concern. Torvard was seldom to be seen but for night-time when he came to collapse next to his wife and sleep like death because Freydis had left him to manage her usual affairs. Demasduit seldom saw anything that did not have Freydis around it. Not the inside of the longhouse, not the village, and not the route of her walk that either Casper or Gustav took her on while Inga held her chain as always. Freydis was with her everywhere.

Watching and worrying.

Demasduit walked with them. But every day, little by little, she felt her energy fade. Breath was gone before they reached the ruins of the village she'd come from. Mind gone most of the time. Demasduit found that, as she trembled and regained herself amongst the ashes and ruins and bones, she could not remember who else had lived here. What they'd called her. Faces came and went like sunlight that winked off the melting icicles but there were no names.

Shanawdithit. She'd remember it now and then. A little girl. But nothing more. Nothing of what became of the real person or what the real person ever meant to her.

She woke one morning full of intent she'd not possessed since her memory could recall. Like an echo of a life she'd led before this one, a time before cages and Pale Ones and chains, reached out of the abyss that had swallowed everything she knew and everything she was and filled Demasduit with dreams and desires and needs again. There were her family. Oonban. Shanawdithit. Chipchowinech. Yaseek. Odensook. Madawaak.

All alive and in her mind again. Their faces, their voices, their scent and the feeling of them near. As real as though she could get up and run to them and see them and talk to them and touch them again.

It was a dream. She knew it had to have been a dream she couldn't remember. Lost things from her mind had snuck up in dreams and tricked Demasduit into thinking their presence surrounded her again.

'You look thoughtful this morning,' Freydis said as she watched though the bars. 'Much more alive than I've seen you of late. Perhaps you're getting better?'

Demasduit said nothing. Suddenly the thought was horrifying. In her stasis she could do nothing but waste away but in health she knew this half Pale One would come out of her in time. Soon. It wasn't far off. And then Demasduit would be healthy but her people would be doomed.

Aeda brought her food for the morning. Freydis had explained Aeda. She'd come from a land called Sicily. Her country was called Syracuse. Demasduit wondered what it was like before and after the Pale Ones came to it. It didn't have Aeda anymore, for one thing. How many others? How long did they hold the Pale Ones off before people like Aeda became their thralls?

Demasduit knew she could never allow it.

The meal stayed down so Gustav and Inga came with the collar and chain. They took her from her cage and walked her through the longhouse. Freydis didn't join them today. She stayed at her table while karls crowded and meandered around and Freydis' guards worked to form them into an orderly line.

They walked out of the village and through the grass that had yellowed and become coarse against their ankles as they swished through it. The leaves on the maple trees had turned golden. As Inga led her up towards the Icelander's village, the first of the big maple leaves were fluttering down to the ground. The forest had an amber shade. It smelled rich and ripe and already there where whispers of the coming winter on the gentle breeze that rustled the brittle treetops.

Demasduit was out of breath. Her back ached. The bulk she carried at her front pulled her down towards the ground. But she pushed on. Careful not to let sturdy Inga or Gustav see the discomfort. She wiped the sweat from her brow. It stung her eyes as it dripped into them. But she pushed on.

The dead village. Its occupants had come from a world called Iceland. Freydis told Demasduit she was born there as well, during a battle between different clans of Pale Ones. Freydis was born of the heat of war. Her first years were lived amid destruction and violence. Demasduit looked down at the bulge in her front. Worse still for this little one.

They walked until they were high on the cliff's edge and then headed towards the scant, ashy remains of Demasduit's home village. There, the cliffs were high and the ocean raged below them. Gently she moved closer as they ascended the hillside. Inga and Gustav didn't notice. She walked a few more steps and walked closer to the ledge again. Still no notice. Demasduit didn't feel the fatigue or the sweat that cascaded down her body anymore. Not even the agony in her back. She moved closer. Her heart thudded hard against her chest. Now Demasduit could look over the side and see the white rolling caps smash and burst into the air on the jagged rocks below.

It won't hurt, she thought. Nothing hurt anymore.

She took another step closer. Only then, like a wave, did her body suddenly feel the immense fatigue. Like it had built up all this time. As though her bones were suddenly gone. She stumbled.

Quickly!

Demasduit threw herself towards the cliff edge. Her feet felt the tufts of grass that thickened before the massive updraft of salt air, ready to leap into it...

The massive arm of Gustav caught her. Swept her clear off her feet and cradled her. Inga curled the chain around her wrist and stood close by. Demasduit was carried back to Straumfjord.

* * *

At last the tide receded enough. Madawaak carried his canoe out from the caves and laid it out on the surface of the water. It bobbed up and down. Out beyond the mists, the swells rose like mountains and died down again without breaking. It was the best chance he'd have.

What was dying anyway?

The Pale Ones still have sentries up at the cradle, waiting for me. They won't come looking for me, Madawaak thought. *I can stay a little while longer...*

But the sea was seldom so kind as what he looked at. No breakers. No roaring foam or crashing droplets sparkling in the Autumnal amber sunlight. This was as good as it got.

Madawaak took the oar and pushed the birchbark canoe he'd spent months building off the stones and out into the icy water. He jumped in. Immediately, the daggers of freezing water plunged into his thighs and feet. But the canoe didn't flood. Madawaak rowed into the onslaught of swells and watched as his bow rose skyward and then plunged down into the unforgiving abyss. But it held. He rowed onward. These were the little swells. Out there, between him and the Island People, were the mighty walls of water. Smooth and blunt. They would not stay that way for long.

Madawaak rowed.

* * *

The seemingly endless hours of ragged screaming stopped suddenly. Freydis looked at the arras and Torvard put his hand on her back and she shrugged him off. The nigh-empty longhouse was silent.

'She's dead,' Freydis whispered, breathlessly. 'She's taken my baby with her...'

As though in response, the tiny cries of a distressed infant issued. Freydis shot to her feet. Torvard stood beside her and tried to touch her again, moved as he was by this sudden childlike eagerness. He'd never seen her so human. She put her fingertips over her mouth and stared at the arras.

Finally, Inga stepped through. Aeda, with red-stained sheets bundled in her arms, stepped out and hurried across the longhouse to the door. Freydis leaped on Inga and gripped her collar in white fingers. Those huge green eyes sought answers in Inga's face before she could ask them.

'A son,' said Inga. 'You have a son.'

Torvard's hand slipped from Freydis. His heart sank. *Wrong,* he thought. *Deeply, deeply wrong.*

Freydis shoved past Inga and hurried behind the arras. Torvard followed her. Thrall women pulled the soiled sheets out from under Demasduit, who lay sweat-streaked on her back. Torvard saw she was still bleeding. Torn open. Badly. But the child was in Freydis' arms.

A terracotta-coloured boy nestled at Freydis' breast. She stared down into its sleepy face, now at rest, and Torvard watched her. He looked at Demasduit. The skraeling's eyes were closed. Her head lolled from side to side on the pillow. He wanted to touch her. Wipe the sweat off her. Comfort her in some way.

'Put her together,' Torvard said to the thralls. 'Stop the bleeding. Can't you see she's bleeding?'

Freydis stood entranced. Her absolute focus never left the boy's face. She didn't even blink.

Demasduit was awake. Her head was raised suddenly and her eyes were open and fixed on the child. Freydis must have seen, because she quickly left through the arras. Demasduit crashed back down into her blankets. Torvard's flesh prickled. The emotions surged in an incomprehensible deluge.

The boy, he suddenly thought. There was nothing he could do for Demasduit and he wanted to meet his son. Though he felt the kick of shame as he left the skraeling, it felt him as soon as he'd crossed back around the arras and seen the child awake in Freydis' arms as she leaned against the table with him. His little eyes squinted and explored the world. His little mouth opened and closed. When he looked at Torvard, a hot shiver ran through Torvard's body. His body no longer inhabited his own heart, it was there in Freydis' arms.

[250]

And yet he felt sickly still. Wanted to look at the boy, but not to touch. Not to hold. It was wrong. As though all the world suddenly slanted inexplicably and constantly. This was wrong.

Freydis finally looked at her husband.

'Eirik,' she said. 'For my father. And because he shall conquer worlds. Torvardsson. Because you gave him to me.'

Torvard wanted to faint.

'I thought he was to be Freydisson in the event of a boy,' Torvard said. His voice sounded weak and frail.

'You gave me my son,' Freydis said. 'I want you to see that I am grateful. Eirik Torvardsson.'

'Thank you,' Torvard coughed. Then turned and crossed towards the door.

He needed air. Air would clear his thoughts.

* * *

Makdaachk looked at his tiny council. Still more Fathers had failed to show even though he'd told Mekwek not to inform them that this council had been called at Freydis' request. Still, Shendeek sat with them this time. That was one more. And the most respected of the River Fathers. If Freydis offered them truth...

'Perhaps they won't come tonight?' Kukuwes offered as she shuffled uncomfortably again. 'Perhaps they lied to us.'

'Then we kill them all,' Makdaachk said. The archers that surrounded them in the forest would not be seen. His boys. Taught by Mooaumook to be silent and unseen hunters. Today, if Freydis came to them without a half-breed...

One boy looked through the curtain that was the door of Makdaachk's mamateek.

'They're here,' he reported, breathless and wide-eyed.

The council, without Keathut or Ninejeek, followed Makdaachk outside into the crisp air of the young winter. The riversides were thick with fallen leaves. There on the banks stood the horses with their riders atop. They waited patiently. The council approached slowly and with caution. With them, mounted on the horse of a huge man, was the boy Moosin, who had been sent to see Demasduit and verify that there was no child but hers.

Freydis had a bundle in her arms.

'Where are the rest?' she asked.

'Gone,' Makdaachk said. 'Perhaps to join Wobee.'

Freydis snorted and smirked.

'They will not last long.'

Gently she unwrapped the skins from the baby. A chubby, healthy little boy was slowly unveiled, and she held him up for the council to see. Moosin didn't have to speak. All their breath left them the second they laid eyes on the curious child whose hands grasped at the air, whose feet kicked and whose eyes were deep and brown with the ageless wisdom and unnerving strength that Demasduit's eyes had possessed all her life.

'Kneel,' Freydis ordered.

Makdaachk went first. They had never kneeled before, not one of them, but his knees touched the earth and the council followed. Only Shendeek stood, brow furrowed and eyes downcast.

'Defy me, skraeling?' Freydis asked him. 'Defy the God Spirits?'

Shendeek shook his head and slowly raised his weary old eyes that peered from beneath heavy wrinkles. 'I only want to know of Demasduit. Is she alive?'

'Alive, Shendeek,' Moosin answered. 'Alive.'

Shendeek looked down again and nodded. Then, gently, he eased himself down to his knees and bowed his head towards Freydis.

* * *

Kaia's hands trembled as they always did for an Althing. She hadn't spoken to Jannik but to collect his tributes and she'd avoided the others as much as she could since she'd got back, but still every time... every single time, she expected to be dragged out before the Althing and then tried and sentenced by Freydis.

The half-breed child was asleep. But as it's skraeling mother wandered about with the other thralls who served their ales, wines and platters she still looked around it. The first few months Freydis had always had the child with her. Even asleep. Althings were held in hushed tones. Demasduit had never taken her eyes off the child.

Kaia wiped a bead of sweat from her brow.

'Nine years,' Freydis said. 'We have nine years before my brother the King will send the numbers I asked for. Nine years to round up the skraelingjar of Helluland. To their last. I have already sent one family of Markland skraelingjar to Thorfinn the Karlsefini's settlement aboard a faering for him to use. They will read the land and track their natural enemies. Thorfinn will then capture them and send them home. For sale to whoever wants them. Perhaps the Christians will name a price and we may come to an accord. But we aren't finished. Beyond a narrow straight lies the mainland.'

Demasduit had stopped serving. She stood there and stared at Freydis as though she could understand what was being said. Freydis took no notice.

'It will take generations to conquer,' Freydis said. 'And the skraelingjar there will not...'

Demasduit turned and ran. Freydis could only stand there and watch as the first ever skraeling thrall threw itself into the fire pit. The furs on Demasduit's back flared up with flame. Other thralls rushed in and pulled the flailing body out. Demasduit screamed. But as soon as they had her out, she rose, still flaming, and leaped headlong back into the glowing red coals.

'Keep them back!' Freydis screamed. Her champions moved in to restrain the rescuing thralls by the wrists lest they leap in after her.

The skraeling screamed and flailed and writhed until it could scream no more. Then the bright tongues of flame raged. Demasduit writhed and twisted and turned.

Finally she was still. Aeda let out a cry of horror as the carcass burned before their eyes and the stink of the furs it wore and its

bubbling flesh filled the longhouse. Smoke from the fat and skins filled the room. The Althing quickly evacuated outside.
Freydis wasn't with them.

20

Nine Years Later

The fish doubled onto itself as the spear pierced through its scales and the ruby blood billowed up to the oily surface. Madawaak stumbled to the edge of his canoe. The water sloshed and the flimsy boat rocked and bumped under his weight. The unusually calm day was forgotten. Madawaak struggled to keep the spear straight and hold the fish steady as it thrashed and sent pink foam bubbling around the long wooden shaft. He bent his knees, placed one hand midway down the length and the other at the end and hauled the catch up. Madawaak felt the canoe sink deeper beneath him. The fish flopped over the fragile wooden gunwale and he heard it crack beneath the weight, but he had his catch aboard.

The fish flopped and the flanks of the canoe rippled and creaked under the assault of its strength. Madawaak quickly braced one foot against its slippery skin. He drew out the spear and rammed it into the fish's eye. It tensed and curled over. The mouth gaped and closed as though it gasped for air. The tail thwacked against the bow of the canoe twice, four times, five times and then flickered and stopped.

Madawaak collapsed into his canoe, exhausted, and looked at the great fish. *Ten passings of the seasons,* he recalled. Ten since he'd brought his feeble ability to catch smelt from the rivers with his bare hands to the Island People and been laughed at for not being a fisherman. Ten since he'd taken his tent and set up a small home on the windy cove on the southern end of the island. Away from the others.

The great salmon was nigh half the length of his canoe. Victory ran sweet through his veins. It would grant him some respect, at least, if not cure him of everything that kept him far from the greater community of the smallest and most isolated islet of the archipelago between the Broken Lands and the Forest Lands.

Suddenly he wanted to throw the fish back. Let the ocean heal the wound over and the great, muscular body pitch itself into the depths where Madawaak's spear could never reach it. There was enough meat beneath the shimmering scales to feed the entire village of his little island. But they would only accept it so that a being did not die in vain.

'Oh, fish,' he breathed as he rubbed his hands over his face. It was an unusually clear day and sunlight reflected off the gloomy ocean surface and shone through his fingers a pinkish glow. As he parted them, Madawaak saw something pass between his stretch of water and the craggy, black coast of the Broken Lands. An ominous cloud moved through his flesh before he looked.

For a moment, Madawaak could not breathe.

The giant canoe was carried on bulging sheets and flanked with their round shields. The great wooden hull scythed through the water on the slight breeze while the carved monster at the bow bobbed up and down and stared vacantly ahead. It was them. They were close enough to see him.

Though he trembled, Madawaak looked over his shoulder. His island refuge was not visible even on the clear day. The dark, gently lolling sheet of water stretched all the way to the still and straight horizon.

He looked back at their canoe. They moved still towards the open ocean beyond the north-western peninsula of the Broken Lands and had not changed their course. But Madawaak had no doubt in his mind they'd seen him. His flesh seized and he could not row the canoe back home.

Shouldn't anyway, he thought. Maybe they were waiting for him to do just that and then follow him. Why steer off course for one? There were many where he came from. Lands yet unconquered by them.

Madawaak moved the fish down below the gunwale and sat still. Watched the huge vessel. It rocked longways as it went and the water split with long white wounds at the sides of its bow and spread across the surface in its wake. It moved fast.

Silently, Madawaak cursed *Aich-mud-Yim* for giving him a clear day. One so very rare. And then to fill it with these devils!

He told himself he would wait them out as his flesh slowly settled and that old rage began to bubble inside him again. That old rage that never went away but bubbled when he thought about them. When he saw something that reminded him of them... dried grass like the hay in their shiny hats, a glimmer on the water's surface like the sunlight winking on the edge of their axes, blood red as that which had stained the snow on the cradle top, the shape of his wife's eyes when she looked innocently up at him, it always came... That rage that made his tongue taste of blood and hatred. That balled his fists and made them shoot out at any soft thing around him. The hay. The water's surface. The bleeding being, dead or alive. Her face.

Hot air blasted Madawaak's top lip as he snorted at them. The cold air that carried the ship felt coarse and foul against his skin. The big water mocked him with its serenity. Madawaak wanted to row towards them.

They'd run me through with their spears and arrows before I get close enough to see their faces, he thought. *But still a good death. Better than leading them home.*

Visions ran through his mind. Bodies split or dismembered. Mouths open as ragged screams issued from the bloodied throats. Bodies in the snow. Dead flesh that once throbbed with life and radiated warmth and was his friend and his family. *Them.* The hatred for them.

Madawaak thrashed as the fish had. Beat the sides of his canoe and roared and kicked the dead fish at his feet. The sights of those he'd killed flashed through his mind. The screams of the children. The surprise in the eyes as they looked upon the last thing they'd ever see. The way the faces fell still as he chopped his tomahawk into them. The silence after those last screams. His skin felt hot. Mind buzzed. Skin flushed deep red...

Then, as though the bubbles burst to his surface, he stopped still. His fists were bleeding. On Madawaak's mind there was nothing but a face that had not appeared to him in so long he couldn't believe how clear it was. How clear *she* was. Her big brown eyes that seemed to look knowingly into some distant place nobody else could see. The way they'd flicker side to side as he spoke... The smooth, soft skin despite the punishment she dealt it. The flat nose. The pouted lips. The oval face.

'Demasduit,' it left his lips. The word wounded him. As though he'd ignored someone he loved for all this time and now felt the pain of his own betrayal. A sickly stab deep inside. Tears flooded his eyes.

When the tears dried, the Pale One canoe was gone. Madawaak seized his oars and rowed towards his island. *It won't be long. If they had come this far, it would not be long.*

* * *

Adothe's sprightly eyes flickered around the rocky outcropping that formed a fortress-like wall around his village just southwest of the centre of their island home. Cold wind whistled through the peaks as it picked up while the sun began to set. The frosty twilight was dim and deep. Fires ignited around the village while the hunting party waited for their Father as the small man with a deeply wrinkled face leaned impatiently on his bow and awaited more from the breathless Madawaak.

When he saw no more was coming, he croaked; 'But they weren't coming this way?'

'Not this time,' Madawaak responded. 'But they were close enough to have seen a hint of our shores.'

The wind whipped the fine strands of white hair around the old man's head. He nodded and turned upon his heel with youthful energy in spite of his apparent age and narrow, wiry frame. The hunting part took the tail of the huge salmon from his grip and carried it towards the largest bonfire in the camp, at the center of the village, where the women and girls stood by with their toughened skins to wrap it in. Smoke from the wet wood wafted thick around them.

'Thank you for the catch,' Adothe said. His voice was deceptively deep and gravelly.

[259]

'Call the Island Fathers together,' Madawaak urged. The strain on his voice echoed the urgency that he'd made the request with so many times so many years ago. Before he'd given up. Become a village unto his own. 'Grant me an audience.'

Adothe had already turned away again. He stopped midstride and slapped his bow against his skinny thigh. 'We do not call each other together. We do not have audiences.'

'Adothe, Father,' Madawaak said. Stopped himself from seizing the old man by the arm. 'What I told you was true. I was young and I did not know patience yet and I am sorry for the offences I caused. Take my next catch as an offering. But heed me. Please. They will come. They came from farther away to find more families and they will come here as well. When the mainland has fallen. If it has not already. And there are none of us left anywhere else but here they will come. With them weapons...'

'...of shining stone...'

'I have seen few of them lay waste to many great warriors.'

'Then we have no chance however many of us there are,' Adothe said. He sighed and looked down to Madawaak's feet and slowly back to his eyes again. 'Becoming a man in my country has not taken the bloodthirst from you. Time has shown that. Tonight proves it. I forgave you already for your offences. I forgave you when you forced my niece to breathe through her mouth for the rest of her life. I forgave you because I believed you would grow up. That becoming one of us would take the hatred and the war out of your spirit. But it has not. You come before me tonight and offer me fish to start war. Even now. As a man. All you've shown me, Madawaak of the Forest, is that we are different people. Yours are war mongers. Full of violence. Our forefathers were right to exile themselves. I was wrong to allow you to stay here.'

'What will you do when they come?' Madawaak bit back as he felt the blood rise to his skin so the shame would colour his face. 'Hide? Run?'

'We do not make violence,' Adothe said, firmly. 'Violence will not come to us.'

* * *

Madawaak's hands shook as he struck the small fire in his flimsy mamateek. The constant breeze battered the thin walls and distorted the frame again, only, this time, he gave no thought to fixing it. He huffed and tears filled his eyes. The fire would not spark. He threw the flint aside and crawled out of the mamateek and watched as the calm waves gently swilled and flooded the rock pools below his home. The wind was cuttingly icy. Tears felt hot against his face, then cooled quickly. Madawaak closed his eyes and stood still as the wind whipped around his skins and chilled his flesh.

'Demasduit,' he whispered. The name felt heavy in Madawaak's mouth and weighted his heart down as it spilled from his lips. 'What has become of Demasduit?'

Taken, he mused. *Taken by them to make their child.*

A stumbling on the rocks behind him called Madawaak's attention and he turned slowly, uncaring as to what or who had followed him home. With a yelp, the small body slipped and fell and crashed down onto the dirt and then leaped to his feet and crossed his hands to hide his embarrassment. Then he just looked at Madawaak with those little, half-moon eyes that seemed constantly to smile even when angry, just like his older sister.

'Adothe would not be happy you've come to visit me,' Madawaak said.

'Adothe doesn't know,' Shensee said.

Madawaak turned back to his little mamateek and gathered the small clumps of tinder to try again at the fire. He knew already there was no sending Shensee away. And in truth he didn't want to. Though he'd never truly loved his wife, rather sought refuge in her flesh from Demasduit who haunted his heart and the Pale Ones whose slaughter of his people and whose deaths at his hands still ravaged his mind like frantic beasts that lurked in the darkness between his thoughts, the company of her younger brother seemed to comfort Madawaak with a sense of true forgiveness. The boy would get himself in trouble, but Madawaak would let him stay.

He was already crouched next to Madawaak. Waiting for the warmth.

'They always said fire wouldn't burn here.'

'It rarely does.'

'But it does. When you make it.'

'Your people like things the way they are.'

'You're my people.'

'You know I'm not.'

'Well I don't remember when you came from somewhere other than here, so that makes you my people.'

Madawaak scraped the flint.

'And I don't like things the way they are. I like fire to happen where I want it to.'

'In the rain?' Madawaak smiled. He looked at the boy, then looked away. The horrors that lived in him had caused him to mutilate Shensee's sister. Caused her to flee her home. He would not hurt the boy. He would die before he hurt any of her family again. But he was afraid his eyes would show the boy something that lived beneath their surface if he looked too long.

'Not in the rain,' Shensee was saying. 'Doesn't look like it's going to burn tonight.'

'It doesn't,' Madawaak said as he dropped the flint to one side. 'You should go back before you get cold.'

'Don't you get cold here?'

Madawaak sat back on his furs and said nothing. His stomach growled.

'I want to talk for a while,' Shensee said as he climbed to his feet. He was able to stand upright in the mamateek, even younger now than Madawaak was when he survived the massacre on the cradle top. 'I don't have a big sister to talk to anymore.'

Madawaak closed his eyes and swallowed the wound. The boy didn't mean it.

'It's cold.'

'Won't you get cold?'

'I live out in the cold because I hurt someone I shouldn't have,' Madawaak hid the tremble in his voice as images flickered across his mind while he spoke. Hid it behind force. Aggression. He winced as the memories of striking Tashedtheek blended with skulls that crushed and split open beneath his tomahawk or the blood and viscera that spilled over his hand as he plunged a dagger into the soft flesh of bellies and sides. Some of those bodies were younger than Shensee...

He caught the thought.

'You should go.'

'Are Pale Ones really coming here?'

Madawaak looked at the boy gently. Kept his eyes focused on Shensee's elbow or arm.

'I've seen them close.'

'I have heard they're giants. With strange weapons that are sharper and colder than stone.'

'You'll give yourself nightmares.'

'Why do you think they'd come here?'

Madawaak said nothing and looked at the floor.

'The Elders say that the Pale Ones come from the god spirits to punish the violence of the Forest People and the People of the Broken Lands. We of the Islands never hurt the Farther People. The Farther people never hurt us. Why would Pale Ones come here to punish us?'

'I don't know,' Madawaak half-whispered. The howling wind swallowed his voice while the frame crackled and the hut tilted even more.

'Hm?'

'I said I don't know.'

'Oh. I didn't hear you.'

Shensee picked something up off the floor and wandered about the tiny space.

'I thought you knew everything.'

'Not everything.'

The boy snapped a small twig in half and crouched down to stab at the dirt with the broken ends.

'You scare people when you talk about Pale Ones.'

'People should be scared,' Madawaak said.

'You killed some though.'

'I did.'

'Maybe they're only coming here to get you.'

Madawaak looked the boy in the eyes now.

'Will you have to leave us?'

Madawaak knew he would. Some painful recess of his heart knew ever since he'd arrived that one day, he'd have to leave them again. That he couldn't run and hide and forget everything. Of course they would come. They came with him long before they came on their canoes.

Demasduit, his thoughts wondered off for a moment.

'Yes.'

'Will you go where Tashedtheek is?'

'No.'

'Where then?'

'Back,' he said. The abyss that loomed beyond life lived in the trees and the plains of his home. But he knew he had to go back. Not to be their slave. Only to know what happened and what became of his people before he could die.

'But they'll get you.'

'I'll fight.'

'I don't want you to die.'

'It will be a good death.'

'The Elders say that the only good death is old age.'

'Your elders are not my people.'

Shansee stood up and dusted his hands on his trousers.

'I'm cold.'

'It is cold.'

'Will you get the fire going?'

'No.'

'I'm getting really cold.'

'Go home.'

Madawaak didn't watch the boy leave.

* * *

'You will leave us then?' Adothe's voice asked in the bitter but clear morning.

Madawaak rose from the half-built canoe and held out his hands so the sea breeze would ease the burning of the raw skin on his palms. The sea growled and barked behind him. Icy brine reached ever closer to the bow of his unfinished vessel.

'Not today. It isn't safe.'

'I don't need safe,' Madawaak said as he crouched down and plunged his hands into the shallow water. The cold numbed them instantly.

Adothe stepped up onto a boulder and looked out at the teeming swells that smashed in quick succession against the natural rocky breakwater.

'I am sorry for what I said last night,' he spoke low and his voice carried over the sounds. 'It is right that you suffer. You have done violence to one who loved you. That is unforgiveable even for your people. But it is the violence of your people that haunts you and their sin you answer for with these Pale Ones. But it is wrong of me to send you to your death.'

'It is right that I go,' Madawaak said as he looked out at the water. Somewhere beyond those waves were the Broken Lands and the bones of everything he once knew. 'It was right that I should have died at the cradle with Gobidin and the others.'

'But you lived.'

'I wanted revenge so much,' Madawaak breathed as he stood and flexed his fingers. 'My hatred sustains me. Here I am nothing.'

'There you are a murderer.'

'I murdered them,' Madawaak snapped. The rage rose in him slightly and heated him. 'It was right when I did. My purpose was to murder them. To kill them off until they finally killed me...'

'Even their children?'

'I will make it right.'

Adothe nodded and rolled his tongue in his mouth.

'Then you should come with me.'

Adothe led Madawaak back to the village and into his mamateek where Debine and her cousins tended to a small woman. She was bound in skins stained with blood. Her breathing was shallow but her knowing eyes looked bleakly up at the ceiling as her face twitched with the pain that seemed to claw up and down her entire body. Debine ordered the woman back when she saw Adothe enter.

'We found her floating amongst the remains of a smashed canoe,' Adothe explained. 'She and a number of others were trying for the distant islands but the Pale Ones intercepted them. There were no others.'

Madawaak stopped before they got too close.

'Will she live?'

'We will ease her passing.'

Madawaak approached the woman and gently touched her brow. She felt cold. Her flesh was hard as though dead already. She looked up at him.

'I am Madawaak of the Forests,' he said.

'Enemy,' she croaked immediately. A Farther Person.

'You have no more enemies, child,' Debine said softly as she caressed the dying stranger's hand.

'You were trying to escape them,' Madawaak said. 'They are everywhere, then.'

'They take,' the stranger said. 'They take our children... they take our cousins and our families in nets and drag them to their villages. In bonds, they take us to their canoes.'

'Across the seas?'

The stranger nodded as tears welled in her eyes.

'How many?'

'They track those of us who hide. Enemies help them.'

'Forest People? Never.'

The stranger nodded.

'Forest People help them find our hidden villages,' she said. 'They tell them our ways so we can't fight them.'

'My people would never yield to them.'

'They are kin,' the stranger said. 'There is a child born... half Forest Person... half Pale One. A son. The Demon Woman raises it. But it was born by her husband and Demasduit.'

A dark shudder assailed Madawaak. He tasted sick in his mouth and gagged as the dizzy spell almost knocked him over.

It worked, then. Demasduit bore them a child. They were kin. Against their will they became kin. A child had by Demasduit. Against her will.

His mind drew him images and conjured sounds that he knew would haunt him in nightmares. The horrors he could imagine. Her suffering. Madawaak weakened and crashed to his knees. Tears poured from his eyes and pain cried out from his heart. Adothe's hand fell upon his shoulder but it was no comfort. Amidst the storm of horror and pain all he could wish was that he'd died at the cradle and never known any of this. Never lived to see it happen. Gobidin. Oonban. They were the lucky ones.

'What became of her?' he asked weakly. When he couldn't hear his own voice, he asked again. 'What became of Demasduit?'

The stranger looked up at the ceiling. Her mouth slightly open. Eyes glassy and vacant.

'Dead,' she whispered. 'By her own hand, they say. Too late not to have the child.'

'The hatred that has existed between your people...'

'It isn't all of us!' Madawaak screamed as he shot to his feet to silence Adothe. 'There will be others. Keathut would never yield no matter who bore whose child. Never! There are others out there who resist. Only the weak ones have turned.'

'Belief is strong. The spirit breaks easy,' Adothe said.

'Not for all of us,' Madawaak seethed. 'Not for me.'

He stormed out of the mamateek and headed back to his canoe. Such was the hate that pressed against him from inside that he no longer felt the cold. Not the wind. Not the sun. Not the gazes of those he passed as he made his way out of the village. Nothing but hatred. Nothing but fury. He forced out thoughts of Demasduit's final days and so thought of nothing but them.

Killing every last one of them.

21

Eagle Who Hunts in Darkness

'Oh, I dropped it!' Eirik said. He stood over the narrow opening in the rocks near Erland the Boatmaker's yard. 'I can see it...'

'Maybe you should make another one?' Torvard suggested. He gently set his very average looking horse aside and put the knife next to it. 'Where is your knife?'

'It's here but I think I can get it.'

Torvard leaned in and peered into the little cave.

'I can't even see down there.'

He reached his hand in and found he could stretch out his whole arm and touch nothing. When he withdrew it, Eirik had already pulled the belt chord off his trousers and was tying the end into a loop.

'Here,' he said. Torvard shuffled aside and Eirik lowered the chord down into the hole. He peered as he carefully manoeuvred the snare. 'The string is too slack!'

'Come on, let's make another one,' Torvard moved back towards his horse and knife. 'I need to try again anyway; mine's no good.'

'No, it's fine,' Eirik said as he searched around on the ground.

'What are you looking for? Here I have more balsa...'

'This!' he picked up a small, crescent shaped pebble.

'What's that for?'

Eirik had already begun to tie a second bow in the chord through which he slipped the pebble and then tightened the bow around it. Torvard couldn't help but smile as he watched.

'Now I'll get it,' Eirik said as he lowered the chord down again. 'There!'

He drew up the wooden horse and took the chord from around its neck.

'That's extremely clever,' Torvard said. 'Where did you learn that?'

Eirik just looked at him in a way that seemed to ask where he would have learned such a thing. Torvard smiled even more broadly.

'Very good. Very clever.'

Horse's hoofs crunched closer in the stones. Soon Freydis and her champion guards looked down on Torvard and Eirik from atop their enormous horses. Gifts from King Lief back in Greenland. Torvard saw she'd brought Eirik's horse, no smaller than hers, along with her and in a quiver on its saddle was a bow and arrows.

'You'll practice riding and archery before night,' she said sternly to Eirik.

Torvard could see Eirik had shrunk with fear. He said nothing.

'Come on, boy.'

Eirik took ginger steps towards her.

'Is your arm feeling better?' Torvard asked him.

Eirik stopped and looked back at his father.

'Of course it is,' Freydis answered for him. 'You are a little boy, aren't you? Or did we mistake you for one? Are you a little rodent?'

'Freydis...'

'He's a little rodent who falls off his horse and cries.'

'That horse is too big for him...'

'You'll shut your mouth!' Freydis snapped at Torvard. Eirik's chest rose and fell with distress but he fought back the tears. 'Get up on your horse.'

Eirik hurried over and lifted his foot to the stirrup. It was too high. Torvard got up to help him.

'Stay there!' Freydis' sharp voice stopped Torvard in his tracks. He sat back down again.

Eirik grabbed onto the saddle and jumped and hooked his foot up at the same time. The horse moved. He cried out.

'You have too much skraeling in you, child. Weak and scared.'

Eirik tried again and managed to get upright on the stirrup.
With yet more effort he managed to crawl up onto the horse's
back and mount himself in the saddle.

'Take him,' Freydis ordered her guards. They led Eirik's
horse off around the boatyard towards the incline while Freydis
trotted over to Torvard and gazed down at him with that burning
green intensity that melted flesh from bone. 'Do not ever
question me in front of the boy. Do not ever.'

'He's a child.'

'He is our future here. Our future is more important than your
pity or your life. Remember that.'

She turned and rode after them.

* * *

Eirik squeezed his legs against the horse's flanks so hard his hips
felt like they would burst. By the time the ground levelled out
and the forests enveloped them and the sprouting ferns
blanketed the ground he was sweating. But he kept focussed on
his mama. She rode her horse ahead of them and led the way.
Behind Eirik the three champions followed; Casper, Gustav and
young Hakon, who still hadn't sprouted a proper beard. Eirik
was still getting used to Hakon. It had seemed too strange for
one of the champions to stand down and another man to take
his place. Hakon wasn't a child. He'd been a servant of Freydis
before Eirik was born... but he'd never been a true champion of
hers until only a season ago. It had thrown his young life out of
order.

Now all his focus was on his mama not seeing his pain.

Once he couldn't feel gravity tug behind him, Eirik was
confident enough to slacken his thighs. The horse seemed to
buck his little body with each step. His hands were white against
the reigns all the while and his teeth ground against each other.
But he could not disappoint Freydis.

She didn't turn. Just rode on. A spectre upon her horse, with
bright red hair that poured down from her head between her
shoulders. Fire against the coal of her pleated leather tunic.

He needed to pee.

It was enough to make him want to cry. But he remembered what happened when he cried when the tender spots left where the bruises had been seemed to alight with pain again. He held steady and kept it in. His mama led them to where the forest thinned. Soon they were in the grassland again and the agony in Eirik's bladder felt like a dagger that slowly turned around and around. He tried holding his breath. That kept the pain at bay for a moment but he grew dizzy. Squirming didn't help.

If he got off the horse, he'd have to get back on.

Eirik only realized he was whimpering when Freydis suddenly turned her heart-stopping gaze back towards him. She turned her horse side-on and stopped.

'What's the matter with you?'

Warm fluid pooled in the saddle and ran down Eirik's legs.

'Nothing.'

His mama stared at him.

Please, Eirik squirmed internally, *don't notice...*

'Don't play silly games,' Freydis turned her horse and continued leading their way.

Soon Eirik's legs were itching as though the skin on them might peel right off. But the ache inside his bladder was gone. Snickering sounds came from the men who followed them but he ignored it as best he could. They would not stand up to Freydis either. Still... he felt each whisper...

Freydis stopped them again. Eirik's horse came up alongside his mama's under its own direction and she pointed up towards the cliffs.

'Look, boy.'

A small group of riders trotted towards them. Four... five. No, four. The fifth was on foot. Tied to the back of the lead rider. He tripped and stumbled now and then and got dragged until he could force his feet under him again and get upright. The three riders that followed keep their spears low. They rode close and jabbed at the prisoner. Freydis kept Eirik and her champions where they were and the group came towards them. As they approached, Eirik could see that the prisoner was smaller than an average person. And darker of complexion.

His breath tightened and a cold tingle tickled down his spine. 'Skraeling,' he whispered.

Eirik knew there were skraelingjar who helped them and skraelingjar who hunted and tried to kill them. But he'd never seen in person neither. If he ever saw a skraeling, friendly or foe, he'd been told to report it straight to his mama, his papa or whoever of the Jarls was around. Nobody lesser, were the instructions. Karls didn't know one skraeling from the other.

The group drew near enough for Eirik to see the blood that poured down from various gashes and cuts in the skraeling. He was out of breath and his knees trembled and his hands were tied and one eye was lost beneath a swollen blue bulge. He was badly out of breath. And scarcely larger than Eirik. The boy felt cold shivers and hot flushes all at once as he realized that parts of the skraeling's legs and arms were showing raw muscle tissue covered in dirt and blood where the skin was entirely flayed.

Still, the small man stood upright.

'This one had red patterns on his chest,' the leader of the group said. Eirik recognized one of Lord Sigrdrifa Astridadottir's champions.

He missed Astrid. Missed that icy blue of her eyes and the airy, soothing voice.

Freydis was talking to the skraeling in his own language that Eirik wished he could understand. Even speak. He knew from his mother's words that his importance was to the Norse, but every time he saw his reflection in clean steel or on the surface of water, he saw their high cheekbones, their black hair and their fierce eyes looking back at him. But his eyes were green and his skin was too light. Eirik was not one of them. But he knew his true mother was. She who birthed him. Who burned alive rather than love him like Freydis, his mama, always promised she did.

The skraeling spoke back. A surprisingly deep voice. His eyes glared with furious rage and Freydis dismounted. Eirik stared at the man. The sight and sound of such anger filled Eirik with fear that Freydis was down from her horse, on equal footing with him. But his mama drew her sword. Then the man changed. He stood upright and rigid, face tensed and lips twitching and eyes filled with ready hatred. He spoke one sentence. Loudly. Eirik's mama repeated it. He said it again and again. Repeating it over and over.

Freydis turned to Eirik and pointed her sword towards him.

'Watch me. Don't look away,' she turned to the champions. 'If he looks away, tell me so I can flog him.'

Eirik watched. Fear held his gaze steady.

Freydis turned the sword towards the skraeling, who kept repeating the phrase over and over again. One of Sigrdrifa's champions leaned forward and rammed his spear into the back of the skraeling's leg. The captive fell to his knees, but he did not stop shouting the sentence. Over and over.

'We sell them,' Freydis said to Eirik as she moved up alongside the downed skraeling. The spear still stuck in his leg. 'If we can. We send them off to Thorfinn who sends them to your uncle in Greenland. But these ones... they'd kill us all if we let them go. So there's only one way to deal with them.'

The champion twisted the spear and the Skraeling moaned with pain but still that one sentence, over and over. Freydis said something in his language. Then she raised her sword and swung it.

With a thwack, the head came off and plopped onto the dewy grass. The body arched forward and a spray of blood appeared before the shiny, gooey neck hole before it collapsed on its side. Then it was still. Incredibly still. Like a nightmare.

Freydis sheathed her sword and mounted her horse. She stared at Eirik.

Eirik trembled inside. He felt sick. He looked at the head with its eyes still open and its expression frozen in that furious hatred. When he closed his eyes, Eirik could still see it against the darkness. When he opened them again, the body had not moved. Nor had the head. Nor the eyes. Sweat broke out under Eirik's clothes again.

'Enough for today,' Freydis said. She turned her horse. Eirik's horse turned and followed the champions and he felt his mama follow him.

A dull rustle issued from where Sigrdrifa's champions had come. It grew louder as it drew nearer. Eirik looked back and saw the ripple pass through the grass towards them and then a freezing arctic blast hit them hard enough to numb their faces and sink through their clothes to their flesh in an instant. Sigrdrifa's champions were headed back in the direction whence they'd come.

As quickly as it had come, that breath of ice was gone.

'Come boy,' a champion said. Eirik's horse followed them back towards Straumfjord and he rode obediently upon its back. But something was missing...

He looked back over his shoulder and saw Freydis was still there, watching the grass and the sky.

* * *

"'My Helga, good arm-serpent's staff; dead in my arms I did clasp. Hel carried off the life of the linen-Lofn, my wife. But for me, the river-flash's poor craver, it is heavier to be yet living,'" Baldar recited. "'And thus ends the saga.'"

Welch was fast asleep, but of the glow of the coals left in the fire dish Baldar could still see the reflection in Byrnhildr's eyes.

'That's a sad story,' she said.

'Well, it probably isn't true,' Baldar said as he gently stroked her brow.

'Did you have to fight anyone for Mama?'

'No. I didn't,' he leaned in close. 'But she had to fight a few for me.'

Byrnhildr smiled.

'Go to sleep. The more tired you are the colder you'll be tomorrow. Good sleep keeps you warm.'

She yawned.

'I'm not sleepy.'

'Oh, really?'

Her eyes were closed. Too heavy to keep open any longer.

'Do you hear that?' she breathed.

'There's no sound...'

'There is,' she whispered.

'Dreaming already...'

'No,' she peered out from under her heavy eyelids. 'I heard it last night as well.'

Baldar raised his head and cocked an eyebrow to show her he was truly, deeply listening. But there was only the breathing of her brother and Baldar's wife, the soft sighing of the ocean and the dull hiss that issued from the coals.

'I don't think...'

He stopped. Did he hear something?

'Papa...'

'Sh...'

Nothing... Baldar wondered if he was losing his mind...

There it was! A clicking. Three soft clicks from somewhere outside.

'I'm scared.'

'Go to sleep,' Baldar ordered as he stood and crossed the lodge to his quiver of arrows and bow.

'What is it?'

'Just some bird or something,' he said. 'I'll get it for breakfast tomorrow. Go to sleep.'

Baldar pushed through the door and stepped out into the icy night. The clouds were still thick and no stars shone above the flat, icy landscape. Soft orange light peeked through the doorways of surrounding lodges. Baldar waited.

Three more clicks.

He followed the sound down towards the beach where the karvi and knarr rested on their hulls in the low tide. Rows of torches lit paths between the grounded vessels. Baldar peered into the orbs of lights that radiated around the oily flames but saw only the white foam that skirted the rising and falling water and the curved edges of the vessels' flanks.

Baldar plucked the string of his bow.

'Who's there!' the gravelly voice of Nari barked from behind.

'Baldar,' he answered. Then turned to see Nari and Orm approach, Nari with an arrow primed at his bow.

'You heard too?'

'My daughter did,' Baldar said.

[275]

'Do you know what it is?' Nari asked as he and Orm joined Baldar at his side and looked out at the abyss beyond the rows of torches.

'A bird or something.'

'That's no bird,' Nari objected. 'Listen.'

They stood still. No more sounds came.

'Hey!' Orm suddenly gasped, and he pointed down along a row of torches that led along the beach beside the water. Nari and Baldar both looked.

The farthest torch went out. Then the next one along. Then the next. One after the other. Coming towards them where they stood. Nari primed his bow.

'Who goes there?' he shouted.

Another torch went out, but no more. Then, three clicks issued. Baldar squinted and thought he could just see the small shape of a person in the dimmest light of the farthest flame. Three more clicks.

Nari held his bow and arrow and marched towards it. Baldar and Orm both followed the ten paces he took, then stopped alongside him. Baldar primed an arrow. Nari prepared to draw back and aim.

'I asked you who goes there,' he growled. 'Skraeling?'

Three clicks issued.

'Alright then,' Nari said and he fired his arrow. In the darkness Baldar saw movement and he too drew back his arrow but just as quickly, something flew out and smashed his bow in two. He screamed out as he saw his arm smash against his chest and felt the bones snap and crack. The impact knocked the air out of him and threw him on his back. By the time the ground hit him, both Nari and Orm fell, both with long skraeling arrows shot through their bodies. Orm writhed and screamed out in agony. Baldar tried to breathe in. He couldn't. His lungs were trapped in a squeezing fist. Blood bubbled up in the back of his throat. Agony roiled up and down in his arm and he looked to see what happened.

A tomahawk. A skraelingjar weapon. His hand was under its blade which was stuck in his chest.

Baldar tried to scream. It only choked him more. He heard his own gurgled cries at the same time as Orm fell suddenly silent. He couldn't move. The pain made his vision throb and spin as though he was drunk. Cold prickles ran through his body.

In the firelight, he saw it stand over him. A skraeling. Small, even for one of them. Baldar's mind could process only small details. He saw the full lips. The sharp nose. The broad cheekbones and the eyes...

The eyes!

There was no iris but deep, red lines that ran right through the center of the white eyeballs. The red aligned with scars that went through both of the skraeling's eyebrows and trailed down to its cheeks. Its head flicked side to side. Unseeing. Listening.

Baldar felt the foot kick his leg.

The pain eased like a receding wave. Time seemed to slow. All was blissful ease and Baldar was freed from the tightening, crushing grip of agony to observe his attacker slowly and leisurely. A woman. Young though. Still with firm, plump flesh in the face. But blind. Blinded. Eyes cut through with human precision. *Shot,* he noted with leisurely detachment, *by a blind archer. How?*

The skraeling leaned down and pulled the tomahawk from Baldar's chest. The pain hit him all at once. All over his body. Like he was being pumped full of pain with a bellows of fire. With every breath he tried to take, more pain filled him. Until he was ready to burst.

The skraeling woman... girl... raised the tomahawk high and brought it down on his face.

* * *

Torvard opened his eyes in the darkness. Freydis' sharp breathing filled their little room and he felt the tension radiate off her. He rolled over and saw she was awake. Eyes fixed upon the dark shadows in their ceiling. Lips pursed. Thoughts flickered across her brow.

'What's the matter?'

'Go back to sleep.'

'Is everything alright?'

'Go back to sleep.'

Torvard knew when he wasn't getting anywhere. He rolled over and closed his eyes and tried to ignore her.

22

One Has Come

The one they called Night Eagle felt the warmth of the sun bring her back from the dreamworld. She lifted her head from the tree root. Birds chirped piercingly in the forest canopy and the light felt soft and milky. Still twilight. She clicked her tongue mechanically and turned her head from side to side. The sound echoed back to her. In her mind, it built an image of the surrounding forest. The tree trunks. The canopy. The mounds of snow that clumped in the larger spaces between the redwoods. No movement. But they were sure to track her.

One of those men had been important. The one who died last. His dress was finer than the others. The patterns gave her a more confused echo as she'd stood over him and yanked her tomahawk out of his skull. The snow was heavy and still. It wouldn't be hard to follow her trail, if they didn't have Forest People to help them track.

But she knew they did anyway.

Night Eagle stood and folded up her robe and tied it up and slung it around her shoulders. Then with her bow and quiver she ran. Ran as she had last night. Clicking with each step. Sometimes avoiding the tree trunks or low brushes only by just enough.

If only the birds would shut up! She'd know how close they were...

Then, Night Eagle stopped. Still. Heard her breath as the gently caught it. She turned in a circle and clicked and heard the vibrations of the tree trunks and the undergrowth... nothing else. The birdsong distorted everything. The land seemed rugged and sharp when Night Eagle could feel that it was covered in a sparkling sheet of snow. Fear prickled through her.

This would happen quickly.

Night Eagle turned and clicked. The trunks of the trees shook and the pines seemed to rustle their needles but she could hear their echo. There was something else out there. Night Eagle hunched. Braced her legs. Forced her breath to steady. Clicked again. Feet crunched in the snow. Softly. Lightly. In a way no Pale One knew how to step.

A soft breeze rustled the forest canopy. The birds shrieked and Night Eagle's clicks echoed back to her as fuzz and white noise. She faced the direction one had come from. There would be others. Coming from her flanks. If they were Farther People... the Forest People were different in their ways. Night Eagle didn't want to believe it was Forest People who helped the Pale Ones. Now she'd find out.

The breeze past and she clicked again. Something... clicked... *An arrow.*

Night Eagle hurled herself awkwardly to one side. The breeze in the wake of the wooden shaft and its tail feathers smacked coldly against her face. Another came from behind. Night Eagle clicked.

There were three.

She ran sideways. Kept her front towards the one who'd fired the first arrow. He was the leader. Night Eagle turned in a circle as she sidestepped and soon didn't need to click. His footsteps scrunched in the snow before her. The tree trunks and shrubs passed perilously close but Night Eagle kept her focus on him. She remembered this place.

A tomahawk slipped through a calloused hand.

Swiftly, the Night Eagle primed an arrow and fired. Then suddenly stopped. Primed another. The confused hunter stopped and turned in time for her to shoot it through his collar...

...footsteps...

Night Eagle primed and fired upward. The leaping hunter screamed and clutched his thigh where the shaft ran him through. She drew her tomahawk and ducked to her knee. The dagger that was thrust at her face passed over her head and she chopped into her assailant's soft belly. With her free hand, she seized the dagger and ran it deep across his throat. Warm fluid poured over her hand and the young hunter gurgled out a pained scream. She let him drop. Heard his writhing limbs scrape against the hardened snow. Night Eagle clicked. Crimson had its own echo when it stained pure white.

All the birds had suddenly taken off in a great crescendo of fluttering that turned Night Eagle's echoes into a kaleidoscope of ripples. When finally it settled, she began to rise. Caught. The bow string creaked as he began to draw back the arrow. The boy shot through the thigh was upright and now he took aim. But Night Eagle was facing him. That's why he hesitated.

Night Eagle clicked softly. Twice. Saw his trembling hands and the arrow not drawn back. He was barely ten paces away yet she could stand firm and he wouldn't hit her. This boy was a Forest Person, as were her other attackers. Though the reality hit Night Eagle heavy in her heart, it meant that the older ones might see her face and remember who they were unforgivably betraying. She clicked. This one was older. Nigh twice her own age, by the sternness of his face. But his spirit was broken. As he looked at her, the man weakened.

'You're dead,' he breathed.

Night Eagle shook her head slowly. Memories from those few years in which she had eyes recalled for her the whiteness of snow and the colour of her people's skin. The sight of their faces when fear touched their spirits. She didn't need to click now.

'You are,' she said. Suddenly dropped to one knee as the hunter's arrow flew past her by more than her arm's reach. By the time her knee hit the snow, she had her bow. Arrow primed. He could never out move her. In shock he could only open his mouth as her arrow shot between his teeth and drove into his skull.

Pale One voices called after their trackers. They echoed through the woodland and Night Eagle could see their vibrations as they swept between the trees.

* * *

'My Lord, your Karvi is ready...' the tawny eyed thrall from Klarjeti said in her soft little voice.

'They haven't come back yet,' Thorfinn said. He paced up and down the limits of his settlement, waiting as the sun grew higher. 'They should have been back by now.'

The Klarjetian just watched him with her big, vacuous eyes. Thorfinn stopped and looked back at her and paranoia shook his flesh. Caucasian thralls were expensive. Young ones were the most expensive in the world. This one was fine. With her silvery hair and thick, tanned skin, she was a rarity and to have got her at birth cost Thorfinn an unthinkable trade.

Stupid!

How could I be so stupid? He started pacing again as he cursed himself. Toli stood guard. He saw the champion shrug stupidly at the thrall. Neither of them understood. It had been Baldar, Nari and Orm last night. It could have been one of the expensive thralls he'd been stupid enough to bring with him to this godless place. It still could be...

'Where are they?' Thorfinn roared. Stomped his foot. 'What happened? What? Did some creature come out of the sea that is immune to arrows and axes? What?'

'I'm sure they will find the assassin, my Lord,' Toli said.

But the smell of smoke had already touched Thorfinn's nostril. He turned back to the forest and saw the thin white trail that rose from the treetops.

'There, see? They've made a fire...'

'Mount a horse,' Thorfinn ordered. 'Bring one for me.'

The thrall still watched him.

'You get on the karvi and stay there. You are not to leave the sight of my boat crew.'

He stormed all the way to his lodge in a huff, fists balled, and quietly cursed the gods. Were they laughing? Was this funny to them?

A clump of snow had fallen and blocked his door. He kicked at it angrily.

'To the bottom of the sea with you all!' he roared at *Odin* and his bullying family as he kicked at the snow until it was clear enough. Inside he retrieved his sword. Worth a hundred of Gunnlogi, he was sure he could buy the chieftainship of Vinland back from Freydis with it and most of Greenland from Lief. But he'd never part with it. It had travelled too far to reach him. Twelve Caucus slaves he'd traded for it he'd never get back and he'd never used it to strike flesh since he'd come to possess it. But this was the occasion.

The Song jian was light in his hand. A weapon thin and sleek and elegant from the farthest reaches of the world. Beyond the grasp of any other Norseman. King or otherwise. He would avenge Baldar with it. *Yes,* he thought. *This is the day!*

Out in the cold, he mounted his horse. Armed men had gathered around him and Toli and some others were already atop horses.

'Those of you mounted come with us and keep watch,' Thorfinn said. 'The rest of you guard the village. Guard the thralls.'

Toli led the charge across the snow-covered meadows and into the forest. There the horses darted left and right to dodge the trees or leaped into the air to clear the low-lying bushes and young pines. Vapor spewed from their mouths and from the horse nostrils as they ran. The air was densely humid. Quickly the smell of smoke died down. But they knew where they were going and so they rode on.

There was something ahead... it looked big...

They rode towards it. Thorfinn stared ahead and he was the first to pull his horse up. The others quickly followed. A cold shiver ran through them that had nothing to do with the icy, damp air of the day. Thorfinn was afraid to blink, lest he still see it in the darkness. So he could not look away.

One of the trackers. His hide. Stretched between two trees as though tanning to be worn.

'Ohhh...' Toli shuddered.

Another was stretched out nearby them... another from the other direction. They were surrounded. Watched by the empty, stretched eye sockets of human skins.

'They did this to their own?' someone asked.

[283]

'Not their own anymore,' Tryggr, the old hunter said.

'Where are the rest of them?' Thorfinn shuddered, wanting only never to see them.

'Over there!' Tryggr said. He turned his horse and trotted over to a circle of low brushes where the dissipating smoke still issued. The others slowly broke off and followed.

Thorfinn didn't want to leave them. He never wanted to stop staring at them, convinced as he was that the image would follow him whether they did or not. But then the thought occurred. Someone did this. Whoever killed Baldar did this. And they were still out there.

Fear spirited him to join the others. But every time he blinked there they were. Mouths pulled to hideous distortions, hands and feet outstretched and tied...

They'd gathered around a burned-out pine. The charred legs of four men stuck out from underneath the dead, blackened tendrils. Tryggr dismounted. With his axe he brushed away the char that fell apart and blew away on the slight breeze as ash. Beneath it, the men were tied together. Tied to the trunk. Their burst eyes ran as liquid down their faces and their mouths were twisted in distortion frozen in ash.

'They were alive,' Tryggr said.

'How did we not hear their screams?'

'They're gagged,' Tryggr didn't point to the mouths, though. He pointed between the legs. Black stains further darkened their singed trousers and Thorfinn knew that it was blood.

'Christians,' Toli blurted out. 'Only they would do such a thing.'

'Don't be stupid,' Thorfinn said. 'I have dealt with Christians. They would not have come here in a number small enough to sneak around us like this.'

'We have to find them.'

'Whoever did this is gone,' Tryggr said as he let his axe drop by his side and dawdled back to his horse. 'They just wanted us to see.'

Toli looked around at the still, empty, snowy woodland with big, frantic eyes. Tryggr tapped his knee.

'They're gone.'

'So are we,' Thorfinn said. 'We're going. I'm taking my thralls and all my goods with me...'

'Shall I go to Straumfjord then?' Toli questioned, now trembling visibly.

Thorfinn concealed the flash of rage.

'No,' he said. Slowly anger seeped through his flesh and he bared his teeth. 'I'll go to Straumfjord. We'll see what Her Majesty does about this.'

* * *

A northern goose landed in the water while Wobee braced to catch a smelt in the shallows of the crystal-clear lake. Quickly the ripples enshrouded his target. The fish was gone in an instant. He breathed a sigh of relief as he turned and ambled over to the where Gheegnyan and young Posson sat and watched.

At least they wouldn't see how slow he'd become.

'Those were the old ways anyway,' he said as he eased himself onto a smooth boulder and waved his hand dismissively at the lake.

Gheegnyan was hardly paying attention. He stabbed at the rocks with his little dagger and wore away at the chert.

'Adyouth died a good death,' Wobee reassured the young man.

'So everyone keeps saying,' Gheegnyan said. 'But they say he was on his knees. His head taken off from behind.'

'It is not the nature of one's death that makes a good death,' Wobee said. 'It is the life that led them there. Adyouth was strong for us. We will miss him. Our resistance is weaker without him. That is a good man. An honourable death leaves holes in both camps.'

'Two Mi'kmaq proverbs.'

'The older I get, the less sense it makes that we were enemies,' Wobee said with a half-smile.

There was a moment's silence.

'But... how do you catch the fish?' Posson asked.

Wobee opened his mouth to answer, but Gheegnyan caught his eye again. He was not chipping his chert anymore. His stern, almost frightened face was fixed on the goose that had disrupted Wobee's fishing. Wobee looked at the bird.

It paddled back and forth. Watching them.

Gently, Wobee rose to his feet.

'What is it, goose?' he asked, softly. Slowly, he approached the water's edge. 'What are you so eager to tell us?'

Gheegnyan and Posson watched as the goose stopped paddling and bobbed up and down on the water. Never did it look away from Wobee. From behind, they saw as his shoulders stiffened. The goose paddled to the edge of the lake, climbed up, and fluttered off. Wobee turned slowly. Behind them, the goose disappeared into the sky. Wobee looked gravely at the two young men.

'The birds are singing late this year,' Posson said. 'The forests should be silent by now.'

'The forests will not be silent for some time,' Wobee said.

'What do you know?' Gheegnyan asked.

'Someone has...' he stepped as he spoke, and his foot slipped on the wet rock. Both boys heard the crack of the old man's skull as it crashed down on the rocks and his body thrust and gyrated in convulsions. Blood spilled out from under his hair. Gheegnyan jumped up and held the old man on his side, while Posson was already running for the village.

'Get Keathut!' Gheegnyan screamed. 'Get help!'

* * *

Posson put his arms around Gheegnyan and they held each other while the wives bustled about beyond the curtain of Wobee's mamateek. Keathut kept vigil from nearby. While all of it was happening, Gheegnyan couldn't help but look at Keathut and how grey his hair had become and how much smaller he seemed as the years passed. Life before this was like some distant dream. A hazy never-never when Pale Ones did not rule their thoughts and were not even known to exist.

But their lives did not wait for these years to pass so they could go back to how they were. They aged. They died. Wobee spoke often of being with his wife in the Spirit World. Perhaps he spoke of it so often that the god spirits decided to grant him his wish... no... couldn't think like that.

But Keathut was getting old. Neither he nor Wobee might ever get their lives back the way they were. *Nor might anyone,* the thought occurred to Gheegnyan. He looked down at Posson. Gentle, young Posson, son of Popsaruk. Too young to really remember a time before Pale Ones.

Ebauthoo emerged from the mamateek. Young as well, but what she'd seen and endured could never be forgotten. Keathut prickled up and looked at her.

'He is awake,' she said. 'You have some time.'

Keathut quickly followed Ebauthoo into the mamateek and Gheegnyan's eyes dropped and flooded with tears. Wobee would die. They all knew it now. Die without ever seeing his home back to itself again and his people safe. Dark, hopeless clouds loomed over Gheegnyan's mind. His father... his own father...

...what was taken from them could never be given back. No victory over Pale Ones would ever equate to what Pale Ones have destroyed.

Moments crept by. Posson felt weak against Gheegnyan so they both went and sat on the log near the bonfire pit. Ninejeek hovered nervously near them. Gheegnyan felt him look at them now and then as though intent on asking them something, perhaps just to fill the heavy silence that hung above them with his voice. But he didn't.

Finally, Keathut emerged. The weight in his steps confirmed what they'd all feared and a collective grief erupted from everyone in the village. Women stopped their work and cried openly. Men gathered around the mamateek or found their wives and wept with them as Gheegnyan looked around, his vision blurred by tears. Amidst all the grief, there hunted the poisonous agony of lost hope as well.

Keathut stood before Gheegnyan and Posson.

'Come with me,' he said.

Posson's mother staggered over and gently took the burden of her son's grief from Gheegnyan. Keathut led Gheegnyan to his mamateek and held the door flap for him. Inside, they were alone. Keathut looked at the ground, paced slowly around Gheegnyan and touched his fingertips to his mouth as he thought.

'I heard the news of Makdaachk,' he finally said.

Gheegnyan looked at the floor.

'I hope for you that our stories remember him fondly,' Keathut said. 'The warrior and hero he was before... this,' he raised his hand weakly and slapped it to his thigh. 'Your brother as well.'

'If not for them,' Gheegnyan spoke in a voice stripped of its depth. 'We could have driven Freydis and her people out long ago.'

Keathut looked down and nodded.

'Wobee had news from the Farther Lands,' Gheegnyan said. 'A late bird migration stopped by the lake before he slipped.'

'He only told me one has come,' Keathut said. 'That was all he could manage. Does it mean anything to you?'

Gheegnyan shook his head no.

'It doesn't matter,' Keathut replied. 'With this and Adyouth we are...'

He pursed his lips and shook his head, lost for words.

'The children of Makdaachk's brothers, of Shendeek, Moosin and of Kukuwes remain with the Pale Ones,' he continued. 'We are outmatched. But they do not hate us. They only follow their faith in the god spirits and that makes us enemies.'

Gheegnyan could hardly stomach the defeat in Keathut's voice. He hadn't the strength to both stand upright and listen to it, so he eased himself onto the furs and held his head.

'If not for that child...' Keathut said. 'I have spoken with Ninejeek many times about that child. He agrees with me. Wobee didn't. He didn't believe it was possible to get rid of that child without losing warriors and he didn't believe that Freydis would lose the support of the other Forest Fathers if the child was dead.'

Gheegnyan looked up at Keathut. This he had not expected...

Keathut looked Gheegnyan sternly in the eyes.

'The child has to die,' Keathut said. 'I will allow no more raids. They have been far too costly for us and still no sign them having worked at all. No more raids. Just the child.'

Gheegnyan felt his throat near close over.

'Me?'

Keathut just looked at him.

'To save my family's name?'

'We will remember whoever does it,' Keathut said. 'Even if it does not win our brothers back to us, Freydis will not have that child anymore. Other Pale Ones will become nervous. They won't feel safe as they do now. That's if it doesn't work. If it does, this war will be over and we will have our homes back.'

Gheegnyan's eyes fell upon the blank wall behind Keathut and stayed there.

'Our big, empty homes,' he said, softly.

'Every day that passes they only grow emptier,' Keathut said. 'If you will not go, I will ask the others. I mean not to single you out. But Adyouth made you a strong warrior and I believe that you would be able to do this. You are not the only one among us. I will ask the others...'

'Don't,' Gheegnyan said as slowly everything he missed of his old life flashed before his eyes. He saw little that he would have back without Pale Ones to fight with anymore. 'I will go. It will be an honour.'

'Take your time, Gheegnyan,' Keathut said. 'Plan carefully. Tell as little or as many People of the Lakes as you like. Talk to me. Talk to Ninejeek about it. But do nothing rashly. The only way we will know you did what you set out to do will be what we hear of it. So take every caution.'

'I will.'

'I know you will.'

Gheegnyan left the mamateek and Posson, with his eyes red and face wet with tears, ran into his embrace.

'I'm going away soon,' Gheegnyan whispered after he had taken all he could of Posson's warmth.

'A raid?'

Gheegnyan looked at Posson's innocent brown eyes and thought about his answer.

'Yes. But alone.'

'What kind of raid will you do alone?'

'It doesn't matter now,' he said. 'What matters is the time we have before I go.'

'You sound as though...' Posson's breaths quickened until they stole his words.

Gheegnyan caressed the young man's face gently.

'I won't leave you,' Gheegnyan said. 'Only to do what must be done, and then I will be near you. Always.'

Posson's innocent eyes darkened with comprehension he didn't want but he didn't object. Instead, he threw his arms around Gheegnyan again and said nothing. Gheegnyan looked over the boy's shoulder at the treetops. The gathering clouds. The air that was dry and crisp before the first snowfall of winter.

Sensations and sights he knew he had to take with him.

23

Into Darkness

Everyone I find, Madawaak concluded as he worked furiously with bleeding hands to finish the last knots to hold his canoe together. He had decided he would kill everyone he found. His own people. The thought kept rolling through his mind. *My own people! With them! Kill everyone,* he thought. It was the only way to be sure. *Everyone on that mainland is an enemy. Everyone.*

Now there was no Demasduit then who was there to protect or worry about anyway? If she did not deserve life, then nobody did.

'I will go with you,' the gravelly voice of Adothe interrupted him.

'You cannot fight,' Madawaak spat without looking up. 'You will not anyway.'

'It is not about fighting,' Adothe said as he looked out at the water and found another large rock to stand one foot on. 'You were right. And you were trying to protect my people as best as you knew how. I owe it to you. To keep you alive for as long as I can.'

'To burden me with a pacifist.'

Madawaak pulled the last two lengths of chord tight and washed his hands in the icy water. Thinned blood ran from the cuts and wounds. He dropped his hands into the water again and held them there.

'I can hunt,' Adothe said. 'I can use a bow and a tomahawk. I am no burden.'

'I can too. Better than you.'

'You can't even make a canoe without ripping your hands to pieces,' Adothe said as he stepped down off his rock and gingerly approached Madawaak. 'Since the falcon told you of your lost Demasduit you have been filled with anger so blinding you struck out at your own wife. Now you know she bore them a child.'

Madawaak bit his own teeth so hard they hurt.

'Look at you. You can't even hear about it without flushing in a rage. How long do you expect to last?'

Madawaak lifted his hands and flexed his fingers until he could feel them again.

'Your enemy has had nine summers and nine winters to grow confident and calm,' Adothe continued. 'They have lived amongst your people. Learned from them. It will not be the same as last time. You need balance.'

'What happened to your beliefs?' Madawaak asked and finally looked at the sprightly old man. 'Do no violence and no violence will come to you.'

'Letting you kill yourself and accomplish nothing is violence in itself,' Adothe said. 'Besides... there is a time to put aside personal beliefs and engage with reality. We are surrounded. I want to see these Pale Ones.'

'You will not come home to tell anyone about it.'

Adothe swallowed hard but kept firm.

'I don't need to.'

Madawaak started to push off the canoe.

'Patience feeds the hunter,' Adothe said. He jumped to join Madawaak at his side. 'Not anger.'

'What do you think I'm going to do?'

Madawaak leaped into the canoe. Adothe followed him and they both began to float out amongst the rise and fall of the swells that carried the canoe back to the rocks then out again. Madawaak picked up his oars but didn't use them while Adothe was aboard.

'I think you're going to kill as many of them as you can.'

'As many as I can.'

'That will be a lot more if you listen to me.'

'What difference will it make?'

'What difference?' Adothe seized the other end of the oar and held it as well as Madawaak's gaze. 'What difference is it if one

mad warrior runs upon an enemy garrison and gets slaughtered
before he can swing his tomahawk or fire his bow?'

'You underestimate me.'

Madawaak tried to yank the oar free but the old man's grip on
the oar was stronger than both his arms. It barely moved.

'What difference is it between that, and two who made a
calculated and measured stand against many?'

Madawaak scowled.

'The difference is what they'll tell their friends,' Adothe said,
calmly. 'We cut down some lone mad dog, they could say. Or
beware those two hunters. They fought well and we lost brothers
against them.'

Madawaak's face softened ever so slightly as the meaning sunk
through.

'You underestimate me,' Adothe smiled.

'If you can keep me sane,' Madawaak mused. 'Why only
now?'

'You didn't need or want to be sane before,' Adothe said. He
let go of the oar. 'Now I've prevented you from killing yourself
on the waves, will you paddle us out before the next set rolls in?'

Madawaak looked over his shoulder and saw the trough in the
oncoming waves. He quickly dipped the oar in the water and
paddled them out past the breakers. Adothe sat back and
watched with a wrinkly grin.

'One step at a time, young man.'

* * *

'It was only one, my Lord,' Tryggr said from behind Thorfinn.

'One?' Freydis said with raised eyebrows. 'One skraeling
killed six of ours and three other skraelingjar?'

Thorfinn glanced back at Tryggr to silence him. She seemed
to be mocking them and he didn't like it.

'We don't know what it was,' he said. 'It left no arrows...'

'But it used arrows,' Freydis said. 'And an axe.'

Thorfinn nodded. His eyes fell upon the half-caste boy that
sat at her side. He was blank with a child's ignorance. Only
Torvard seemed stirred by the news Thorfinn delivered, and

[293]

that came as no surprise. How could Freydis be so blasé about it?

'My settlement is afraid,' Thorfinn added.

'No doubt,' Freydis said. 'Burning weeds and the chanting spells in every superstitious tongue from every uncivilized world you gathered them from.'

'Not just the thralls!' Thorfinn snapped. 'The karls. The jarls. Everyone!'

'Then they need a strong chieftain,' Freydis said slowly. 'Not someone who will leave them and run for Straumfjord with piss stains on their pants.'

'I came to collect.'

'And to complain,' Freydis snapped.

'Do you not want to be warned when my men are slain by a creature that can fire arrows in pitch-darkness?'

Freydis broke into a soft smirk.

'Then you're finished here,' Freydis said. 'Tryggr Olafsson, you are now Chieftain of Helluland...'

'What?' Thorfinn shrieked at such volume that Casper and Hakon both raised their atgiers at the ready.

'Thorfinn Thorsson, you have a greater responsibility now,' Freydis slowly rose. 'You will take your loaded knarr back to Greenland and remind my brother, the King, that ten years has passed. I have fulfilled my obligation to him. I demand one hundred knarr of settlers. Lords and their karls and everything else they own. Tell him we have made room for all of them. Tell him I am to be made Queen of Vinland and will be passing chieftainship of Markland to Gustav Kristoffsson upon appointment of my new title. Tell him that. And tell him that my first order of business as Queen will be to expand my territory into the mainland and to keep expanding it until we find the sea on the far side of it. And tell him that not one of these terms is negotiable. Or Vinland will declare war on Greenland. With all the allies we have made in the skraelingjar trade at our side.'

Thorfinn was, for the first time in his life, dumbstruck.

Freydis sat down again.

'The mainland territories will need chieftains,' Freydis said. 'Those who know how to trade and sell full-sized skraelingjar thralls.'

Thorfinn wanted to object but could find nothing to object to.

'Don't worry Thorfinn,' Freydis smirked. 'I don't think one archer who can see in the dark will cause us much harm.'

'Yes, my Lord,' Thorfinn said weakly. 'One hundred knarr. We have room. Queen of Vinland. Expand territory... do I threaten him with war immediately or just in case he objects?'

'For a trader you make an excellent messenger boy,' Freydis said. 'Get out.'

Casper and Hakon raised their atgiers as Thorfinn and his men turned to leave.

'Just Thorfinn,' Freydis called. 'Those going back to Helluland stay.'

They all stopped. Thorfinn stopped himself from looking back and then took his leave. Once the door shut behind him and the light of day was kept out of the lodge, Freydis stood, walked around the table and crossed to Tryggr.

'Find this archer,' she said, closely. 'Take my trackers if you need them but find it and kill it. Bring me the head.'

'Yes, my Queen.'

'Lord,' Freydis said with a smirk. 'I am not Queen yet.'

She nodded towards the door and Tryggr and his men marched to it, pulled it open and exited as well. Freydis turned back towards her husband and son.

'Are you concerned about this archer, my Lord?' Hakon asked as he followed her.

'No,' she said. 'I want to see its eyes, that's all.'

'It's eyes, my Lord?'

Freydis touched Eirik's shoulder as she returned to her seat.

'I want to see eyes that can see in the dark,' she said. 'What's next?'

'Kaia Svenungursdottir,' Torvard said. 'To explain why her tributes have been low yet again.'

'Ugh,' Freydis rolled her eyes. 'You deal with it. I want to go riding with my son.'

* * *

The sun shone behind the lakeside hideaway and Gheegnyan
crept off with his bow and quiver of arrows and spear and
tomahawk during the silent moments in which Posson wasn't
around. He left the mamateek he'd lived alone in for a few
passes of the night since Adyouth had been captured. Inside its
darkness, a loneliness dwelt that had taken on a presence of its
own. Gheegnyan almost said goodbye to it. He crossed the
village through the maze of toiling gatherers who brought their
baskets to their wives and daughters with their sons in tow and
helped them skin or peel or otherwise prepare them before they
set off again. Birchbark satchels held their boons for later. The
women half-submerged them in the icy lake water or buried
them in the light snow to preserve them that much longer.

Nobody paid any attention as he slipped bye.

He hoped they wouldn't. As Gheegnyan reached the edges of
the village and the homes thinned and the people grew more
and more scattered, he left greater distance between them. Felt
his flesh cool and his heart quiver. What would become of that
mamateek where Adyouth's presence was so deeply absent that
the absence itself had become a companion? Would it be left
to fall into disrepair? Would the roof cave in and cut out the
spirit of that darkness so complete and that silence so intense
that it had become sentient and watchful?

Gheegnyan heard his breath quiver as he entered the pine
forest and that fresh, sweet smell in the still air enveloped him.
Sounds still issued from the village behind. Hammers
thwacking, wood on stone or wood in preparation for the
coming night, voices that called not to him but just to each other.
Gheegnyan walked on and tried to think of the child. He knew
Adyouth had seen him. A small boy. Dark hair. Eyes the colour
of peeled chestnuts. Features lost between Pale One and one of
their own. But that's all he could manage. Gheegnyan could not
form a living image of this boy in his mind. Only a concoction
of Adyouth's descriptions. No life. No sounds. No flicker and
pulse. Nothing like what he knew he'd find.

His weapons felt so heavy. Gheegnyan had never wanted to harm or kill anything.

'Nobody ever wanted to,' his father had told him and Mooaumook when they were little and he'd come home with flecks of blood still on his face from a Farther People raid that had come too close to home. 'If the day comes when you do want to then... my boys... all you can do is wander off into the forest or the broken lands or take yourself out to sea and stay there. Because your spirit is gone. But if you know it then the god spirits will guide you to where you need to be. Not in this life. In the next one. Where you can't hurt anybody.'

'I'm going to kill someone, Father,' Gheegnyan said. 'But I don't want to.'

Thoughts of children from around the village haunted him. Some of them weren't from the village... some of them were Mooaumook when they were boys. Mooaumook when he'd been the age of Eirik Torvardsson and Gheegnyan had looked up at him in wonder at the wisdom and the physical prowess he'd embodied. When his papa wasn't around, Mooaumook was head of the house. Gheegnyan thought his brother could lead the village at that age and nobody could have told him otherwise.

'I don't understand how this is going to help,' Gheegnyan said as he imagined Mooaumook looking down at him in that way he used to. Superior, but encouraging. Come on, brother. Let's get into trouble. But he didn't answer. Didn't seem to hear. Mooaumook just faded into the forest and the shafts of golden mid-afternoon light that reflected on the snow and formed shimmering prisms like spirits in the forest.

The silence was complete. Only the crunching of Gheegnyan's moccasins in the wet pine needles and slushy snow. Nothing else. Not even a hint of a breeze. Gheegnyan stopped and felt the isolation, like a cocoon of invisible cold all over his body that seeped slowly through his flesh. He'd never been so alone in all his life. It was like all that existed had suddenly fallen away and nothing remained but this prism-filled fantasy version of it.

Some dewy dream he could walk in. Going nowhere. Accomplishing nothing. Never to return.

Gheegnyan stopped to eat some nuts and grain from his pouch as the forest ahead grew denser and darker and the sunlight began to abandon the sky to the first twinkles of stars. He slipped some snow into his mouth and resisted lighting a fire. Ahead was the deeper forests where he'd pass by the lakes and his old home, though nobody who knew him would live there anymore. With his father went the last memory of him from that place. Gheegnyan shook his head with a melancholy smile.

With Adyouth went the last memory of him at all. Unless he could kill this child.

From there was the dense undergrowth. Then the land rose up and formed gullies full of fern trees that pooled beneath the towering redwoods and concealed the ground entirely. It was easy from there. He'd walked that way twice. Followed his papa and mama to watch the Forest Fathers gather and honour Mooaumook. He'd seen Demasduit then. Again before they'd all gone off to fight the Pale Ones. He'd seen Demasduit a second time. First she'd been another face amongst the crowd, distinguished only by the little sister who'd hovered around her endlessly. The second time she'd slain a polar bear.

'What was she like?' Gheegnyan asked the memory of Mooaumook he let conjure behind his eyelids as he rested his head against the tree trunk. But he couldn't hold the memory. And the memory wouldn't answer him anyway. Nobody would.

Demasduit walked these forests, he thought. *All alone.* Stories of her wanderings spread after her defeat of the bear. He'd heard them around campfires and as bedtime stories for younger kids he'd been left to care for. He wondered if she'd come by this way to the lakes she was said to have gone to, right where Gheegnyan had lived until his father had sent him away. She'd been so close so many times. Close enough to fall in love with his brother.

Now he would murder her son.

* * *

The Night Eagle turned on the spot and clicked three times. Her trail remained. She continued up into the hills where the tree limbs began to curve downward and loom over her like sentinels that waited to strike. Starlight felt silvery and soft. There was no warmth from the velvet moon. She picked and pulled her way through the mossy roots and limbs that were spiralled and curled all around the ground as though they were tentacles frozen in bark mid-writhe. Wet clumps brushed against her from every angle as she went. For a moment, it felt like they might suddenly catch her in their grips and drag her down into the earth.

Still, when she broke through the other side, Night Eagle stopped and gingerly clicked. She'd prepared for this moment. Readied herself every day since knowing what her calling would be and that it meant coming back to this place... but when the echo came back to her, The Night Eagle was a lost and crying and screaming child again.

Maybe it was preserved in time having waited for her to return or maybe her own memories corrupted the image that came to her ears but what she saw in the echo was no different than what she saw with her eyes the last time she had them.

A steep rise on the edge of a mountain, levelled off like a shelf and surrounded by willows like curtains. This time no fire glowed from within. Breathless the Night Eagle approached and wiped the blood that fell from her eyes in place to tears. The air felt dense with the ghosts of memories. Spirits who haunted this place and they were doomed always to relive the hideous deaths they suffered. Night Eagle climbed up and reached forward until her fingertips found the soft branches of the hanging willow. One last pause to gather herself. Then, Night Eagle stepped through.

In the near perfect darkness, her echoes showed her mamateeks that seemed to have melted into the earth, slowly consumed by where they had come. The bones of the dead were long gone into dust and soil but Night Eagle knew that nearby one feature still stood. A spear. Rammed in the ground.

Gently, she reached out and clicked her way to where her hand would find it.

On the ground to her right, once she'd turned and put her back to the spear, that was where mama bled. Where she'd died. Shanawdithit watched the earth drink the crimson life as it had poured from mama's open neck. Then in front of her. Directly in front. Demasduit. Screamed and reached for her. Then fiery hair fell before her face. Then eyes green like no other green she could remember. Then the blade. For a moment, everything the *na'gipugtaqanej* had taught her was gone. Darkness. Only darkness. Darkness she'd never known. All light, colour and complexity suddenly gone. Not taken. Not extinguished. Gone as though never to have existed.

The agony!

All the sounds of the world were consumed by her own screams. Screams that did nothing but echo back at her for the longest time. For forever. Until little Shanawdithit had died.

Night Eagle stopped. The memories relented. Touched her cheek and felt it was thick with blood. She'd staggered a few paces from the spear in her delirium. Now was not the time.

The rotting, dry rooftops and walls of mamateeks crumbled in her hands as Night Eagle pulled them off and piled them in one of the circular scars in the earth left by a long dead fire pit. She placed a few larger sticks over the top. Then ground her flint until some warmth lingered in a little flame. With a few breaths, the fire caught.

Then she moved away from the flame. Into the edge of night. The squirrels foraged nearby and their little scratches and shuffles issued to the hunter's ears. So still her pulse almost stopped. The squirrels foraged. A low sigh. Already Night Eagle could sense them in the echo of her breath. She clicked. The squirrels froze, startled.

Everything was more confident at night. Eased into the belief that hunters couldn't see, except for owls. And the Night Eagle.

'I take your flesh,' she whispered. 'To feed myself. I thank you.'

The squirrels were silent. The Night Eagle clicked one more time. Before their image faded from the echo, Night Eagle put an arrow through one. Back at the fire, she ripped the skin off. Cooked it over the flame. Tongues of fire licked high into the dark air and swirling funnels of ember lifted up into the stars. Night Eagle could feel it and hear it.

Pale Ones would see it. Those who helped them, her own people, they would see it too. See it first. They would lead the Pale Ones of the Farther Lands to her. In time.

She would wait. This place was strong with the memories of Demasduit. Night Eagle hoped her sister would visit her in dreams.

24

Returning Home

'The demon walks this land.'

The words slipped out of Madawaak's mouth automatically as he sat atop the cliffs and looked over the Broken Lands that stretched out before him. The snow was still light. It had not yet become the pure white tundra he'd left behind. The scattered lakes that spread across the lush green grasslands still caught the orange light of the dawn and shone like beacons in the fields. Near him tracks led south along the coast. A wolfpack. But no animals were in sight. No life whatever. Madawaak had to remind himself there were Pale Ones here. He knew none of his own people remained but had not imagined that the world could go on as serenely as it had without him or his kind and not be completely overrun by Pale Ones.

They'd defeated Gobidin with so little. They still were so few. How fragile a way of life truly was...

'Do you believe in demons?' Adothe asked from beside the fire.

Madawaak looked back at the old man, embarrassed to have been caught speaking to himself. He stoked it with wet sticks to last night's embers again. If the Pale One saw it, so be it. If they'd brought Forest People down here then they would certainly see it.

'I used to,' Madawaak said as he joined the old man by the tiny fire. 'Now I believe in Pale Ones.'

Adothe gave a faint smile that accentuated the creases all over his face.

'God Spirits?'

For some reason, Madawaak could only think of Demasduit. Young and beautiful as she'd sat beside him on the cliff's edge near the village of Oonban and they'd talked about their dreams. Darkness surrounded them. Beyond it was white light, as though night radiated from them, and the spirits of those who'd been there passed facelessly in and out of their darkness and disappeared in the light.

'No.'

'I thought all of your people believed in such things.'

'If God Spirits are why my people hunt their own kin and choose allegiance with monsters instead of the Farther People, then I choose not to believe in God Spirits.'

'I never asked you these things before,' Adothe said inwardly as he poked at the fire again. 'Should have.'

'Why?'

'Something to like about you,' Adothe said. He dug his stick deep into the ashes and unearthed the leather parcel they'd buried in there the night before. Carefully, they both unwrapped it. Steam billowed out and the seal meat inside was almost liquified.

They ate with their hands.

'Do you think the Forest People will go back to war with the Farther People once the Pale Ones are gone?' Adothe asked with his mouth full.

'Demasduit would have been a guarantee of peace,' Madawaak said. Tears taunted the backs of his eyes but he held them at bay.

Adothe watched him blush.

'She's gone though,' Adothe said. Then he cocked his head. 'Or she might still. Who knows?'

'How might she?' Madawaak asked, unable to hide his annoyance.

Adothe looked down and shook his head as he chewed on the last piece of seal meat.

'Tell me what you mean.'

Adothe swallowed sharply.

'A common enemy is a powerful broker.' He looked out at the rising sun, now golden and standing halfway up from the icy plains like a distant dome of light. 'Ready to go hunting?'

Adothe stood upright and offered his hand to Madawaak who shoved what was left of the meat into his mouth and took it.

* * *

The two of them walked as the sun emerged and rose high above the lands and the snow softened under steps. Adothe fell behind more and more every hour. Madawaak started to stop and wait for him to catch up as he knew they were nearing the sea again. They would follow it around. Though his veins pumped hot with the lust for blood, there was now frustration diluting his rage and he didn't want it there. He wanted Adothe to see something. Maybe he would finally understand why Forest People did violence and war.

The fire that morning had given him an idea. He didn't want to just happen upon some roaming Pale Ones or pick off farmers from the fringes of their village yet. First another thing. Something to let them know what had returned to the shores they'd stolen.

Past noon, they reached the coast. A single bird flew high overhead and was obscured by the vibrant sunlight that shone through the cotton clouds. Adothe had fallen behind again. Madawaak stopped to watch the bird while he waited for the old Island Father to catch up.

'We'd have reached the other side by now, if this were home,' he complained as he slowly regained ground on Madawaak.

'I'm not used to it either,' Madawaak said. He let Adothe pass him a few paces, then Madawaak walked beside him. 'It's been a long time.'

'I wonder what Gobidin thought when he came to our island.'

'I wonder what Demasduit would think of it...' Madawaak stopped himself. 'Gobidin?'

Adothe breathed a few husky breaths and kept walking north along the beaches.

'When did Gobidin come to the Island?'

'Long ago,' Adothe replied. 'You'd have barely been born.'

'What did he come for?'

'What do you think Demasduit would have thought of our islands?'

'I asked what he came for.'

'Those were different times. The Farther People were at constant war with your fathers, and many feared that they would form an alliance with the Mi'kmaq.'

'You're not answering me.'

They walked on. Adothe panted loudly and raggedly.

'We should rest,' Madawaak said. 'You don't want too much of this air in your lungs.'

He stopped. Adothe stopped as well. Both men licked their cragged, numb lips. Their bodies sweated into their furs while their faces were nigh frozen. They sat to catch their breath.

'I'm slowing you down,' Adothe coughed.

'That's okay,' Madawaak said, as he considered all the ideas he'd had on the long walk. If the Pale Ones found the Island now, there was nothing he could do about it. If they did not, then everything else that mattered was already gone and so there was no reason to rush. 'We'll wait.'

'You've been thinking.'

'I have.'

'About Demasduit.'

'About Gobidin visiting your Island and you avoiding telling me why.'

'Demasduit never set foot on my Island and she never will,' Adothe said. 'What was it that made you think of her?'

Madawaak bit his top lip and looked out at the snowy emptiness.

'This land was where I last saw her,' he half-whispered. 'And where I knew I'd never see her again. I wonder what I could have done. Claimed her. Told her I loved her. Begged her father to let us love each other... if she ever loved me.'

'Of course she did,' Adothe said. 'Maybe not in the same way but... love is love.'

'How do you know?'

'I don't know. Does it matter now?'

'I suppose it doesn't.'

'You loved her very much.'

'Yes.'

'Remember that,' Adothe said. 'These feelings may not exist on the other side. If there is a spirit world. I don't think there is. To be safe, you might as well enjoy them now. You don't know if they exist beyond life.'

'Pain does not exist anywhere but in this world.'

'Do you believe in the afterlife?'

'I don't want to,' Madawaak admitted, carefully.

'Why not?'

'Because then she'd never be at peace.'

Adothe leaned in close.

'Neither will you,' he said. 'There would always be that one you didn't kill in time. Or at all. That hut you didn't burn. There is no peace while we think of these things.'

Madawaak put some snow in his mouth and let it slowly melt on his tongue.

'But why you tried,' Adothe said. 'That's what's important. That's all there is now. Is why. Not what you didn't. Not what you could have. Only why you tried.'

'It's too late for trying.'

'Is that how you feel? Why did we canoe all the way over here, then?'

Madawaak did not answer. He looked at the old man's big, brown eyes with their youthful flicker framed in such an old face. Madawaak's heart thumped once deeply and for a moment he hoped Adothe would never leave him. Would always be there. For a moment he didn't want to doom either of their lives this way, if only because of the danger it presented Adothe.

'Let's keep walking,' Madawaak suggested.

* * *

The fire crackled and hissed on the wet earth while the dry ocean breeze bent it sharply towards the west. They'd rounded the deep bite that cut into the south end of the Broken Lands. Tomorrow they'd reach their destination. Adothe sat with his eyes closed. His long, grey hair swept across his still face and he breathed slowly. Madawaak wondered about the bird he'd seen. What had it seen? Where had it come from?

'I think...' Adothe suddenly said, and then he trailed off for a moment. 'I think Demasduit would have walked from one end of the Island to the other and then from the top to the bottom and... and maybe she wouldn't have said anything but in time... not in a long time... I think she would have withered there. Wilted like a flower in bad soil.'

Madawaak just looked at him, though he felt his pulse quicken to hear her name spoken by another without prompt.

'Flowers don't grow on the Island,' Adothe said with a crooked smile. 'Too much sea air.'

A sharp wind blew and sparks flew off the top of their fire and whirled out into the darkness that veiled the interior of the Broken Lands.

'Her Farther husband would not have let her wonder either,' Adothe said. 'Probably even less far than she could have on the Island. There she'd have wilted too. I wonder if it would have been worth it, in the end.'

'She used to dream of Mi'kmaq country,' Madawaak said over the swelling ball in his throat. 'And the countries beyond it. The worlds that exist out there... I wonder how much of it has fallen to Freydis and her kin?'

'I don't wonder that,' Adothe said. 'When I wonder about Freydis I wonder... I wonder what she's running from.'

'I don't care.'

'That's the demon woman, is it?' Adothe asked. 'You've never said her name to me before.'

'That is the demon. Why are you talking about Demasduit?'

'I just wonder.'

'Do you think it is best that she died?' Madawaak asked. The tremble in his voice was clear and obvious.

'No. Never. Of course not. And not the way she did.'

Madawaak nodded and looked down into the fire. After a few moments, he eased into his robe and wrapped it around himself.

'I wonder if she's... out there now. Now without any oceans in her way or marriages or polar bears.'

'There is no life after this one.'

Madawaak heard Adothe retract.

'I'm sorry I never knew her.'

'When are you going to answer me?' Madawaak asked while he nestled his cold face into the fur. 'What was Gobidin doing on the Island?'

'It was a long time ago,' Adothe grunted as he pushed his feet down into his robe.

'What was he doing there?'

Adothe took a deep, gravelly breath.

'He demanded we help his warriors to the northern coasts of the Farther Lands,' Adothe said. 'He wanted great seafarers and knew we were the best. He didn't want peaceful exiles.'

Madawaak turned and looked across the fire at Adothe. His face was half obscured in night but his eyes were open as he stared up at the deep blue sheet of velvet night.

'When we refused, he attacked us,' Adothe said quickly.

'Gobidin? Attacked you?'

'He'd have wiped us out if the tide hadn't changed and smashed his canoes on the rocks,' Adothe said. 'Only those who'd already landed were left. Not enough, even as skilled warriors, to take us all. We sent them back. They never returned.'

'Gobidin was a proud and noble warrior...'

'Noble warrior,' Adothe softly repeated. 'Like when someone says they'll win a battle. Like you say Freydis has already won.'

'What are you saying, Adothe?' Madawaak raged as he lifted himself up on his elbow.

'I'm saying Freydis isn't here because her people won anything, she's here because they lost something,' he said, still softly as though he were ignorant of Madawaak's offence. 'I'm saying nobody wins a battle.'

'...That there is no such thing as a noble warrior?'

'What is a warrior if he doesn't kill people?'

'I've killed people,' Madawaak warned while the heat bubbled up inside him. 'I intend to kill more.'

'...And do you feel like you've won anything? Do you feel like you're going to win anything?'

Madawaak's fists were balled and he was half pitched out of his robe, but he stopped there. He could do something. Could take up his tomahawk and smash the old fool's head in. Or his spear. Or his arrows and bow. But Madawaak couldn't respond. As though it were fire doused with water, Madawaak's rage sank back down into the dark recess of his spirit where it hid, and he eased back into his robe like a kicked pup.

* * *

'What is this place?' Adothe asked as he staggered breathless up to the top of the flat hilltop that was Gobidin's cradle. He kicked the rusted dome of a helmet. It didn't budge, half buried in the earth. 'What happened here?'

Madawaak heard his voice for the first time since the night before and ground his teeth as he paced around. Visions of what had happened there assailed his mind. Memories of the massacre of Gobidin's people. Memories of his massacre of their hunting party. The heat bubbled up to his surface and Madawaak felt his skin flush and his muscles tense.

'This is where your enemy fell,' Madawaak stomped his foot on the spot where Gobidin fell and the snow had melted away under his marching feet, now darkened by the scant remains of a horse that decomposed there long ago. 'They came up here. He was the first to die.'

'I have no enemies. Alive or dead.'

'This is where Oonban fell,' Madawaak stomped again. 'I killed one of theirs here as well. Later. When they tried to hunt me down. One of the heads I mounted on stakes out there,' he pointed inland of where they were. 'I scared them off. I kept them scared back long enough to get away. I shouldn't have run. I had a whole hunting party here and I slaughtered them all. Some I burned,' he pointed over the edge of the cradle where he'd burned the thickets while they'd screamed tangled up in them. He could hear them. See their faces. 'The rest of them I got right up close and I felt their blood warm my face and my hands and I killed them. I bashed their skulls until they shattered. I rammed their heads on stakes and I...'

'Madawaak...'

'And you!' Madawaak shouted and pointed at Adothe. 'Gobidin's people weren't smashed on rocks. They were slaughtered here. Here along with the women and the children and the Forest Fathers who'd stayed behind. While you were on your Island laughing.'

'I never laughed,' Adothe said with a haunted expression.

'My family went home. They're dead too. Freydis got them. My mother and my father and my sister...'

'Madawaak...'

'Dabjeek!' Madawaak shouted with his hand in the air. 'Eenodsha. Ebauthoo. That was their names. Pale Ones never even knew their names.'

'How do you know they're dead?'

'I covered their children,' Madawaak said as he lumbered back to the inland vista and looked out at the slowly freezing tundra. Across it was their settlement. Their farms. The graves of the children he'd... 'I covered them with skins before I bashed their heads in with the back of my tomahawk. It was like... breaking eggs under a sheet.'

A wave of nausea came over Madawaak and the rage darkened from a fiery frenzy to a deep, black malaise that seemed to harden and depress him at once.

'Their children, Madawaak?' Adothe asked, softly.

'Help me gather the thickets,' Madawaak said. 'We need to light a fire.'

He turned and stormed towards the regrown brushes of thistle and thorn that surrounded the cradle and blocked most of its entry points. Adothe stepped in front of him. Madawaak didn't break his stride, intent on walking right into him.

'Debine,' he said. 'Shansee. Bashedtheek...'

Madawaak grabbed Adothe by the arms and frowned into his eyes.

'What are you doing?'

'We're naming the loved ones we'll never see again, aren't we?' Adothe said. 'So we don't forget why we're doing what we're doing?'

Madawaak scowled and breathed sharply through his nose.

'They're mourning me already,' Adothe said. 'They didn't cry when I was leaving but they're crying now. Getting it all out. To them, I'm dead already. Because they don't know when I'll die. Only that I will.'

'They're not dead.'

'Are they any less gone to me?'

Madawaak's furious visage broke but his rage did not subside.

'Help me light this fire, will you?'

* * *

As the night fell, Runa Carlsdottir plucked the last of the brown little roots from the hardening soil and dropped it into her basket. She'd have to boil them for days before anyone could eat them...

Runa turned to take them back to the house but something dull caught her eye on the horizon. She ignored it and walked a few paces. A bright star or...

... but there weren't any stars tonight.

She stopped and looked back. There was light across the darkened plains. Something dull glowing in the great distance... What was out there? Theirs was the innermost farm on Hop. Had someone gone out farther?

Another thought prickled up her spine and haunted the back of her mind. When she was a little girl her father had told her tales of when he'd hunted the lone skraeling who'd haunted Hop. How he'd set out with a hunting party, one of two. And they'd sent him to deliver a message and when he'd come back with more fighters, they'd found the heads of his fellows mounted on spikes. Mighty warriors. Tricked to their deaths at the hands of one little skraeling. The only reason her father had survived was because he was the lucky one to be sent on an errand. The second party dared not go any further.

The stories had given her nightmares and made her afraid of the dark until she'd realized there was no lone skraeling... not anymore...

But fire burned. Somewhere out there a fire was lit. And the distant orange light spread farther across the night sky with its otherworldly turquoise glow. A fire lit by someone.

Runa took the basket and hurried back to the house. Carl sat near the fire dish and drank from a horn while Helga washed a pot in a bath that was heated over it. Little Erlanh played on the floor with a carved horse. Runa put the roots down by the doorway and crossed to find her peeling knife...

'What's the matter with you?' Carl asked.

'I saw fire.'

'I see fire too,' Carl said as he raised his horn to the dish.

'Out there,' she said, foolish though it felt. Runa wanted him to go look and confirm that some distant childhood nightmare hadn't just surfaced for a moment while she was awake. 'Out across the plains.'

Carl's face immediately lost all of its colour and his eyes whitened with a terror that struck icy fear into Runa's heart. The horn shook in his grip and then fell on the floor. Carl was upright in the same instant and he marched to the door and threw it open. There he paused for a moment. Runa hurried to him but he stepped out. The door slammed in her face. She pushed it open and followed him.

The fire was truly burning. It had grown.

'Father...'

'Get inside!' Carl screamed as he whipped around as though to beat her. Runa was out of his reach. So he stormed behind her as she ran back for the house and he slammed the door behind them. Helga had picked up Erlanh and cradled him on her bed. Carl picked up his axe and atgier and kicked the bow and arrows.

'Pick it up,' he ordered Runa.

Runa's hands shook as she took them. She knew how to use them and had killed their dinner more than once... but this was a figment of her terrors. A ghost that haunted her father. How could she shoot a ghost?

'You two sleep,' Carl ordered his wife as he stomped back to the door and slid the latch home. 'We leave for Thorvaldafjord at first light.'

Runa held the bow and tried to control the shivering panic that shot up and down her body.

'Listen for any sounds,' Carl told her as he joined her by the fire. 'I'll guard the door. You listen for any sounds and shoot whatever makes them. It could be him trying to get in.'

'Who is it father?' Runa asked, and she hoped he'd answer her with a Norse name. Even a skraeling name that wasn't his.

Carl didn't answer her at all.

25

The Wolves Awaken

A red glow ignited before the darkness, as though the firelight pierced her eyelids and Night Eagle could see it again. But she couldn't see it. Only feel the radiance of its warmth. She knew this was a dream.

Come whoever may, she thought. Her heart quivered.

'It's a wolf,' came a voice that melted Night Eagle's spirit and brought her to her knees. 'Impersonating my baby sister.'

The light grew intense and rimmed with bright flame and in the midst of it stood Demasduit. Her eyes were sad but they were always sad. Her face was dirty and glossy with a sheen of sweat. Exactly as Shanawdithit last saw her. Surrounded by flame.

'I am home, Dema,' Shanawdithit said. Her voice was small and girlish. Could see again. Was little again. 'But you aren't here anymore.'

'What do you catch sculpin with?' Demasduit asked.

'A net.'

'Is this a net?'

Night Eagle looked down into her hand where her bow was gripped.

'Go home, Shana,' Demasduit said. 'Go home.'

The spectre faded just as it had come, and the light dimmed down and Night Eagle was in darkness again. The darkness in which she lived.

* * *

Few stars lit the night sky, but Tryggr could see the thin column of smoke the issued faintly from the pointed treetops up ahead. The looming black forms of the mountains brooded above them. Tryggr knew where the skraeling was. They kept the terrified skraelingjar trackers mounted on the spare horse towed behind Folkvar and Tryggr led them into a gallop through the dark woodlands.

In a thunder of galloping hoofs, the hunting party tore up the undergrowth and sent snow and dirt and debris hurtling in their wake. They wove through the trees. The smoke disappeared behind the canopy that engulfed them but Tryggr led them on with the certainty of a hunter on the trail.

The ground rose steeper and steeper beneath the riders. They passed flowing brooks and waterfalls there the mighty river to the east gathered. The horses' hoofs splashed in the muddy banks and bogs where the snow melted and the dripping canopies turned the ground into slush. Horses grunted as they worked to push themselves along. One of the skraelingjar cried out in fright but Tryggr led them on. Folkvar didn't even look back to see that they were both still there. When the ground dried again the horses regained their confidence. They galloped on.

Toli's horse sidestepped in fright as a doe caribou suddenly leaped up from the undergrowth and fled in fright with a fluffy white calf struggled to keep up and whine loudly at the same time. The horse slowed and veered off path. Toli fought to regain it. Suddenly, the stupid animal reared up on its hind legs and let out a piercing cry. He fought the reigns. The horse bucked and leaped around in the small patch of woods and Toli lost sight of the rest of the group.

'Stop it,' he shouted.

The horse grunted and bellowed but it managed to regain control of itself and start to slow down. Toli let it calm itself. He'd dropped a few arrows but didn't dare dismount to retrieve them now.

'There, now,' he said as he turned the horse to pick up the others. The horse obeyed. Toli rode through the dark forest alone, only able to guess exactly where Tryggr had led them. Then, suddenly he'd rode right into the middle of their group.

Tryggr's huge hand reached up and seized the reigns of Toli's horse right out of his grip. The mighty Norseman jerked the horse's head down and it froze still in obedience so quickly Toli tensed his thighs to keep from being thrown. He quickly dismounted. The pain of the sudden and urgent strain flooded his legs quickly.

'What are you doing?'

'Shut up!' Tryggr hissed. Toli's horse still stood frozen at Tryggr's command. 'If this thing makes one more sound, I'll slit open its belly and leave you to walk.'

Toli caught his breath but said nothing.

Tryggr stared at him as though he dared the boy to object.

'Let them off the horses,' Tryggr said without looking away from Toli. It took a moment for Folkvar to realize the order was for him and then he picked the two skraelingjar trackers down from the horse. They stared as though dazzled at something higher up the mountainside. Folkvar tied the horses' reigns to the pine trunks one at a time and all the while, the animals did not move.

Tryggr gently let go of Toli's horse as Folkvar came to get it while Toli looked ahead at what had the skraelingjar spooked. All he saw was that a faint orange glow issued from between the trunks of trees that were black in the night. The pines thinned ahead. In their way stood a spindly mass of leafless branches that reached skyward like bare talons.

Tryggr nudged one of the skraelingjar with the sharp end of his atgier. The savage looked at the other and they hesitated while their nerves made the pulses in their necks throb visibly. Tryggr turned the atgier and nudged the skraeling again. A tiny drop of blood ran down the maple-coloured forearm.

The skraelingjar looked at each other again. One nodded towards the glow and the second nervously led the way. Tryggr held his atgier in front of the two Norsemen before they could follow.

'If you slip, slip quietly. If you fall, if you break your ankle, I don't care. One scream. One cry. One loud utterance and I'll ram this through either of you as readily as I would them,' he nodded towards the skraelingjar.

Toli nodded nervously and the atgier moved aside. Tryggr went after the two guides and Toli moved to follow him but looked back at Folkvar when he realized the other older hunter stood still.

Folkvar stood there with both hands on his axe, white-knuckled. Eyes fixed on Tryggr.

'What are you doing? Come on.'

Folkvar looked at Toli. Without releasing his tense grip on his axe, he started to walk and Toli continued behind Tryggr. The brushes and ground were soon lost. Instead, Toli found himself grappling his way through fallen logs and winding roots and branches that seemed to grab at his leathers with the intent of dragging him into the darkness.

His foot slipped. Toli pursed his lips before he even braced to stop his fall and crashed down with a thud. A log dug into his ribs. Up ahead, Tryggr stopped and looked back. Toli took a few deep breaths and lifted himself up again. The axe on his back seemed to catch on every available piece of foliage and he was glad he'd left his bow and arrows back with his horse.

Folkvar was suddenly beside him.

'I won't let him hurt either of us,' Folkvar whispered.

Toli turned panicked eyes towards Tryggr, but their leader kept pushing ahead behind the skraelingjar.

'Now isn't the time,' Toli whispered.

'He spoke to her,' Folkvar said. 'She destroys men's minds. They ought to have killed her long ago...'

A harsh whistle came from ahead. Tryggr had stopped and now looked back at them. His axe gleamed in the dim light from ahead where it was slung at his hip. Toli could think of nothing else but to keep climbing. Folkvar fell behind him again. Tryggr turned and kept going on ahead. Toli breathed a soft sigh of relief and did not stop nor look back towards Folkvar again.

Finally, Toli heard a few scratches and a stumble from Tryggr and the fur-clad hunter fell out of sight. Toli could see the clearing. He hurried ahead and fell twice more, ignored the splitting pain that shot up his hand, and fumbled his way out and onto the hard, level ground. Tryggr held him steady with a powerful hand on his shoulder, then nodded in the direction of the glow.

The skraelingjar waited for their masters. Behind them was a rise in the mountainside wreathed in willows from behind which the firelight shone. The skraelingjar stood unusually still with their backs to the strange sight. Their eyes were wide and their hands were pressed firmly against their sides.

'They seem scared,' Toli whispered barely above a breath as Folkvar climbed out of the mess.

'Maybe there is one from the mainland in there?' Tryggr whispered. 'They must be scared of the mainlanders. Why else would they live on this shithole of a rock?'

Folkvar climbed to his feet and brought his axe to his front. Tryggr nodded to the skraelingjar. They didn't move. He pointed to them, then to the willows. They still didn't move. Neither one looked at the other but somehow, they both knew neither one was willing. Tryggr clenched his atgier and gestured with the blade.

Toli felt his teeth begin to chatter so he clenched his jaw to make them stop. He stayed close to Tryggr. Folkvar, with his huge axe and shield, dawdled behind them. The skraelingjar climbed up the embankment and Tryggr again whistled through his teeth to stop them.

Both of them froze.

Tryggr climbed up beside them and the three of them reached the top together. Toli reached up and pulled himself up and didn't look back to Folkvar. Tryggr slid his atgier between the two skraelingjar and nodded for the one closest to the willows to go through.

The fire crackled from the other side. The glow was strong and hot.

Shaking, the skraeling pushed through the willows and disappeared. Tryggr parted the hanging reeds with his fingers and looked in. Satisfied, he nodded to Toli. Then he slipped through as well. Toli held his breath and stepped after him. Folkvar followed as he pushed the other skraeling along in front of him.

The fire was as tall as three men and had a large base in the centre of what looked like the old ruins of a village. One of the skraelingjar's. No strong turf bricks were anywhere, only the flimsy bark and mud structures of the nomads. Tryggr moved a few paces out in front of them, hunched and fixed on something and then pointed near the fire.

A robe, thick with the sleeping form of a small human, rested near the fire. It must have been hot. Toli could feel the heat of the flame where they were at the edge of the village.

Tryggr looked back at one of the skraelingjar. He reached out, grabbed his shoulder and pushed him towards the robe. The skraeling looked at Tryggr with frightened eyes. Tryggr held up his atgier. The skraeling turned and walked towards the fire slowly. Toli could see how tense his shoulders were and the painful hesitation in each step as he got closer and closer to the bundle...

...Another sharp hiss from Tryggr.

Toli wished he'd brought his arrows. They could just kill it from here and go home.

Folkvar nudged his skraeling and sent him out after his fellow. They kept apart from each other, but Toli saw the glances between them.

'Terrified,' he breathed.

'Quietly,' Tryggr sighed.

On his gesture, the three hunters stepped lightly and closed in on the robe. Toli saw that it was wrapped up over the creature's head. From different angles the three closed in. Tryggr struck the first blow. He rammed his spear through the furs and Folkvar followed by chopping into it with his huge axe. Toli never took a swing.

He saw it first.

The attack stopped as soon as it begun. The robe hadn't moved. Tryggr pulled out his atgier and the blade was clean. Folkvar lifted his axe. He kicked the robe open and saw only a bundle of straw.

Tryggr turned and looked back at the skraelingjar just as an arrow ran through his jaw. He cried out. A second arrow hit Toli in the chest and Folkvar raised his axe in time to block the third. Before Toli could fall, Folkvar seized the weakened, dying boy and held him like a shield. Tryggr rolled onto his hands and knees in the dirt. He raised himself to his feet with his axe in his hands but a fourth arrow burst through his gut and knocked him down again.

Folkvar saw where it came from.

With his arm around dying Toli's neck he lifted the body high and ran forward towards the source of the arrows, battle axe held high.

Between the two rotted shells of cottages he found nothing.

Toli vomited blood over his forearm. He let the body fall. Tryggr cried out. Folkvar turned to see one of the skraelingjar guides with a rock in his hand. He leaped on Tryggr. Started to beat the hunter's skull. Folkvar roared and ran back to Tryggr and brought his axe down on the skraeling with a heavy wet thud. The skraeling's body crumpled. Blood sprayed lightly from the wound in his back as Folkvar dragged the axe from his shoulder blade. He turned just in time to see the flash of Tryggr's atgier in the firelight.

The other skraeling rammed the blade into Folkvar's gut. A pain that boiled his flesh brought Folkvar to the ground and he forgot his axe as both his hands grappled to pull the atgier out of him. The skraeling did it for him. In a frenzy from the blinding agony, Folkvar grabbed his axe. But he couldn't stand. The pain made his limbs flaccid. He looked up. Saw the skraeling raise the atgier and ram it down into his chest. Folkvar saw the blade sink through his body before the darkness took him.

* * *

Moosin felt the shaft pierce through his thigh as he drew the spear out of Folkvar's body. He looked down and saw it before the pain hit. Then crumpled to the ground as the pain sunk its talons through his flesh. Breathless he tried to crawl away. A spear landed in his path. Moosin turned and clambered to his feet. Limped as he tried to run. But another arrow swept before his face and the pain and the fear were too much. He buried his face in his arms and hunched down low. Cried.

A presence loomed over him.

He looked up through his tears and saw who stood over him, arrow at the ready.

* * *

'Please!' the tracker cried with his hands raised. The Night Eagle heard the language she'd almost forgotten over the years spoken again and relented. The wounded man had stopped still. He lay before her. She could hear the terror in his plea. 'Please Shanawdithit.'

Night Eagle kept the arrow ready. But did not draw it back.

'I know it's you,' he said, softly. She could sense him trembling. 'I saw you when our families went to battle together. I stayed in your father's village. My family were with you in the Broken Lands.'

'Who are you?' she asked, nervous to speak lest she get something wrong.

'Moosin of Shendeek's Family,' he answered. The bitter odour of death slivered through the haze of smoke and heat. 'Everyone thinks you're dead.'

'How did you know it was me?'

'You came here,' Moosin said. The terror had faded but there remained the searing pain of the arrow through his thigh. 'Here, of all places, to wait for us.'

'Why spare me then? What am I to you?' the anger in her question made her tighten her grip on the bow and arrow again.

'You're Demasduit's sister!' Moosin yelped. 'That makes you kin to Eirik Torvardsson...'

'That is not his name!' Night Eagle paced forward, drew back the arrow and pressed her foot onto the soft flesh of Moosin's thigh. The young man cried out and writhed in the dirt. 'Not his name!'

'I don't know what else to call him!'

'The child!'

'The child! The child! The child!'

Night Eagle removed her foot and took a step back. She felt the Pale One spear at her foot and kicked it aside.

'When they see you're alive,' Moosin strained to say. 'When they see... you... they'll realize they were wrong. They'll come back.'

'What? Who will?'

'The Forest People who went with Pale Ones.'

'Like you did!'

'My whole family did! I was sent to them by my own grandfather. I was a child. Barely older than you were... ohh...'

Night Eagle clicked softly and saw that Moosin was looking at her eyes.

'What happened to you?' he whispered.

'Your Lord,' Night Eagle said. 'She cut out my eyes and left me here.'

'Yet you live,' Moosin said. 'That you survived as a child left alone here is the will of the god spirits... that you did it with no eyes...'

'It was not the will of any god spirits,' Night Eagle growled. 'Your fantasies are all lies. It is lies that your family followed to the Pale Ones.'

'We are your people.'

'You are not my people,' Night Eagle seethed through her teeth. 'None of you are my people. The only person of mine on this land is the child, all the others are rotted away in its soil.'

'Don't say such things,' Moosin shook his head in disbelief. 'With you they'll come back. They'll fight against the Pale Ones as I just did. They'll see they... they got the message wrong. It was dark magic that made Demasduit birth a Pale One child...'

'It was the failure of her people to protect her that made Demasduit birth a child,' Night Eagle said as she slipped the arrow away and turned from Moosin. 'And the Pale Ones.'

'What have you come to do?' Moosin asked as he sat upright. He winced with the pain.

Night Eagle clicked and found the big axe. She picked it up.

'Which one was the leader?'

Moosin just sat there, dumbly.

'Point. I'll know.'

He pointed to Tryggr's body. Night Eagle moved over to him without even facing Moosin's direction and swung the axe down on his neck. The body rippled. Night Eagle chopped again. The thwack squelched. She swung a third time and heard the axe hit dirt. Discarded the axe. Drew her dagger. Picked up the severed head. Carved out the eyes with her dagger. Walked with it back towards Moosin.

'Can you walk?' she asked.

'Yes...' he told her, uncertainly.

'Take this back to his village,' she threw the head at Moosin's feet. 'Tell them I was headed south.'

'They'll kill me.'

'Good.'

Night Eagle turned to gather up her things.

'They'll skin me alive or burn me for what I've done...'

'What I did,' Night Eagle corrected.

'They'll still kill me,' Moosin said.

Night Eagle picked up her robe and paused.

'It will be a good death,' she said. 'You will find redemption. More than you will if you don't leave me right now.'

She heard as Moosin gathered up the head, got up, and staggered off.

* * *

There were only a few darkened patches in the clay left where Oonban's village had once stood. Left alone at night, unable to start a fire there, Gheegnyan played a game. He walked around in the dark that let his imagination paint whatever he wanted over it and tried to piece together the village again. When he thought he'd done that, he tried to add the people.

Mostly just Demasduit.

But all he could remember was the bonfire pit where Mooaumook had stood and been painted in red ochre. And where his father had stood beside him. He couldn't even remember the face of Oonban. The great Oonban. It frustrated him to exhaustion, like every other night, and he climbed back down to his little cave in the cliffside and settled in amongst the bird guano and cold dirt to sleep.

Night's biting cold followed Gheegnyan into the dreamworld. It numbed his face and every breath stung his sinuses while his flesh quivered. Thoughts of Demasduit flashed and flickered across a bare tundra under a pale sun. White on white. Gheegnyan tried to curl back up into a ball but his body would not move. The howl of wind reached from inside the cave into his mind and filled his dream with whipping winds and freezing gusts like pins piercing all over his face and hands. The visions stopped. For a moment, bright light was all there was. Pure mist. Like the gloom of the spirit world.

There was a low growl from somewhere close behind Gheegnyan.

He wanted to turn but couldn't.

A growl. A snort. Gheegnyan knew what it was. He closed his eyes while his flesh prickled in preparation for the strike. An agony he couldn't imagine.

With heavy footsteps that thudded under each powerful stride, the massive creature moved around to his side. The head was enormous. The mouth big enough to swallow a whole leg off him. The top of his head barely came up to its jaw while it walked on all fours and when the body followed, he wanted to collapse, dizzy from its sheer size.

The enormous creature turned and stood right in front of him. Then it reared up. As tall as four of him. It bellowed. He could only think of Demasduit. She was bigger than him when he'd seen her. But now would be smaller. Smaller than Gheegnyan who was dwarfed by this monster and yet it was this monster she slayed. Gheegnyan couldn't breathe in. He couldn't blink. His terrified eyes were fixed on it and yet the snow didn't sting them as it normally would...

...of course. He was dreaming.

'Creature,' Gheegnyan said as he forced himself to remain calm and remind himself again and again, it's only a dream. 'Why have you come to me now?'

The bear roared again. Light winked in the spittle as it oozed from the monster's fangs. The thought of Demasduit as she battled such a beast kept coming back into his mind...

'Demasduit?' he finally croaked.

The bear closed its mouth and looked down at him.

'You know what I've come here to do, don't you?' he said, as the fear simmered down.

The great bear looked down at him.

'Do you know the doubt in me?' he said, softly. A voice frail as the snowflakes that fluttered down past the mouth of his cave towards the waves that smashed mercilessly against the rocks below. Somehow, he was aware of them. Both the waking world and this strange limbo of his spirit. 'Do you know the... I don't think I can do it.'

The bear stood up and roared again.

'He is a child. He is one of us. He is your child.'

The bear fell back on its forepaws and looked up over Gheegnyan's head. The giant feet padded on the white snow but left no mark as the giant, fleshy body moved around Gheegnyan again and disappeared behind him. Slowly, the snorting faded off into nothing.

Gheegnyan woke up.

The dim blue light of the night's final moments filled the east-facing cave. The tiny snowflakes fluttered down like a veil that danced slowly and then rapidly and chaotically with the surge and fall of the ocean below. Gheegnyan shivered and his teeth chattered. Chilled to his bones, he stood up as far as he could in the tiny cave and danced about until the ache in his skin subsided. Ice prickled at the wetness in his eyes.

Sickly fear still haunted him from the dream. It had seemed so real. Every fibre of the bear's fur had moved as its muscles rippled before him. The heat of its breath still tingled his nape. The size of it...

In the darkness, he'd seen Demasduit. The night before. Big in his memories because he'd been so small, but he knew she was small. Smaller than usual. Next to that creature she'd have been...

...Gheegnyan stopped and thought about the child. He'd watched them from a distance or from behind the hilltops or tall grassy tufts and once from the fern forest when they'd come close enough to it. That little boy on his horse. Armed men had flanked him every time. With them... that face he couldn't forget. All that he'd heard about the demon woman from Adyouth and the others... he'd expected something terrible. Something inhuman. But she'd seemed so calm. The way she'd watched the child had been cool and almost nonchalant. She didn't guard him with fierce wildcat's eyes or the steely watchfulness of a mother wolf. She hadn't been gigantic either. Big, but they were all big. Most of the Pale Ones were bigger than her. She'd seemed small with them flanking her.

But what haunted him the most was her face.

A woman's. The men were half wreathed in beards and straw from under their helmets, but she was... soft. Delicate even. Her hair wasn't like fire at all. It was bright red and fell down her shoulders from under her helmet like a fountain of warmth.

She was a woman. A human woman. No demon at all.

Though he couldn't figure why, that thought made his hands shake more than any of the mythology he'd heard built up around the demon woman. Freydis. How could such a thing possess such power?

Gheegnyan thought of the polar bear then grabbed his bow and quiver. He'd prove it today.

* * *

'What are we going to do?' Adothe asked as the hilltop burned into daylight, as though the earth it was made of had caught fire. 'Wait here for them to come and kill us?'

'We trap them,' Madawaak said as he paced around the crags and rocky outcroppings that made up the west face of the hill, searching for something. 'Just like last time.'

'Do you expect that's going to work?'

Madawaak stopped and looked at him.

'It doesn't matter if it works,' he spat.

'I really think it does,' Adothe said as he followed Madawaak, who'd turned to pace off again. He had to jog to keep up. 'I think they'll expect a trap. They'll come at you from all angles and you'll be lucky to scratch one of theirs.'

'Me? What about us?'

'I didn't come here to die the first time I saw a Pale One...'

'But you came here to die.'

'Stop, boy!' Adothe shouted as his breath ran out.

Madawaak stopped and turned his furious, frenzied eyes to the old man.

'Boy?' he seethed. 'I haven't been a boy since...'

'Maybe they don't come at all,' Adothe said.

Madawaak frowned at him.

'Why would they not come?'

'You've got their attention. You're expecting them. Maybe they outwait you and make you do something even more stupid.'

Madawaak took a threatening step towards Adothe.

'Suppose they do come. A lot of them, like last time. What will the others do? Back in their village?'

Madawaak paused again. His brow was furrowed, but his eyes lost their rage.

'Wait for their warriors to come home...' he grumbled.

'Will they expect you to come home instead?' Adothe asked.

Madawaak looked at the hillside and Adothe saw that his brow was furrowed and his eyes were wild and unfocused.

'There will be children,' he said.

Adothe's heart sank.

'There will be guards... there will be warriors... there will be food and supplies for you to steal and livestock to slaughter...'

'... and their children.'

'Madawaak!' Adothe said, firmly. 'Don't go this way.'

Madawaak turned and continued around the hillside.

* * *

They had always said Lord Asny didn't look like a chieftain. Runa had been too young to know any different, but as she sat

at the Chieftain's table with old Gottfried at one side and her
champion, Eostre, at the other, she not only looked too small
but too frail. Soft and exposed there. With nothing but a turf
lodge and a wooden door to protect her from the ghosts that
roamed outside.

'Lord Asny, Carl the Karl,' said the bearded man who'd let
them in with a crooked, mocking grin. 'Urgent terrors.'

Asny prickled up. Runa motioned to bow but her father stood
right up in front of Asny. A sliver of panic tingled up Runa's
spine to see Eostre tense as her father got close to the Chieftain.
But Asny's small, pixie-like face with milky skin and light blonde
hair did not so much as twitch. She leaned forward.

'The cradle,' Carl said. 'I saw fire there last night. Enormous
fire. Was there anyone out there last night?'

Asny sat back in the chair. She looked at Gottfried.

'Did you go to investigate?' Gottfried asked.

'And leave my family?'

'No,' Asny said curtly. 'No, of course not.'

'They're outside,' the guard said.

Runa began to quiver with urgency. She'd expected them to
leap to their feet, take up their arms and storm out to besiege
the cradle. What she saw instead was her chieftain and her
chieftain's predecessor and advisor struck dumb with nervous
fear. Only Eostre sat calm and still. Her square, bull-like face,
thin lips and permanently-squinted eyes all firm with the same
stoical severity she'd greeted them with. But that didn't help
Runa. As though she picked up the sudden tension in the room,
her mind began to go wild with visions of what this skraeling
really was. Fanged beasts and furry wolfmen haunted her young
imagination. She tingled while her back was to the door and
ached to know her mother and little brother were out there.

Finally, Asny spoke.

'You will lodge here with your family,' she said to Carl. 'I will
call an Althing.'

Gottfried leaned close to the Chieftain and whispered into her
ear. Asny closed her eyes and took in his words. She took a deep
breath and opened them again.

'My Lord,' Carl started, cautiously. 'If that skraeling has returned... time is of the essence.'

'Carl insists on haste,' Asny said. 'My advisor insists on sending every able-bodied soldier out there to find him, pending a vote from the Althing.'

Asny looked at Runa. Stopped the young girl's heart with her delicate but icy stare.

'How good are you with that?' she asked, with a glance down at the bow Runa held before her.

'I've brought down meals for my family,' Runa forced herself to say. Still could only conjure a faint whisper, barely beyond a breath.

'What about skraeling?' Asny asked.

'She's strong enough,' Carl said.

'You of all people,' Asny interrupted him. 'You were there. You saw half my strongest dead. All by one set of hands. What chance has she got?'

Runa felt warm tears push to the backs of her eyes. Her lips began to tremble uncontrollably.

'Not if we're all there with her,' Gottfried said, having abandoned secrecy. 'We should lodge nobody. Send them all. Attack the spot where the skraelingjar of these lands fell in full force.'

'You have a son as well, don't you Carl?' Asny asked.

Carl hesitated.

'Yes.'

'How is he with an atgier or a bow?'

'He's a child,' Carl said.

'The skraeling will not get past us,' Gottfried said. 'If you're going to call an Althing, do so to muster all our force...'

'And leave my settlement unguarded?' Asny protested.

'We've had ten years to prepare for him,' Gottfried said.

'He has had ten years to prepare for us,' Asny said. 'It will be a debate for the Althing.'

'That will only take longer,' Carl said.

'None of us will be going anywhere until sunrise of the morrow,' Asny affirmed. 'We acted in haste last time.'

Gottfried looked away from her, eyes towards the ceiling.

'I will not make the same mistake. And I will encourage against sending our entire force and leaving our village unguarded.'

'But... my home...'

'You will lodge here,' Asny said. 'Your family cannot be rebuilt.'

She nodded towards the door. Runa took it as a cue to leave and was already striding breathlessly towards the door when the guard shot a sharp few words at her father. He stayed back.

When Carl met them outside, Runa couldn't stand still. Her flesh crawled with the fear she'd absorbed in the lodge with the elfin chieftain and those others whom Runa had been raised to revere and respect. There were no politics that could have hidden their fright. All except Eostre.

'We will go to Lord Viveka,' Carl said to Helga, who held Erlanh to her side against the biting cold mist that had whipped through the settlement. 'She will lodge us. I have to attend an Althing tonight.'

Helga nodded.

'Plead to Eostre,' Runa suddenly said, as though she'd caught the thought amongst the swarming mass and quickly delivered it before it fluttered away again. 'She was firm. She wasn't afraid like the others.'

'Gottfried was not afraid,' Carl said. He pushed her arm to get her walking with the rest of the family. 'Gottfried has slain whole villages.'

'He was afraid, father,' Runa said more quietly. Now she felt as though their survival itself hinged upon Eostre. 'She will send everyone.'

'Maybe we shouldn't send everyone...' Carl's eyes were on the tuft of his son's hair that peeked over his wife's shoulder as she walked ahead of them.

'I don't want to be left behind!' Runa said as the frantic thought taunted her again. 'Do not leave me behind.'

That was it, she had to admit to herself. That was her fear. She would never see this thing and put an end to the horrors. Or that she would be left here to imagine the horrors the warriors were facing while she sat with her mother and brother, exposed in the white snow. The more guards she had, the less force they had.

Carl said nothing.

'Promise me, father.'

'I can't promise you.'

'Promise me!'

'It will depend on the Althing!' he snapped and stopped midstride. She stopped as well. Defeat weighed on her and brought the tears back. He walked on.

Then she would go to the Althing.

26

An Assassin's Arrow

Gheegnyan decided on the ferns because they hadn't come that way in a while. It was early in the day and Freydis tended to take the boy riding and for his practice in the evening so he used the time to amble down to the babbling brooks that ran down through the ravines into the lakes to catch fish. Some hardened sap from a maple tree was sweet on his tongue along the way. The time allowed Gheegnyan to wonder if it would be Freydis who would kill him.

He could picture it...

The child dead by his hand. Before he could even feel the flush of guilt on his conscience, she'd have that long steel shaft of shining stone out, just like he'd seen her do in practice. That sword. She'd cut him in two with it. Would it hurt? How long would she let him suffer? Her fury would compel her. She would not have time to punish him. Then he'd be free. His spirit would break away from this awful world and he could be with Adyouth again...

Gheegnyan had to stop. He was blinded by tears that ran freezing down his cheeks.

Would he see what his actions would do for his people? Would he know life again, the way it had been before the Pale Ones came? Thoughts didn't hurt...

...How would the child die?

He couldn't walk and consider it at the same time. But the polar bear. The polar bear that had been a hundred times the size of Demasduit and fallen on her spear.

Gheegnyan kept walking and knew he had to eat something before the hunger pangs and thoughts drove him crazy. He could not walk away now. Too close. Too much was gone. Where would he walk to?

It was past noon and Gheegnyan was almost doubled over with agony from his hunger. The thought of eating put a foul taste in his mouth. But that was his mind. Scattered. Had to focus. Not eating would only make him die before he could do anything to the child.

What is it like to kill a child? Their skin so easy to break... their little bones so fragile...

The thought weakened Gheegnyan and he dropped amongst the clumps of ice that had gathered on the brook's banks. He looked at his hands. At his legs. Felt his pulse. Felt all the emotion and aimless, meandering thoughts and sick feelings of all the idle moments of his life move through him. Lost in his memories. Gheegnyan felt the joy, the love and loneliness. The exhilaration that came before every fall. *It wasn't a long life, but it was rich with so many sensations,* he thought to himself. *All lost.* Would he take them to the Spirit World? Would he feel as strongly about those he'd loved in that gloomy unknown?

Was there a Spirit World at all?

Either way, he thought, *the last thing I'll know aside from the devastating pain that would mark the end of my life would be the horror of murdering a child.* Gheegnyan cursed Keathut. Why him? Because he was alone amongst them. Why not one of the others who was alone? Because without Adyouth he was idle. Useless. The others still had use. The others could repopulate...

'How could I do this?'

A freak gust of wind rustled through the evergreens. Gheegnyan thought he heard a low growl. He looked over his shoulder. A wolf pack? No... it was deeper...

It was a gust of wind.

'I can do this,' he said. He looked down into the water. A trout hovered in the running water, clear as air, right below his feet.

With a whip of his well-honed hand he caught the slimy creature. The squeeze of his hunter's fist kept it from flopping clear of him and he bit into the top of its head. With a slimy crack, the fish fell limp. Gheegnyan was at his leisure to eat it.

When the bones and inedible pieces were discarded to feed the mighty pines, Gheegnyan headed back. He knew what was next. There was nothing else in the way. Demasduit had not asked to be set upon by a polar bear and Keathut had not forewarned her that would be her fate. And though there was time between, it had spelled her doom. Gheegnyan would not suffer as she had, he promised himself. He would put up too much of a fight. Freydis would have no choice.

He still hunted his way back. Soft steps. His movements did not so much as squelch in the wet, muddy snow or snap the damp twigs. All his weight on the toes first. Then the rest of the foot. One step. One portion of the foot at a time. He held and distributed his weight as though it was in his hands to manipulate. Stopped every few paces. Listened. Searched the ground. Hunting. His polar bear would not sneak up on him. Gheegnyan was the hunter.

The sun became its strongest and cast the shadows of the trees across the meadows that were patched with snow and grass that had turned brown and all but suffocated under the blanket of snow that had sat on it for two days. Soon winter would come. All the fields would be white. Gheegnyan would not see them. Nor would he see the sparkle this later sun would ignite across those snowy fields or the way it all turned into powdery blue by night.

Neither would the child.

Everyone had been innocent once. Adyouth, himself, Mooaumook... Gheegnyan remembered the look in Ebauthoo's haunted eyes when she'd come to them as a girl. That was how innocence died. The child would have that look. But not for long. Gheegnyan closed his eyes and prepared himself to see it.

He quickened his pace through the fern gully and climbed a maple tree. Up into its canopy, one branch at a time, until he could see the meadows, the incline up to the cliffs and even the dark patch where Oonban's village had once stood all from his vantage point. Beyond it, the azure sky had a misty haze. Over the ocean. It would be a freezing night. A cold that two people, at least, would never feel.

The sun blazed without much warmth. Soft northern gusts caressed the canopies with slow rhythm that rustled the leaves and Gheegnyan sat straddling a thick branch. There he waited and watched as the shadows progressed towards the hillside and began their way up.

Maybe they weren't coming? Would Gheegnyan be able to muster this bravado again tomorrow? Or the day after? Lack of sleep had already made his thoughts fleeting and manic. His eyes stung so easily. A gooey film covered his face...

Dark shapes moved along the cliffside.

Gheegnyan gathered himself yet again and peered through the leaves. Four horses. What looked like only three riders. The child was too small to see from so far back. There was no cover between him and them. No way of getting closer.

All Gheegnyan could do was wait and watch.

The horses stopped at the old village and the riders he could see — the two big ones and the smaller one that was Freydis — dismounted. They stood for a moment. Gheegnyan had seen this before. The child often struggled to dismount, again later to remount, and his mother and two guards would do nothing but sit and watch him.

Why did they come out here? Surely there were enough places to practice down at Straumfjord, he wondered. What was the significance of this place? Did she want the child to see that the other half of his bloodline had been trampled into the ground? Did she want... a skraeling like Gheegnyan to see them?

A chill prickled all over Gheegnyan that had not come on the breeze.

* * *

Eirik and Ingebjorg helped Snorre off Eirik's horse. Freydis watched them. Capser and Hakon trotted about on the hillside and watched the distant trees. Finally the stupid boy was off.

Ingebjorg dusted off Snorre though he hadn't dirtied himself getting off the horse and Eirik automatically joined in.

'Why are you doing that?' the glassy voice of Freydis cut in. Eirik jumped.

'I'm sorry.'

'You're sorry? What for?'

'I...' he stuttered.

'Kings don't stutter, boy. You said you were sorry and I asked you what for?'

'I don't know,' Eirik answered in despair. Then lowered his head and awaited the strike.

'You don't say sorry,' Freydis said. 'You don't ever say sorry. Not to me. Not to anyone. Ever. Understand?'

Eirik nodded while his cheeks burned.

'Why were you dusting the boy off?'

Eirik looked at Snorre. He and Ingebjorg stood back and watched on with wide eyes and pursed lips.

'Answer me.'

'I don't...'

'Because the girl was doing it?'

Eirik said nothing.

'Would you do some stupid thing a stupid girl does just because she's doing it?' Freydis demanded. 'Answer me.'

'No.'

'Then why were you doing it?'

'I won't do it again.'

'What will you do?'

Eirik thought about his answer. Every lashing he'd received in the past year livened with tingles until he found the response he thought would please her and make her stop and love him the way papa did.

'I will think for myself.'

Freydis squinted at him. The green of her eyes seemed to intensify as though they burned. She could look inside him. See his deceits... but all his energy was on resisting the urge to cry. If she saw that...

'You're a smart boy,' she finally said. 'I wonder if you're too smart.'

She opened a leather saddle bag on her horse's hip.

'I've had these made for you and your friends.'

When she turned back, she had a small axe in her hand, held by the head. She offered it to Snorre.

'Go on,' Freydis insisted.

Snorre gingerly stepped forward and reached out. Then, once he had the handle in his hands, he jerked it away from her and retreated five paces back to where he'd stood. He held it close. Looked at it as though he would never look away.

'Thank you,' he said.

Freydis slid a short, downsized atgier from a leather sock behind the bag and held it out to Ingebjorg.

'Go on girl,' she said. 'My first weapon was a life size atgier when I was smaller than you. I snapped the head off and used it as an axe.'

'Thank you, my Lord,' she said as she took the weapon and bowed. 'It is an honour.'

'Yes it is,' Freydis said. 'I had to use mine right away. It was still stuck in my first suitor's face when they found him.'

Ingebjorg looked at Freydis and bowed again.

'And for you,' she said as she reached back into the saddle bag. 'An exact copy.'

Freydis pulled out a miniature version of Gunnlogi and held it hilt-first to Eirik. He took it in his trembling hand. The sight of it made his flesh tense and now to hold it he could not but quiver.

'What's the matter boy?' Freydis asked. Then she drew the real Gunnlogi and held it up so the sunlight caught its blade and burned the children's eyes. 'That cost me a fortune. And one day you'll wield the real thing.'

Eirik looked up at her. With all his might, he pulled back the fear and the tremble and the daunted feeling but he knew he looked ridiculous. She snorted and sheathed Gunnlogi.

'You're scared of it,' Freydis said.

'No I...'

'You two!' she snapped at his friends. 'That replica sword could buy your families a knarr. I'll give it to the first one who can draw blood from Eirik.'

'Mother,' Eirik gasped.

'Careful boy,' Freydis said.

Eirik turned in time to see Snorre draw back the axe. He leaped backward and fell on the ground and the swing missed.

'What are you doing?' Eirik squealed.

'I want that sword.'

He swung again. Eirik scrambled to his feet and the axe hit the slushy grass where he'd lay so hard it dug into the cold earth. Snorre didn't stop. He came again with the axe drawn back and Eirik ran to hide behind his mother. Freydis turned and mounted the horse. Eirik stopped before he fell under the hoofs.

The axe...

Eirik brought the sword up and felt it smack into something. Snorre screamed. He dropped the axe in the clump of snow. Blood ran from his fingers.

'I'm sorry...' Eirik apologised. Snorre shoved him with both hands and Eirik slammed onto his back. Snorre screamed and picked up the axe again.

The blade of Gunnlogi came from above and stopped in front of him like a gate. He froze. Looked up at Freydis.

'You lost,' she spat.

Snorre squatted down, crossed his arms and began to cry. Freydis put Gunnlogi away. Eirik climbed to his feet, tears in his eyes and Snorre's blood smeared on his leather. Freydis looked down at him.

'Well, what about you?' she demanded of Ingebjorg.

Ingeborg dropped the atgier and shook her head.

'He's my friend.'

'Girl,' Freydis ridiculed. 'Why don't you have any other boys for friends? Ones that don't cry like babies when their hands are cut.'

Snorre's cries instantly became silent. His face was red and half covered.

'Redeem yourself, boy,' Freydis said. 'Pick up the atgier and...'

A flick caught her attention and Freydis looked at Casper and Hakon. Both were still, having watched the fight. A whistle arched through the air.

Snorre let out a gust of air. Eirik looked at him. He was still as he was. Nothing but...

...an arrow.

An arrow had struck through his back. Longer than he was tall. Ingebjorg screamed as Snorre lurched to one side and fell on the ground. Blood bubbled up from his lips. Eirik was frozen still. He barely noticed as Freydis stopped her horse in front of him and held up her shield. Something thudded against it.

Casper and Hakon charged their horses into the fields.

'Bring him alive!' Freydis screamed after them. 'Alive!'

* * *

Deep horror rattled Gheegnyan as he realized he'd hit a child. As soon as Freydis moved her horse, he knew he'd got the wrong one. The second arrow exposed him. The two guards broke off in different directions and arched around to ride towards Gheegnyan from his flanks. He primed an arrow to fire at one but there issued a snap through the air.

Move!

Gheegnyan rolled aside as Freydis' arrow rammed deep into the earth where he'd laid in the snow. Adrenaline flooded through him. Run, he thought. Run at her or run away? Gheegnyan looked up at Freydis just as she loosed another arrow. He leapt to his feet and turned and ran as the horses closed in from either side.

Gheegnyan ran away.

The trees from which he'd crept so slowly and so quietly now seemed so far away. Behind him, the two guards crossed paths and both turned broad to come at him again from the sides. Gheegnyan ran with all his might. Still the distant trees seemed to come no closer. All he could hear behind him was the pounding of the horse's hoofs and all he could see ahead of him a giant expanse of snow. Gheegnyan ran though his lungs burned with icy cold. He dropped his bow. Tore off the quiver of arrows. Ran and ran. The snow which had seemed thin and slushy now slipped beneath his strides and slowed him.

One horse closed in behind. Gheegnyan turned. Freydis. She'd charged right between her two guards and now flew at him on the horse with her sword held high. Behind the horse a tunnel of dusty, filthy snow kicked up. Gheegnyan screamed in terror. With a last rush of blurry adrenaline, he pushed to get to the trees...

...something flickered at the bottom of his eyes...

...They seemed to get closer... closer... but Gheegnyan looked down...

There was an arrow through his thigh.

Pain and shock struck through Gheegnyan's entire body all at once and the ground smashed into his face and chest. He crumpled around the arrow. Before he could scream, the huge horse, Freydis perched on top, ran over his legs. Gheegnyan felt them whip around under the horse's hoofs. Bone snapped. Cartilage twisted and tore in a succession of pops and crackles.

Gheegnyan opened his mouth to scream but the shock stole his voice. All he could do was wretch. The huge horse ran over his legs again but this time he felt nothing. Gheegnyan's body stopped tumbling but his mind kept rolling around in the snow and he clutched the slush in his fists as though he could keep himself on the surface of a capsizing world.

That was when he lost consciousness.

27

Two Assassins

'Where is it?' roared Rangvaldr as he pushed himself against the crossed atgiers of Gustav and Casper and leaned his head through towards Freydis. 'Where? I want to skin it alive!'

Freydis held little Eirik by the shoulders and stopped midway across the lodge. She turned and looked back at the raging hunter with his shirt torn asunder. Blood ran in streaks down his pectoral muscles from where the atgier blades pushed into his skin. His wife wailed and screamed outside. She still cradled their dead son and her din drowned out the chains that slithered on the other side of the wall, in their privy.

Almost.

The giant, wild-haired man's head twitched as he listened. He held up his axe.

'You've got it locked up,' he turned to charge back out. Casper and Gustav, the seasoned guards, seized him by the shoulders and the force of the wild man's stride almost tore them off their feet.

Torvard watched from their arras. He looked at Eirik, the ashen face, the terror in his eyes, and he knew something awful had happened to his boy. He hadn't been there to protect Eirik. Freydis looked at Torvard. She tapped Eirik on the shoulder and mouthed 'Take him.'

Torvard hurried across and took his son by the trembling hand, then led him silently to the arras and slid it across and blocked them out. Eirik sat immediately on the foot of his and Freydis' bed, huddled himself, and began to cry.

Freydis' glassy, songlike timbre was too quiet to understand from behind the arras.

'I'll kill you both!' roared Rangvaldr.

'Then what?' Freydis snapped. Then she fell silent again.

Torvard cursed himself for not knowing what to say to Eirik to comfort the boy. Not even knowing how to begin. How could she do it? Why was she so fast with conviction and persuasion? She who would use it for nothing but her own gain... it wasn't fair.

Torvard finally sat next to his son and put his hand on the boy's back. Eirik dropped to one side and buried his face in Torvard's shoulder and put one little arm up across his chest.

'My son,' Torvard breathed softly. 'My little boy. You saw something terrible today, didn't you?'

'When you finish,' Rangvaldr roared. 'When you know where its kin are you will give it to me? Me and only me. Right away. Immediately!'

Freydis said a few soft words and then something that sounded like 'Done.'

Then there was silence.

Eirik suddenly pushed off his father, sat upright and rapidly wiped his eyes with his sleeve. Torvard listened for Freydis' footsteps.

'Son, it's okay,' Torvard said. 'It's okay if something really hurts. If you don't know what else to do, it's okay...'

The arras was thrown aside and Freydis stepped in. Her eyes fixed on Eirik. Then they flickered at Torvard so he knew what she said was for him:

'Get out.'

'What happened?'

'Get out!' she ordered.

Torvard slowly stood, but did not break his unblinking stare at Freydis. He stepped closer to her.

'Don't you punish him,' Torvard hissed. 'Not for this. I've never seen him so distraught, so don't you dare punish him...'

'If you ever threaten me again,' Freydis boomed at him. 'I will have you drawn and castrated like the Christians do.'

Torvard paused.

'I'm not threatening you, Freydis, I'm...'

'*Don't I dare?*' she spat. 'Who do you think you are? Get out!'

Torvard stared at her with his fists clenched. Without darkness in his mind, he realized he could do it right now. Hit her. Smash her across the face with all his might. She wouldn't fall down. Freydis would barely react. But she'd know the hatred he felt for her in that instant. As pure and truthful a hatred as the love he'd always felt for her until that point.

But he left them alone. Torvard crossed the lodge towards the doors and the howling woman. Over the cries and screams he heard his wife's voice, stripped of its songlike melody and instead rough with rage she seemed to reserve only for Torvard and Eirik.

'You do not cry! If they kill me and your father in front of you, you still do *not ever* cry!'

He heard the faint slaps of her hands across the boy's face and back. It brought tears to his own eyes. But he kept walking. Before Torvard knew it, he was outside and faced with a silent crowd that had gathered around Rangvaldr and Hilde as they built a funeral pyre for their little boy Snorre. Torvard pieced together what had happened that day. What the new skraeling prisoner in their privy have done and why Freydis wanted him alive.

For one nightmare moment, he looked at the pyre and saw Eirik's lifeless body laid upon it. It was enough to make the tears run freely. His face flushed. In sadness and fury he wondered if he could go one further than to strike her...

Snorre was a good boy. Beloved. The faces of the crowd were all wet with tears, hollow-eyed and ashen in their deathly malaise. Men, women and other children. They'd kill their own if they knew one of their own was responsible. Torvard knew they thought that the skraeling chained up in the privy was the one responsible.

Torvard wondered if he could tell them why Freydis took Eirik practicing out where she did every day... tell them the truth... would that break the spell she had them under? Would they kill her?

If they didn't...

Torvard turned and staggered away, hunched over the stabbing ache in his heart. He knew he couldn't watch Snorre on the pyre. Soon there'd be no telling Snorre from Eirik. Too much to bear.

* * *

Madawaak stayed low as he crept towards the silent village. It was eerie without the hum of life. A still and lifeless anomaly on a landscape completely alien to it. Their homes... ripped up from the earth and stacked... it was haunting to see them all empty.

Adothe crouched and ran clumsily behind him. He held himself correctly, but his feet were not balanced, weight not distributed to his feet and his gait much too uncoordinated and quick. The old man stumbled and hit a pile of logs and let out a yelp. Then propped himself up against it to catch his breath.

Madawaak smiled. Not to mock him, but to suggest how wonderful it would be to find all their settlements like this. Even the big one in the Forest Lands.

Adothe continued his fumbled attempt at silent running and staggered into Madawaak. The young hunter caught the old man in his arms. Chuckled aloud.

'I think it's okay,' Madawaak whispered.

They looked around. Both still felt the thick tension around them in the air. The promise of death was liberating either way. They knew the end was coming. They'd caused chaos amongst the Pale Ones. Now there was only some death to dole out before their own came and they'd have done what they came to do.

The homesteads and domiciles thickened beyond the small cluster of structures and the land between them grew narrower. Still there didn't seem to be a stir of life. *They're all gone,* Madawaak thought. *All after me.*

'Are you okay?' he breathed to Adothe.

'Let's get this over with,' the old man said, gravely. There was a hollowness in his face that Madawaak had seen since the cradle had burned.

[344]

He knew why. Adothe could not accept the way things were.

Madawaak continued deeper into the village, past the empty domiciles. Their doors were closed. Like sleeping eyes shut. Adothe fumbled along behind him. The darkness welled up inside Madawaak and the fire began to bubble up in his blood.

Adothe didn't understand the way things were.

A low rumble and rhythmic squeaking stopped them both. Madawaak and Adothe crouched down by a pile of unused turf at the side of one of the smaller domiciles.

'I don't understand...'

Madawaak hissed at him to be quiet. Adothe recoiled and closed his mouth.

A large, heavily tanned man emerged on the wider street. He pulled a tray mounted on wheels and stacked with jugs and plates behind him. He was old. Grey haired. Hunched. But great muscle still flexed and rolled beneath his loosened skin. He wasn't a true Pale One. Too dark-skinned. One captured from somewhere across the waves and brought here. Slowly he dawdled right past them. The old slave's ailing eyes had failed him.

It was a start.

Madawaak clutched his tomahawk and leaped out from his hiding place and jumped up onto the cart and the old slave turned in time for Madawaak to smash the tomahawk into the side of his head. The chert blade embedded in his skull with a crack and knocked his jaw loose from its hinge and popped one eye out. The old slave was dead instantly and the weight of his body pulled away from the tomahawk as it fell.

The dog cart fell under Madawaak's weight as the screams issued from all around. No... not screams, he realized with an icy shudder. A war cry. He crashed to the ground as the Pale Ones spewed out from the domiciles that had been silent seconds ago. He rolled and leaped to his feet as the bows thwacked. The arrows hit the dirt behind him. Madawaak leaped towards Adothe.

'Run!'

The old man turned and ran hard ahead of Madawaak. They wove between the domiciles as the arrows flung through the air behind them. Every whizz and thud blasted Madawaak with another jolt of lightning-like adrenaline until he ran with fevered intensity and ground his teeth. Adothe kept in front. More of the doors burst open ahead of them and more of the Pale Ones emerged.

Women... they were all women!

Adothe ducked low and ran ahead. Madawaak's eyes darted around and his heartbeat rang out loudly in his ears. A door burst open and a giant Pale One stepped out. She swung her axe high and Madawaak ducked and slid across the snow. Another appeared in front of him. Blocked his path. He dodged the stab of her atgier and grabbed the pole. She jerked it back. The splinters drove through the skin of Madawaak's hand but he did not let go. He chopped the pole with his tomahawk and snapped it. With another swing, he cleaved her chest.

He drew out the tomahawk. Turned. Knew she was right behind him. Ducked the swing of an enormous woman's blade. But she followed through. Her knee rammed into his face.

Hot pain flooded his lips and his skull and numbed his mind while blood flooded the back of his mouth. Madawaak crashed backward onto the snowy grass. The first breath bubbled and choked in his throat and Madawaak coughed and blood and teeth burst out of his mouth. On the other side of the haze, the giant Pale One woman raised her axe to deal the death blow.

A cry scythed through the air.

The blurry form of Adothe rammed into the woman's front. Right under her axe. The weapon dropped from her hands and landed on its side in the snow beside Madawaak. Adothe swung his tomahawk again and again. Beating it against the giant woman's armour while his legs braced around her midriff and held him in place. Finally she fell backward. Face bloodied to a pulp and neck chopped down to the bone.

Another Pale One was right behind her.

Madawaak grabbed the huge axe and lifted it as Adothe let out a gasp and spun with the force of the arrow. It had pieced his collar. Madawaak roared and spat blood until he could gasp air through his mouth. But Adothe sprang to his feet again. The arrow that flew towards Madawaak rammed through Adothe's ribs from behind. The old man staggered but did not fall.

'Run away!' Adothe screamed. Blood bubbled from his nose and his lips turned red.

The old man turned and raised his tomahawk. Another arrow jerked him and he threw the tomahawk only a few paces.

'Run Madawaak!'

As a fourth arrow sent the old man to one knee, Madawaak saw the archer and as if time had slowed Madawaak could see her there behind her bow. See the anger. See the terror. The revulsion as she primed a fifth arrow. Madawaak saw her young face and made sure she saw his. Then, he turned and ran for the forest. The arrow shot at him whizzed by and hot air slapped his face but Madawaak didn't look back.

Blood filled his gullet. Agony zigzagged up and down his legs, hips and sides. The world dipped and swirled and almost faded into darkness. But Madawaak didn't miss a stride. Didn't collapse until he knew he was out amongst the lakes with their icy sheen atop the water and the slight hills and the tufts of frozen reeds that could shelter him.

There, he collapsed.

* * *

Eirik's mama led him towards the closed door of the privy. They went around the new one built for the servants and approached the door of the old one, where now only one thing was kept. He felt short of breath. Dizzy. Aeda opened the door for them and held it.

The festering smell would have stopped Eirik in his tracks but Freydis' powerful hand remained clasped on his shoulder and pulled him along. They stepped into the dark little space. As they moved through the dark room, Eirik saw in the light cast by the open door one of the limp, bloodied hands that hung from a shackle. It dug into the flesh and blood ran down the

[347]

brown arm. Eirik closed his eyes. He knew they were inside when the cold, nauseating odour enveloped him.

'There he is,' Freydis whispered.

Eirik knew he had to open his eyes. Slowly he did. The sight filled him with a deluge of terror and nausea and his body instinctively turned him away with a deep shudder. Freydis held him tight and forced him to face it.

'Look!'

He looked again. The small but muscular body hung with his hands clasped in irons and nailed to the ceiling beam. A tall stump was placed for him to sit on. The creature's legs hung over the sides and through the ripped trousers Eirik could see they were swollen and blue. Red in some patches. Dark, deep red. The stench was of human waste, rotten meat and some miasma of other things Eirik didn't want to imagine.

'There he is,' she said again. Her fingers dug deep into his shoulder. 'Do you want to say anything to him?'

'I can't...'

'I can. Say what you want to say.'

Eirik took a breath in that made his stomach tense and his gullet fill with slime.

'Snorre was my friend...'

Freydis translated his words.

'You...' Eirik stopped to swallow the ball that lurched up in his throat.

'Cry now,' Freydis threatened, 'and I'll lock you in here overnight.'

'You killed my friend!' Eirik blurted out as quickly as he could.

The skraeling said something half mumbled and slurred.

'He said he was trying to kill you,' Freydis said as she squeezed Eirik's shoulder even harder. 'He thought Snorre was you.'

'Why?' Eirik asked.

The skraeling answered Freydis' translation.

'Because,' Freydis said, 'the people who hide from us and won't help us want to kill us. They want to hurt us. And they think that if they kill you, all the thralls we gathered here will turn against us. Help them, you understand?'

'I understand,' Eirik said as he felt the tightness in his chest and the heat under his skin. It rose from his gut. Clutched his heart. 'Where are the others who hide?'

Freydis released her grip. Her vice-like hold on him melted into a proud caress as she translated the question. Amid the anger and fury, Eirik felt a warmth in his stomach. She loved him. He'd won her over at last and this was all it took. Rage was all she wanted, all along.

'He said we can kill him as slowly as we like,' Freydis said. 'But he will die before he tells us anything.'

Eirik promised himself he'd never stop raging. Not ever. Never lose this love he'd earned at last.

'What do you think we should do?' Freydis asked Eirik, gently.

'Hurt him,' Eirik said, high on the moment. 'Hurt him until he does tell. But don't kill him. Otherwise he won't.'

Eirik felt her smile.

'Go on, Eirik,' Freydis said. 'Go comfort Ingebjorg. She's very sad and needs someone strong like you to look after her.'

Eirik puffed up and headed off to see to his duty.

* * *

Freydis stared at Gheegnyan as the child closed the door behind her and left them in darkness.

'What is your name?' she asked.

Gheegnyan said nothing.

Freydis moved in the dark space and Gheegnyan heard a soft scrape and then she clasped her hand against his exposed, bloody knee. For a moment, he felt the sharp pain pressed between their skin. Then it sunk into his flesh with twisting, stabbing agony that made him scream as though his eyes were about to explode.

'Gheegnyan!' he cried.

Freydis released her grip. The pain brought tears from him.

'Don't make it so easy,' she whispered.

[349]

He saw only a momentary blur of light as Freydis left Gheegnyan in the darkness.

28

Coming Home

Madawaak ate what he could scrape out from under tree bark or pull through cracks in the ice over frozen ponds, slept on beds of leaves and twigs gathered from under trees and spread in caves, warmed himself in his own clothing and felt his own body fester underneath the furs that kept the cold off. Slowly strength returned. Thoughts returned. Always the sight of the Pale One girl who'd killed Adothe. If what he could force himself to swallow did not bring the strength that slowly coursed through his body little by little, then the memory of her would.

The clouds darkened over the days. White mist fell upon the open fields at night and provided cover for Madawaak to sneak back to the scattered homes that skirted their village. That was where the strange beings were kept behind fences and fed and grown to be killed for food without the hunt. The homes were dormant.

They'd come back soon.

One home was farther out than the others and their cows stood in a paddock nearby it. Madawaak watched it. Kept his eyes on the horizon that swallowed the sun every night and waited to see their hunting party come back over it. By now they will have spread out. They were searching the forests and the jagged south-eastern coast.

As he kept his watch one evening, he saw a lone Pale One atop a fast horse gallop out of the mist. He rode past the dormant domicile and disappeared in the direction of their village. Madawaak wrapped his skins around his head to stay out for the night. When morning came the thudding of the hoofs woke him as the rider went back out. Back to join the hunt for him. Snow had fallen overnight. Madawaak was half buried in it when he lifted himself up.

Winter had arrived.

He knew that Pale One would tell the others about Madawaak and Adothe. Tell them there were two ghosts, not one, and that one of them was slain. They might even reward that girl. They would come back. They would search around nearby; the forests he'd run into and the rocky badlands and hillsides that surrounded them. They'd find his hiding places before long.

Madawaak spent one more day foraging. He ate roots that slept beneath the ice and awaited the warmer days. Found fish. Sharpened his tomahawk. Thought about the Pale One girl. She was young and fit and strong but frightened. Without the steady watchfulness of a seasoned fighter. It might have been her first human.

It would be her last.

Madawaak hacked through the pond ice again and watched as the water settled and waited quietly until one of the little blue crayfish appeared and then he snatched it. Dived his numb hand into the ice and grabbed it. Madawaak threw his catch aside and padded his hand on the thickening snow. The crayfish fell into a cold coma. He picked it up and bit the head off with his remaining teeth and sat on a snowy hillside to chew through the shell. His gums had healed but were still tender. The slimy taste was foul. But it would bring him back to himself. He had recovered enough.

Soon they would come.

The evening mists gathered and filled the twilight with imposing walls that wreathed all of the land. Madawaak fixed his gaze on the opaque glow of setting sun. The only way to find the settlement in this was from memory. That way was west. The village was east. He made a marking in the snow with his heel.

Still the riders did not return.

Maybe they were waiting for him?

Madawaak got up and walked in the deepening night until the dark blue became thick, inky blackness. Their home could be arm's reach away. He wouldn't know. But neither would they and they would use firelight. At least Madawaak would see his hunters before they saw him.

He stopped walking. *Might as well rest here,* Madawaak thought. He hoped that he'd wake at their return...

Then a sound. A deep, melodious sigh.

Madawaak picked the direction. Heard something move about in the distance. The scrunch of wet hay and the snort and moan of a large animal. One of theirs.

'Speak again, strange spirit,' Madawaak called. 'You know what I've come to do to your captors.'

There was silence. Madawaak huffed and decided that Pale One animals knew no better than Pale Ones how to understand him...

Then another moan.

'I hear you,' Madawaak said. He followed the sound. 'I hear you, strange spirit. You know why they keep you and feed you, don't you? You know what they'll do to you... and you'll never have been free. I will set you free, strange spirit. Maybe you will not last long, with the wolves, but at least you will know freedom.'

Something solid knocked against Madawaak's chest. He coughed. Felt it. Wood. The fence!

The slow, laborious trots of one of the Pale Ones' captive beings drew near and he felt a wet nose nudge against his neck. Madawaak reached out and touched the coarse fur. The being lolled its head as it chewed on the dry grass in its mouth.

A memory built in Madawaak's mind. As he relaxed and remembered how the domicile stood so it overlooked the fences and the paddocks, the image conjured slowly in his mind. Soon he could look and see the structure they lived in and he touched the cow's face one more time.

'I will keep my promise,' he whispered.

Madawaak left the being and the fence and plunged back into impenetrable darkness. As he walked, he placed one foot in front of the other and felt the toe of his moccasin touch the heel of the other foot with each step. The structure was close. He reached out before him and kept the slow pace up until his hand touched the cold dirt of its outer wall. His heart started to thump and gather pace.

He felt his way along the wall until he came to the solid wood of the door on its tanned skin hinges. Madawaak pulled it open. He stepped inside and took his flints out of his satchel pocket. As he rubbed them together, they generated sparks. Like a blink brings brief darkness to day, so the sparks of the flints brought momentary vision to the inside of the domicile. Madawaak found the dish in the centre. Ashes and burned limbs of wood filled it.

As he rubbed the flints together, Madawaak found their stash of dry wood. Then carried it to the fire dish. Then stuffed light tinder between the logs and lit them with the flints.

Light.

A small axe leaned against the wall near one of their beds. Madawaak hurried over and lifted it and found it was still heavy and cumbersome. But he had a promise to keep. With a long branch from the fire, he lit his way back outside. The shining dots of their big, dark eyes as they caught the firelight and reflected it back at Madawaak led him to the fence again. He set the torch down. The axe blade was thin. Madawaak found the joint where the beam met the post and chopped there at the leather straps that held it. The leather snapped and the log fell.

Madawaak didn't have time for the other.

The cows hurried to the break and leaped out. Madawaak stepped out of their way. The huge beasts stood out in their freedom on the edges of the firelight for a moment. They looked at him. All at once. Then one of them turned and bounded into the darkness. The others did the same. Two, three, then all of them.

Madawaak listened until the thuds from their hoofs faded into the abyss. Silence fell about him like the absolute blackness. Then he picked up his torch and went back inside to wait.

Sharp tasting meats were kept in a pouch near the fire. Madawaak ate them and then went outside and collected snow for water. Then he went back inside and lay down on one of the beds. The sleep that fell upon him was as deep and inescapable as the night.

* * *

'One of them came back to us,' young Konal said as his fingers flexed by his side towards the basket he'd brought in with him. 'He delivered this.'

'Show it to me,' Freydis ordered.

Konal bent down and lifted the lid off. Behind him, Casper and Gustav clutched their atgiers. Eirik craned to see. From the pungent stink of rotting meat, it was a body part. Konal took it by the hair and lifted the decomposing head out. The face was deflated. Bruised where the cheekbones and jaw rested against the slackened skin. But the scars on the eyes called their attention.

Eirik shuddered.

Two vertical scars down through the eyebrows to the cheeks. The eyes each split in two. Konal dropped the flaky head back in the basket but Freydis remained silent. Eirik looked up at his mother.

She just sat there and stared at the basket.

'We killed the messenger,' Konal said.

Freydis opened her mouth to say something but stopped. Eirik squirmed in his chair.

'Do you know what it means?' Hakon whispered from the chair on the other side of her.

Freydis regained herself. She looked piercingly at Konal and a smirk crept across her face.

'Get rid of that head before it stinks out all of Straumfjord,' she ordered. 'Go home. Thank you. You've done well. Casper, give him some gold.'

'Thank you, my Lord.'

Konal bowed deeply over and over as he backed up towards the guards with the basket clutched in his hands. He almost backed right into Casper. When Konal turned to face the great wall of man that blocked his path, Casper greeted him with two gold coins, then stepped aside. Konal turned and bowed to Freydis again.

'Thank you,' and then he was gone.

[355]

Freydis hand flexed on the tabletop. Her fingers stretched out, then slackened. Eirik watched. She breathed in a few times as though to speak, but each time simply exhaled and flexed her fingers again.

'What is it, my Lord?' Hakon asked.

'There is another assassin,' Freydis said, softly and slowly. 'This creature that came from the water. It's one of them.'

'We'll rub more salt on Gheegnyan,' Eirik suggested, hoping to earn another smile of approval from his mama.

'No...' she said. 'Well, yes... but he won't tell us about this one. He doesn't know about this one.'

'How do you know?' Hakon asked.

'He'd be more confident if he did.'

Freydis stood and held Gunnlogi in her hand as she slowly made her way around the table.

'What did the eyes mean, Mama?'

'This is a very special assassin,' Freydis said as she slowly turned to face Eirik and Hakon. 'One who can see in the dark as plainly as she can see in the day.'

'She?' Hakon asked. 'Their women aren't warriors...'

'This one is,' Freydis said with a smirk. 'She's had to be.'

'I don't understand my Lord.'

Freydis stared at Eirik. He looked at her. Looked away. Squirmed. Looked back. Didn't know what to do. She just kept staring.

'We should send them,' Hakon said. 'Send them to stop her.'

'No we shouldn't. That would be a disaster,' Freydis said, without breaking her stare at Eirik. 'I want you to go, Hakon. Take one tracker. A young one. A child, if he knows their ways. She'll be coming this way. Find and pick up her trail.'

'Yes my Lord,' Hakon stood.

'Bring...' Freydis said loudly to keep Hakon's attention. 'Bring her back alive. She's very important to me.'

Hakon nodded.

* * *

Madawaak's eyes snapped open. There was no light from outside but he knew it was daybreak from the unease in his blood. Seldom had he slept so long in his adult life. Something had woken him...

A noise. Small.

Madawaak sat up and saw the little bulge under the sheets on the bedding laid out across the domicile from him. It raised its head and looked at him with vacuous curiosity and little golden curls tufted out from under the hood.

A child. A Pale One child. Not more than three summers sold.

The door flung open and Madawaak met the terrified eyes of a Pale One woman. She cried out and charged him with a small axe held high above her head. Madawaak took up the same bulky weapon he'd used last night and rolled forward out of the bed and rammed it into her soft gut.

She huffed and fell on top of him. Madawaak kicked and struggled out and swung the axe down onto the back of her head. A scream caught his attention. At the door. And arrow pointed at him.

Madawaak dove out of the way as the shaft buzzed through the domicile and embedded up to the feathers in the turf bricks of the wall. He grabbed a burning stick from the fire and threw it. The girl withdrew from the doorway. Madawaak leaped and swung his tomahawk. Smashed the bow out of his path. The arrow fell harmlessly. He seized the girl by the collar and dragged her in.

The door swung shut behind them.

The girl stumbled on the meat pouch and fell. Madawaak landed on top of her and rammed his fist into her mouth then cupped her lips to stifle her scream. Warm blood spattered his palm. She looked up at him with bulging eyes and gasped for air and he saw who she was.

She'd killed Adothe.

The rage in him flared up and seized control. He held the tomahawk high. Lifted his hand from her mouth. The girl cowered. Turned her head. Waited for the blow that would plunge her into nothingness...

Madawaak looked down at the black hair cast across her face. The creamy tan. She was bigger than him by only a little. For a moment there was no distinguishing her from Demasduit, as she had been when they both knew each other.

A moment that was enough to stall Madawaak's hand and extinguish the fury in him.

Slowly, she turned her head and looked up. Madawaak saw the blue eyes. But he couldn't move at her or blink. Couldn't catch his breath. Couldn't look away.

Finally, he dropped the tomahawk and moved off her. Crawled back a few paces. The girl eased up and stared at him. The child called out something. Runa. Madawaak looked. The girl grabbed his tomahawk...

Madawaak shot upright.

He rammed his elbow into her face and knocked her down again. Grabbed hold of the tomahawk by the handle but she wouldn't let go. Madawaak stomped and kicked her wrist until her fingers limpened and he could lift it from her hand. Turned. Beat her with his elbow again and knocked her on her back. Kicked her side. The girl coughed.

Thoughts darted through his head. Madawaak couldn't keep up. Couldn't stay here. Couldn't come back. Panic flooded him. How could he come back now? What if he came face to face with this Pale One again?

Madawaak had to make them come out to him. They could kill each other in the forest and away from this girl so she would not become another Demasduit.

The child.

Madawaak seized the child. The girl screamed and staggered to her feet and stumbled towards him. Madawaak sheltered the boy. He kicked her in the knee and knocked her back down. Then ran.

Ran out of the structure. Into the white mists that shrank beneath the sunlight. Out into the wilderness towards the forest. He looked behind him as he ran. Saw how far behind the domicile had shrunk. Then ran more. The child grew heavy in his arms. He didn't complain. Didn't make a sound.

It wasn't until Madawaak could see the dark forms of the treetops brood over the mist on the horizon ahead that he stopped and looked down at the confused face. No tears. For a moment he thought he could take it back...

...the rumble. Hoofs. Madawaak turned. In the distance, the hunters galloped toward their homes.

Madawaak fell on his knees, stricken with fatigue and dizziness. What had he done? He held the warm little thing that was not so little in his arms close to his chest and looked at the trees ahead. There was only one way...

He got up and kept walking. Sick deep in his heart.

* * *

A settlement lay ahead. Night Eagle smelled the slight smoke in the air over the wolf scat she'd come across in the mountains. *The lakes,* she thought. Every settlement had to be avoided but one, Night Eagle knew this much. One that was on the ocean side of the Lakes. She readied herself and followed the steep downward slope towards it. Clicked and navigated her way towards the anomaly that showed itself in the echoes that fluttered between the thinning trees ahead. It was either the right one or the wrong one.

This was unknown land.

Night Eagle had followed the same path she'd taken as a child down from the where the Great River gathered but there'd been settlements then. Villages. Forest People's villages. Her own kin once but as she'd stood near them, it had been obvious they were different. Their song had fallen silent. A guilty, bottomless silence wherever she found them. It was how Night Eagle had known to go off the path she knew. They were all once her kinfolk. But her kinfolk had sang and talked and filled the forests with their life.

Silence was for the Pale One slaves.

As the trees continued to thin and more of the sunlight fell upon her Night Eagle slowed her pace. Crouched low. Prowled.

Felt her weapons hung all over her body with her fingertips. One at a time.

'You,' an old voice came.

In a flash, Night Eagle had an arrow set and aimed. She clicked. Saw the echo of the old man as he recoiled from the end of her arrow. Something struck in the image. Night Eagle clicked again.

She knew this man.

'I am not... with them,' he said. Night Eagle remembered the softness, even though it had degraded and become husky with age. She knew the face. The mouth hung open as it did when he'd been stumped. The eyes full of honest naivety age could not dull. Honest people always looked that way. Night Eagle knew this from the first honest face she'd ever seen. One of the only that lived in her memories of sight.

'Say your name,' Night Eagle ordered.

'Ninejeek.'

Night Eagle removed the arrow and slipped it back in its quiver.

'I was tracking the wolves,' he said. 'You were as well.'

Night Eagle shook her head no.

'Is it you?' he asked, as his shaky hands slowly lowered and moved closer to her.

Night Eagle touched her tomahawk. He stopped.

'Your eyes...'

'Cut out,' Night Eagle said. 'I am looking for Wobee.'

'I...' Ninejeek babbled, struck dumb. 'I... I... I don't believe it. They said you were dead.'

'Left for dead,' Night Eagle said. 'Not the same thing.'

'Can I come closer so I know you're real?'

'No.'

Ninejeek swallowed nervously.

'Wobee is dead,' Ninejeek said.

'But there are others.'

'There are. Keathut is leading them. Do you remember him?'

'Do you know where they are?'

'I do... they don't welcome strangers.'

'Am I stranger to you?'

'I mean they don't allow anyone they aren't sure is one of them into their village,' Ninejeek said. 'The last time anyone saw you was... with the party that was taken by Freydis.'

Night Eagle heard the honesty in his voice.

'Then I can go no further,' Night Eagle said.

'I'll tell them you didn't see...' Ninejeek stopped himself. 'I'll tell them you don't know about us. That I was deeper in the forest and that you never saw... or... knew I was there.'

'They won't believe you.'

'Then they will try to stop you reaching Straumfjord,' he warned. 'They will think you're a spy.'

Night Eagle knew that if she killed him here, they'd come after her anyway. His people would think she saw. They would hunt down anything that was headed from this place to there.

'Let them,' she said.

'I will stay out two nights,' Ninejeek said. 'I will keep following the wolves.'

Night Eagle turned towards Straumfjord and started to walk.

'Shanawdithit...' he stopped her. 'A village lies between us and them. It is Bidesook's now. He is with Freydis. They all are. Everyone else.'

She kept walking.

'Shana...' she stopped again. 'How did... how?'

'They know more than you think,' she said. 'They watch all the time.'

'The Farther People? Did they find you?'

'It wasn't Farther People,' she said. Then, Night Eagle kept walking.

'Then who?' he called after her, but she didn't stop. Didn't turn around. In a few moments, she was gone.

29

Only Flesh

Carl wandered up and down the main street of the village while the families of the hunting party came and collected each of them like a net unto a shoal of fish. His legs ached and belly rumbled painfully.

Soon he was wandering up and down alone.

A small group gathered around the spot where they'd burned Viveka so he crossed over to them.

'Was anyone else killed?' he asked with a trembling voice.

Nobody seemed to hear. But Gottfried turned his scarred face and icy blue eyes back towards Carl and saw his distress. He placed a hand upon the hunter's shoulder.

'My family,' he said, as he shook his head.

'They went home,' a pubescent boy next to him said. The blacksmith's apprentice. Carl couldn't remember his name. 'Some of their cattle appeared around town so they went to see what happened.'

Carl's blood ran cold. He looked at Gottfried. Gottfried turned and patted Lord Asny on the shoulder, whispered to her, waited for her approving nod, then shuffled with Carl out of the mourning crowd. They quickly mounted their tired horses again and rode for Carl's farm. Soon Eostre was on her horse and she rode alongside them.

They passed from the clustered houses and out into the sparser edges. Carl's eyes stung. He cursed himself for living so far out. For not being afraid of that ghost skraeling enough... or too afraid... so much so that he had to prove something to himself.

The fence was broken. The cows were gone. Carl was off his horse before it stopped running and he stumbled in the snow.

Eostre followed and Lord Gottfried kept watch with his giant battle axe in his hands. Carl pushed through his door.

Helga laid dead. Dried blood darkened in a pool under her stomach. The axe in her skull turned her head sideways and Carl could just see her glassy eye. He squeezed his atgier tight.

A sob.

Runa sat crouched on the bed. Her face was spattered with dry blood and her lip and cheek were swollen and blue. She looked up at her father. He filled with rage.

'Where is my son?' he demanded.

Runa's bruised lip quivered.

'Taken.'

'I'll summon Lord Asny,' Eostre said as she turned and hurried out the door.

Carl stared at his daughter. Dark thoughts welled inside his mind and chilled him to his bones.

'Did he...' he was unable to finish the sentence.

Runa shook her head no.

'If he did... you could have one inside you. You have to tell me. Did he?'

'No...' she gasped.

Carl's eyes filled with tears.

'He did.'

'No... Papa, he didn't.'

Carl looked at her belly. Felt the crawling revulsion under his skin.

'He did!'

In a rush of rage, he seized her by the hair. Runa screamed but he dragged her outside and threw her onto the snow. Gottfried turned in confusion.

'What are you doing?' Gottfried demanded.

'She has one inside her!'

'I don't!' Runa screamed as she shot upright on her knees. 'I don't! He didn't...'

Carl drew a dagger and dragged it deeply across her throat. Her words disappeared into a gargle. A light pink spray burst from her veins. She fell and writhed as the snow around her slowly turned red. Carl stood stiff for a moment. Then he leaped onto her back and thrust the dagger in again and again. Still Runa gurgled and gasped and spluttered. Finally he shoved the blade into the back of her neck and she stopped.

'What have you done?' Gottfried shuddered with horror.

'She had one inside her...'

'She told you she didn't!'

'Why did she let him take her brother?' Carl screamed.

'Carl... you're insensible. This child was yours!'

The thudding of horses' hoofs issued and in seconds Asny led the Althing on horseback to the farm. Her blue eyes fixed on the body of the girl. She dismounted and looked down at Runa, then at Carl. Ingolf and Eostre dismounted for a closer look. Their brows furrowed at the scene.

Asny looked at Runa and then looked at Carl.

'He escaped,' Carl gasped.

'This girl was alive when I saw her...' Eostre said.

'He was here...'

'He killed her,' Gottfried said as he pointed his axe head at Carl.

Asny glared at Carl. Ingolf and Eostre's shoulders tensed and their hands flexed towards the atgiers sheathed on their horses' saddles. The rest of the Althing moved in closer.

'She had one inside her,' Carl repeated. But his voice shook. 'She...'

He broke down and cried. Then he fell on his knees.

'The skraeling took my son!'

'You've murdered your own child,' Asny said. 'What would do you to skraeling then? Thank him?'

'No! I... I... I'm confused...' Carl blubbered as he reached up towards Asny's knees. 'I thought... I don't know... I didn't... I don't know!'

'Carl Jurgensson, you are no longer of this settlement,' Asny said. 'Your Jarl...'

'Me, my Lord,' Ingolf said.

'He is outcast,' Asny said. 'Sentenced to exile on one condition; he brings the head of the skraeling to the Althing. Then we will reconsider his punishment. Do you object?'

Ingolf shook his head. 'No, my Lord.'

'Motion that Carl Jurgensson be exiled until such time as he can bring us the head of the skraeling,' Asny projected over the small crowd. 'Then we reconsider.'

A unanimous 'Aye.'

'I go with him,' Gottfried said.

Asny stared at Gottfried.

'Not out of pity for him, though Carl was taken by a temporary madness,' Gottfried looked pitifully at Carl. 'But for myself. Carl may fail. I will not.'

'As long as you accept that Carl's resentencing is a condition of him bringing the head back, not you,' Asny said.

'Then he'd better hope he gets to skraeling first,' Gottfried said. 'Before any of my champions. The skraeling has one of our children.'

'I approve,' Asny said, though the reluctance was obvious. 'You have until sunset to gather your supplies, feed your horses and muster your help. At dusk, I cut off the head of Carl Jurgensson if it is still within my reach.'

Gottfried bowed.

Asny mounted her horse. She turned it and led the Althing back towards the village.

Ingolf mounted his horse last and waited.

'Ivers, Katla and Steinar,' Gottfried said, when the others had thundered off.

Ingolf nodded and rode after the Althing.

* * *

'What have you got there?' Torvard asked Eirik, who emerged from the trees without any wood. Torvard had nearly finished his seal statue already. But the boy cradled something in his hands...

'One of theirs,' he said, and he held up a chert knife with a grip of wood bound in tanned hide. 'The one who killed Snorre. It's his.'

Eirik held it in his hand and thrust it from his waist.

'I thought we would make things again...'

'I don't want to make things!' Eirik squealed. He threw his hands down by his side and paced around as though in pain. 'It's boring!'

'Y... you're so clever at it.'

'Then why do I need to do it?'

Torvard set his knife and statue aside on the old log he sat on.

'What do you want to do then?' Torvard asked. He wanted his son to stop thrusting the knife around.

'Stab him with this,' Eirik said. 'The way he wanted to do to me.'

Torvard tensed and his mouth dried. Eirik walked up to a collapsed turf brick and stabbed it. Torvard wanted to look away. He didn't want to see his sweet, sensitive son turn into this thing that Freydis wanted him to be... but he had to know...

'Eirik,' Torvard said. 'Son... will you talk with me a minute?'

'What's the point of talking with you?' Eirik exploded. 'All you want to do is sit and make things and talk about nonsense poetry.'

'Poetry is our history, Eirik...'

'Our history is war.'

'Not all of it,' Torvard said, hot in the face to hear Freydis' words come verbatim out of his young mouth. 'The Norse are merchants. We're explorers. Your grandfather founded Greenland without ever killing a soul.'

'Because there was nobody there to kill,' Eirik said. He looked down at the knife which he held in both hands again as though to cradle it. He spoke softly, almost to himself. 'It wasn't like that in Iceland.'

'Freydis told you about Iceland?'

'Mama did,' Eirik looked at Torvard sternly. Then his eyes fluttered back down to the knife. 'She told me how she was made.'

'Conceived?'

'She told me that could never happen to a man, no matter what another man does to them,' Eirik said. 'Only a woman could end up with a baby inside her. But women ride out and meet the enemy anyway and that makes them stronger than men but still more weak and...'

'...and it involves another life. When it happens.'

Eirik nodded.

'Nobody ever did that to Frey... your mother,' Torvard said. 'What happened to her mother. Nobody. And she fought many battles.'

'Your mother killed everyone who tried. She's strong. I want to be strong like her,' Eirik gripped the knife hard. His knuckles turned white.

'Strong people don't just go around hurting other people,' Torvard tried to reason. 'Strong people can be smart as well. They can bargain with other people. They can reason with them. Even make friends of them. The person who discovered this land never killed anyone in his life and he is a king now.'

'He should have killed them!' Eirik yelled, in another eruption of anger. Torvard reached forward, worried he'd cut himself on the knife in his hands. 'If he had, then Snorre would still be alive!'

'I want to talk to you,' Torvard tapped the log beside where he sat.

'I don't want to talk. I want to hurt the skraeling. I want to hurt it! I want to kill it!'

'What has she been doing with you?' Torvard sat up and reached out to try and calm him. Eirik pulled away.

'She's made me strong!' Eirik squealed as he pulled away. 'Not weak like you. Not a weak, little man who sits around thinking and playing with dolls. I hate you! Stop poisoning me!'

Eirik turned and ran into the forest. Back towards Straumfjord. Gustav hurried after him. Torvard sat on the log and held his head as the wave of dizziness came. The sickness in his gut. The stabbing in his heart. It was too much. To hear her words come from Eirik was one thing, but to hear the harsh things she said only to Torvard was another. She'd turned his boy against him. Tears filled Torvard's eyes as he thought about it. He watched the little drops fall and make little holes in the snow between his feet.

He'd lost his boy.

* * *

Eirik opened the privy door and found it empty. Only the odours lingered. But he had the knife in his hand and still puffed and raged and so he stormed towards the lodge door. *Mama moved him,* he thought. Annoyed. *But she'd have her reasons,* he thought. *Where? Where would he be?*

Eirik tore open the door and marched right down the line of people who stood waiting to talk to his mama and up to her table. Slammed the dagger down in front of Freydis.

The man complaining to her fell silent.

'What are you doing, Eirik?' Freydis asked, her eyes flared.

'Where is the skraeling?'

Freydis looked back at the door. Gustav stepped through with his atgier in his hands and the line took a cautious step out of his way and he looked at Freydis with fearful eyes and mouth agape.

'Eirik, go and play with your father,' Freydis ordered. 'I have business to attend...'

'I want to know where he is!' Eirik rammed the knife into the tabletop.

Freydis clasped her iron hand over his and squeezed it hard against the handle. The electrifying pain dulled his rage. Eirik cried out as tears flooded his eyes and he heard himself wail, embarrassingly.

Freydis stared at him while he twisted in agony.

'Go and play with your father,' she ordered, slowly. 'The more you weep, the harder I'll squeeze.'

She gave him a sharp crush just to show she was serious. Then released. Eirik's palm bled where the edges of the wood handle had dug through his skin. He held it tight and breathed through his teeth. But he didn't cry. Eyes were hot. No tears fell. Did not cry.

'Go,' Freydis ordered. Then she looked again towards the back door and spoke with venom. 'Casper will take you. Gustav will mind the line.'

Eirik heard Casper march up behind him.

'He wants to speak nonsense,' Eirik said. 'You said I shouldn't listen to him.'

'You shouldn't,' Freydis said. 'But appease him.'

'I don't know what that means.'

'Go listen to his nonsense and find out,' Freydis looked up at Casper. 'Get him out of here.'

Eirik felt the huge hands come for his shoulders. He leaped forward to grab the knife first but it was swept up before his eyes by the swift hand of Freydis. Casper clasped him by the shoulders. Eirik was dragged back out to his father.

Freydis looked at the skraeling knife, then set it aside.

'You were saying, Jannik Asmundsson?'

'The cattle are contaminated,' Jannik repeated. 'Worm of the liver. It's in all of them and it's infested my thralls. I've pulled worms out of their eyes longer than my forearm. It must have come from Greenland.'

'Pigs?'

'Not breeding,' Jannik said. 'We'll be through them in a day if I substitute their meat for the cows'.'

'Gustav,' Freydis called. Gustav stepped forward. 'Send a karvi down to Hop and find out why Chieftain Asny has failed yet again to ship us any caribou. If her hunters are too weak to catch them, maybe she can send the cattle back to us. Can you manage that?'

'My Lord,' Gustav bowed, turned and hurried outside.

'It's only the beginning of winter my Lord,' Jannik warned. 'If we get no caribou, there'll be nothing but fish meat and dried provisions to last us. If King Lief's knarr arrive with more infested cattle then I don't know how we'll feed all the new families...'

'I'll worry about the new families, Jannik,' Freydis said as she sat down. 'You feed the people that are here.'

Jannik bowed, turned, and marched outside. But made sure he made eye contact with everyone in the line on the way out. Then he was outside. He walked towards the hillside and up towards his butchery.

As the jarls gradually disappeared from around him and were replaced with the karls of the outer properties where the lands were worked, he heard footsteps behind him. One jarl that followed him. Hood drawn over her head. As they passed through the trees, she stepped up next to him and they walked side by side.

Jannik felt her expectant eyes on him. He said nothing. Didn't want to.

'Any day now...' she said.

'I saw the boy,' Jannik told her. 'He's more far gone than his mother.'

'He's young. Children are easily influenced.'

Jannik kept walking. Kaia was gone and he was walking alone.

* * *

'How strange,' the voice said loudly. Night Eagle stopped walking. 'I thought I'd have to go all the way to the lake before I found game. It must be my lucky day.'

It came from all around. Night Eagle spread her fingers and touched the low fern fronds that wet her hips as she walked through them. The sun shone down nearly uninterrupted by any forest canopy. Night Eagle remembered this place...

'I wonder what it could be... A fox? I'll have to aim well to hit a fox...'

Night Eagle clicked. Heard the echo of the fern tops that flooded the gully and kept the forest floor in perpetual shade. The trees parted and the wet greenery shimmered. There was no telling memory from what the echo carried back to her. Both visions were as vivid.

'Too small to be a seal,' Demasduit's voice continued. 'Too clumsy to be a Great Auk.'

[370]

Night Eagle's lip twitched and her face grew hot...

'Maybe a baby seal that got lost? Maybe even a baby caribou... I've got it! I'll just take careful aim and...'

'No,' Night Eagle whispered softly. 'Don't shoot me, sister.'

But there was no Demasduit. Just the Night Eagle in an empty fern gully. Alone.

She kept walking the familiar way towards the incline... but this was not the way to Straumfjord. Night Eagle would have to...

...she stopped walking again. A tingle ran up her spine. Clicked. Nothing to hear. But there was a sound. A breathing. A soft breathing that grew quicker and quicker.

Eyes were looking at her from straight ahead.

Hidden. Pale Ones could not hide. Night Eagle touched the cheek of her tomahawk. Clicked again.

He was right in front of her. A boy. Not much older than she, if at all. His lips parted as he gasped for air and his eyes bulged as he stared at her in blood-curdling horror. Night Eagle faced him and her grip tightened on her tomahawk...

The rope snapped tight around her neck. Night Eagle grabbed at it but the sudden force from behind crushed the air from her throat and jerked her backwards with agonizing force. Night Eagle fell on her back and huge hands tore the bow from its quiver and the tomahawk from her belt. The rope tightened the more she struggled.

Night Eagle stopped struggling. On the cusp of consciousness, little Shanawdithit was helpless again.

* * *

'My son complains constantly of pain in his gut,' the old-looking woman wept. 'I'm afraid he has the...'

'The worms, yes,' Freydis said, as she shifted in her seat. 'There's really nothing I can do about it.'

'Perhaps you could lessen our tributes?' the old woman asked. 'He can't work like that and his father died last winter...'

'Help is coming,' Freydis said as she held up her hand. 'Help will arrive any day now.'

Casper stepped through the door. He nodded, breathless.

'Get out,' Freydis ordered the older woman. Then she stood. 'Get out all of you. Gustav. Casper. Get them out. Now!'

The woman looked at Freydis, wounded, but bowed her head and hurried out as the rest of the line filtered through the door. Freydis grinned at Casper when they were finally gone. The guard stood aside. Gustav held the door.

Hakon dragged the pelt sack inside and hauled it to the centre of the lodge. Freydis hurried around the table. Ran to it. Hakon opened it. The pelt opened up and fell to either side of the captive...

Freydis stopped and her eyes widened.

'You...' she whispered.

The skraeling blindly turned its face back and forth and made a dull clicking noise through the skin gag in her mouth. Freydis held up a finger.

'Wait,' she ordered. 'I've got to get my son.'

Hakon saw the minute twitch in the skraeling's face at the words.

Eirik sat on the end of the bed and sulked. When he heard Freydis footsteps, he took a breath, winced, and braced for the flailing and screaming that would certainly follow...

She cast aside the arras and smirked at him.

'I want you to come and see something.'

Eirik felt faint as he followed her out into the lodge. Then, as they crossed the tables, she moved aside and Eirik's eyes fell on the creature half in a torn bag. With a man the size of Hakon behind it, it looked tiny. Though its head moved side to side and up and down in a strange, almost haunting manner, it struck him as almost familiar. Not in any way his eyes saw. It was her presence. To be near her felt softening and frightening at the same time.

As they got closer, Eirik saw the eyes.

'What happened to her eyes?' he shuddered as his body involuntarily withdrew. Upon the sound of his voice, the head stopped moving and the creature's face turned directly to Eirik and turned his blood cold. He wanted to run away.

Freydis held out her hand and drew him closer. They stood over the skraeling as she knelt in the bag, her hands and feet bound in ropes. Hakon held his atgier behind her. There was no escaping, no doing anything to harm anyone for this strange skraeling. And yet Eirik wanted to hide behind his mother. Nobody had answered Eirik's question. He wanted to ask again but he couldn't speak while that face was turned towards him.

That face...

Something beyond the eyes... the whole of it. The chin. The cheekbones. The nose. The hair. There was a horror that lived in them that reached out and grabbed Eirik and gagged him at the same time.

'Mama...' he managed to whisper.

The skraeling girl tensed and seemed to focus on Eirik somehow without sight. He stepped back. Freydis pulled him forward again.

'Mama,' Freydis said, slowly. The skraeling turned her face towards Freydis and Eirik could breathe again... only just. 'This one knows our word for mama. It knows your voice, Eirik,' she bent down and leaned close to the skraeling's face. 'It knows my voice.'

The skraeling seemed to shudder. Eirik's mouth fell open and his blood warmed slowly. It was afraid. Afraid of his mother. Eirik squeezed Freydis' hand and glanced up at her as she stood upright again with a smirk on her face.

'It was trying to make a clicking sound,' Hakon said. 'Through the gag.'

'Hakon,' Freydis said without looking away from the skraeling. 'Bring it with us.'

Hakon grabbed the sides of the slashed bag and scooped up the skraeling in it. It didn't fight or make a sound. Freydis held Eirik by the hand and led them out of the lodge into the evening of blackened blue. Light mists poured out of the forest above Straumfjord and rolled down towards the water. Freydis led them to a hut behind the lodge that had not been there a few days earlier.

Of course. Eirik cursed his slow mind.

He pulled his hand out of his mother's grip as they walked. Tension ran through his shoulders as hatred heated his face and body up again. His fists balled. Eirik hoped he'd see it in pain. He now could think only of Snorre.

The sight of Snorre as he'd died.

He sensed his mother was still angry at him about today. Eirik wanted to win her back. He didn't have to think about it anymore; he'd trained himself well. She'd trained him well. All he had to do was hate the skraeling and do what she told him to do. Then he'd win her back.

Freydis opened the door but no foul odours hit him. Instead the smell of seawater. Seawater and meat. Eirik's eyes adjusted to the darkness and he saw the skraeling where he lay... on a bed! On a bed with skins soaked in seawater bound around his mangled legs.

Eirik took a sharp step into the corner. Hakon entered behind Freydis, still with the bag in his hands, and Freydis turned and looked at Eirik.

'You're helping him...'

'Of course,' Freydis said. 'I said we'd keep him alive, didn't I?'

'But you're helping him!'

'He would have got infected, if he'd stayed where we'd left him,' Freydis said, with patience what was so alien from her it disturbed Eirik. 'Infected. Do you understand what that means?'

Eirik nodded.

'What does it mean?'

'Sick. From something...'

'Something like injuries,' Freydis nodded. 'Good. And an infection would have killed him.'

Eirik began to feel the sting of shame but he didn't want to lose the anger. The anger would make up for everything.

'We'll put him back,' Freydis assured him. 'We'll put him back in the privy when he's all better and then we'll cut little pieces off him and burn him until he's on the edge of death again... and *then*?'

She looked at Eirik, expectantly.

'Help him again?' Eirik squeaked, sheepishly.

'Help him again,' Freydis touched the end of his nose with her finger. 'But I don't think it will come to that anymore. Because I think this,' she nodded towards the sack in Hakon's hands. 'This is going to help us. And I want it to help us. I want to hurry things along.'

'Is my uncle coming?'

'No... what did I say? He's sending ships. He's not coming himself.'

'Oh...' Eirik withdrew. 'But you want to find the rest of the skraelingjar before he comes?'

Freydis nodded slowly.

'And then,' she reached into the little satchel at her hip. 'You will get to do the honours. For both of them.'

Freydis held out Eirik's skraeling knife. Eirik took it. Held it. Let the fury that compelled him rush through his hand and fill it with his rage again. He looked up at Freydis.

'I will.'

He looked at the skraeling whose name was Gheegnyan. Gheegnyan, tied by one hand and one ankle to the wall, looked back and his eyes flickered from Eirik's face to the knife and back again. Eirik felt a quiver deep inside him. Something that slowed his heart and filled his head with mist. But he held his ground. Held his breath. Waited for Freydis' command.

'Hakon, would you open the bag? And take the gag out of its mouth.'

Hakon crouched down and untied the strap from around the skraeling's mouth and slid the gag out from between her teeth. Eirik watched. He wanted to hear it speak. But it didn't. It just made clicking noises.

Gheegnyan started to shout at it. But the skraeling gave a long hiss and he fell silent and Eirik saw his eyes move up to Freydis and then back at the skraeling. Eirik looked at Gheegnyan. The fear on his face trembled and blazed like a lightning strike. Eirik's heart pounded once. Heavily. He held the knife weakly in his fist.

'This,' Freydis said to Eirik as she waved her hand over the skraeling in the bag, 'is Shanawdithit. Can you say that Eirik?'

'Shanawdithit,' Eirik whispered. The skraeling cocked her head towards him. It heard. Eirik shuddered.

'She has come to help me and your father take care of you,' Freydis said with a smirk at Eirik.

'Why?' Eirik asked.

Freydis nodded towards Gheegnyan.

'This one doesn't want her to take care of you,' she said. 'He wants to hurt you still. Wants her to hurt you, but Shanawdithit would never do that. Never. She won't even try to stop you hurting him.'

Eirik clutched the knife and looked up at Freydis.

'Get him here,' Freydis said, and patted her chest just below the shoulder. 'A few times. Just like you wanted to earlier. Go on.'

Eirik looked at Gheegnyan. The skraeling man stared back at Eirik with bulging eyes and teeth shown and his chest pumped up and down furiously. Eirik looked at the skraeling's shoulder and chest. *Yes,* he thought. *There.* He clutched the knife hard. Breathed sharply through his nose. Hot waves rolled up and down his back.

'Go on,' Freydis said, impatiently.

He knew he had to. Eirik knew that if he didn't, he'd lose her again. The skraeling looked at Shanawdithit.

Shanawdithit just sat there. Expressionless with those dead, ruined eyes.

Eirik screamed and charged at the skraeling. He rammed the knife into the flesh and felt the stone clash against bones underneath. A ball rose in his throat. Faintness almost stole his mind from him. But Eirik drew back and stabbed again. The skraeling screamed and convulsed on the bed while his chains rattled and Eirik kept stabbing him. The frenzy of terror and anger took control. Rammed the knife. Again and again. Hit ribs. Hit bone. Squelched through flesh. Blood spattered up and felt hot on his hands.

A firm tug drew Eirik away. The skraeling fell back on the bed and roared through his teeth. Eirik caught this breath. Guilt closed its burning jaws over his back and sunk deep into his flesh and the tears came. But Eirik held them back. He remembered Snorre. He looked at Shanawdithit.

Still just sat there.

Freydis caressed the boy's hair.

'Let's go for dinner,' she said.

Eirik staggered before her through the door.

'Bring that,' he heard Freydis say to Hakon. 'She can share the same bars as her sister.'

The words meant nothing to Eirik.

30

Across the Divides

'Here,' Madawaak said as he set the child down on a mossy log in the root bed between two large redwoods. 'They'll find you here.'

The boy stood up from his robe. His disproportionately large eyes welled with tears and Madawaak pulled up a sleeve to wipe them away.

'Don't. Don't... it's too cold.'

The boy said something in their Pale One language and a sorrowful, frightened tone. Madawaak looked at his uncomprehending face. Pink and soft. The most vulnerable life in all of the forest and it caused a tremble in his heart that ached. Madawaak took the boy by the arms and he felt weak and fragile and suddenly he wanted to wrap the boy up and protect him from the movement in the trees and the nameless echoes that surrounded them.

'How can I make you understand?' he asked, shakily. 'Your people are looking for you. They're after me. They will find you. I left a trail even your people could follow.'

The boy's lips quivered. His soft yellow curls were exposed and his skin turned icy. Madawaak wrapped the robe around his shoulders and pulled the hood over his head.

'Stay here,' Madawaak said. 'They'll find you soon. Before nightfall.'

Madawaak took a sharp breath, turned and ran. But the icy air scored his throat and lungs and he stopped at the first tree to cough. The cry of the child caught up to him. A mournful objection that would not be lost in any language. Madawaak looked at the sky.

Darkening. Quickly.

Go, he thought. Madawaak pushed off the tree and kept walking. The child called to him, this time in a frenzied pitch that forced him to stop. He closed his eyes then fought back tears and swallowed the ball in his throat.

'Give me strength, Demasduit... Oonban... someone. Give me your strength. I have none of my own left...'

In the distance, a wolf howled.

Madawaak turned and ran back for the boy. His feet clambered over the snowy banks and he stumbled with arms outstretched to the crying, sobbing boy and seized the little, soft body in his arms. Madawaak looked around, eyes wide. His heart pounded. The boy cried. The forest seemed vacant, but a chorus of mournful howls flooded the emptiness between the great redwood trunks and stout pine trees and seemed to come from all directions. Madawaak crouched low and raised a bare finger.

It trembled above his head but a soft breeze carried their scent to the south.

'We can't stay here,' Madawaak whispered, though he knew hungry wolves would follow them for days if they needed to. Suddenly, he wished the Pale Ones would find them. Madawaak looked to the shortest stretch of forest before the clearing.

The clearing offered nothing. No shelter. He had to find shelter. That meant wandering... the child had fallen silent. Madawaak softened his grip and looked down at the wet, frightened face and felt the little hands clutch at his sides desperately.

'It's okay,' he said. 'I'm going to try to keep you safe. If I can't... I'll kill you first.'

He picked up the child and sought the densest forest around them and then carried the child towards it. The howls haunted them. They rang out again as Madawaak walked and the branches closed in around him and the boy.

A hunt. There was hunger in that howl... but no bloodthirst yet. None of that savage certainty of having found a target to home in on. The wind would find them soon. Then the howls would change and the wolves would be onto them.

Madawaak ignored the flashes of urgency that jolted up and down his spine. He walked at a steady pace. The forest grew darker and darker and everywhere he saw flickers of the starlight caught in predatory eyes. But he kept walking. Kept steady. If he missed some kind of shelter, he'd not find another one in time.

Darkness sheathed the expanse around them quickly.

The wolves had fallen silent. Every crunch of Madawaak's feet on the crisp snow sounded as loud as a scream. His heartbeat was deafening. Swift sounds issued from the abyss that stared at them from all directions. Madawaak searched with wide eyes. The deepening night offered nothing but bare tree trunks and dense pines...

From nearby, came a low rumble.

Madawaak's eyes locked onto the dark silhouette of a pine, rimmed with silver in the moon's glow, and he rushed towards it.

Don't run, he thought. That was their signal. They wanted him to run.

Under the shadow of the vast base, Madawaak lifted the boy up into the network of branches. The boy started to climb. They came from all directions, all at once. A savage rattle from deep in the throat of the alpha wolf shot through Madawaak's flesh and he leaped up to the branches. Hot air blasted his ankle and he lifted it. The teeth snapped on his skin and agony twisted its burning tendrils up his thigh. Madawaak screamed.

The boy said something breathlessly from above.

The wolf shook its head violently from side to side and sent ripples up through Madawaak's body. He roared as he flexed his shoulders and tried to pull himself up. Held his other leg high and felt the hot blasts of their breaths as their jaws snapped shut below with each failed lunge. The enormous weight of the alpha tore at Madawaak's shoulders. He felt his strength failing and the rough, sticky bark shredded his hands.

With another shake, the wolf loosened Madawaak's muscles and both his legs dropped. The wolves rushed. Madawaak let out one more roar and pulled his leg free of the jaws. His flesh tore and skin ripped with a shuddering pain that churned Madawaak's stomach and made him sweat through crawling skin. But he was free. Madawaak pulled himself up.

Blood poured from his leg and rained down on the wolves. They bunched up and lifted onto their hind legs to snap and tongue the air and catch as much as they could. Madawaak felt faint. But his body wouldn't let him go. He crawled up. Found the boy.

'Go up! Higher!' Madawaak choked out the words. The boy understood and climbed one branch after the other.

Below them, the ravenous gurgle of the wolves lurched closer. Madawaak looked down and saw the alpha frantically grapple its way up through the branches while the others behind it attempted to follow. In the low light, he could see the gaping jaws. The jowls stretched back to reveal the full length of the fangs. The salivating gums. The eyes seemed to glow an unearthly yellow in the starlight.

Madawaak stopped climbing and reached for his tomahawk.

The wolf scrambled towards his feet. Though one foot was numb from blood loss, Madawaak dropped down a few branches until he was almost next to the animal. He drew the tomahawk back. Swung it over a branch. The chert blade smacked against the hard skull and the wolf let forth a squeal of such pitch that Madawaak's ears rang. The massive body fell limp and dropped down. With a hard thud, the body landed sprawled on the snow and the rest of the pack leaped down and enveloped the body.

The boy sat on a branch with his arms braced hard around the trunk. Madawaak heard his sobs and climbed towards him slowly while the adrenaline died down and the pain in his foot took hold. Madawaak's vision throbbed and little lights danced before his eyes. When he reached the boy, he saw that the pine needles had cut and scratched his delicate, pale skin. Fear rattled the boy's face and made him quiver.

Madawaak sat next to him and put a comforting arm around the boy's shoulders. Below them, the sound of teeth that scratched across bone, flesh that tore and pulled and jaws and tongues that lapped blood and stringy meat were inescapable and sickening, coupled with the low growls of satisfaction from the pack.

It wasn't right. Wolves never ate their own. Never. Madawaak had always been told that a wolf would die before it fed on its own. Something was wrong...

The boy was silent. Madawaak looked at him and saw the stars shine in the whites of his eyes. The boy listened. He was frigid with fear. *Pale Ones,* Madawaak thought. *They overhunt the caribous and now drive the wolves of the Broken Lands to starvation.* The wolves of the Forest Lands would migrate north and swim to the mainland. Even out to the islands. But the wolves down here were too far away. They relied on the winter caribou.

They would never have attacked like that otherwise.

'Try not to listen,' he said to the boy. But even as the night stole the last features of the boy's face from Madawaak's vision he could see his words were lost. Madawaak gently covered the boy's ears.

The boy shuffled along the branch and curled up against Madawaak's chest. Madawaak looked up through the thinner needles near the top and saw the stars fade behind the ceiling of strata that spread quickly across the sky. *Adothe,* he thought, *is this your doing?*

The faces of other Pale One children crashed through Madawaak's mind amid memories of screams and blood and the sound of skulls as they cracked and the flushes of horror that always followed. The long nights spent in tears. In confusion. In blood-fuelled frenzy. He remembered the inside of a Pale One structure back in the Forest Lands. In the cove near where he'd grown up. Remembered the pale little bodies that hung lifeless from some old warrior's hand and the cold look on his pitted face as he'd struck the life out of them in a few simple strokes. But remembered the babies that were flung from the cradle as well. Remembered the massacres. Barely the size of root vegetables in the Pale One hands... thrown to their deaths.

Madawaak closed his eyes and put his arms around the boy and covered his ears between his sleeve and his chest. Silently, he thanked Adothe. Then he held the boy for all of the children like this one who had no time, no power and no voice to stop the tides that swept them away.

* * *

Night Eagle sat in the darkness and listened to the footsteps. A small flame drew near. One of them walked towards her. Lighter footsteps. The steps of a strong, controlled, and powerful body.

'Freydis,' Night Eagle said.

'You speak,' Freydis whispered. In their language. Night Eagle heard her sit down in front of the bars and the soft slap of one of her hands as it took hold of the bars. Night Eagle clicked. Took stock of where the fingers were. Let herself think about breaking them. 'You've come to take my son from me.'

Night Eagle said nothing.

'You understand? My son,' Freydis said.

'I understand,' Night Eagle replied.

'That's an interesting dialect. I've heard it before but not here...'

Night Eagle did not respond.

'I knew you'd survive, Shanawdithit,' Freydis said with a tone of such admiration it sickened Night Eagle to hear it. 'I knew you'd survive and that's why I spared you.'

'You wanted the Farther People to find me,' Night Eagle said.

'They didn't though, did they?' Freydis said. Her smile altered her vowels slightly. 'It wasn't them... it was someone else.'

Night Eagle again resorted to silence. She could sense the way Freydis picked through every nuance in her voice. There was an intensity to the way she listened that Night Eagle could feel as it radiated off her like a vibration in the air.

'Did they send you to take my son?' Freydis asked. 'Eirik Torvardsson isn't one of them. He shares blood, that is all. It was my desire that made him and my hands that have raised him. As you have seen, Shanawdithit. Tonight. You saw.'

Night Eagle said nothing.

'He won't go with you,' Freydis told her. 'He'll never see you as family. Had your sister been strong enough to stay alive he might have, in time, but she didn't. Demasduit was weak and broken. Whatever relation Eirik had to her burned in the fire.'

The words stung at Night Eagle's skin, but in her silence, she forced them back.

'All he remembers is her screams,' Freydis said. 'The way she screamed in the flames. I tell him, "That's the woman who helped make you born. She is why the skraelingjar will be loyal to us and help us. The good skraelingjar. The ones who recognize how important our friendship is and how important what my son represents is. The bond between our people." It is all he knows. It is all most of your people know now. There are just a few out there who think killing my son will bring the rest back to savagery and competition with us. Maybe they're right. They will kill him, if they get the chance. Gheegnyan, that one you saw today, he came to kill Eirik. And you don't want that, do you?'

'I will protect the child,' Night Eagle said.

'His name is Eirik.'

'I will protect the child.'

'Even from your own people?'

'I have no people.'

'But you do,' Freydis said. 'We share a common goal. My child's safety. Your devotion to him has kept you alive, even though you never met him until tonight. Your love for him sustained you. A blinded child in the depths of the forest. He gave you life. Knowing he was out there gave you back what I almost took away from you. You thought it was love for your sister. But she abandoned him and you. Now all that remains is Eirik. You can be family to him. Even if he never sees you that way, I will give this to you. I gave him life. I brought him to the

[384]

world. And now I will give you a place with him. You can love him and care for him until the end of your days. Safe and secure with us.'

'You keep using our language to try and tell me he is your son,' Night Eagle said. 'But it does not work. There are no words to own a human in our language. Not in any way. Not even as a parent. Every adult is the parent and every child theirs. I know what you mean to say because I have seen the way you and your kind own people. But you can't say it. Not in our tongue.'

Freydis was silent for a moment. Night Eagle heard her ease back from the flame into the shadows.

'I'm glad you understand anyway,' Freydis said softly. 'Nevertheless, he is my kin. Not yours. The only way you will be near him is through me. Consider what you've lived for. And maybe one day I'll even let you see him without bars between you.'

Freydis got up to leave.

'*Drottning*,' Night Eagle said, speaking their tongue.

Freydis paused.

'I will earn your trust,' Night Eagle said, in the Forest People's language again. 'I will protect my nephew from anyone who tries to harm him. I have no people. Only the child.'

'Prove it,' Freydis said. 'And you will have a family again.'

Footsteps. Someone else approached.

* * *

Freydis held the burning torch near the dark shape in the cage, unused since Demasduit, and showed Torvard the new occupant. A shudder ran through him that almost shattered his bones. That face... That hair... That little, wiry body, small even for one of them... it was her. Tears filled his eyes as they looked over her lips down her neck to her narrow but taut shoulders. *It is her,* he thought, and only then did he finally see her eyes.

They stared unseeingly. Into nothing. Unfocused. All white but for two thick red lines that ran down the middle. They aligned with scars that ran through her brows. Down her cheeks.

Torvard could tell that she knew he was there. He didn't know how exactly... there was just something in the way she held her face towards him and sat rigid... as though she knew it would intimidate him. Her brow even flickered with the emotion of recognition. And hatred.

'It's her sister,' Freydis said in a snide, bragging tone she'd never grown out of. 'We have her back, in some small way.'

'What happened to her eyes?' he asked, though the cold place in his heart knew Freydis had something to do with it. That cold place she occupied all the time now. He heard the unloving frigidity in his own voice but she didn't seem to.

She just said nothing, like always when asked a question that she didn't credit to be due a response. There was no shame in Freydis' stoic evasion and lack of eye contact. It was stubbornness. Torvard heard the younger, less reserved Freydis' voice in his head answer him:

'Can't you tell?'

Torvard wanted to ask how old she was. Where she came from. What Freydis had in mind to do with her. But as he stood beside his wife and knew he'd share a bed with her tonight yet again he felt nothing but revulsion. And Freydis wouldn't answer him anyway. He decided she wouldn't know and let it go.

'She's going to help us,' Freydis said. There was a vulnerable softness now that Torvard decided wasn't going to fool him this time. 'She's going to make it safe for our son.'

'I doubt that,' Torvard said as he numbly moved over to the bed and threw the skin sheet aside. 'She'll throw herself in the fire first chance she gets. Like the other one.'

He said the words with a silent wish that it wouldn't happen. A silent wish Demasduit hadn't...

'You wouldn't want that,' Freydis said softly as she carried the flame to her side of the bed and stuck it in the turf to extinguish it. 'You're in love with her already.'

Torvard said nothing.

'I saw how you grieved for Demasduit,' Freydis said. 'You wouldn't miss me like that.'

'I grieved for the way that child spent the last months of her life. That is all.'

'That child,' Freydis echoed. Then she said something in skraelingjar language and Torvard waited for merciful sleep to take him away from her.

31

Closer

The door burst open. Asny pushed her spare breakfast of smoked mackerel and mouldy bread aside. The assortment of sailors flanked by her own frantic guards and members of the Althing poured in through the little door, led by one in the front. Her crewmates fell into line behind her and they approached Asny's table while her people stood guard by the door and shook their heads apologetically.

Asny knew they were the trading crew of the karvi that had come from Straumfjord.

'My Lord...' the captain bellowed as they crossed the narrow hall.

Eostre burst out from behind her arras, a battle axe braced in her hand. The intruders stopped immediately and reached for their weapons. Asny held out her hand and Eostre stopped immediately.

They were carrying weapons. Had they expected resistance? Or something else?

'My Lord,' the captain repeated as she bowed impatiently while her crew grumbled indignantly. 'How long did you intend to keep us waiting?'

...The crew had not brought shields...

'Long enough to see that we cannot offer what you've come for,' Asny said, softly. She flicked a glance at Eostre.

Esotre slid the axe into her belt.

'Then Chieftain Freydis will...'

'What's going on here?' Hrafn burst in between the guards and behind the messenger crew. 'Who are you?'

'We kept our guests waiting too long, Hrafn,' Asny said. The crew from Straumfjord parted slightly and she looked at Hrafn's face. Her pulse gathered speed. She could only hope the sailors didn't notice. 'It's okay. We'll see to them now.'

Hrafn bowed his head and said nothing.

'Any further interruptions?' the captain asked.

The captain had a shield. It was slung over her back.

'Please continue,' Asny said as she felt the top of the shield beside her own chair and the short handle of the axe that rested on it.

'What became of your hunt?' the captain asked. 'You say you have nothing.'

'Our hunt was unsuccessful,' Asny said. 'The caribou population has thinned.'

The guards crept out to either side of the lodge and prowled their way down the walls. Eostre stayed where she was.

'Very well,' the captain was saying. 'Then we have been ordered to take back the cattle that were sent to you.'

A few of the crew started to look around. A nervous energy began to buzz around the lodge. It spread across the group and Asny glanced again at Eostre. A brief plea to her not to move.

'We can't,' Asny said, forcing the strength in her voice.

Eostre stayed where she was.

Hrafn was still hidden behind the group. Ingolf appeared on the far corner from Eostre and Asny wished they'd stop. Enough... enough!

'And why not?' the captain asked.

'You can take them if you want to please the Chieftain,' Asny said. 'But you'll have to hunt them down. They escaped.'

'Captain...' one of the sailors hissed. Asny's mouth was dry.

'You just got back from a hunt,' the captain said to Asny. 'Did you not think to catch them? Did you not see any? Cattle aren't that clever, Chieftain Asny... I wonder what that makes you?'

'Don't come here and insult me,' Asny argued angrily and won back the attention of the crew that she could see. 'Freydis is not chieftain on Hop, I am. Remember that.'

The warriors had managed to surround them. Partially.

'Freydis is not chieftain anywhere. She is Queen of Vinland.'

Asny's people locked their focus onto the crew. Nervous glances darted over them and the crew behind their captain stirred ever more.

'Sir,' the crewmate said more forcefully while the others tensed and clutched at their weapons.

'What?' the captain asked angrily.

Asny breathed in.

'Hrafn!' Asny shouted.

The warriors swept in with axes drawn as they charged. The crew raised their weapons. The axe heads dug through the flesh and clashed against the bone and the attackers quickly hacked into the group with the wild abandon of hungry wolves. The captain charged forward with some at her sides. Eostre leaped in and struck on in the side of one's head with her axe.

Asny raised her shield and axe and leaped over the table and smashed the end of her shield against the captain's. Screams filled the lodge with the sudden surge of heat. And the wet cracks of sharp steel against flesh and bone. Asny drove her shield into the captain's. They pressed and clashed against each other and pushed and manoeuvred to make an opening. The captain's axe flew at her face. She evaded. Pulled back. A swing missed. Asny saw the shield move to one side and she beat it hard with her shield and sent it further. Exposed the captain's shoulder. Swung.

The axe dug into the bone with loud snap. The captain squealed. Hrafn drove the end of his atgier into her face and knocked her backward. Both he and Asny struck at her head and shoulders until she was bloodied rags and jagged bone.

The hall was littered with bodies split and spilled open. Life oozed from their still forms. One of them moved. Ingolf rammed the end of his atgier into the face of the man and he made no sound. The head caved inward.

Asny looked around. Not one of hers had fallen. She smiled over her people as they looked at her with the haunted faces that always came fresh from battle. The quiet hollowness that horror would pour itself into her later when the adrenaline subsided and the stoic discipline was no longer needed. She caught her breath.

'Drag them out into the fields,' she ordered. The champions and Althing delegates set their weapons aside and tiredly gathered up the bodies. Asny turned back to the table and took a piece of fish in her bloodied hand.

'They'll kill us all for this,' Hrafn said softly behind her as he went about his work.

'Only if she lives.'

Asny put the fish in her mouth and let herself feel the high of success.

Eostre approached Asny and wiped her hands. Asny plucked a piece of fish and slipped it into Eostre's mouth. Eostre looked at her with devoted faith. Then they both went to join Hrafn and the others.

* * *

Eirik relaxed his thighs without even noticing as he rode up beside Freydis on their way up to the cliffside. It was only when he was beside her that he could look and smile. All without the loss of absolute focus that he was sure was the only thing that kept him on the animal's back. His mama gave him a smile.

Something warmed inside him.

Eirik could ride. At last he could ride. He let himself smile but the icy blue gloom of the snowy day ached in his teeth so he kept his mouth shut. All around them, snowflakes fluttered and twirled down from the stark white sky and a soft white mist partially obscured the forest edge down across the meadows. Eirik cast a brief glance back at Shanawdithit.

She sat on the little horse with her hands tied. Hakon rode directly behind her while Casper and Gustav pressed their horses so hard against her sides that she couldn't fall even if she tried. Eirik kept his mind on his riding. If only to keep his mind off her and not be haunted by those uncomfortable feelings he couldn't quite place. Was it fear? Did he hate her like he hated Gheegnyan? He wondered if Freydis wanted him to hate her... but it was better that than fear her.

The horse's hoofs ploughed through the light, fluffy snow until Eirik's mama brought her horse to the front and turned side on to stop them. The waves crashed like thunder below. Gusts of icy wind sliced up the cliffside and cut through their skins and all the way through their flesh. Eirik was already shivering by the time his feet landed on the ground. Up to his knees in snow.

He looked at the spot where Snorre had died. Even with it buried under the powdery mass Eirik knew exactly where it happened but still could not get the image out of his mind. How limp Snorre's body had become and how still his eyes and face were after he'd fallen.

Freydis dismounted and held his slackened bow in her hand. He took the cue and retrieved his quiver from his horse's saddle and excitedly took the bow. He'd hit something today. Here, he'd hit something for Snorre. All Eirik had to do was imagine it was Gheegnyan and he'd hit it.

Freydis' champions took Shanawdithit off the horse and placed her in the snow. Still with her hands tied. She took a few steps towards Freydis and said something in her own language. Eirik's mama answered.

Eirik watched Shanawdithit for a reaction. The skraeling closed her mouth and swallowed like people did when they were afraid... had Freydis scared her? She stumbled a few paces closer. Eirik didn't like her that close so he took a few steps towards the hillside and watched Freydis in case she saw this one act of cowardice and took him back home without even allowing him to prove himself with a bow at last. Eirik looked around for the post that served as his target.

It wasn't there.

Could it be buried under the snow?

Suddenly, he felt a presence behind him and Eirik looked quickly to see Freydis standing over him with her eyes fixed on the skraeling. Quickly the skraeling ran out into the fields. Eirik watched as a dark feeling came over him. Freydis called out to the skraeling and she stopped running and turned to face them.

'This is a test for both of you,' Freydis said. She put her hand on Eirik's shoulder. Eirik's knees began to tremble as he stared at the blind skraeling that seemed to stare back at him even without eyes. As though she stared at everything. All at once. 'Shanawdithit has come to prove her loyalty to you, my prince. And you are going to test your new mettle.'

'What if I kill her?' Eirik asked quickly and breathlessly.

'Then we'll know she was true to her word,' Freydis said.

'What if she runs away?'

'She could right now. That skraeling lived alone in the forest as a little girl, younger than you, without her eyes. Her hands being tied shouldn't stop her.'

The skraeling twitched left and right spasmodically awaiting the first arrow. Eirik recognized the tension as though it was mirrored back at him and he didn't want to shoot her. But why not? One of them... one of Gheegnyan... but she'd come to help.

'Did you test all of the skraeling this way?' Eirik asked. He felt stupid immediately as the words came out of his mouth.

'No!' Freydis laughed. 'We'd have none to help us! Just this one.'

'But...'

'I don't think you'll be able to hit her,' Freydis said. 'But I'll be happy if I decide you made a good shot.'

Eirik looked at the skraeling. He lined up his arrow and prepared to draw back...

'I want something if I'm able to,' Eirik said. Heat filled his face. He was overstepping his bounds and knew it but...

'Alright,' Freydis agreed as she touched his shoulder and stood beside him. 'What?'

'Teach me how to talk to them,' Eirik said. Freydis let go of his shoulder and he felt that familiar sting of the coldness towards him she radiated so often. Eirik tore his eyes off the skraeling to look at his mama. She kept her eyes on the skraeling. Lips pursed. An unnerving seriousness suddenly all over her.

'We'll see,' she told him, darkly. 'If you hit her, I will start teaching you to talk with them. Only if you hit her.'

Eirik looked back at the skraeling. He wanted to talk with her
so she could reveal herself to him and not be so mysterious and
maybe tell him how she survived with no eyes, let alone in the
forest as a child younger than him. Eirik wanted to lift the veil
around her. To understand why she stirred him in a way he
never had been stirred before. If he hit her... she'd never talk to
him.

Eirik looked back at Freydis. She'd receded to the cliff's edge
with her horse and watched on with a frigidity to match the biting
ocean breeze. There was no more bargaining with her.

'Go on!' she ordered.

He'd hurt her feelings. Eirik knew it. Now he had to make it
up to her whether he would ever be able to speak with
Shanawdithit or not. He looked at the skraeling. Lined up his
shot. Drew back the arrow. Heaved against the resistance with
his shoulder held high, aimed and fired.

The skraeling barely moved. A twitch upon the flick of the
bow but nothing else. The arrow flew by and harmlessly buried
itself up to the feathers in the snow somewhere behind her.

Eirik snorted and drew another arrow. He let his frustrations
drown the thoughts of emotions and fear and curiosity. It was
time to hurt someone.

He drew back another arrow. Another miss, but closer this
time. Near the left shoulder. The skraeling still didn't move and
Eirik seethed through his teeth as he armed another arrow and
loosed. Missed. Armed another. Loosed. Missed.

Finally, he drew one, glared at her with blazing eyes and roared
as he took aim. Unleashed. The skraeling ducked to one side
and the arrow sailed past. Eirik screamed and threw the bow in
frustration...

...Clapping.

Freydis clapped her hands for him. Eirik turned at her and grit
his teeth and roared again.

'It's not fair! She can move!'

'They all move,' Freydis chuckled as she approached him.
'Had that been a real bow and arrow, and if you were strong

enough to fire it, that would have hit her. It's only because they're so slow you missed.'

'How can she do that when she can't even see!' he stomped his foot and fought back the tears.

'She can see,' Freydis said. 'And now I know how...'

Freydis looked at the skraeling and clicked her tongue three times rapidly.

Eirik looked back at Shanawdithit with a snort and saw her approach them cautiously and slowly. Hakon and the champions hurried over. They grabbed the skraeling and carried her over to the little horse she'd rode up on.

'That wasn't fair,' Eirik shouted. He trembled with rage.

'No it wasn't,' Freydis bent down and flicked his nose. He snorted and turned away. 'Oh, come on. You've made me very happy. You did what I wanted you to do and showed me what I wanted to see in you. And I got what I wanted from Shanawdithit. You've pleased me. Very much.'

She put her hands on Eirik's shoulders and doused the rage slightly. He looked at his feet. Soon, all his energy was dedicated to trying not to cry in front of her. That would ruin everything...

'I won't teach you skraelingjar, because you didn't hit her,' Freydis said. 'But I will give her to you.'

Eirik quickly looked at Freydis and then over at Shanawdithit. 'A thrall?'

'Just for you,' Freydis said. 'Your first one. Of many, many more.'

'But if I can't speak to her...'

'Speak our language,' Freydis said. 'She'll understand.'

'How?'

'She'll have to,' Freydis shrugged and smiled as she stood upright. 'Are you grateful?'

Eirik knew the cue.

'Very much,' he said. 'Thank you, mama.'

'You're welcome. You did a fine job.'

* * *

The boy held his stomach and started to blubber. Madawaak looked down at the forest floor from the treetops where they'd shuddered through the night. The wolves were gone. The snow was scarred down to the black earth beneath and stained with blood but nothing else of the alpha wolf was left behind. Madawaak looked out at the sky. Saw the distant black shape of a great bird in the pale sky. It patrolled like a vulture. But by the way it carried its enormous span Madawaak could tell it was an eagle.

Around them, the treetops were thickly blanketed in white snow. Madawaak had brushed the layers off himself and the boy through the night to prevent them being cocooned.

The boy moaned weakly.

He was curled against Madawaak's side with both his little hands pressed into his stomach. Madawaak knew his complaint. It was mirrored by the stabbing pains for food in his own stomach and the weakness in his limbs and the faintness in his head. Madawaak petted the boy to try to reassure him.

'I'll find us food,' Madawaak said. The boy looked at him sleepily. Madawaak pointed into his mouth and then his stomach. 'Food.'

'Food,' the boy repeated in Madawaak's language. '*Gjor.*'

'*Gjor,*' Madawaak repeated, then nodded his head. 'Food.'

'Erlanh,' the boy pointed to himself.

'Erlanh,' Madawaak repeated. 'Madawaak.'

'Madawaak. Erlanh.'

Madawaak looked down at his foot. The pain still flared hot up his leg but the cold had stopped it bleeding. A piece was missing from his leg. Madawaak could fit his fist in it. He scooped a handful of snow out of the canopy and pulled a strip of pelt from his satchel and stuffed the snow into the wound. The red icicles pressed into his flesh. For a moment, Madawaak's body was seized with pain and he let out a cry. Quickly, he left the snow and tied it against the wound with the pelt while Erlanh watched closely.

'Erlanh,' Madawaak said, firmly as he pointed to the branch that Erlanh sat on. The boy nodded.

Madawaak climbed down. The snowfall had covered the trail left by the wolves but he could see beneath the canopies where the wolves had dragged the pieces of their alpha away. His feet touched the ground and Madawaak stumbled. Leaned against the tree. Moaned through the shock of pain that raged in his wound. A few deep breaths. With nervous eyes, Madawaak looked around for the wolves.

They knew weakness. They knew a wounded being when they heard one.

All Madawaak had left was the tomahawk in his belt. The satchel was empty but for a few more strips of pelt, flints and spare gloves. He had to find food. Madawaak looked once more up at Erlanh to reassure the boy. Erlanh looked down at Madawaak. Fear flickered beneath his stoic face.

They were brave, the Pale Ones.

Stabs of pain made Madawaak limp with every step as he ventured from under the tree. As soon as he was under the pallid sunlight, he knew there was no escape from the pack if they came back for him. So Madawaak hobbled farther. Around him the forest brooded with a predatory silence as though every open space between the trees watched and waited. Madawaak looked back towards Erlanh.

The tree was quiet. Erlanh might just as well have not been there at all.

Madawaak quietly wished to the silence that the wolves and the Pale Ones who hunted him would find each other. Buy him time enough at least to recover a little bit. Then Madawaak distracted himself by searching for frozen ponds or birds' nests.

'Some luck,' he whispered. 'If not for me then for the boy. For Erlanh.'

Madawaak looked back again but he had wandered too far from the tree to see it. Around him, the forest had closed in. He came upon a downed tree and started to walk around it and he measured his half-steps as he went. The pain dug its claws in deeper. Madawaak had to stop. He sat on a thick root and waited for the throbbing pain to subside and closed his eyes.

Take the boy back, he thought. *It is over...*

They'd kill Madawaak as soon as they saw him and he knew it. But the abyss beyond life's veil wasn't daunting anymore. If Demasduit, Adothe and Ebauthoo weren't there to meet him then at least darkness and nothingness were not the suffering that had come upon himself and his home. At least he would not be embroiled anymore in conflicts. The living could hurt each other all they liked. He hadn't the heart for it anymore.

Madawaak had avoided wondering why he had lived while so many others hadn't since he'd first left the Broken Lands for the Island. He knew the madness that followed. But still he could not help but wonder...

A small clearing opened up before Madawaak. In the centre of it, bathed in the dim but unbroken daylight, stood a red maple.

'Oh, thank you,' Madawaak almost ran towards it. The sickening pain that grabbed him by the foot stopped him immediately. Still he stumbled breathlessly. Almost hugged the soft trunk. 'Thank you.'

Madawaak sank down to his knees and took his tomahawk out. With all the strength he had left in him, he slammed the blade into the tree. The day had warmed. Sap began to run almost immediately down the chert blade and Madawaak held his hands under it to catch it and drank it quickly. As the sweet syrup lathered his throat, he took a glove from his satchel. Madawaak held it under the axe until the pelt pouch was full.

32

Small Mercies

Eirik sat amongst the thralls who buzzed around the lodge in preparation for the Althing tonight. Torvard spotted him by the head table and started to manoeuvre through them. They scrubbed the tabletops and mounted iron block holds to light tinder in and give them light. The main fire dish was being stocked with wood. He wondered how Freydis would provide the illusion of abundance, or if she would bother. The fishing boats had come back with little. The winter had claimed their game. The other two outposts, on Hop and Helluland, had all but ceased contact and Freydis' last messengers sent to Hop had failed to return at all.

Even amongst the thralls there hummed that same nervous, frightened tension that had become evident and normal all around Straumfjord. He'd overheard Viggo's remark as he'd passed the forge the other day...

'The skraelingjar only have to wait us out.'

Torvard had seen the knarr that had taken the captured Helluland skraelingjar away get more and more empty. Still the thought of it saddened him.

'Hello papa,' Eirik said when Torvard reached him and looped a finger through one of the ringlets on the back of his head.

Before him was a wooden bowl of a strange looking pudding.

'What's that?' Torvard asked.

'My new thrall made it,' Eirik nodded towards the corner where the blind skraeling stood by like a sentinel with no sight. Torvard shuddered and looked away. In the blur of his peripheral vision or across the dark distance of the lodge, there was no telling her from her sister.

Eirik held up a spoonful of the little that was left. Torvard took it and tasted it. Sweet and slimy.

'Shall we go?' Eirik asked.

'When you're finished.'

'What will we do today?'

'I thought we could try some fishing...'

'Good. Some kind of hunting.'

Torvard nodded and automatically looked again at the skraeling Shanawdithit. Still she watched... somehow, he felt her gaze... as though it came from everywhere at once. The guilt that ravaged his heart flared painfully.

'Alright,' Eirik said. 'Let's go.'

He turned to Shanawdithit.

'Come on!'

She approached them and Torvard shuffled uncomfortably.

'You're bringing her?'

'She knows things, Papa,' Eirik beamed. 'Not just how to get food from trees and the ground. There are tricks she has for everything. She should come with us.'

Torvard felt faint. Eirik didn't know...

'Yes, okay.'

They started to cross the lodge. A sharp grab at Torvard's arm spun him around to meet Freydis' gaze.

'If she gets anywhere near Gheegnyan,' Freydis said softly. 'If Eirik hears anything... I'll kill all three of them.'

Torvard's blood ran cold.

'Your son...'

'We won't need him much longer,' Freydis said. 'I keep him for you. Don't let yourself forget that.'

She tenderly released him and gave Eirik one of her crooked smiles before she turned and headed back into the bustle of the thralls. Torvard turned and looked at Eirik. His sweet, soft face had a monsters' brooding underneath. Planted there by Freydis. Torvard fought back tears as all doubt in his mind that she would do as she threatened instantly disappeared from him.

'Are you going?' he asked, impatiently.

'Yes. Come on. You mustn't fall in the water today. It's very cold.'

'When have I ever fallen in the water?'

They walked and Shanawdithit followed behind them all the way down to the boatyard where Erland hurried out to greet them. He froze when he caught a glimpse of the skraeling who walked behind them.

'Is that safe?' he asked with eyes that bulged.

'This is Shanawdithit,' Eirik said, enthusiastically. 'She's my thrall.'

'Good for you lad,' Erland said with a lingering glance at Shanawdithit's eyes. 'A faering for you, my Lord?'

'Yes, and two poles if you please...' Torvard followed Erland to pick out a faering while Eirik looked over his shoulder at Shanawdithit.

Every now and then, Eirik noticed how people looked at him. He was aware of how different he was with his olive-coloured skin, hazel eyes and black hair. And he was small for a boy his age. People never said anything. But they made him feel it all the same, in ways he didn't really understand. The way they looked at him. The way they spoke. Tinged with doubt over him or suspicion or something. Just unsettling things. Sometimes he'd lay awake at night and think about it and get upset... then there was his mama...

But until just now, he'd never seen or noticed such behaviour towards anyone else. He wanted to say he was sorry. That he understood. But Shanawdithit just stood there and stared into nothing and waited for him to start to walk.

That's what he did. When mama insulted him or hurt him, he stood just like that.

'It's okay,' Eirik said as he moved back over to her. She was his height. Just about his size. He touched her hand. Her fingers were so hard and rough they felt like stone. But Eirik felt them flex in his grip and something moved across Shanawdithit's face that only Eirik's heart saw, so he held her hand. 'People don't want to be mean. They just don't understand what it's like to be different. My dad told me that.'

Shanawdithit lightly squeezed his hand.

'Eirik!' Torvard called in a way that frightened him. 'Come on!'

Eirik let go of Shanawdithit's hand and led her down to the water's edge where Erland held the faering steady in the dark, icy brine. Torvard stopped Eirik.

'Go on,' he said to Shanawdithit.

'You first then, is it?' Erland said as she climbed aboard the little boat.

'Don't talk to her,' Torvard whispered to Eirik. 'Order her around like you would a thrall, but never talk with her.'

'I can't,' Eirik said. 'She doesn't speak our words and I don't know hers.'

'Still,' Torvard said as he gripped Eirik's shoulder firmly and looked into his face with wide, frightened eyes. 'Don't be with her unless someone else is there. Me or your mama. Okay?'

Eirik wanted to cry. He frowned and scowled instead. He wanted to protest and tell him that Shanawdithit was his friend and that she'd proven herself. But he was shaken by the fear in Torvard. Eirik didn't know what else to do.

'Okay,' he muttered.

Torvard nodded and slackened his grip.

'Good. Get on the boat,' he said.

Eirik hurried through the icy water and seared his feet and hurled himself into the boat. Torvard followed. Erland pushed the off the shore and Torvard started to row. Shanawdithit sat up on the upward curve of the starboard quarter and the ocean breeze lifted her fine dark hair around her face. Eirik wished he could speak to her. Just the sight of her made him feel so... at home. The fear was gone. Maybe he'd only feared her because she was a skraeling...

...like Gheegnyan.

Eirik's mind started to buzz. *If Shanawdithit is so human and so like me then are others like this too?*

'Eirik,' Torvard said as he rowed and the slight swells raised and lowered them on the inky surface. 'Take some bait out.'

Eirik opened the little wooden pot lined with straw and reached into the fetid confines to pull out a portion severed squid tentacle. Torvard stopped rowing and lifted one of the iron hooks.

'Now, I'll do this,' he said as he slipped the tentacle from Eirik's fingers. 'I don't want you to cut yourself.'

Eirik looked at Shanawdithit. She seemed to be looking at him, albeit in whatever way she saw things. There it was. A belittling prediction of his inability.

'See if you can tie that onto the end of a line,' Torvard said. 'Be careful.'

'I am careful,' Eirik mumbled as he did what he knew how to do and had done many times before.

In his frustration, Eirik looked up at Shanawdithit. Just to see...

She seemed to be focused on his papa. Her lips ticked slightly and Eirik thought she might very softly have been making her clicks. The ones his mama had mocked.

Eirik's hands started to shake. He looked back down at the hook as he squeezed it tight between his fingers and his heart beat fast and his blood ran hot. Teeth caught the cold air. Freydis revolved around and around in his mind. The way she'd tease him. The way she'd hurt him. The sting of her slips and the ache of her kicks. Her eyes as she watched him furiously and intensely with a smirk on her face and awaited any little slip up. Anything that made him seem weak in Freydis' own mind.

Torvard stopped rowing and picked up his own hook to bait.

The shock of his own thoughts settled Eirik again. Then he burned with shame to have for a moment hated his own mother so much. It had arisen unexpected. Just as quickly it settled again.

Something sticky ran over his fingertips. Eirik looked and saw they were red with his blood.

'Now see? See what you've done?' Torvard said as he tied the hook to the string line that connected to his wooden pole.

'It doesn't hurt,' Eirik looked up at Shanawdithit when he became aware of her attention. It was like a gentle hand on his shoulder. Soft warmth against his face. Torvard dipped Eirik's finger in the freezing water to stop the blood.

They bobbed in the black water and watched the great white monoliths that floated around them bump and sway and Eirik wavered between teeth-clenching rage and eye-watering sorrow until the elements made his face numb and all he wanted was a warm fire and four walls. He looked at Shanawdithit constantly. Her stoic countenance never changed, she didn't shuffle and she never uttered a word.

The strength of her astonished him.

When the sun grew low, Torvard rowed them back to the boatyard where Erland greeted them again.

'How'd we do?'

'Not a thing,' Torvard answered as he splashed in the ankle-deep water.

'Must be bad luck,' Erland nodded towards Shanawdithit as Torvard plucked Eirik from the gunwale and lowered him to the ground.

How those moments of hopelessness when he was being carried twisted in Eirik's gut. How he hated Erland. Enough to want to ram a fishhook into his mouth and drag him around the stony shore.

'Well, I was going to say we should build a fire to cook the fish but...' Torvard said with a shrug as they walked back towards Straumfjord in the murky twilight. The yellow lights gleamed like beacons in the darkening cove.

'I want to go home,' Eirik complained. His feet hurt from the cold and he was so fed up his own thoughts had a painfully bland taste to them. More than anything, Eirik wanted to get Shanawdithit away from these idiots.

She followed behind Torvard silently.

'You can't go home just yet,' Torvard said. The words crushed Eirik's patience and it bled rage through him.

'Why?' he stopped and faced his papa.

'Because there's an important Althing tonight,' Torvard said. He and Shanawdithit both stopped as well.

'I'm allowed to sit at Althing,' Eirik said with his fists balled. 'Mama says it's good for me.'

'Not tonight, Eirik,' Torvard said. There was a weakness in Torvard's voice. Tinged with some cowardice or another.

'Why not tonight?'

'Because they're making a decision about your mama.'

A light came on inside Eirik. She'd spoken about the voting... that they might vote her out of her position. Thus Eirik out of his. Mama had told him that this would mean the skraelingjar would all turn on them. Even the ones in their villages and their homes.

Torvard had started to walk again. Eirik followed. Shanawdithit walked beside him. Eirik looked at the side of her face. The almost square nose, the prominent chin, the high cheekbones... there was a ferocity to her appearance but none of it towards him. He couldn't imagine how these people were ever bad.

Gheegnyan, he thought. And for the first time, he wondered why.

'We'll buy some meat,' Torvard said half to himself. 'Cook in the village centre. Maybe some of your little friends will join us.'

Torvard reached back and nudged Eirik's arm.

* * *

'Go on, go with them,' Torvard urged Eirik as the children who'd joined them for their campfire meal urged him away from them. 'I'm watching. It's okay. Don't leave my sight.'

Eirik snarled and went off with his friends. *A few minutes,* Torvard thought, *he'll be himself again.* But it was obvious the boy was upset... *Was it the skraeling? Couldn't be,* he thought. *He was happy about that. Something else... maybe the fishing. Does Eirik not like fishing?*

The skraeling sat across the fire from Torvard and he tried not to look at her, staring into the lapping red flames instead. But her blind gaze drew his eyes back up to her and there she sat on the far side of tongues of flame that flickered and danced all around her as though to frame her face. For a moment it seemed her dead eyes glowed red with the reflection.

Demasduit. Arisen from her own ashes.

'What does Freydis want with you?' he asked. Torvard didn't know why. What he wanted was for this Shanawdithit to run away. Run back to her people. Stay out there in the savage forests where Torvard could imagine she didn't exist until Lief Eiriksson's boats came and...

...And annihilated them all.

'Really,' Torvard asked in a sombre tone. 'What does she want?'

The skraeling raised one small hand and moved it across her face, then threw it towards the fire.

'Your sister,' Torvard said. 'I have hated myself more every day since...' he looked into the fire again. 'Since I did what I did to her. I know you know. That's how Eirik was born and... as sick as it may sound... for that I'm grateful. He's given me something to love in this world and I love him more than I ever thought I was capable of loving. I certainly don't love Freydis. You know that, don't you? She's the only thing in this world I hate more than myself. But with that boy,' Torvard pointed towards Eirik, 'to me he makes things seem right the way they are. I'm sorry. I don't think you feel the same way because he's only your nephew...'

Torvard looked at her still face. Like a stone carving.

'I'm sorry. That's all I should say,' Torvard coughed. 'Sounds pathetic.'

The skraeling got up and walked around the fire slowly. Prowled. Came right up and sat down beside Torvard. His hands started to tremble. His flesh quivered. She sat right beside him and leaned close, mouth-first.

She spoke. Her language. But so low Torvard would never have understood no matter what she said. And yet he did understand. Maybe it was the tone or the need or the pure love he recognized as his own but he knew what she said.

'Tell him who I am. Tell him who he is.'

'I can't,' Torvard said. 'Freydis would kill us all.'

The skraeling got up and prowled back to where she'd sat. A few clicks led her the way. Then she was again back across the fire.

'But I can take you somewhere,' Torvard said.

* * *

Night Eagle smelled him as soon as she stepped into the darkness. A click revealed him. Frail and broken-spirited and chained to the wall, he could barely lift his head to look at her. Living death. A body with its spirit crushed and destroyed. But he lifted his head and looked at her and she took a stride closer.

Torvard said something. Night Eagle knew he meant for her to hurry.

'Do you know who I am?' she asked.

'I know who you are,' Gheegnyan said. His voice weakened by the strain of his suffering but darkened by the awe and fear of looking upon what he doubtless perceived as the living dead itself. 'I knew as soon as I saw you.'

'I will free you from this place,' Night Eagle said. 'Soon. People from Keathut's tribe followed you and they watch from the forest. The Pale Ones haven't seen them yet. They will stay there until you are dead or they are caught.'

'Posson,' Gheegnyan said with a quiet moan of agony. 'Stupid, stupid boy.'

'You will go to him. Crawl if you cannot walk. Go to him and go back to Keathut. Tell them Freydis is coming. She will kill them all if they do not stop her. Keathut will know what to do.'

'How do you know this?' Gheegnyan asked, desperately. 'I can't. I can't get out to them. They'll catch me.'

'You will,' Night Eagle said. 'Or your kin will be destroyed for all time.'

'How do you know about Freydis?'

Night Eagle turned and stepped around Torvard, who closed the door on the last desperate hiss from Gheegnyan. She directed her face toward Torvard. The only way she could thank him. He led her back to the fire where the voices of the playing children danced around in the night like the flames. She sat with him again.

* * *

Kaia's mouth ran dry and her heart pounded as the Althing voiced their concerns to their Chieftain one at a time. She couldn't keep count. There was only hope... hope that everything that was to come could be avoided. That Freydis could just be voted out.

'You have disgraced us!' Astrid boomed. 'I have kept faith in you through a lot of things, Freydis Eiriksdottir. But torture is something we do not do. We do not want a haven from the spread of Christianity if it means behaving no better than them. If you must kill, then kill. But we do not torture.'

There was a cheer that was loud and yet desperately thin and distant to Kaia. The rest remained silent. As though they knew something the others did not.

'My response!' Freydis called over the sea of murmurs.

Hakon turned and nodded to her from the centre of the lodge.

'I have resisted these tactics for over a decade,' Freydis said. 'But the rogues threaten my son. I will not allow danger to come to him. Not when our survival hinges upon his life.'

'My response!' Sigfrieda cried out from beside her predecessor. Hakon nodded towards her. 'Over a decade? Do you say that you did not torture that poor girl you forced to bear your son?'

'My response,' Freydis said, breathlessly.

Hakon gave her the nod.

'I agonized over what I did to that girl,' Freydis said. 'I agonized over my husband being with another woman. I agonized when he fell in love with her. But that girl was a spoil of combat...'

'It is the combatant who reaps the spoils of combat!'

'And how am I supposed to do that?' Freydis barked.

'The Chieftain has the floor,' Hakon scolded.

Freydis stood.

'I want to close this now,' she said. 'By addressing the men of this room,' she snarled at Astrid and Sigfrieda, 'even though it's these two women who don't seem to understand.'

They both looked at her angrily. Kaia allowed herself a small sliver of hope...

'How many of you men have reaped your so-called spoils?' Freydis asked. There was an uncomfortable silence. 'How many of you men came back to those spoils to see if they'd become pregnant with your children? How many of those spoils came back with you as thralls to live on your lands and enjoy the comfort of your protection? You've all called me illegitimate. Either with your tongues or your minds. How many bastards have you made? Or women, how many have your husbands made? Did you stand up and insist, then, that the bitches they'd spoiled came back with you as thralls and lived within arm's reach of your husbands and raised their children? Or did you wish they were dead? Were you relieved when they stayed away?'

The discomfort grew thick enough to stifle Kaia's breath.

'Were you relieved when they died in labour?' Freydis said. 'Hypocrisy. My husband took my dues from this battlefield. I kept that girl. I helped her deliver her baby and I raised it as my own. I had her in my home. Behind my arras with my husband and I. And when she threw herself into a fire, I raised her son.'

'That son,' a man Kaia couldn't see said, 'who also gave you power over the skraelingjar.'

'That son is the reason over a hundred knarr are sailing towards Straumfjord,' Freydis said. 'To finish what I started here and begin anew on the mainland. What I did, I did for him and for her and for all of us. How many of you can say the same of your spoils?'

There was silence.

'I torture,' Freydis admitted. 'Yes. To protect another woman's baby. And all of you and yours. Show me how many of you, or your husbands, have done the same. I was the child of spoils. Taken by the beloved Eirik the Red. He took my mother home. Gave her a life on his fields in spite of his wife. I

had to fight to prove who I was. But I learned from him. I
learned what a difference you make when you take your spoils.
And that difference can be all for the good, or simply pushed
aside and forgotten. I wonder what torture my life would have
been had one of you or your husbands been my father instead
of the great Eirik the Red?'

Kaia's heart sank.

'Motion to vote now.'

'Second!'

They voted. Kaia kept her hand down. There was no
opposition.

33

The Fallen

Madawaak chipped the top corner off his tomahawk to make the carving dagger. Sustained by the syrup, he and Erlanh staggered back toward the maple tree.

The boy looked up at him as they walked together. And imitated his limp. Madawaak stopped. So did Erlanh. The two stared at each other. Madawaak took another step. Erlanh did as well. Madawaak took another five steps. Erlanh imitated him. Limp and all. Then opened his mouth all the way, buried his chin into his chest and gave a devious little chuckle.

A smile crept across Madawaak with a warm feeling. He took another step and then what he wanted caught his eye...

Flat snow. Undisturbed by stone or fallen branches.

'Come on,' he said and led Erlanh to the pond. Madawaak pressed the boy back with his hand and shook his head. Don't stand there, boy. Then Madawaak carefully lay down on the edge and lowered his ear to the water and tapped with his tomahawk. The muffled echo of liquid water replied. Madawaak smiled at Erlanh.

With the tomahawk he chopped a hole through the thin ice to the water below. Erlanh sat down on some soft vegetation and waited while Madawaak watched the water slowly settle. The boy sighed. Time passed. The sun grew higher.

Erlanh sighed again. Then he started to sing to himself.

A silvery flash shone up from the dark water.

Madawaak plunged his hand in and seized the fish. He brought it up and Erlanh nearly jumped out of his skin with surprise. With the dagger Madawaak quickly stripped the fish's flesh and stuck half of it in the snow and split the other half in two and then gave one to Erlanh. The boy had it in his mouth before the slime could fall down his fingers. Madawaak ate his slowly.

They walked around the woods. Erlanh imitated his guardian's search until Madawaak found something else he wanted.

A birch tree stood ghostly white against the ashy trunks of the slumbering forest.

He took out his dagger and Erlanh watched with sleepy fascination as Madawaak carefully carved off a patch of birchbark. He folded it into a parcel. Just like the satchel he had at his side. Then Madawaak led Erlanh back to the fish that he'd placed in the ice and Erlanh watched as he took out the rigid, stark white strips and put them in the bag.

Madawaak handed the bag to Erlanh.

'We won't be hungry tomorrow,' he told the child. Erlanh nodded as though he understood even though his weepy expression said he didn't.

They limped together back towards the clearing where Madawaak had seen a dogwood. Beside him, he heard chewing. Erlanh was eating the rest of the fish out of his satchel.

'Maybe *you* will be hungry tomorrow,' Madawaak mumbled.

They crossed the clearing past the maple and Madawaak almost reached the dogwood when he felt that Erlanh's presence had fallen away from his side. He stopped and looked back. Erlanh stared at the maple tree with the last morsel of fish pinched between his finger and thumb. Madawaak glanced around the clearing. The distance between them made his flesh prickle with readiness as he sought the staring eyes of wolves or the prowl of a polar bear... even a fox would not be too small to take this boy.

'Erlanh,' Madawaak called.

The child looked at him, then at the tree again. As though he was transfixed by this thing he didn't even know had given him life for the day. The sun shone at them sideways. Twilight would fall upon them soon and that's when the hunters would be on the prowl.

'Erlanh,' Madawaak called as he continued to the dogwood and took out his tomahawk. He'd spend the night at work. Chop out a piece of dogwood and make a bow and arrows with the dagger. The skins in his satchel would be enough to pleat into a string.

Madawaak chopped at the tree. The wooden clacks of the chert as it cut into the tree's flesh reverberated loudly around the clearing. Erlanh took a few paces towards Madawaak, then looked at the tree again.

What was the boy doing?

'Erlanh!' Madawaak said more firmly as he slowly carved out the six foot of dogwood he'd need.

Then he saw them.

Madawaak ducked behind the tree and sank down to the base of the trunk where the undergrowth would conceal him. The pain sank through his foot but he held his breath. He looked up across the clearing...

Erlanh still stood there. They were on the far side. Five of them. One was old with a white beard but his frame was enormous.

'Go to them, Erlanh,' Madawaak whispered. As he watched, tensely. 'Go to them.'

The Pale Ones seemed hesitant to emerge from the forest edge. They huddled under the snow encrusted canopy and looked around at the sun-bathed clearing with its sparkling white mantle. Erlanh didn't seem to have noticed them.

'Erlanh!' one of them finally called. He broke away from the others and had both a bow across his back and an axe clenched in his fist. Erlanh looked and saw him then.

Madawaak clutched the wet twigs and leaves beneath his hands as he watched. The boy and the Pale One stared at each other for a while and the other Pale Ones primed their bows and kept watch. The Pale One, maybe his father, held out his hand. Shouted.

'Go, Erlanh,' Madawaak mumbled. 'Go!'

Still Erlanh did not move.

The Pale One clutched his axe in both hands and his teeth shone through his beard as he stormed towards Erlanh. Madawaak wanted to stop him. His body urged to leap up and order the Pale One to slow down. To not frighten the boy. But the Pale One stormed forward with his axe in his hands as though he intended to use it.

Erlanh turned and ran. His face was red and his mouth was open and Madawaak threw himself out into the sunlight with both his hands up.

'Erlanh!'

The arrow whipped past his head so close the feathers scratched Madawaak's face. Still he crawled forward. Other arrows came. They slammed into the ground beside and in front of him. One landed close. Madawaak felt the shaft slide through his hand. With a roar, he lifted his hand and freed himself to keep crawling while his blood stained the snow. The Pale One caught Erlanh with an arm around his waist. Erlanh fought and cried.

'Madawaak!' he screamed.

That hideous, shuddering sensation ran through Madawaak again as an arrow slid into his shoulder. He fell on his side and clutched it. It had pierced through his arm and hit his side and blood flowed immediately.

The Pale One shook the boy hard as he turned and hurried back to his people. Madawaak saw through the haze of pain the Pale One shrink back towards the forest and the others come out towards him. Erlanh was back with them. Madawaak heaved himself to his feet and hobbled back for the trees. He ducked his head. Arrows flew over the top and rattled through the forest. Finally he reached the undergrowth and threw himself in.

* * *

Gottfried led Ivers and Katla across the clearing into the forest on the other side. There he stopped. Erlanh kept screaming and screaming, calling out the skraeling word.

'Madawaak!'

'Shut up, boy!' barked the voice of Carl.

They all heard the cracks of his hand as he struck Erlanh.

'Why does he brutalize them like that?' Ivers muttered.

The boy's screams reached a higher pitch.

'He murdered the other one,' Katla whispered.

'Well it's turned the boy skraeling now...'

'Shut up!' Gottfried hissed as he turned his gaze slowly back and forth around the thick forest that surrounded them. The skraeling could have been an arm's reach away. Behind some tree. Crouched in some undergrowth. Either way, it had the upper hand here.

But Gottfried wasn't about to go now. This one wasn't going to escape him a third time.

'Madawaak,' he sang softly as the boy's screams softened as Steinar and Carl carried him off to safety. 'Madawaak.'

'We should go,' Ivers said.

'Keep tight,' Gottfried ordered. He felt Ivers and Katla move in close against his flanks. They faced outward. Bows ready. Gottfried had his axe. 'Madawaak.'

They could still hear the screams of Erlanh.

'That's driving me mad,' Ivers hissed.

'Be quiet!' Gottfried said. He led them forward. Prowled with them deeper into the undergrowth until the naked branches scraped against their faces and shoulders.

'The boy doesn't want to go!'

'Would you?' Katla whispered. 'Be quiet.'

'Madawaak,' Gottfried said.

'What for?' Ivers said. 'He's watched us from wherever he is.'

'He's injured,' Kaia said. 'We've got him.'

Ivers suddenly loosed an arrow. A large bird in the canopy squawked and fluttered up into the air. A clump of snow fell from where it had been.

'Sorry.'

'We should have brought Steinar with us,' Katla breathed.

Gottfried made a short, sharp whistle and stopped still. Katla and Ivers kept their focus off to the sides while Gottfried hunched down and stared unblinkingly at one of the larger brushes.

'Katla,' he barely breathed.

Katla looked out of the corner of her eye at where Gottfried wanted her to shoot. She counted to three. Then drew back her arrow and turned as Gottfried dropped to one knee and she fired into the brush. Before her arrow hit, Gottfried leaped up and swung his axe. The axe head disappeared into the undergrowth beside them and something let out an inhuman howl.

Gottfried stood upright and dug with his axe. An old fox rolled out. Nearly cut in two, it writhed and showed its fangs as they slowly opened and closed. Gottfried delivered it another chop. The head split and the eyes popped out and the animal was dead.

'Feed yourself on that, skraeling,' Gottfried said as he kicked it. 'We have the boy.'

'Think he'll follow us?' Katla asked as Gottfried turned and ushered them back towards the clearing.

'It's all he has left,' Gottfried replied.

The hulking old warrior stepped between the two confused younglings and continued in the direction of the howling child. They followed. Casting nervous glances over their shoulders as they went.

* * *

Madawaak fell where the dead fox lay and felt around until he felt the cooling fur. The night had fallen. Darkness flooded the forest while a dazzling sky of stars peeked through the forest edge from the clearing. Madawaak lifted the fox up to the light. It festered and stank. The exposed flesh had turned grey. The screams of Erlanh had finally fallen silent.

They'd waited for him. Not nearby, but close enough to see the flames from the fire he'd have had to build to make use of the fox. But he'd ignored it. Despite the urging ache in his flesh and his gut to eat something real he'd resisted. Waited for silence.

Madawaak threw the fox aside and crawled up to the clearing. Once there, he fell on his back. High above the canopy and the turquoise snow that blanketed the open space and the lone maple tree the dome of stars seemed to twist and move. The snow hadn't stopped his bleeding. One arrow was still stuck through his arm and that had yet more bleeding to do. Blood still stained the snow where he'd been.

The wolves, he thought.

He took the goose feathers that had brushed against his face while he'd crawled from his hiding spot and gripped them tightly in a trembling hand. With his other hand he held the arrowhead. Hard. That shining stone. He gripped it and snapped the top off. The pain rang through him as though he'd snapped off a part of himself.

No sound. No sound.

High on the adrenaline, Madawaak pulled the arrowhead and drew the shaft through him and threw it away. Blood spattered the snow. Black against the glow from the stars. As Madawaak held his breath, he pulled the last few strips of skin out of his satchel and compressed his wound. Darkness wavered before his eyes. Deep unconsciousness threatened him. Time leaped forward with each blink but Madawaak fought with all his might to...

...Someone grumbled...

Madawaak raised his head and peered around the blurry clearing. A huge shape stumbled around and yapped and barked to itself with human tones.

A Pale One.

Madawaak stayed still, yet unseen. The Pale One paced around and wiped his face with his sleeve again and again. Madawaak dropped his head down onto the snow. Waited.

A phase of darkness swept through Madawaak and suddenly the Pale One was silent. The steps were close. The snow shuffled right beside Madawaak's head. He kept his eyes closed. Lay still. The Pale One stood over him and looked down.

Madawaak opened his eyes.

The Pale One just had time to gasp and Madawaak whipped his hand around and drove the arrowhead into the tendon of his heel. With a scream, the Pale One fell and raised his axe. But

Madawaak reared up to his knees and swung his tomahawk into the side of the Pale One's head. With a dense crack, the head snapped to one side and fell onto the snow. Madawaak drew the tomahawk out and turned it backward and swung again and again down on the skull. Blood sprayed out and darkened the snow in the shape of a clutching talon. The body tensed and released and finally rolled flaccidly to one side and Madawaak caught his breath.

The chert head of the axe dropped from the end of his handle and thudded on the snow. Madawaak picked up the Pale One's axe. It was small for the Pale One. Light. Still big for Madawaak but astonishingly light. Madawaak dropped down on top of the corpse. The pain seeped through him and held him down.

He waited for more Pale Ones to appear.

Unconsciousness came first.

* * *

When he awoke, the soft light that filtered through deep creamy clouds fell upon Madawaak's eyes and his body shuddered with terror. He stood up. His head ached beyond fury and his body felt drained of all its strength. But Madawaak was upright. Breathless. Dizzy. Utterly focused.

The wolves circled around. Showed their fangs. Gargled at Madawaak, and he raised his hands and avoided looking at their eyes.

'I will not keep you from your meal,' he said, softly. 'I will not fight you.'

He backed away slowly. The wolves rushed the body and seized clumps of flesh in their jaws and tore and pulled. Madawaak staggered out across the clearing. Away from them. More emerged. They came from all directions and joined in the rabid fray that enveloped the Pale One's body.

The weight of pain and fatigue came crashing down on Madawaak again as he made it out of their sight. Down a slight embankment, he collapsed against a tree.

Madawaak heard his heart beat heavy and hard.

[418]

But a single coherent thought found its way into the detached corner of his mind; what had made the Pale One come back alone? He seemed to have forgotten about Madawaak...

Something wasn't right.

He still held the Pale One axe in his hand. Madawaak clutched it and dragged himself back to his feet.

'Leave me alone, wolves,' he said as he walked back out into the clearing where already the pack had reduced the carcass to rags of offal. 'Leave me alone.'

He collapsed again beside the maple tree. Then dug the axe into the flesh.

* * *

When the wolves finally left, there were only shreds of the Pale One's clothes that remained. Madawaak tied the strips of skin he had left in his satchel over his wounds. No more bow... but the shaft was almost carved out of the dogwood tree.

A spear.

Madawaak grabbed hold of the axe in the tree and lifted himself up. Then he edged the axe out and looked at the thin, sharp blade made from the shining stone. He chopped into the maple tree sideways. When he pulled it out, he saw the sharp edge of the axe head had been bent by the blow. These were only weapons for flesh. Useless against the land.

In the patch of bloody snow, Madawaak found the head of his tomahawk. With that in both hands, he carved at the tree until the strong piece of wood was free and his wounds bled through his skins as though fresh. Then he sat and with the dagger he'd made slowly whittled out his spear. Even as the hunger weakened him. Even as the sun set and darkness stole his sight away. No stars anymore. A thick sheet of white cloud had moved in and Madawaak felt the soft tingle of snowflakes as they fell on the back of his neck and brushed his face.

Then, when he had his spear shaft, Madawaak got up and went back to the place amongst the brushes where he'd hidden. He found the pup foxes who still waited for their mother. With the back of the Pale One's axe he broke their necks one at a time, as quickly as he could, and made a small fire of their dry, loose tinder nest where he singed off their fur and cooked their flesh.

* * *

Morning gave Madawaak a stark white sky but not enough snow had fallen to cover the trail left on the earth by the Pale Ones. Five walked away. One laboured by the burden of a child under his arm. A child who fought. Who'd screamed. Now and since yesterday there was silence. Somewhere water dripped. It didn't make sense...

Madawaak followed the trail into the forest that led the way eventually back to the Pale Ones' settlement. One had come back. He wanted to know why. It was all there was left. All his life, the love he'd only known as pain and loss, the idle times, everything that could have been and everything that was centred around one question. All of Madawaak's life narrowed down to one answer. Then he could die.

He wanted to die. Then and there, just lay down and close his eyes and wait for the jaws of the wolfpack to find him. His wounds ached. By now the pain had spread from the holes their arrows had made out through the flesh of his limbs. Madawaak felt the tenderness of infection. But something in his heart was stronger.

A need to know what became of Erlanh.

The trail began to break apart. Heels dug into the black soil beneath the white mantle and swept the decaying leaves of summer in every direction. The fight had intensified. Madawaak found the feet that imprinted the deepest and stayed on them. Followed them in spirals and scuffs. Had Erlanh fought so hard? The Pale One had been thrown off balance. Madawaak couldn't breathe as he watched. He could see the conflict as though the marks on the earth projected the ghosts of what had happened up at him. The Pale One as he fought with a child. Erlanh as he'd grappled at his captor's shoulders.

What boy is so afraid of his own father?

Then, Madawaak saw where they'd stumbled. Where they'd fallen. A bush was broken. Madawaak looked through it.

Eyes looked back at him. Frozen. Still. Dead.

Erlanh's eyes.

Madawaak cried out and fell to his knees. The wounds opened again and he felt the hot blood spurt out. He didn't care. Erlanh was dead in the snow. The mouth he'd fed pinched tight in a final moment of pain. The eyes he'd looked into wide with shock. His body was pinned under the corpse of the Pale One who'd taken him. Shot with arrows. In the back.

Gone through, Madawaak saw as he reached out and touched the tips of the arrows that had taken that little boy's life. He threw his head back and howled. Howled all his spirit out into the sky as Erlanh's innocent face appeared before him. Like the ones he'd killed.

It didn't matter if they heard. Madawaak wanted them to hear.

He wanted them to come for him.

34

The Fury of the Morning

It looked as though Torvard would spend another night alone. Deeper and deeper into the night and Night Eagle still heard his shallow breathing and his uncomfortable fidgeting hour after hour and still Freydis did not return. Twice before this had happened. But Freydis always appeared before the dawn. Always.

Night Eagle could hear the abysmal stillness that always plunged in around them before the break of dawn and could feel the gentle vibration of the first light as it edged towards their horizon. Freydis wasn't coming home tonight.

Eirik's soft snores issued through the arras from his portion of the longhouse.

Torvard got up and fumbled his way towards her cage and knelt right in front of her. Night Eagle clicked. Tears streaked down his cheeks. He spoke to Night Eagle. Said something. She didn't know what it was but she could hear the heavy sadness in his speech. Now was her chance.

Night Eagle reached forward and touched the lock of her cage. Torvard said one word. Then she heard him open it.

They snuck out of the longhouse into the freezing night. Snow tickled their cheeks and brows. Torvard led Night Eagle towards the lodging where Gheegnyan was kept...

...footsteps. The warmth of fire.

Torvard froze. Night Eagle clicked. The guard stood before them. Torvard said something. His words were short and shaky, as though braced for pain. But the guard held his torch high. Waved it side to side. Night Eagle looked back and clicked. It was as planned.

Around the forest edge, lights ignited and waved back and then went dark again. The guard who stood in front of them stepped aside. Torvard nervously led Night Eagle the rest of the way to the hut and opened the door for her.

'Be silent,' she said quickly as she stepped in. Still a din of shuffles and tensions exploded from the stagnant space before her. But he didn't make another sound. Gheegnyan lay still while Night Eagle hurried to his side and felt for the bonds that held him. It was a chain made of their iron.

What Mooaumook had given all their world for.

Torvard hurried up and unclasped the iron cuffs with a blade. A horse's hoofs pounded up to the door. Torvard picked up Gheegnyan and carried him to the rider and Night Eagle clicked to see that it was Kaia. She covered him in a cloak. Positioned him on the horse in front of her. Torvard asked Kaia a question. She did not answer. Instead just turned the horse and galloped off across the village.

'Every night they've waited,' Night Eagle said as she gave Torvard an encouraging nudge back towards the longhouse. 'They have made sure one in league with them has been on the night watch every night since I came.'

He said something back at her. Neither one understood a word from the other but the fear in his voice betrayed him. Night Eagle reached out and squeezed his hand.

'It will not be forgotten, what you've done,' she said.

At the longhouse, he entered the door and began to close it in front of Night Eagle. She reached out. Stopped it with her hand. Then shook her head at him no, a gesture that was familiar to both of them. He asked a question. Night Eagle pushed through the door and clicked as she led the way back through the darkness to her cage.

'No,' she said as she climbed into the cage. 'I did not come here to save him. I am not finished yet.'

She closed the cage door slowly on herself. Torvard slid the bolted latch home and hurried back into his and Freydis' bed. Eirik's nose had started to whistle. Torvard lay awake.

* * *

Sleep teased Torvard's eyes as he lay there and waited. Memories of the man he was only a year or so ago came and reminded him about what state he'd be in now. Nervous. Horrified. Ready to burst open and spill the details of what had happened all over Freydis. Then he'd have watched in shame and guilt as Kaia Sveninungursdottir and probably her entire karldom suffered whatever horror Freydis would have for them. He'd have realized again the monster she was. No better than the violent one-god barbarians who burned people alive and flayed them and tore them to pieces slowly. And he'd have wished he could be as strong as he was now.

Now Torvard felt nothing. Maybe he was too tired or maybe the question of where Freydis had been and its obvious answer were too much for even what had just happened to supplant. But Torvard didn't care anymore. After he'd seen that child on a pyre... after he'd seen good Norse people vote to allow her to torture someone... after she'd forced him to torture a girl... *No,* he thought. They were pieces of the hatred he felt for her. But it was the way she made Eirik behave that silenced and strengthened him.

Freydis made his son like her.

Enough light shone between the turf that Torvard could see Shanawdithit in her cage. He could only wonder how many had turned. Not enough to vote an Althing. But they were only jarls and not the many more karls who if anything held truer to the Norse way of life than their lords...

The door thudded and heavy footsteps strode quickly across the longhouse. Torvard got upright. Ready. Freydis burst through the arras in her pleated leather with Gunnlogi at her side. She looked first at Shanawdithit. She knew. Then she glared with those toxic-green eyes at Torvard.

'Where were you?' Torvard asked quickly.

'What happened to the skraeling?'

Torvard nodded towards Shanawdithit.

'Not her!' Freydis snapped and in two strides, her face was right in front of his. 'What happened?'

'What did happen?' Torvard asked without the bat of an eyelid.

Freydis' eyes narrowed and departed from his to scan around his face and body. Then she turned to Shanawdithit and asked her a question. The skraeling didn't answer. Freydis kicked the bars of her cage and they hummed as she screamed her question again. Still Shanawdithit said nothing.

'Mama?' Eirik's voice came. 'What's wrong?'

Freydis stared at Eirik a moment as the rage turned her face purple.

'Your skraeling has to die.'

Eirik stared up at her with his sleepy eyes, open-mouthed.

'I don't know why you kept it in the first place,' Torvard said.

'You...' Freydis turned wildly towards him and pointed her gloved finger. 'Don't you. She got a message to him somehow. Gheegnyan can't be getting far the way he is. There are skraelingjar in the forest waiting for him. There have to be or he wouldn't have even tried. It's too far.'

'Do you think I relayed a message to...'

'I don't know!' Freydis interrupted. Then she looked at Eirik. 'I don't know who did this to me.'

Eirik rapidly shook his head.

'Neither of you?' Freydis feigned shock. 'Well that's quite incredible. It wasn't me! I'm fairly sure of that.'

'Mama...what are you talking about?' Eirik asked, softly.

Freydis looked at him again. Suddenly a chilling wave of calm came over her.

'It's alright, son,' Freydis said with a smirk. 'I'll know very soon that I can trust you again. Before we even have breakfast, I'll know.'

'What are you going to do to him?'

'You shut your mouth,' Freydis hissed and shot him a venomous look. 'You're coming too. Don't worry.'

* * *

Eirik watched through silent tears as Freydis dragged Shanawdithit across the village towards the hills where the forest watched over them. Everything was white with snow. Even the sky seemed to be blanketed. They left a thick trail behind them as Freydis led him, Torvard, Hakon, Capser and Gustav past the sparser edges of the village and out amongst the trees. Behind them, Aeda and the longhouse thralls led their horses.

As Freydis' party walked by them, people around the village livened. Eirik couldn't see their faces. Eirik always saw people watch Freydis, whatever she did, and he always thought it was because they loved her and wanted to please her like him. But now their glances chilled his flesh. But he didn't know why. All Eirik could think about was Shanawdithit.

What was Freydis going to do to his friend?

They reached a small clearing where the trees were scattered and a few homes were still visible behind them. The shadowy figures of onlookers appeared but kept their distance. Freydis threw Shanawdithit to the ground. Then she barked an order in Shanawdithit's language. Shanawdithit lifted her head and then climbed up to her feet and stood there. Freydis gave the order again. This time there were more words and Eirik saw her flick her sword towards him as she spoke. Shanawdithit clicked towards Eirik.

Eirik saw the fear in her. Just the same as what Freydis made him feel. But Shanawdithit didn't cry. She stayed firm and turned and walked away from them. Further and further. Until Freydis whistled.

Shanawdithit turned. Eirik heard her soft clicks and Freydis pointed her sword towards Eirik again.

'Run away,' Eirik whispered in desperation. 'Run away and never come back.'

But Shanawdithit didn't run. She just stood there.

'Come here, Eirik,' Freydis ordered without looking at him.

'Don't hurt him,' Torvard growled. Casper and Gustav stood close at his sides.

Eirik didn't move. He'd heard what Freydis had asked of him but couldn't do it. Didn't want to lose sight of Shanawdithit.

'Eirik!' Freydis barked.

Aeda led Freydis' horse to her side. Eirik forced himself to join his mama and as soon as he was in reach, her talon-like fingers closed upon his shoulder and sent stabbing pain through his chest. Eirik suppressed the scream.

'They're watching us,' Freydis hissed at Eirik as Aeda hurried back to the other thralls. 'Right now. From all around. The ones who killed Snorre and tried to kill you, they're here. Watching. Are you going to cry in front of them?'

Eirik held his breath, forced it all down and shook his head. Freydis stood over him. Dominated him. The gleam of her sword winked in the corner of his eye.

'Your skraeling lied to us,' Freydis said. 'She helped Gheegnyan escape.'

'How could she have?' Torvard asked but Eirik saw the sword move slightly towards him and Torvard made no more sound.

'She came to free him,' Freydis said. 'Now he's been in Straumfjord. He knows where you sleep and where I sleep.'

Eirik stared at Shanawdithit. The skraeling girl just stood there though he wished with all his might she'd run. Freydis shook him and his attention snapped back to her.

'They'll come back to save her,' Freydis said. She pointed her sword at Shanawdithit. 'They'll kill me and kidnap you.'

Eirik reached for words but his mind was blank. Northing but terror. His eyes darted around at the surrounding trees but he couldn't see any sign of the skraelingjar. But... they'd snuck up on Snorre.

'I think,' Freydis said. Then she leaned down closer and whispered. 'I think you and your father helped her.'

'No!' Eirik cried.

'No?' Freydis echoed, mockingly. 'Then prove it to me.'

She took from her saddle bag Eirik's bow and an arrow and slipped them into his hands. Eirik looked at Shanawdithit. His heart trembled and his breath ran cold. But she faced him stoic and firm. Could she not tell what Freydis wanted? He hadn't heard her click.

'Kill her,' Freydis said. 'This time I mean it.'

She took a few paces back and left Eirik to stand before Shanawdithit with his little bow and downsized arrow. Behind him stood his mama and papa. Then their guards. Then their thralls. Then the villagers who gathered more and more at the forest edge and watched on from a distance, too afraid to come any closer. All the eyes of Straumfjord were upon Eirik. Yet he felt the cold winds of a barren and empty waste blow through his flesh as though he stood alone in the world.

There was Shanawdithit. Where she waited for him. Why wouldn't she run?

Eirik tried to swallow but his mouth was dry. He primed the arrow. Next, he had to aim and he looked at her where she stood. The same size as him. Alone as well. *Shanawdithit might have helped Gheegnyan,* he thought. But the thought didn't arouse his rage. There was no rage. Only hurt. That lonely hurt of other people's expectations, of their judgement and of Freydis' wrath that Eirik shared with his friend Shanawdithit.

In his heart, he knew it all along. Eirik wouldn't do it. It was worth the beating. He cast the arrow aside and turned and faced Freydis. Her eyes flared. Eirik's heart raced and he trembled but he wasn't going to back down.

'No, Mama.'

Freydis bared her huge teeth as she took a few paces towards him. The rage that blazed from her being scored Eirik's heart but he would take it. He didn't care.

'She's my friend,' he blubbered.

It was then that he realized Hakon had come up close behind her. The shine of steel caught his eye. Eirik's reaction was automatic.

'You...' she snarled.

'Mama!' he screamed.

It happened so fast...

Freydis turned and had Gunnlogi from the sheath and swung the blade high. There was a wet crack. Something dark hit the snow between their feet and Hakon made a high-pitched sound but, in the same motion, Freydis brought the blade back down.

A thin crescent of blood appeared on the snow beside them.
Hakon fell as his throat opened.

'Eirik!' Shanawdithit shouted.

Torvard ran towards him. The distant onlookers scattered and
riders upon their battle horses charged out from between them
and obscured them in the opaque white cloud of their snowy
wake. Their atgiers pointed down as they closed in an arch
around Freydis. Casper and Gustav dropped behind their
shields on one knee and fired arrows from their bows. A rider
fell with the scream of a horse and disappeared into a billowing
cloud of snow. The others kept coming and Freydis turned
towards Eirik as Torvard seized him by the arm and ran with
him towards Shanawdithit.

Shanawdithit hurried closer and met Torvard and took Eirik
by the arms. Eirik ran with her a few paces but the screams that
issued from behind were too much. He turned back. Freydis
stood at her horse while Casper and Gustav alone thinned the
swarm of riders. She drew a bow and arrow. Primed it.

'Mama!' Eirik screamed in fear for her.

Freydis drew back the arrow. Aimed at Eirik. Torvard looked
back and saw what she was doing and leaped in front of his son.
The arrow pierced through him.

Eirik turned cold. He screamed out as his father fell to the
ground. Freydis stood stunned. Blood bubbled up between
Torvard's lips and stained his beard as he looked up at Eirik.

'She isn't you mother,' Torvard gurgled. 'She'll kill you. Run!'

'Eirik!' Shanawdithit cried again and pulled at the back of his
tunic.

Freydis looked at Eirik with a white hatred he'd never seen or
felt for anything and a sharp pain pierced through him.
Shanawdithit urged him on. Fear flooded his body as Freydis
reached back for her horse's saddle. He turned and ran with
Shanawdithit.

* * *

The pain swelled inside Torvard like a blooming flower as he
clung to life so he could watch his son run away with

Shanawdithit. They started up the hillside. The snow-covered pine trees obscured their bodies and then blended together on the giant white hillside.

'Protect my son,' Torvard breathed. He spat the blood from his lips and turned his head. Stabbing pains shot through him with every inch of the motion but he had to see.

The horses screamed as the champions of Freydis cut the last of them down and then swung their atgiers onto the splayed riders. They gave a weak, despairing cry and raised their hands in vain. Then with splat fell still. Their blood ran into the vast red patches that dotted the bed of ice between the pines.

Freydis drove her sword into Kaia's axe. The jarl had lost her horse and blood ran thickly from her long blonde hair but she faced off against Freydis. Swung her axe at the shield. But Freydis was stronger and bigger and beat her shield against Kaia's to form an opening. Kaia swung her axe but Gunnlogi was faster.

Kaia gave a retching moan and turned away from Freydis. Blood erupted from her jaw and neck and she dropped her shield and fell to one knee. Freydis came up behind her. Torvard winced and waited but Kaia raised her axe and deflected. Spun and stood shakily. Dealt a follow up blow that Freydis sliced through and sent the axe head spinning aside. Then drove her sword through Kaia's chest.

Kaia fell to her knees. Freydis pressed the sole of her boot against Kaia's face and drew Gunnlogi out of her.

Torvard struggled to gasp in shallow, fast breaths.

Before him stood Casper, Gustav and Freydis. She hurried to his side and dropped the sword and lifted his head and cradled him in her lap.

'Torvard... Torvard...' she said, suddenly frantic. 'I didn't mean to...'

'My son,' he cut her off. But words were too small and too weak so he looked at her. Told her with his hateful glare that he knew what she was doing. That she wouldn't fool him now. But the pain swelled and his breathing grew so rapid that all he could do was give in and plunge into shadows and silence.

[430]

* * *

Gustav and Casper caught their breath. The cold air stung their lungs as they panted. Their Chieftain let her husband's head fall to rest on the snow. With both hands, she clutched the arrow she shot through him. The blood ran through her fingers. She stared up the hillside and her flesh began to quiver all over.

The villagers began to reappear where the limits of Straumfjord met the forest. They moved tentatively. Looked over their shoulders back down towards the longhouse.

'We should go back to the village,' Casper said while Gustav looked at the bodies and the blood on the ground. 'Tell them the assassins have been suppressed before they get any ideas...'

'You go,' Freydis said softly without a break in her unblinking gaze up the hillside.

'I go where you go...'

Freydis clawed her fingers and smeared the blood on her hands down her face. Eight red lines of her husband's blood. She picked up Gunnlogi and slid it back in its sheath and then marched towards her horse.

'If we let Straumfjord...'

'Straumfjord will fall back into line when my brother's knarr arrive,' Freydis said as she mounted the horse. Still she stared in the direction Eirik and the skraeling had run.

'If you aren't there to greet them...'

'Are you champions or not?' Freydis somehow looked at both men at the same time. Then kicked her horse into a gallop and sped up the hillside in pursuit.

Casper and Gustav stepped over the shattered bodies to their horses.

35

The Ghost in the Forest

Madawaak didn't have any ochre to bury Erlanh in. He cut the end of the new spear off and carved a small canoe like the one they might have escaped in and let the child keep his satchel. On the bed of soil, he placed these meagre things. Then he lowered the cold, light Erlanh in.

'Adothe,' Madawaak said as he sat back beside the pile of rocks and stones he'd managed to amass. 'Help this boy to the god spirits. Give him their red ochre so he knows he belongs with us. Tell him why I can never join him there. Tell him what I did. Father... mother... your names were Eenodsha and Dabjeek. Ebauthoo is with you. So are Oonban, Chipchowinech and Shanawdithit and... and Demasduit. I'm sorry I have never spoken of you. I have let your names go unsaid in this land and maybe in this world and I am sorry. Help me now. Take this boy where I can never go. Let him grow and live and hunt as one of us and give him the family he should have had. My heart aches. Take this boy. Please. Take this boy.'

Painfully and slowly, Madawaak piled the stones on top of Erlanh until he was buried. His wounds didn't bleed anymore. But they had not healed over either and holes in his body blackened and stained the flesh around them yellow. There wasn't much time.

Early morning had not passed yet. Madawaak foraged for food and found an abandoned nest with some little blue eggs and dug up a root which he washed in the nearby pond. He ate and then turned to the other things he'd need.

He stumbled back to the clearing and collected more sap and then cut more of the dogwood. Two long shafts twice the length of his body. Smaller branches made noggins between them and he had enough left over to make another spear for himself. He

[432]

broke his tomahawk up on a sharp rocky outcropping that jutted out from under and snow and fixed more of the sharp chert with pleated skin he'd stolen from the dead Pale One adult. Madawaak pleated a long string and tied the noggin and the two lengths together so they pointed at the head. Then he carved the first wooden spike.

The day wore on quickly, so Madawaak took his two spears and his fence with its spikes and went back into the forest to where he'd left the naked Pale One. The dried meat he'd had in his skin pouch had been revolting. But the pouch itself had two more flints and some dry tinder tucked inside it so Madawaak slung it over his shoulder and took off his birchbark satchel.

Weak and out of breath, he stuffed the dry tinder into the birchbark satchel and cleared away a circle of snow. Then, with the damp wood he could collect, Madawaak built a structure around it. He left it there. Took his fence and the last of the pleated skin and wandered deeper into the forest.

When he returned, it was nightfall. Madawaak was dizzy and his saliva tasted foul and bitter but he worked on. Crouched down by the fire, he ground the flint sparks into the tinder in the satchel until it alighted with small tongues of flame. He blew his sickly breath over it. The damper wood whistled and popped and smoke billowed into the darkening sky. Madawaak piled more of the damp winter wood onto the fire and the sparks danced up into the air and extinguished quickly.

'See my fire,' he gasped. 'See my fire.'

Madawaak picked up the thicker logs. He could barely lift them and their bark felt painfully coarse against his hands. But with a cry, he hurled them onto the flames. Then he collapsed against a tree and watched as the wood sizzled and the foam and sap bubbled out of the cracks in the broken edges and the flames climbed higher.

He cupped both hands over his mouth and bellowed with all his might.

* * *

Grabs of sleep took Madawaak throughout the night. He left it to chance. If they came when he was out, so be it. But something inside comforted him. Something told him that it wouldn't happen that way and that he'd wake up even if they crept up as silent as the Autumn.

An ambrosia light through the trees stole the stars from the sky. Madawaak waited. *They will come,* he told himself. *They will come.*

Madawaak's eyelids closed over again and a heavy blanket of sleep fell over him that was suddenly interrupted with an icy gasp. He shivered and his eyes darted around the forest. Then, again... a rumble. Thunder on the ground. Madawaak could feel the vibration where he sat.

Horses.

Madawaak steeled himself and used the spears to get upright. His face was numb and the cold filled him from his blood down to his bones and his face ached. But Madawaak moved to position.

* * *

Katla rode behind Steiner and he behind Gottfried. Her snarling resentment commanded her horse more than her body did and the distance between them grew. Behind them, through the forest and across a frozen tundra, were her boys and husband that she'd ached to hold and smell and speak with again just last night.

Carl was dead. There was no reason for the rest of them to suffer out here any longer. And then Gottfried had seen a fire.

'Lord Asny sent us to kill the skraeling,' was all he'd said. Steinar had said nothing against him, of course, and Katla's objections had gone unheeded. That was that. Home was off the agenda. Apparently, one skraeling was worth all this trouble.

'Our Lords are elected by the jarldom and the jarldom are supported by the karldom. The decision of the Lords is everyone's decision and duty to see through.'

Well, Asny didn't have Katla's vote anymore. Not as long as she kept this Gottfried at her side. Katla kept hearing his words.

His actions kept playing out in her mind, particularly the night before last.

Carl was an idiot. But the boy didn't have to die.

The anger rose so high Katla found her hand had reached for her atgier and her horse had dropped far back enough from the men that she could only just see the domed helmet of Steinar through the thickening foliage. It bounced around as the horse negotiated the rough country. Katla snorted and kicked her horse to catch up to them.

'He took the child,' Steinar mumbled when Katla found them.

Carl's body was half buried in snow, a naked hip, leg, hand and half his head peeked out from the mantle as though he were embracing it. Erlanh's body was gone. Gottfried trotted slowly around a smouldering pile where the fire had burned. He dismounted. Kicked around and set white clouds of ash and leafy strips of burned bark twirling in the gentle northern breeze.

'Ate him,' Gottfried grunted, then looked at their surroundings with squinted eyes. Silence surrounded them. Gottfried's axe was in one hand, his spear in the other. In all the years she'd known him, Katla had never seen Gottfried carry a shield.

She slid her spear from its restraints and held it atop her horse.

'What do we do now, my Lord?' she asked.

Gottfried said nothing. He prowled slowly out of the ash and left his horse as he continued into the deeper undergrowth.

'Spread out,' his voice issued once the rest of him had disappeared.

Steinar's normally mellow brown eyes were stricken with fear. He held his shield tight and lowered his head and looked around wildly in wait for the attack as though it would come from everywhere at once.

'My Lord, I think we should stay together,' Katla called out. She reached for her shield as well.

Gottfried's horse stared at them. No answer came from the old man. Katla stared back at the horse and slowly Gottfried's thoughts began to form in her own mind. She looked at Steinar and dismounted.

'What are you doing?' Steinar hissed.

'He wants the skraeling to attack the horses,' Katla made a gesture with her fingers to her eyes to say that they were being watched.

'Why would he attack the horses when we're all on foot and alone?' Steinar's eyes widened and his skin grew even more pale.

'He can't get all of us at once,' Katla said. She held her shield and her spear then picked a random direction and walked off. It wasn't until she started that Katla realized she was prowling in the direction of home.

Steinar remained on his horse. His eyes darted around and he gripped his axe painfully hard. Katla whistled at him. Steinar looked at her. She could see the rapid rise and fall of his chest from where she stood. Katla nodded towards a random portion of the undergrowth and mouthed 'on foot.' Steinar looked at it. Then back at her. Katla nodded yes. He looked again.

There was no denying her own fear. Katla could feel her heart pound against the pleated leather she wore. But she kept steady. Kept her husband's soft blue eyes and warm voice in her mind. Kept the feeling of her sons in her heart.

'Steady,' she whispered towards Steinar as he shakily dismounted.

He bent his knees and held his shield out before him and waded his way through the undergrowth. Katla turned away before Steiner became too obscured to see. She trod lightly. Kept her breathing under control so nothing would obstruct her hearing. It was all they could do. They had to hear the skraeling make a move for the horses.

Soon all Katla could hear was her pulse, the slight whistle in her cold lungs and the slow, soft crunching of boots as they came carefully down onto the snowy forest floor. The shaft of her spear hissed as it slid through the low foliage ahead. Irregular bursts of mist billowed out from between her lips. Katla felt the trembling beneath her leathers.

A noise.

A twig snap? A bird hop? The last thing Katla would ever hear?

She froze and her wide eyes darted around and stung in the cold air.

Then, a scream.

Katla turned and sprinted back towards the horses. As she leaped over the logs and fallen things she'd carefully navigated on the way in, the screams continued. Dull and droning. Pain. The first had been shock. They weren't the horse screams she'd expected but the raspy howls of a man. It wasn't Gottfried. Gottfried wouldn't scream.

The horses stood in the clearing and looked around with the same calm vacant expressions they had all along. Steiner kept screaming. It was disjointed now, as though he were moving or being flung around. Katla charged behind the head of her spear. Shield up. It knocked the low branches out of her way as she hopped and skipped after the screams which had dropped a pitch into growls and roars of aggression.

'Keep fighting!' she cried. 'Keep fighting Steinar!'

Katla's spear was rammed aside by a sudden force and Katla quickly pushed her shield forward. Beneath it was Steiner. Gasping and bellowing uncontrollably, he writhed about and swung his axe wildly. Katla stood back. She realized it was he who'd knocked her spear in his madness. She looked around to find the attacker. But all around, nothing looked back but the empty spaces between the trees and the bushes.

'Stop!' she snapped at Steinar. 'Be calm! Calm down, will you!'

There was no way to hear if they were being snuck up on with Steinar thus insensible. Katla took a step back and crouched amongst the bushes. Looked around. Again saw nothing but snow and brown bark and dark shades of evergreen.

Steiner settled and lay on his back. Blood streaked and spattered over the foliage around him and as he looked at it, he started to hyperventilate. Katla looked and saw what had been done. His heel. Slashed across. Both of them slashed right through.

'Oh, Katla,' he gasped. 'Oh, Katla. Oh, Katla...'

'Quiet.'

'Don't leave me here,' he whined as his voice went up to his falsetto. 'Don't leave me.'

There was no way he was going to walk out of here. Nor could Katla carry him. She looked around again, this time in search of a hulking old man with a great, grey beard.

'Where is Gottfried?'

'I don't know... Katla... I'm hurt badly...'

'Where is he? Did you see him?'

'I said I don't know!'

'The skraeling?'

'I didn't see any skraeling,' Steinar started to cry. His hands were up on either side of his belly and his fingers curled in agony. 'Please don't leave me here.'

'We are both going to die if you don't shut up...' then an idea hit Katla and cut her off mid-sentence. She looked at Steinar. He looked at her with eyes set to burst. Katla bit her lip. Felt that pain instead of what she was about to do. 'Wait here.'

'Don't leave me!' Steinar screamed. 'Don't!'

But Katla was up. She turned around. Started to prowl back towards the horses.

'Katla! My mother! I have a mother and father... Katla!'

His voice hit a fevered pitch and made Katla's heart pound frantically but she kept going. *Come on,* she thought. *He's all alone. Get him.*

But Steiner's screams and cries didn't stop and so Katla worked her way back to the horses. Hers trotted about. The other two dug their snouts about in the snow as they grew hungry. Katla's horse, Embla, trotted right over to her side.

'Katla!' Steinar screamed.

Embla muzzled Katla's shoulder. Could she? Gottfried was missing and Steinar didn't have a chance. Katla was alone. As the thought came to her, the forest seemed to close in even more. Every invisible pocket that surrounded her housed a spear that was ready to pierce through her or slice some tendon so she couldn't get away. The skraeling... it wasn't human. It wanted them to die slowly and screaming. Why should Katla as well?

'I'm sorry Steinar,' she whispered, and mounted her horse. Turned it towards home. Suddenly a force struck Katla from behind. Enough to shatter her. Katla looked down and saw the bloodied end of the spear suck through her guts. Blood spattered onto her horse's fur. Shock and pain hit all at once and in a daze, she fell from her horse. She hardly felt the ground hit her.

* * *

Madawaak ran from the bushes and grabbed his spear. The Pale One gasped through a blood-filled mouth and feebly reached up at him with bare hands. He grabbed the spear, tore it through her. Blood and intestines spilled onto the snow. Quickly he rammed the sharp end through her ear, tore it out again and ran back into the undergrowth before the Pale One stopped writhing.

'Katla!' the other one kept screaming.

Madawaak ran back to him and quickly pushed the spear through his neck. Between his collar bones. He gurgled and sputtered blood over his chin and Madawaak again tore the spear out and turned and hit the dirt. He crawled in amongst the undergrowth. The third one... he hadn't come for his friends... Madawaak had to...

With a crash that shook the earth a wall of shining stone smashed down in front of Madawaak's face. He could see his reflection in it. And the huge hand that reached down and gathered the back of his neck in a crushing force and tore him away from the ground. Madawaak hurtled through the air and slammed into a tree. The fog swilled around in his head as he collapsed down to the cold ground. But there was an enemy. As the warm slime oozed down the side of his face, Madawaak grappled to his feet. That crushing grip closed around his throat. The ground left his feet again and the bark of the tree smashed into his back and he hung there while the mighty hand cut off his breath.

The old, wrinkled eyes stared at him steely blue. The mouth beneath the grey beard was twisted in snarling hatred. Madawaak kicked and fought and punched at the Pale One's arm. But it was useless. As well he might have tried to punch through the trunk of a redwood. The world began to turn white...

But the hand released. Madawaak fell again. Gasped for air and turned to crawl away. That grip again. His ankle. Suddenly he was hurtled through the air. Arms flailed. Screamed. The trunk of the tree collided with his ribs and he felt them pop and snap and give out. Madawaak crashed down again. Agony stabbed and tore through his side. He coughed hot and bitter-tasting air and gurgled and wheezed. A huge force from behind jolted Madawaak's spine and sent him somersaulting over and away from the tree.

A moment. The world turned around him. A kaleidoscope of brown and black and green and white. Blinding agony bit into his body. Every patch of him. Bored into him with sheer pain.

The giant beast stomped towards him. Behind, an opaque wall of haze and throbbing pain. But Madawaak gathered. He rolled over. Saw the red drops between his hands as he crawled away. Another huge force propelled him further. He smashed headlong into the ditch he'd dug and curled up at the far end.

Coughing, ruined, broken... Madawaak turned to face the monstrous Pale One that stood at the other end of his ditch. The giant stepped one foot down. Madawaak cried out to muster his strength, turned away, reached up and smashed the carved stump aside.

The fence flicked out from the shrubs. The giant Pale One looked up just as three of the barbs that the fence side was lined with burst through his flesh and pierced his chest. Both huge arms wrapped around it. He roared as blood bubbled up from his gullet and ran in thickening streaks through his beard. The monster fell on one knee. Looked at Madawaak. Then crashed down in a heap and dragged the whole fence trap down with him.

Madawaak didn't know if he lost consciousness or not. He lay there for what felt like forever but never knew when the giant Pale One stopped moving or breathing or wheezing. It just happened. Time seemed to leap forward with every blink and soon it was mid-morning.

* * *

A bohemian waxwing hopped about near his face. Madawaak looked at it. Wondered if this would be the carrier that would take his spirit into the gloomy underworld.

'Where have you been, bird?' he slurred, weakly.

The bird looked at him. Rapidly cocked its head from side to side.

'What has become of my home?'

Shanawdithit. The name struck Madawaak's heart even amid the unbearable pain that wound tightly around his chest. She was alive? That morning. Ran away with the son of Demasduit. Freydis chasing them. That morning. They hid.

The little bird fluttered away. Madawaak's eyes were wide open and some unearthly energy rolled through his veins. Shanawdithit. Alive. Madawaak rose painfully to his feet and spat away the blood in his mouth and staggered out of the ditch. He staggered past the body of the Pale One and followed the trail they'd left back to where his double-sided axe lay embedded in the hard winter earth.

Madawaak pulled it out, slung it over his shoulder, and started to hobble towards their village.

[441]

36

Cometh the End of Times

Night Eagle listened to the thundering hoofs move past them. Barely a hundred paces afield. There were trees and shrubs in the way and the hollow, rotten log sheltered both she and the child completely but they would not stay hidden for long.

The tears that streaked down Eirik's face softened the echo that bounced off him when she clicked. The frown. The anger and confusion that curled him into a ball and filled him with hateful thoughts. If only Freydis had taught him their words. If only Night Eagle had the time to learn theirs during her captivity. She could tell him Freydis deserved this. Tell him she was not his mother.

But she'd raised him. A boy would forgive the woman who raised him for trying to kill him. Night Eagle knew it.

'I am your aunty,' she said, as warmly as she could manage. Heard him flinch. 'Hear me. Please. Your mother was my sister. Murdered by Freydis.'

Eirik sniffled.

'Those people...' Night Eagle didn't know the Pale Ones' word for themselves. It didn't matter after all. But maybe she wanted it to. Night Eagle wanted to say the right thing so as not to offend him because that meant he could understand her somehow. 'Those who rebelled against Freydis...'

Eirik flinched again. He understood "Freydis."

'Before either of us were born, Freydis had another brother who was chieftain of their settlements in this land,' she told him. 'He sent her far away. Further than the Farther Lands... Helluland...' she played out as much as she could with her hands. 'Where she found the mainland. The people there... the skraelingjar there... they are larger than us. Closer in size to Pale Ones. She met one and he fell in love with her. Taught her their ways. Taught her how to speak to other skraelingjar. One day she abandoned him. He found her and tried to stop her but she killed him. Two other Pale Ones were with her. Hakon and Asny. They were both very young then and they saw what she did. They were the first to know what she planned to do to the skraelingjar. They told others. Quietly. But Freydis always suspected. She sent away or killed most of those she thought would turn on her. The rebellion died down.'

Night Eagle clicked. He was still there but stone quiet. Hearing, but unable to listen.

'Until one-night, Hakon went with Freydis to hunt down my mother, sister and me,' she continued anyway. Though her flesh tingled. They didn't have much more time. 'He saw her do this to me,' Night Eagle ran her fingers down the scars on her brow and cheeks, across her eyes, 'and couldn't live with it. He snuck away and came back as soon as he could with Kaia. They did what they could for my eyes. Then he returned and she smuggled me through the Far... through Helluland... until she found skraelingjar there who could take me across the water to the mainland. She found men there who still spoke the Pale One tongue. Sworn to avenge their dead son, they took me in and promised Kaia that one day someone would come from the Mainland and take revenge on Freydis.'

Night Eagle swallowed. She felt the heavy sting of blood-tears that pooled in her eyes as she remembered Kaia. Her final rebellion had failed. Her faith in Night Eagle had been misplaced and it got her killed. Now there was only one hope. For Kaia, there was none.

'They planned,' she said. 'They ran through every possible scenario in secret and in quiet so they'd know what to do whoever came and however they came. When they realized it was me... I don't know how that must have felt. But they stayed the course. They were brave warriors and strong to make such a stand. Like your father. Torvard. Brave.'

Eirik sniffled again.

'Come, child,' she held out her hand. 'We haven't finished yet.'

Eirik recoiled. Night Eagle let her hand drop down onto her knee.

'I was sent to kill Freydis,' Night Eagle said. 'I chose to save you because we are family. My sister who haunts my dreams and whose memory fills me with grief is your mother. Demasduit. Demasduit. Demasduit. I know you are hers. I will abandon everything I came for to keep you safe. Or I will die trying.'

She held out her hand again. Eirik recoiled.

Night Eagle climbed to her feet, stooped in the narrow opening, and made her way towards the open heavy with defeat. If there was nothing she could do for...

'Torvard.'

She stopped and turned back towards Eirik. He looked up from his arms that were folded across his knees at her.

'Brave,' he said, in the native language.

'Torvard brave.'

'Torvard brave.'

'Demasduit.'

'Demasduit.'

'Your mother. Demasduit.'

'*Móðir,*' he said.

She felt his hand slip into hers. Then he stood. They went out into the cold air together.

'Eirik brave,' she said, and touched his nose. Eirik looked up at her and she felt the watery gaze of lost eyes that flickered as they sought meaning in a world that suddenly had none. Night Eagle clicked up towards the hilltop as softly as she could manage. The echo brought back a vision of rich sunbeams that shone between tree trunks. Not detail. It wasn't far. They'd have to get closer.

'Eirik must be brave now,' Night Eagle said and squeezed his shoulder. He nodded.

Night Eagle led Eirik up the hillside truly blind. She heard Eirik's footsteps follow behind her. Arms outstretched. Tentative steps ready to knock against anything...

A rock knocked Night Eagle's toes. She spread her arms and stumbled and almost fell. But she felt Eirik's hand snap back onto hers. Tightly. He held her steady. A strong boy. Good grip.

Night Eagle clicked softly.

He pointed up the hill as though to make sure that was what Night Eagle had intended. She nodded. Eirik led her around the boulders and tree trunks and the fallen logs up the hillside. Night Eagle kept her other arm out beside her but Eirik led her confidently and all she had to do was follow where his footsteps went. Something moved inside her heart...

The ground levelled out beneath them. Eirik stopped. He asked her something that sounded like a question. Night Eagle pointed around. Look. Come on, Eirik. Look. Then she felt his hand tensely touch her shoulder.

Was someone there?

'Skraeling?' Night Eagle asked and pointed down towards the figure.

'Skraeling,' Eirik responded.

Night Eagle nodded and Eirik led them down the gentler slope. They were headed towards the lakes.

As they descended, a sound tingled Night Eagle's ears and she turned back and clicked. The hilltop. Trees. Sunlight that blossomed as it reached up towards midday. Just as they'd left it. Night Eagle gestured Eirik to hurry up. He pulled on her hand and she followed him with as much certainty to every stride as she could muster... but she was slow. Every time her foot left the ground was like a leap into abyss. Every time it came down again Night Eagle had to gather enough courage to lift the other one and as the hill steepened her steps hovered in nothingness longer and longer.

The thought came to Night Eagle like a whisper. Almost in her sister's voice. *He has nothing but you.*

A wave of calm rolled through Night Eagle and she breathed easier and matched Eirik's pace as he led. He quickened. She was able to keep step. Night Eagle clicked up behind them again.

Still nothing.

It was never going to be this easy, she thought.

They kept their pace until Night Eagle heard the light body nimbly but clumsily stumble down the tree and drop to the earth.

'Gheegnyan?' Night Eagle asked.

'Yes. He lived,' the boy said in a gentle, breezy voice. 'They said to lead you.'

'To the lakes?'

The young man shook his head no.

'Where then?'

'To the trap,' he said with caution in his voice. His eyes were fixed on Eirik.

'What is your name?' she asked.

'I'm sorry. Posson.'

'Lead us wherever,' Night Eagle ordered. Posson turned and sped off into the deepening forest. Eirik took Night Eagle's hand and followed him.

'We must hurry,' he said.

Night Eagle turned and clicked again. This time with every intention of the sound flooding the valley. The long whinny of a horse responded. They were coming. Night Eagle turned and nodded Posson along and he led them.

Night Eagle had to stop again. She turned her head and lifted her face and felt the sound rumble. It issued from below the hills. Down in the gully where they walked. Eirik and Posson waited breathlessly.

'Now we run,' she said.

The three of them charged as fast as they could as the undergrowth thickened and enclosed around them. Night Eagle fell back so Eirik could be in front of her. She followed his steps as she clicked and pressed her hands into his back when he lost pace. Posson soon disappeared. Night Eagle followed the fading sound of his crashing moccasins as he jumped and ducked and wove his way back the way he'd come to find them.

Then he whistled. High and loud.

The rumbling of the hoofs kept growing louder and louder. *Still three of them.* Night Eagle heard Eirik begin to wheeze so she pressed her hands against him but the child was losing step.

'Go, Eirik!' she barked. 'Go!'

Finally, they broke into a low, narrow gully where a creek ran shallow between flanking walls of fern. Night Eagle led the child through the middle of it. There was no sign of Posson. But a figure appeared on the rise ahead and waved at them. It was an older man. Night Eagle clicked. Old. Mutilated hand.

With a final burst of energy Eirik charged towards the old man and Night Eagle followed. Behind them, horses bellowed.

'Go!' Night Eagle screamed.

The older man grabbed one of Eirik's hands and leaped with him into the ferns. Night Eagle followed. The riders charged through the creek so fast that sparkling waves of water sprinkled out in their wake. Freydis led, spear held forward and shield at her side. Another whistle came. Freydis hooked one leg out of a stirrup, swung herself over to the horse's side and let herself fall into the frosty creek bed. A volley of spears came down. With the sudden release of weight, Freydis' horse raced on ahead of it while the other two let out bone-rattling screams as the spears pierced through their necks and flanks.

Casper cried out and clutched a spear that had pierced his thigh. Human blood ran with the horse's.

With a great cry that poured into the ravine, the little red bodies leaped up from the ferns and charged down with their tomahawks or spears held high. They leaped down onto the riders.

Freydis stayed low. The first body that came at her she rammed her spear into his belly, then spun and beat her shield against the face of another. His tomahawk flew over the top and splashed in the water. A surge of screaming issued from behind her as Gustav and Capser fell into the water but Freydis pressed on ahead. Bodies flew at her from all directions. She held up her shield against the spears and arrows and stabbed her spear low into the hordes. Put them down. The creek ran red as the bodies fell and curled around their wounds. One caught her spear with his tomahawk and cut the head off. She had her sword out, before he could reach her and, with a swing, his ribs opened and viscera spilled out. Another mighty blow hit her shield. But Freydis didn't stop. She chopped her way through them as they came. Slit their bellies. Smacked her sharp blade against their shoulders to snap them. Ducked. Wove. Swung. Blood spattered her face. The violence behind her grew to rattling intensity and Freydis pushed on. Hacked through a leg that stuck under her shield. The shield ripped away. Freydis turned and beat her sword against it, knocking it aside, and swung her Gunnlogi into the skull of the skraeling behind it.

Night Eagle realized what would happen just as the old man squeezed her shoulders with one good hand and one crippled.

'We have to go!'

He turned and frantically crawled away. Night Eagle grabbed Eirik. But he watched on, transfixed, as Freydis hacked her way through the attackers in a shower of blood and cacophony of guttural screams. Night Eagle tugged on his sleeve.

'Come on!'

Eirik turned and followed after them just as Freydis cleared the ambush, seized her horse by the reigns, mounted and charged off under pursuit of a few feeble arrows. With a scream, Gustav fell under the chopping tomahawks. But there was silence after. No cries of victory. The survivors charged through the trail of their kinfolk, slashed open, split, screaming or writhing around as innards spilled out of them and slipped through their trembling, clutching hands.

But Freydis was gone.

* * *

Night Eagle listened as they ran up another gentle slope but the galloping of the single horse's hoofs had faded completely. The old man staggered and doubled over. He reached back and took Night Eagle's shoulder as she gained on him. Eirik staggered behind. The old man collapsed onto his knees and coughed.

'I can go no further,' the old man said. Keathut. She knew he was Keathut. Some howl from the depths of her memories reached her as she gasped for air. 'They've arrived.'

'They...' Night Eagle cut her question off as she realized what he meant. If they could have taken Freydis' head to the cliffs and thrown it at them they'd have turned back. But she was alive. They were coming. Instead of going home, all those who'd helped her who were left alive would soon die. Asny. Her settlement in the Broken Lands. All of them. If Freydis lived to order it.

There was only one hope.

Night Eagle clicked towards Eirik. She didn't want to do this to him but it was the only way. Freydis would kill him too. Death seemed the only option for both of them. Night Eagle reached out and touched his hair and then found his shoulder.

'Draw her to us,' Night Eagle said. He nodded.

'I will give you a good start.'

'Not too good.'

Night Eagle nudged Eirik along. He touched her shoulder and whined but she pushed him though they were both out of breath. He whimpered but turned and ran. Night Eagle touched Keathut's shoulder and then ran after Eirik.

* * *

Keathut waited until the sound of their footsteps faded across the forest floor. Then he waited more. Tried to picture where their giant canoes would be by now. Close enough. He looked around and thought about what he might do to get himself killed. His insides trembled.

Build a fire? He hadn't any flint. Keathut fiddled around with some fallen branches that were damp through and gave up. He'd just have to scream. Keathut threw the branches aside and turned and...

Her eyes stared into him from atop the horse. They were framed in a face so caked in drying blood that she looked like she'd painted herself in it. Keathut spread his feet and raised his hands. Ready to fight her and her horse with his bare old hands, he looked up at her and bared his teeth.

Freydis stared at him.

Keathut remembered when he'd last met her. That moment had haunted him more than all the death and all the destruction his life had been responsible for.

So now was the time.

'Come on, Freydis,' he said.

Freydis' eyes sought the ground and then trailed along where Shanawdithit and Eirik had run. She looked at Keathut again. Still said nothing.

'Do you remember me?' he taunted and raised the hand she'd mangled.

Freydis kicked her horse off and charged after Shanawdithit and Eirik. Keathut ran after her. A few paces reminded him of his human weaknesses and he fell to the ground and bellowed with all his aged and withered might.

* * *

Eirik heard the old man as they were halfway up the hill.

This one was without trees and led from a flat meadow up to cliff's edge. He remembered this place. The old skraelingjar village that the earth had slowly reclaimed and now the snow had finished off. The spot where Snorre died. He could hear the rolling waves and their crashing sighs issue from beyond the edge. Eirik felt faint. Unable to breathe in enough. His heart pounded so hard it hurt and the harsh taste of phlegm burned in his gullet.

Finally, Eirik's legs could carry him no more and he crashed against the snow. Shanawdithit came to a sudden stop at the edge and looked out over the ocean. Eirik looked up. Saw her shoulders buckle under the weight of what was out there. Eirik climbed to his feet and coughed violently. Shanawdithit turned and held him steady.

Out on the ocean, the knarr rode the swells up and down while the icy winds billowed their sails and carried them towards Straumfjord. The front row drew nearer as he watched and left

[450]

a white trail behind them that was quickly scattered by the rows upon rows that followed behind. All the way back to the distant icebergs that lolled in the misty distance. As though the whole sea might have been blanketed in knarr.

The wind stung his eyeballs and Eirik turned and buried his face in Shanawdithit's shoulder. She put her arms gently around him. It was too much. Everything today had just been too much to take in and understand. The idea of Shanawdithit dying filled him with horror. It softened him towards the skraelingjar as a people but still he had seen Snorre die here by their arrows... he hated them as well. And hated her a little. And that part of him wanted Freydis to come get her but the rational portions of his mind and heart knew that meant she would kill him as well. Eirik retched.

Freydis rode out from the shadows beneath the trees. Eirik squeezed Shanawdithit harder. Shanawdithit pressed his sides. Eirik released her and she turned and clicked towards Freydis, clicked towards the ground, then slowly started to walk towards the horse as it charged.

Unarmed, she walked. Hands by her sides and with soft clicks that issued from her mouth. Freydis galloped toward her. Across the meadows. Up the hillside with that sword Gunnlogi drawn and held in the air. It caught the sunlight and flashed into Eirik's eyes as he watched her ride closer and closer. He couldn't breathe.

Shanawdithit stood still. Freydis drew close. Eirik could see the thick mist billowing from the horse's mouth.

Shanawdithit dropped onto her back. Her hands plunged into the snow beside her and ripped an atgier up out from under the mantle and the skraeling rammed the back end into the ground beside her and caught the horse in the chest just below its neck. Eirik saw the blade sink into the horse's flesh. The animal screamed as it barrelled forward and Freydis flew through the air and the horse came crashing down over Shanawdithit.

Eirik cried out.

Freydis slammed into the snow a few paces from him and bounced and rolled and left a trail of red blood behind her. She stopped just short of the ledge. Lay there still. Eirik looked at the horse and couldn't see Shanawdithit... *She must be under it,* he thought. As he gasped for breath, his eyes darted back and forth. Freydis. Shanawdithit.

The knarr, he thought. The knarr had to know and then they'd stop whatever Freydis had told them to do. They were coming to kill the skraelingjar. He had to let them know she was dead.

'Hey!' Eirik cried as he waved his arms in the air. There was no telling how they'd turn their knarr towards the cliffs and what they'd do when they got there but Eirik called anyway. Could they see Freydis' body? Would they realize it was all over? 'Hey!'

He saw the pilots of the first few knarr start to move about. Heard the distant bellows of their calls to each other. Eirik smiled. He had their attention.

The familiar stinging pain of those iron hands clasped onto his scalp and seized a handful of Eirik's hair. A force from above pushed him down to his knees and he cried out. The cold edge of Gunnlogi touched the back of his neck and he knew who had him.

'Mama...' he cried.

'Don't you dare call me Mama skraeling,' Freydis' voice said. 'You know who your mama is. You chose your mama.'

She pulled on Eirik's hair to keep his neck straight.

'Look at them,' Freydis demanded. 'Coming to slaughter every last one of the skraelingjar. All of that could have been yours. Those people aboard those ships would have been yours to rule as a king. The first King of Vinland. But you betrayed me. You chose them. The animals who live in the dirt.'

Eirik cried openly. His insides sunk and felt like they'd turned to mush inside him and shame burned him.

'I'm sorry,' he whimpered. Not to Freydis but to Shanawdithit who might have been dead behind them. 'I'm sorry... I didn't mean it. I love you.'

'I never loved you,' Freydis said. 'You were always too weak. Like your skraeling mother who burned herself on a pyre rather than accept who she was.'

'You killed my mama,' Eirik cried.

'I wish I had. Before you came along and disappointed me like this. Look at you. Crying even now. I wonder if those tears will stop once I've cut your worthless head off?'

Eirik screamed out in terror as he waited for the blade to come back and do as he'd seen it done to...

Something crashed against them from behind. A hard thud hit Freydis in the side and she gasped deeply as she was dragged right past him.

Shanawdithit!

The little skraeling had leaped against Freydis' shoulders and rammed the head of the atgier into her ribs. Freydis stumbled over the edge of the cliff. Shanawdithit fell with her and Eirik screamed and hurried to... he didn't know what. Just be there. But as he looked down, he saw that they'd landed on one of the steep ledges and rocky outcroppings that scarred the cliff face.

Shanawdithit flew through the air and smashed into a boulder still with the bloodied atgier blade in her hand. Freydis staggered to her feet. Dark red blood ran down her side and stained her lips. She hunched over the tiny skraeling and swung Gunnlogi. Shanawdithit clicked frantically and hurled herself up to the top of the boulder and kicked Freydis in the face. Freydis staggered back. Shanawdithit slid down and swung the atgier blade but Freydis blocked in and followed through and Eirik screamed but Shanawdithit ducked and then rose and blocked Freydis' swing-back. The force was so strong it knocked Shanawdithit against the cliff face and she had to roll along it to evade another hack.

Gunnlogi dug into the dirt. Shanawdithit spun and slammed the atgier blade into the side of the sword. Freydis tore it free but Shanawdithit struck it again. Knocked it out off to Freydis' side. The side she bled from. Shanawdithit hit again and again and the pain of the blows doubled Freydis over and she clutched the wound in her side. Blood seeped through her fingers.

Finally, the sword hit the side of a boulder and Shanawdithit gave a mighty swing and Gunnlogi made a long whining sound.

The broken blade fell into the icy water.

Shanawdithit swung and Freydis moved to block with but a small shard. Shanawdithit rammed the atgier blade into her stomach. Freydis roared. Shanawdithit drew back the blade and swung again. It carved Freydis across the front. Freydis stood upright as blood erupted from her wound and Shanawdithit rammed the blade one last time into her chest.

Freydis staggered backward and dropped the hilt of Gunnlogi. She ripped the atgier blade from her chest and stood to face Shanawdithit... staggered... buckled... turned and faced the coming knarr and doubled over and without a sound, disappeared over the edge.

Eirik saw the pilots and crews watch Freydis plummet down the cliffside, smash against the rocks and bounce into the water. Blood billowed out in a deep red cloud around her. She floated on the swells, suspended for a moment, until the icy black waters filled her leather skins and dragged her down feet-first. Her arms reached up at the dancing glare of sunlight above her.

Shanawdithit felt her way back up towards Eirik while he watched the knarr. The pilots of the front row shouted to the ships behind them. The sails turned and slowly, one after the other, the knarr behind the front row turned their bowsprits about in an arch until they faced home and the crews worked to catch the winds to carry them back again.

Eirik wiped his eyes as Shanawdithit hurled herself over the edge and collapsed in the snow. Eirik moved over and slid his arms under her and lifted her up and held the strong little body to warm her.

'It's alright, Shanawdithit,' he whispered. 'It's over. We're going to be okay.'

Epilogue

Winter winds blew cold between the structures that surrounded Madawaak. He stumbled around and around and in and out of all of them. As evening set in it was obvious. They were gone. The enemies he'd lived just a little while longer to fight had up and left and there was only empty houses and dead bodies left of them.

Their own. Dead in the street. Slashed or stabbed and left with their weapons of shining stone still in their hands. Madawaak's heart crashed into his guts. Nothing left...

A low grumble issued from near the larger domicile.

Madawaak staggered over and froze when he saw the huge white body and rippling fur. Fear froze him momentarily. Then the enormous head, stained pink with blood, lifted from the corpse it fed on and looked at him. A wave of calm fell over Madawaak. The black eyes stared at him and he stared back at him and a quiver issued from his heart.

'Demasduit,' he breathed.

The bear grumbled softly. Turned to face him but came no closer.

'Take me to you,' he whispered. 'Please. There is nothing left in this world for me now. I am like you. We can never go home. Home is gone. A new world has to be born for our people and there is no place in it for us.'

The polar bear licked its lips, then turned and started to walk away. Back out onto the frozen tundra. Madawaak followed and followed until the Pale One settlement faded over the horizon behind him and the bear had disappeared into the white mist of flatlands before him. Then he stopped. The bear was gone. The Pale Ones were gone.

A hot tear rolled down his cheek and fell into the snow with a gentle tap. Madawaak turned. He walked back towards the forests where Erlanh was buried.

* * *

The tribe from the Lakes met Night Eagle and Eirik in the meadows with Gheegnyan, held by two strong hunters, and Posson at the front. Ninejeek and Keathut followed behind. Night Eagle rested on Eirik's shoulders and the two held each other up.

Night Eagle heard the duller echo off Gheegnyan's face. He was covered in red ochre.

'They made me Father,' he said, softly.

'They were right to,' Night Eagle said.

'Pale Ones are boarding the giant canoes that came to their village,' Keathut said. 'They are leaving. We owe you everything we will ever have in this world.'

'You owe me nothing but to raise this child well,' Night Eagle said. She pushed Eirik towards them. He turned. She felt his big, hurt eyes stare at her in confusion. Night Eagle touched his hair. 'Teach him his mother's language. Tell him stories about her. Make sure he knows who he is and who his family was.'

Posson gently took the child by his shoulders and squeezed him reassuringly.

'You won't stay?' Ninejeek asked. 'You are his family.'

'His family is dead,' Night Eagle said. 'But tell him Shanawdithit loves him and will think of him always. And one day... when he comes to find her... he and the people that took care of him and raised him into a man will always be welcome amongst her people. And there will be peace between them forever.'

Ninejeek knowingly put his hand on Eirik's shoulder. The boy looked tearily up at him. Then back at Night Eagle. He shook his head and blubbered something but Night Eagle took him and hugged him.

'*Vinr*,' she said.

'*Skuldalig*,' he responded, urgently.

'Come find me one day,' she said. '*Skuldalig*.'

'One day very soon,' Ninejeek said.

Night Eagle took a few steps backward, then turned and ran north across the meadows. Eirik ran after her a few paces. But he was still too sore and too tired and he stopped and stood there and cried as she faded into the shadowy forests in the distance.

Ebauthoo came up beside him and took him gently by the arm. He turned and looked at her. She smiled at him warmly.

'Let's talk about your mother.'

THE END

Other Works by Max Davine

Mighty Mary

Mary was a circus elephant. The Star of the West. She could dance, play the trumpet and pleased crowds wherever she went.

In 1916, after a disastrous Wild West show in Erwin Tennessee, acts against Mary the five-ton Indian elephant would go down in history as one of the most disturbing bizarre cases of animal cruelty the world has ever seen.

But, Mary had a life before the circus. She was free once. Part of a wild herd.

During the British Raj, she was captured, trained and sent to America to become a spectacle. Along the way, she loved, she lost, she made friends and formed bonds. She suffered heartache and experienced ecstasy. She was a living being. This is her story.

Angel Valence

Ineke Valence: Single mother of one. Blond. A drinker in spite of prohibition. Resident of Staten Island.

The Angel of New York: The law's gun for hire, the one they send when the job gets too risky, a thief, or bodyguard, or murderess... A former spy of the Russian Revolution.

During the last months of the Roaring Twenties, one woman must play both roles. But when her NYPD contacts throw her a job that's close to home, she finds the lines between the two alter-egos beginning to blur, and her daughter's life in jeopardy. She travels to the small northern city of Rochester to crack the case before the mob cracks her identity, but what she finds will put her violent, tragic history on a more dangerous collision course with her delicately balanced present than she could ever have imagined.

Terra Domina

1885. A ten year old boy is missing. His twin sister encounters a strange old man in the woods near her house. He seems infatuated with her, and displays unusual control over the world around him, over the events to follow in her life.

She is Michelle Augustine, and from this day to her adulthood, the turn of the century, to Australian Federation, from poverty to comfort, love to loneliness, violence to peace and all the passion, joy, death and destruction her life will influence he and his sinister connection to her will never be far behind.

The Red Legion

Prohibition is over, closing the lid on half the crime in New York. Wall Street has crashed, opening it up for a whole new breed of criminal to roam the city streets...not that it's Ineke Valence's problem anymore. She has long since hung up her revolver, replacing it with a soda bottle, her red scarf with a barmaid's threads. That is until her old nemesis from the force Sergeant Fielding decides to make it her problem, framing her for a murder and then setting her up to fall hard. Valence moves quickly to bust the case, but when an old associate from her days as a Bandita down in Mexico resurfaces bringing omens of ill for her, and then someone makes the fatal mistake of kidnapping her daughter Elysia. Valence heads to Mexico to retrieve her, the line between Ineke and Angel never so stretched, never so close herself to becoming what she has always feared.

Dino Hunt
Jimmy Reeves is a down on his luck wildlife wrangler, his career  once saw him traveling the globe, working on relocation programs and starring in documentary films. Now, he and his business partner Paul Franciscus are lucky if they can get a gig wrangling bulls in Arizona. Until one day, when they receive a massive advance payment from a mysterious company based in Florida. In return, they are to do what once brought them glory the world over; trap and relocate endangered animals. Little do they know they're not going to the Everglades to trap alligators, they're going through time and space to rescue great, big dinosaurs! But others have come to pillage the Cretaceous world for its natural resources, and to enslave and exploit the prehistoric inhabitants. They are ruthless, they are well equipped, and they will stop at nothing. It's up to unwitting Reeves to make a stand not just for the dinosaurs, but to save his own life, teaming up with an alluring paleontologist and a helicopter pilot nicknamed "Crash" to save the land of the forgotten from human annihilation.

Off The Map

By 1873, long since the Golden Age of pirates and swashbuckling adventure, the oceans, it's said, were tamed, at least that's what young French orphan girl Chanel Angeli thought when she settled down and married into a rich mining family by means of their charming, gorgeous heir Oliver Aubry. Until, that is, Oliver accepts a business proposition from his old mentors Lord Beaumont, who has begun excavating an island in the Azores Archipelago that holds many mysterious and deadly secrets. When Beaumont betrays and enslaves Oliver on the isolated piece of land, which is thought to be capitol city of Atlantis, Chanel escapes and teams up with the devil-may-care captain of the Margeaux, endeavoring to rescue her husband, but along the way she finds, within herself, uncovering many mysteries of her own...

Connect with Max

www.maxdavine.com
Twitter @max_davine
Instagram @thewriter.max.davine

Printed in the USA
CPSIA information can be obtained
at www.ICGtesting.com
CBHW042318090224
4188CB00036B/514